KINGDOM AT TITAN'S END

Fabled Quest Chronicles

Book Six

AUSTIN DRAGON

Published by Well-Tailored Books, California

Kingdom at Titan's End
(Fabled Quest Chronicles, Book 6)
978-1-946590-11-4 (paperback)
978-1-946590-06-0 (ebook)

http://www.austindragon.com

Book cover design by Humbert Glaffo

Printed in the United States of America

CONTENTS

ARRIVAL...5

From Afar... 6

Entering Titan's Gate 16

Caravan's End.. 42

TREASURES OF ATLANTEA 93

Caravan of the Royals 94

The Goblin Proposal 120

Caravan of the Berserkers 127

Caravan of the Drows 143

Messenger... 155

THE FEAST 159

Reunited...160

Legends...185

The Lamia Gambit 278

The Dying Celestial Elfin Queen 295

RIVERMOUTH REBORN 311

Sun and Snow... 312

The Lost Warriors 324

Selkies and Drows..332

City of Faylen 347

Fae-Man 369

Caravan of the Lost Kingdom...................................381

Things of Night 394

Lady in the Lake 405

WHEN MAGIC TURNS TO DUST...................................431

Where's Oughtred?................................... 432

The Great Alliance...................................469

Letters 480

FROM THE DEVOURING DARKNESS 483

Escape from Atlantea...................................484

Lich Lord 506

REVENGE 531

The Giants of Antaeus 532

Elves From the Ocean Depths 540

The Fairy Sisters of Chrysa 543

Fae-Bloods................................... 550

A Rage Almost As Ancient 555

Hall of Atlanteans 558

WAR OF GIANTS................................... 565

Planet Fall 566

Hordes of Evil 569

Demon Centaurs, War Wizards, and Necromancers ...581

The Accord 587

Demi-Titans 593

Fury at Titan's End 599

THE REALM OF REALMS................................... 607

The Return................................... 608

Atlantea's Fear 618

Faylen's Legacy 627

As Atlantea Sleeps 632

Introduction

Once upon a time...

Beyond the Lands of Man and its Seven Empires, there was the legendary marker known as Titan's Bridge—the sole legendary gateway created by the ancient Titans themselves to the realm of the Magical Lands. Men had passed through the gateway for a millennium since its discovery in search of adventure and, later, unimaginable riches. The destination was the fabled kingdom of Atlantea, coveted by humans and fae alike.

Long ago, before the dawn of man, fae, and beasts of light and darkness, was the Age of the Titans. They were humanoid beings of such gigantic size that their heads reached high above the clouds into the heavens. According to myth, a Titan known as the Maker of All Mountains was so devastated by the death of his beloved that he walked the entire circumference of Pan-Earth, dragging his fabled weapon, the Star Slayer. He carved a massive valley before killing himself by leaping off the world into the void of space. This valley that cut through not only the known world but every other realm, too, was known as Titan's Trail.

Every three years, the northwestern lands of Avalonia became the starting point of the Kings' Caravan. Twenty years ago, the Kings of Xenhelm began this royal ritual journey across the Trail, attracting men—royal, noble, and commoner, farmer and knight, apprentice and warrior—from every corner of the Lands of Man. It was a year-long journey like no other through unimaginable dangers, both mortal and magical, by day and night, and all for one reason—to obtain the limitless riches of its final destination—the coveted magical kingdom of Atlantea. Most brave men would never risk such a venture filled with danger and death, even with the protection of the Kings' Caravan. However, there were plenty of men who would and gladly did so under the auspices of the Four Kings.

But the Kings' Caravan was no more due to their own treachery. Only Titan's Caravan remained under the command of a human, a man called Traveler. He was a caravan the likes of which none had ever seen before—humans, elves, sprites, fairies, giants, other fae races, many magical beasts, and a shape-shifter not from the world of Pan-Earth.

The Fabled Quest Chronicles has reached Atlantea, filled with its untold riches and far, far more!

Has the journey ended or just begun?

ARRIVAL

FROM AFAR

Life at the bottom of the Oceans of Faë-Land—the Oceanus Omnis—teemed with more variety and intensity than any other realm on land. The Oceanus Omnis was called the empires of mermaids, water nymphs, and water fae such as the sea centaurs, tritons, and water elves. But even their great kingdoms and queendoms occupied only a tiny fraction of the vastness of this magical aquatic world.

A merman swam slowly upwards through a tunnel the size of a giant city-ship. The ocean bottom glowed a wintry blue from the many photo-luminescent florae and mollusks below. Strangely, the greater the depths in this part of the ocean, the brighter it became. The merman ascended into temporary darkness, though he could see as clearly in the darkness as he could by sunlight.

There were two species of mermen. The handsome male humanoids with a large fish tail instead of bipedal legs and skin of an almost luminescent light blue or green. Then there were mermen such as he. Male sea humanoids that looked like a brown fish but with the head of a man—blue-green hair, unsightly teeth, and slits for eyes. They were known to be present at the sinking of ships but also, despite their appearance, to magically cure sickness and lift curses. The most revered were also powerful seers. He was one known among the fae of the Oceanus Omnis and the great cyclopes and centaur seers of the Magical Lands.

He had sensed them from many leagues away. Their magic was that powerful.

The nearer he got, the more turbulent the water became. Krakens were everywhere! The monstrous squid creatures had been violently removed from their ancestral territories and lashed out in a frenzy ten-fold against any living thing around them, including each other. The madness of the krakens could go on for years. Only when enough of them had been killed and devoured by each other, thinning their numbers, would their rage subside, and serenity could return to the region. All ocean life of any size would stay thousands of miles away until then. No craft of any water fae, good or evil, would dare venture into the region for decades to come, if not more.

He had only seen a "kraken wall" one other time in his centuries-old life. Kraken tentacles were so long they could reach out high into the sky to snatch winged beasts or flying caravans to their death. But he was too small for any of them to notice. However, he had surrounded himself in a concealment spell. But the magic he sensed was not from them.

The merman stopped mid-swim. The smallest of adult krakens were twice the size of a city-ship of merfolk. Even as a merman of noble upbringing slow to show emotion, his mouth was aghast as the giant foot of such tremendous size came down upon a kraken and pinned it to the ocean floor. The sea creature desperately struggled and futilely ripped at the giant leg that dwarfed its entire body even with all its tentacles. All around, the frenzy of the krakens intensified; the waters were thick with flailing tentacles. When the giant pushed forward, the kraken's body exploded in a cloud of purple ink, fully crushed as the giant marched along the seafloor unimpeded. The merman stared up but could see no further than its calves. He could normally see into the void of space itself with his power, but the magic enveloping them was far too strong.

Already the ink cloud had dissipated, he screamed in shock and darted away for the tunnel as a giant deformed hand reached down after him.

From the surface of Pan-Earth, it would have only appeared as a dot of light to the naked human eye in the fullness of a moonless night. But from the heavens, the shooting star pulsated with fiery flames of blue and white towards the planet. A portal larger than any human or elfin city appeared in the void of space before the vessel, descending like a comet and engulfing it.

The comet transformed into its true form from within the pocket-realm—a golden flying sea ship with neither oars nor sails gliding through the sky. The sky ship passed through one-hundred-foot arch after another, each time passing into another realm.

In the cavernous command room of the ship, a gathering of royals, warriors, and wizards—all sky elves—watched the spectacle outside from in front of a giant watch-mirror floating in the center room. In the center of the group stood an elderly elfess with flowing white hair down her shoulders and back, nearly touching the ground. Her white crown and white collared robe had a slight star-like glow.

She could feel a tingling of electricity in the air even before the main doors opened to the throne room. Celestial elves of her age and power could sense the most minute stirring within the air itself or the movement of magic or energy through it.

"We have word, my queen," said the arriving elfin messenger. "The Kings' Caravan has arrived at Atlantea's gates with its customary fleet of ships."

"Is that what you came to tell us?" an elfin noble asked. "King Oughtred and his prince king sons have been traveling the Trail for decades. What is the news in that?"

"And," the messenger continued, "so has this Titan's Caravan."

"The one of fae and humans?" another elfin noble asked rhetorically.

"Yes, prince, led by the human, with a water elfess and human royal. The caravan flies the banners of the fairies of Chrysa, giants of Antaeus, and centaurs of Chiron."

"Did they arrive before or after the Kings' Caravan?" the white elfess asked.

"Together, my queen, or I should say: they pass across the threshold as one. That is the news of note we thought you should know."

The gathering looked past the messenger with expressions of surprise.

"You seem to be without your companion, queen," an approaching voice said to the white elfess from across the chamber as a new elf entered through the great doors to the throne room with his own guards, to join the messenger.

The white elfess was not unattended. Two tall high elfin warriors stood on each side behind her, elegantly dressed in white silver armor with curved-bladed spears in hand, the ends resting on the black marble-like floor.

She smiled at the source of the electric tingling within the air upon her noble skin. The shadow elf stepped closer, dressed from neck to toe in a black royal battle robe. The skin of his face and hand was a midnight black. Two purple-skinned night drow warriors in armor were at his side, following closely.

"Lord Blak," the white elfess greeted. "What an unexpected and pleasurable surprise. Anytime one can speak with one of our rarely-seen shadow elfin cousins, the day is certain to be special. When did you arrive?"

He watched her with pure white eyes. "You know when I arrived."

"Yes, but my guardian is attending to other matters," she said.

"Of course, queen. It's your affair and none of mine." The skin of a shadow elf appeared as the embodiment of darkness itself. He opened his right hand, and a small pouch appeared. "The wager is yours, and I always pay promptly."

"Wager?" the white elfess asked.

"Titan's Caravan. They reached Atlantea. A caravan of humans, lesser elves, and even lesser fae led by no less than a human. No one expected that it was even remotely possible—save you."

"The folly of an old elfess. I was not being serious."

"But you have won the wager nevertheless and should collect what is owed."

The white elfess took the pouch from his hand.

"Does your guardian await them at Atlantea's gates, perhaps?" he asked.

"No, but we will be there shortly for you to see for yourself," she said. "You can greet your champion—the human Oughtred."

"King Oughtred of Xenhelm ceased being a human some time ago, or we would have had no interest in him at all, which begs the question of why a celestial elf of your stature would be so interested in this human-led caravan."

"I am not."

"Though your actions say the opposite."

"What actions?"

When a shadow elf smiled, few could see the expression as even their teeth were as black as night. But celestial elves were one of the few races that could.

"I must have been misinformed then, my queen."

"Yes, I would say so."

"You are the Queen Mother Anelle of the Celestial Elves of Nimbus, directly responsible for the great alliance of celestial, star, and cloud elves. An alliance that includes shadow elves and night drows. An alliance of nymphs and elementals. The alliance of many ancient elves and higher fae kingdoms over the centuries. It would be blasphemy for me to even think you would work against our noble, glorious, powerful, and feared alliance."

"You make too much of trivialities, Lord Blak. If a mere human, even with his sword of Titan metal and shape-shifter not of Pan-Earth are a threat to our empires, maybe we don't deserve to exist after all. My wager was a jest. We've done so before. Do you not remember? We did so before at the prospect of the human King Oughtred and his three sons and their ambitions. You collected the winnings that time around, I believe. No one seemed particularly excited by that wager."

"Much can change in a year."

"For humans, yes. But not us."

"I also hear we lost many elves of the alliance at a battle at the Cyclops City of Mímir-Spring. Were you equally indifferent upon hearing that news?"

"We don't know what happened there. The cyclopes have been in contact with no one since the battle."

"The Battle of the Siren Storms of Madness. That is what they are calling it. We lost many allies there too."

"Crab and spider centaurs are not allies. They are abominations!"

"They serve a purpose. You as a royal can understand that."

"Of course, I do, but we are high elves of ancient royal lineage. We have the luxury of choosing our evil allies with more care."

"Perhaps. Or when one outlives their purpose, then, whatever happens, happens."

The two high elfin warriors stepped in front of the white elfess.

"Was that a threat, shadow elf?" one of them asked.

"Please, high elf, remove yourself from my face. I might take note of a star elf or celestial elf but not a high elf. Even the lesser moon elves have some abilities."

Queen Anelle grabbed the warrior by the shoulder to restrain him. "Come now, the vessel is landing, so we have no time for childish fighting amongst ourselves lest we be vanished from their realm."

Lord Blak walked right up to the white elfess.

"Why are the Atlanteans closing their kingdom to all?"

"Why ask me?"

"The rumor is that King Oughtred plans to conquer Atlantea," another elf in the group called out, "or seize the lands before its gates."

The white elfess turned briefly to the other elf. "That is ludicrous. Our ancient fae races failed in that effort eons ago. The Atlanteans are our most honored allies now. I know this human-now-lich king believes he can do all, but he cannot. I'm surprised at you to believe such nonsense."

"But it was your human who spread the rumor," the shadow elf king said.

"My human? I have no human, Lord Blak."

"We have worked too hard, too long to be thwarted by duplicitous comrades who have suddenly grown a conscience." Blak looked at his night drow guards. "When do we cross into the Atlantean realm?"

"We cross in mere moments, m'lord."

The shadow elf slammed his hands together. A magic ball of black light erupted and swallowed everyone, then the entire command room.

The elfin sky ship had passed under another gigantic arch into a realm of many swirling lakes, fast-moving rivers, water spouts shooting high into the clouds, and crashing waterfalls. Swarms of flying fish fluttered through the air and in and out of the water. Not far away, a floating tower hung above a cloud—a port for sky ships.

A lone Atlantean herald, clothed in an ornate golden robe covering his indigo skin of gemstone, floated above the raging green river below. Startled, he watched the sky elfin vessel explode in a violent display of black light.

Fragments fell to the connecting lake below in a shower of dust and debris.

ENTERING TITAN'S GATE

Their caravan master Traveler stood upon the bow of their white warship's deck as they sailed forward. They never had to use, thankfully, the new ship's eight cannons at the bow or four on the stern to fight their way in. More than a year later, though it seemed far longer, the fabled kingdom of Atlantea was before them at last.

All had grown accustomed to Traveler's battle attire—a hooded cloak, orange-tinted elemental armor, and his sheathed sword on his back. He already knew the sights that lay ahead. For all others, both human and fae, everything seen was with eyes of wonder and excitement. Their three masts had sails fully extended but were not needed. The current of the sea moved the vessel forward like an invisible guiding hand. The deck remained packed with humans, fae, and animals.

Two columns of their fleet of city-ships followed, each their own crews filling the decks. Two dozen vessels of Queen Geneva of the mermaids, Queen Oluania of the oceanids, King Centauro of the sea centaurs, King Traerio of the tritons, and then the water elfin royals Kings Finlor, Elfred, Agis, Queens Amphitrite, Leena, and Eriana. In another column were the cecaelia commanded by the mermaid octopus Queen Atopia who "stood" on her tentacles triumphantly on the deck of her lead ship. But all of the Titan's crew and their allies were triumphant. Neither siren storms, packs of krakens, nor the treachery of the Four Kings had stopped them.

As everyone was enraptured by what was ahead, Traveler and the dog kept a watchful eye on the other column of ships following—Oughtred's large fleet commanded by other human and fae kingdoms. His wizards floated above their ships in the air and called out to a human head of sun fire descending to them. More than one of them pointed to the deck of the white ship of Titan's Caravan.

The fiery humanoid head descended as it transformed into a tall, fully formed glowing figure of a man, clothed in a robe of light, floating above the water. As he hung in the air, his skin became like a blue gemstone. The being was an Atlantean. He had uncharacteristically large eyes but no hair of any kind.

"I am told you are the human named Traveler and all the ships that I see are of Titan's Caravan," the Atlantean said.

"I am Traveler, but not all are of Titan's Caravan. I cannot stay silent in the face of their deception no matter the negative cost to my own party."

"You lived in Atlantea?"

"I did. For some time to travel and study."

"I can see it in the aura around you. I can also see the same in the polymorph at your side. You both lived in our lands for a time."

"We did."

"Then you spent your time in Atlantea wisely. You remain an honorable man."

"True, though I don't know how you can know this after so many years. But I also know Atlanteans are a race of those with second sight. Again, I must caution the kingdom that served as a home of the dark ones who travel with us now as if they are allies when they are nothing but enemies. Enemies who tried to kill us many times on the Trail."

"Those others who travel with you do not partake in deception but follow our instructions, albeit in a very generous way to benefit themselves. No, it is because of you, the human named Traveler, who many in our city remember well and fondly, that the decision was made. All at the threshold, at this time, can enter together as Titan's Caravan, or none can. It is the only exception the Imperium will agree to, and they do so only because of your previous good history with us. Either you will be the last caravan into Atlantea for some time, or the caravan that entered the day before last will be. It is your decision."

"Then I have already made the decision. We sail forward with your permission."

The Atlantean smiled as he nodded. "The permission is given. But is your crew ready?"

"Yes, or so they think. But I will guide them."

The crew of Titan's white ship remained quiet, enchanted by the very first Atlantean they'd ever seen in their lives. He spoke with his lips, but his words seemed to be inside their heads.

Traveler's eye caught sight of Oughtred on his ship. The caravan master looked away quickly to stave off the sickness and hatred of the man with a self-satisfied, duplicitous grin on his face.

"Then sail forth, human called Traveler," the Atlantean said with a nod. "You and your parties may complete your long journey through Titan's Trail into our realm."

He rose back into the sky and once again took the form of a ball of sun fire.

From the deck, the gathered crew gazed out over the ship. The six Antaean giants joined them, towering above everyone else. They remained weakened as their magical strength came from being upon land itself, not on the great oceans of Faë-Land, where land was several thousands of miles below. But they were eager to see the fabled city, too, with their own eyes. The Tree Shepherds had their three main crawling trees grow above the giants and extend their branches out for men. Gnomes, brownies, and gnomoids scurried up the magic trees first and made their way to the topmost branches; the trees were now as tall as the ship was long. The caravan's giant lizards, all two thousand of them, took to the trees with their human minders breathlessly trying to keep up. Little room was left for any others, but other humans, fae, and animals managed to climb up too.

"Is the ship growing, Mr. Traveler?" Pangolin asked, looking around.

"It is, indeed, Mr. Pangolin. Our new ship is a magic ship too and can change its length and width at its captain's command."

"Your command?"

"Yes, but the ship knows how big it should be for its crew."

Laughter and chatter grew louder as they sailed forward. Their allied fleet of other humans and water fae following behind grew even noisier with spontaneous cheers and song.

"At last, we see the fabled kingdom with our own eyes, Mr. Traveler?" Lady Aylen asked.

"Far more than that, princess. But human or fae, no matter the age, it's a spectacle for any lifetime many times over."

The half-elf, Mr. Elman, saw it before everyone else and alerted others. The sea ahead ended abruptly. All the Oceans Omnis, the great watery expanse of the magic realms of Pan-Earth, disappeared not far ahead in the distance. Traveler said nothing as the crew speculated amongst themselves but settled on the theory that they were about to drop into a giant waterfall.

As they sailed to the magic precipice, Traveler looked back one last time. The royals and others did the same to notice that Oughtred's fleet followed in their long black ships. The further away they sailed, they realized that his ships were much greater in number than they had previously thought. Now, Oughtred's fleet appeared as a solid black, impenetrable wall slowly moving on the surface of the great ocean after them.

However, more frightening in the distance, they could still see long black tentacles like slender fingers reaching into the sky. They were so far away from the cities of Kraken's Wake or White Waters but the giant krakens could still be seen.

"Such a view from one's nightmares," the berserker Nirgund said at the king's side.

"The living dead warriors or the krakens?" Pangolin asked.

"Take your pick, Mr. Pangolin. One has heard stories of a single draugr, not ships crowded with armies of them. We've grown up on the stories of the single kraken terrorizing a single kingdom, not a herd of them so vicious they slaughter each other. If we could only get them to fight each other."

Pangolin patted his comrade's shoulder. "Destroy each other," Pangolin said.

Gwyness held her amulet with her hand. Even from their growing distance, it glowed and she could feel its warmth. The dark magic of the draugr army was terrifying. She prayed that she and Lady Aylen would never have to face such creatures in the future but did not feel the Fates would hear her.

With so many ships following them, the horizon was blotted out. Few among the Traveler fleet realized that the path forward to Atlantea was gone, replaced by a hazy cloud of mist. In this realm, it was as if one could only focus on only one thing at a time.

"What do you think Oughtred's planning, Mr. Traveler?" King Aereth asked.

"Nothing good, sire, nothing good."

"I sense he's playing games with us. A boast or a true plan to conquer Atlantea, as he said?"

"Or something else entirely, sire."

"You no longer believe he plans to conquer Atlantea as he said?" Lady Aylen asked.

"Perhaps, princess. Atlantea closes its kingdom the very same time Oughtred arrives. He had amassed a vast army of war wizards at a new city he called New Xenhelm in the heart of Faë-Land, filled with who knows what other creatures and dark magic. We destroyed it."

"You and your dog destroyed it," King Aereth said.

"Yes, sire. But Oughtred still possesses an army of darkness larger than any fae would think possible to assemble. Perhaps, sire, it is a coincidence, and we worry for nothing."

"Come now, Mr. Traveler. I trust your instincts a lot more than that. You should too," King Aereth said.

"My instincts, sire, say there should be concern, but it is no longer our concern. The Atlanteans have been managing their own affairs before any of our nations were even civilizations, both human and fae. The burden is theirs. Your only concern going forward will be to acquire the treasures of the fabled kingdom for your own." He grinned. "This is why you hired me."

"Yes, indeed."

"Sad, though. After all we've been through, Mr. Traveler," Lady Aylen said. "The journey is over. The story is over."

"Do not say anything of the sort, princess. You have the lost city of Rivermouth to rebuild and purchase the tools, provisions, and weapons for your lost warrior mage clans."

She smiled and nodded. "Yes, correct as always, Mr. Traveler."

"Thanks for reminding her, Mr. Traveler," Gwyness said.

"Steep drop!" Mr. Elman's voice rang from the top of one of the crawling trees on the main deck.

"Are we really going to fall?" Gwyness asked.

"If Mr. Traveler isn't worried, nor should we be, Gwyness," Lady Aylen said. "We are in the lands of magic on oceans of magic in a ship of magic. I doubt there will be any falling."

"We cross into the lands of Atlantea," Traveler said.

"But I thought we did already," King Aereth said.

"Almost, sire."

Their vessel crossed an invisible barrier. The sky and everything around them winked out. Shock and awe paralyzed them as their lead ship sailed on black waters with the darkness of the heavens around them. Stars in the distance seemed only several hundred feet above and around them. The sun was behind them. Ahead of them, the ocean did drop off. Everyone aboard was terrified, but they all noticed the smile on their caravan master's face. Their lead ship sailed off the edge first and then dropped.

The sensation wasn't a violent descent but a controlled fall. They sailed down another waterfall to rival that of even Titan's Fall. At the bottom were distant stars and the water raged as it plummeted. After a time, none could tell how much time had passed, they crashed into the black waters. The splash drenched them all but evaporated instantly as if the water wasn't real at all. One after another, the ships of their convoy crashed after them as they all continued forward in near darkness as the stars and the sun from above were gone. Then they saw it. In the distance was a massive oval portal and within there, the normal sky resumed, and there it was—again. The real castle peaks of the fabled city of Atlantea at Titan's End, not the mirage that they had seen before.

"We're truly here," Traveler said with pride.

"The final bridge into Atlantea, Mr. Traveler. What you had told us before. Their own Titan's Bridge. That was it, was it not?" King Aereth asked.

"Yes, sire. The Trail ends as it begins. Their bridge is made of the black void of the heavens, not a physical bridge, though there is a physical one before the entrance to the port city, built by fae long ago but a very small one. I could not spoil all wonders of Atlantea for you. You need to experience it all for yourselves."

"I cannot argue. Wonders, indeed," King Aereth said.

"Any other surprises, Mr. Traveler?" Lady Aylen asked.

"You know I hate surprises, princess."

She scoffed, and others laughed.

Titan's Caravan had departed the Lands of Man in Avalonia across Titan's Bridge, the first marker of Titan's Trail. Through the Lands Between, they first stepped into the magic realms of all fae. In Faë-Land Minor, the lands of fairies, sprites, and giants, they reached Titan's Step. In Faë-Land Major, the lands of elves, hoofed fae, and goblins, they reached Titan's Arch. Across Titan's Walk, they marched through the Forest of Ancients, known also as the Great Forest or Giant Forest, where as their giants'

put it: "you may encounter a fifteen-foot squirrel and then a swarm of twenty-foot fire ants or a thirty-foot snake." Leaving the continental lands of fae behind, they reached the Oceanus Omnis, the empires of mermaids, water nymphs, water elves, sea centaurs, and tritons. They sailed past Titan's Fall, the cosmic waterfall from the heavens. Then to sail a true cosmic waterfall more worthy of the name Titan's Bridge. More than a year later, Titan's Caravan stood aboard their white ship to reach and behold their ultimate destination.

Humans and all fae stood on the forward deck, gawking at the glowing fabled city hanging above the horizon ahead of them. Even most of their animals were mesmerized by the sight. Their sea convoy sailed across another barrier, and they were in the realm of Atlantea at last. The city appeared to be made of solid white gold and rose from the horizon into the heavens, with both the sun and the moon at opposite ends in the sky.

"We made it," Bragg, the dwelf, said with tears in his eyes. His elfin comrades gathered around him were equally caught up in the emotions of the moment. More than one elf patted him on his broad shoulders. Bragg and his men had waited decades more than the rest, but the moment had finally arrived for them as well.

"Yes, indeed, Mr. Bragg," King Aereth said with Lady Aylen, Gwyness, and Hobbs at his side.

A blockade of Atlantean ships sat on clear waters before them. The vessels were balls of light, a single one larger than any ship in Titan's Caravan's or Oughtred's fleet.

The ships formed a wall from one end of the horizon to another. While all others thought it normal, Traveler knew otherwise. The ships slowly drifted apart to allow their fleet passage. He scanned the horizon. The kingdom reached into the sky, past a ring of thick white clouds.

"We bring our year-long fabled quest to an end!" Traveler said to all.

"Hear! Hear!" Cut-Throats, elves, and sprites yelled out.

Traveler gave a forward motion with his hand, and once past the Atlantean light ships, their white ship increased in speed. Their ally fleet of two dozen ships followed in a single line—mermaids, oceanids, tritons, sea centaurs, water elves, and the seventeen cecaelia vessels.

All eyes studied another tall, bald Atlantean on the deck of the light ship with his skin of blue gemstone—their second Atlantean to be seen. He leaned forward in his golden robe to address Traveler.

"We know you," the Atlantean said from the deck of a ship of light.

"Yes," Traveler answered. "I lived here."

"The one who travels to many realms."

"Yes."

"You travel here with friends."

"Some are friends; some are not."

"You are all children of Pan-Earth."

"I wish I could make you understand that not all those children are worthy of your consideration as they only live for cruelty and to cause harm and destruction."

"Do not trouble yourself with such matters. You have returned to Atlantea. Enter and enjoy our magical city of riches and wonder."

"Thank you. But I must inquire. I've never seen your ships such as these before, and to guard the passage to Atlantea. Do you expect danger?"

"The Imperium deals with any threats to Atlantea, as we always have."

"What of the draugr?"

"Draugr?"

"There is a man called Oughtred who follows us. Many of his ships have gathered just outside the entrance to your realm. They are filled with living dead warriors."

"How can something be living and dead? It can only be one."

"They walk by the power of dark magic."

"They are still welcome."

"Welcome? You have no fear of them?"

"No. All beings are as welcome to cross into Atlantea. However, our realm does not allow dark magic and does not allow violence."

"I know of the prohibition of all violence, but what happens if something crosses into Atlantea that lives by dark magic?"

"They vanish into never-more."

Traveler reflected on the information. "I misunderstood what I was told. I thought evil living beings could not cross into your realm."

"The preventative traits are the dark magic and violence of any kind, not whether you call them living or dead, good or evil."

"Then your ship blockade is not for them?"

"We are here to protect the gateway to Atlantea but fear not."

"But you are closing Atlantea for the first time in all of recorded history?"

"Yes, but for only a short time. A thousand of your years."

Traveler smiled. "A thousand years is not a short time, even for an elf."

"You are fortunate then to arrive before that time then to be welcomed by those already in the city."

"When will Atlantea officially close to outsiders?"

"At the next full blue moon."

Traveler knew his moon charts—only three days away.

The Atlantean smiled; his gemstone face was as pliant as natural skin. "Do not trouble yourself, the one called Traveler," he said. "Go forward."

The Atlantean nodded a final time as their ships slowly moved past the wall of Atlantean ships of light.

Traveler removed his telescope from his cloak pocket while he quickly glanced back.

"Very informative conversation," King Aereth said.

Oughtred's dark fleet still followed. He did not want to spoil the awe of the nearing fabled city for any of the caravan crew, so he returned his gaze forward and peered ahead through his telescope.

"Very much so, sire."

"Does that mean we could come across a manticore within the walls of Atlantea?" Pangolin asked.

"Perhaps, but it would be friendly," Traveler said with a grin.

"Friendly?" Lady Aylen remarked. "Mr. Traveler, we're here for treasure. No more monsters."

The caravan had already magically forgotten Oughtred's fleet as the enchantment of Atlantea was all-consuming.

The dark bargain would come to pass. They could only enter Atlantea if all, including Oughtred, came through as one. They'd officially be the last caravan to enter Atlantea in their time. The news stunned most aboard, but they were glad nonetheless that they would have the honor of entry in the name of their own kingdoms. Traveler knew the Atlanteans well. When they made a decision, it was final. No other party or caravan would be allowed entry into the fabled kingdom for a thousand years. Humans could not remain in any fae city of magic forever, so when those of their Titan's Caravan left, with the coveted riches for their kingdoms, it would be for good. There would be no other Titan's Caravan—or Oughtred's Kings' Caravan—for many human generations to come, if ever.

The enormous circular structure of Titan's Gate neared, literally coming out of invisibility in a wavering effect like a "visual earthquake."

The fleet sailed across the shadow of the one-hundred-foot-tall Colossus of Titan's Point, towering behind them on a flat island. The statue honoring the Titan, or myth thereof, known as the Maker of All Mountains, wore a helmet over his saddened face, clad in chest armor, dragging his fabled weapon, the Star Slayer, upon the earth was the penultimate marker to Atlantea. They had seen statues as tall in Faë-Land, but this one had a much thicker body. Traveler told them that centuries ago, Titan's Point and Titan's Gate were once a continent apart.

"A meteor storm of giant rocks falling to Pan-Earth from the heavens destroyed much of the continent that the Colossus of Titan's Point stood upon, leaving only a mere island. That continent was home to many, many towns and ports that sprouted up over the eons. Some of those fae went to Titan's Fall, and others went to other cities on the sea. Through magic, the Atlanteans pulled the island of the Colossus of Titan's Point closer to the city," Traveler told them.

"Why didn't they all move into Atlantea, Mr. Traveler?" Lady Aylen asked.

"You live in Atlantea; you must live by their rules. Not all fae wish to live by the rules of others, even Atlanteans. Profiting off them and its trade is a different matter."

The final marker of the ancient Titan's Trail to Atlantea, Titan's Gate, was a thick circular structure of stone, fifty or so feet in width, and one-fourth of the Gate was below the waterline. The material of the gate appeared to be carved out of a single piece of solid stone, but as they neared, its reflections suggested more of a metal of some kind. The Gate's entrance was well over a mile high, and once vessels passed through it, the kingdom's shore was clearly visible under a mirror-like blue sky, though according to their caravan master, it was still at least a hundred miles away.

The moment their lead ship crossed the threshold, like they had already experienced, they passed into another realm. Thick billowy white clouds hung in the sky, the lowest twenty feet above, but it was the wildlife in the air that grabbed everyone's attention.

Quillen already had his magic sketchbook open. "That's them, Mr. Traveler, the perytons, or deer birds. Are they friendly?"

"As long as you do not go near their nests, Mr. Quillen, but their lairs are so high up and far away on the side of the cliffs that they should be out of your reach," their caravan master replied, "even to you."

To one side were mountains with steep cliffs. Their outward appearance seemed hazy as if an illusion. They were many miles away, but how far was not clear. The side of the cliffs reached beyond the height of the Colossus outside the gateway, possibly higher, but where they ended on either side was not certain.

"Do these perytons have teeth, Mr. Traveler?"

"They do, Mr. Quillen. Retractable and for fighting, so be nice to them."

The perytons were as large as horses with the antlered heads, legs of a deer, and the wings and body of a hawk. As they circled high above, in many different flocks, their collective birdsong was loud but not frightening.

Traveler walked into the crowd on the deck to the supplies. He reached into one of the food baskets of a pull-cart manned by the pech. When he returned, he gave young Quillen some of the ambrosia fruit. The boy flashed a smile and looked up at the circling perytons above them. He raised his arm with one of the pieces of fruit and shook his hand to attract them.

"Give him some space," Traveler directed. Everyone on the deck moved back from the boy.

"How do I call one of them?" he asked, when suddenly three of the beasts landed right in front of him.

Quillen jumped back a bit. The three perytons stared at him with big black, curious eyes. Up close he could see how beautiful the colors of the feathers on their chest were. The body feathers were brown, but the chest feathers were shiny blues, greens, yellows, and indigo. Their antlers weren't massive but big and sturdy enough to effectively gore a man if they had to.

"They're bigger than I thought," Quillen said. The beasts were taller than him, but he sensed no malice in them and extended his hand. In moments, Quillen had the magical beasts literally eating out of his hand.

The boy could hear applause and cheers behind him. He smiled but didn't take his eyes off them. They were friendly, but that didn't change the fact that the talons of their two feet could slash him in half with little effort. As they chewed the last bit of their fruit, he reached forward slowly to touch the forehead of one of the animals. The peryton stepped forward and closed its eyes to receive Quillen's stroking of his forehead.

"He likes the lad," a man said behind him.

The peryton enjoyed the attention but then opened its eyes. It stared at him, yawned, shook its head, and shot up into the sky with its two other companions to join the flocks above. Next to him, their tucked-in wings seemed small, but in flight, they stretched out wide to carry them along the air without a sound. The one that he had petted made a melodic caw, then all the perytons in unison made the same sound, echoing through the area. With a big smile on his face, Quillen stood there admiring them. Their birdsong repeated as they circled around and around above the boy and finally flew off to their nests on the mountain cliffs.

Quillen would have plenty to sketch in his magic book that night.

"Oh, there's more, Mr. Quillen," Traveler said.

"More, sir?" Quillen asked.

"You'll see, Mr. Quillen. You will be quite busy with your sketchbook in Atlantea."

With both Titan's Point and Titan's Gate behind them, all that was left between them and the shores of Atlantea was a bright blue sea. A network of large white stone piers jutted out from the land, evenly spaced. As they got closer, the shore looked to be crystalline and sparkled under the sun, with the land sloping up to a field of lime green grass swaying in the breeze. Beyond that was a smaller version of Titan's Bridge, which more than a few of the human men remarked on. The first official marker of Titan's Trail was a bridge, and so was its final unofficial marker. At the other end of the bridge was the open entrance of a castle wall of towering keeps into the sky, with the beginnings of the solid white golden city beyond it.

"Are we truly the last caravan to be admitted entry into the fabled kingdom, Mr. Traveler?" King Aereth asked.

"Yes, sire. The Atlanteans are merciful people but when they make a decision, it is unwavering."

"Then our caravan was more fortuitous than any of us could have imagined."

"It would seem so, sire."

"Will their payment to enter be the same, Mr. Traveler?" the king asked.

"Wizard!" Traveler called out, surprising the royals. "I know you listen. Show yourself."

A small cloud formed in the air in front of them and took the mirage–like form of an oval mirror. The face of Oughtred's humanoid lizard man wizard appeared.

Traveler did not wait for him to speak. "Your King Oughtred will pay the full entrance of Titan's Caravan into Atlantea."

A devious smile came over the iguana man's face. "My king was expecting this. Payment awaits at the city's door for you to take charge of. No such trifles will deny all of Titan's Caravan from taking its honorable place within the walls of Atlantea as the last human-led caravan for a thousand years."

The image and the cloud disappeared.

"How did you know?" King Aereth asked.

"They've been listening and watching us!" Lady Aylen said with anger.

"A safe assumption of ones so evil." Traveler turned to the princess. "You can return your payment of entrance to the vaults of Sirnegate or use for a new city," he said. "You as well, sire."

"Oughtred knew what you were going to do," King Aereth said.

"Not a difficult guess on his part, sire."

"Especially if he listens to us even now as we speak," Lady Aylen said.

A single city-ship pulled alongside theirs. The vessel began to submerge, stopping when its main deck was level. The entire water fae royals were gathered— Mermaid Queen Geneva of Kraken's Wake, Queen Oluania of the Oceanids of Kraken's Wake, King Centauro of the Sea Centaurs, King Traerio of the Tritons, the water elfin royals: Kings Finlor, Elfred, Agis, Queens Amphitrite, Leena, and Eriana, and, standing above all on her tentacle legs, Queen Atopia of the Cecaelia. The two selkie leaders,

Queen Nori and King Otari of the Selkie Clan of Therian, stood alongside.

"You may see Nori and I again," Otari said.

"Thank you and good journey, human caravan master of Titan's Caravan," Queen Geneva said. On the deck, merfolk, nymphs, sea centaurs, tritons, elves, and cecaelia stood in formation at attention. All the water fae nodded as the vessels continued the descent and disappeared underwater.

"Our fleet is gone," Lady Aylen said sadly, looking behind them.

Others turned and noticed that every ship of the water fae were gone. All that remained was Queen Issaleth's red ship.

"Atlantea has underwater docks for water fae and those on the clouds for flying caravans," Traveler told them.

Cackling black birds flew over them and grabbed everyone's attention again. The birds had the heads of smiling bats. In the sea ahead of the ship, yellow dolphins swam away in the same direction. The dolphins had the heads of frogs. The pookas!

"Your friends are leaving us too, Mr. Traveler?" Lady Aylen asked.

"They have no desire for treasure, princess. There are many islands around Atlantea for them to explore. For them, the caravan is over too. They did what I hired them to do."

Traveler's eyes locked on the other fleet behind them. Oughtred's fleet was still coming through the Gate. The

Atlanteans told him not to be troubled, but how could he not be. A human who had turned to dark magic to become as evil as any demon had been allowed to casually sail into Atlantea, the ultimate kingdom of the magic of light, with Titan's Caravan as his key to entry. A dark army commanded by a human lich let into the fabled kingdom by him—Traveler.

"Will we ever see them again, Mr. Traveler?" Lady Aylen asked, still watching Traveler's shape-shifting fae fly and swim off.

"Perhaps, princess."

When the two human vessels docked, their caravans departed down gangplanks and gathered together for the last time. Upon a shore of crystal sand, humans and fae instinctively grabbed handfuls to stuff into a pocket or pouch for a keepsake.

"We both had ships that we barely had time to break in," Queen Issaleth said to the king.

"Our substitute ships served their noble purpose," King Aereth said. "Here we are in Atlantea."

"Yes, the sirens can keep our empty ships. Our time together was also short but no less honorable," Queen Issaleth said. "We overcame the great many obstacles placed before us and succeeded where so many others failed. My late father smiles from the heavens, and I know your late wife and son do as well, sire. Thank you."

King Aereth took her left hand and gave it a kiss. "A pleasure and honor to have traveled alongside a royal house of an allied empire, Queen Issaleth."

The queen stepped to Traveler. The caravan master repeated the gesture and smiled.

"If my empire had known of your superior capability and knowledge, we would have joined you at the start. My caravan suffered great casualties along the Trail."

"But you have arrived, queen, for the honor of your kingdom."

"Yes, thanks to you, sir. Are you certain we should not wait for you?"

"No need, queen," Traveler said. "I am sure your crew is as anxious to secure your kingdom's treasure, especially knowing that you will be Baltica's last caravan to the fabled kingdom for a thousand years."

"So true, and sad. Good luck, Titan's Caravan. I look forward to a future where we will all be back in the Lands of Man and enjoy a great feast with all our kingdoms in attendance."

"I would like that very much, Queen Issaleth," King Aereth said.

Queen Issaleth led her chief wizard, knights, domovoi brownies, giant four-armed ant men, and warriors to the final bridge into Atlantea as everyone watched with sadness.

"Mr. Hobbs," Traveler called out.

Their steward ran to him. "Yes, sir."

"Let us march into Atlantea as we did on the land Trail. Have the flag bearers fly our banners high, our Brothers Brimm playing loud, and Mr. Pangolin, can you and your vanguard do the honors?"

Their master-at-arms grinned. "Mr. Traveler, it took you long enough to get us here."

Human and fae laughed as they got into their column formations.

Traveler gave one final look towards the Gate and the growing Oughtred fleet gliding through like a dark, malevolent cloud sitting on the surface of the bright blue sea of Atlantea. No one else was concerned by them anymore. What none of them knew, both human and fae, was that the realm of the Atlanteans was no different than humans leaving the Lands of Man and entering the magical lands for the first time, as when they crossed from the Lands Between into the Mirage Plains almost a year ago. He had lived in Atlantea and, as a result, was immune to the enchanting effect of the realm. All cares and fears were washed away by the magic reverie of the realm. If they were to look back, they would see the splendid Titan's Gate, but Oughtred's fleet would not hold in their minds and be a formless shadow at the outer edges of their periphery. They would not look back because they didn't want to. The fabled kingdom of Atlantea was ahead!

Traveler was no longer their caravan master. He could not see Oughtred but could feel the evil man's presence, likely watching them even now. He believed that despite Oughtred's claims to the contrary, the Xenhelmian king would seek revenge against them for the deaths of his sons even within Atlantea—somehow. Traveler was certain of it, no matter how impossible such a thing was within the timeless power of the Atlantean realm. For Titan's Caravan, his role in Atlantea, along with the dog, would be as their guardian against the darkness masquerading as formless shadows at the edges of perception.

CARAVAN'S END

Nearly a year ago, they first began their quest. For the humans who had been with the caravan from the beginning, the memories seemed to be from decades ago. They had left the Lands of Man behind to cross into the first region of the Magical Lands—Faë-Land Minor, the lands of fairies, sprites, and giants.

Their caravan master had left them behind to rest, or so he said, flying away on the back of the dog who transformed into a giant white hawk with multicolored wings like a peacock, colored plumed feathers sprouting from its head, and eyes the brightest blue they had ever seen. Traveler and animal flew high into a perfect blue sky and disappeared into a sea of massive white clouds.

They rested in their camp on the other side of the Mirage Plains' magical barrier. The first two days were quiet and uneventful. The men told endless stories to each other to pass the time. That and regale at the awe of the luscious land, which twinkled with enchantment, bold and bright colors, and they could not wait until they saw their first fairy, elf, mermaid, or unicorn.

On the third day, however, Lady Aylen had looked out across their five-thousand-man-strong camp and saw why Traveler had left them there. Most of the men were in such a deep state of sleep that nothing could rouse them. For those not asleep, men were sleepwalking, their eyes closed, wandering aimlessly from side to side or in circles. Others seemed mad, laughing uncontrollably to themselves. When she looked into their eyes, their gaze was someplace else. Others had flora or cobwebs growing on their bodies. She didn't know it at the time, but she was immune. Traveler and his dog knew why. She was not human after all but fae.

Now, their caravan master left them again to become accustomed to the great magic of Atlantea. They all had crossed into a realm of magic by beings beyond Pan-Earth, and from an ancient time so long ago, maybe even at the birth of the Titans. For any human or fae first crossing into the realm of Atlantea, they too would succumb to a form of sleep or lethargy for a time. No one was immune.

Her mind had the image of a prancing owl hippogriff. The beautiful golden beast had the hind half of a horse and the front half, including the head and forelegs, of a giant owl. Repeating in her head was the hypnotic harmony of the beast's birdsong, unlike anything she had heard before. The steed belonged to someone meeting Mr. Traveler, but she wasn't sure who.

The land dazzled her with its many colors. Giant insects flew about, as did tiny sprites with glistening membranous wings. They were everywhere, playfully observing the new visitors to Atlantea.

She remembered bright green, yellow and blue trees filled with fruit that could have been apples, oranges, grapes, or all. Fairies, sprites and birds sat on their branches or leaves. Butterflies flew all around them like a benevolent swarm. The river was filled with fish and water lilies. Flowers were growing at the edges on either side of the river—so many beautiful tulips, lilies, ferns, dandelions, and mushrooms too.

Were those treefolk or flower fae she remembered? Or did the trees and flowers look humanoid?

Lady Aylen struggled between sleep and a dreamy consciousness where she could barely distinguish reality from dreams. She wondered if the realm's magic was altering her very memories of recent events. The images of the city-ship of the mermaids, water nymphs, water elves, sea centaurs, tritons, and especially the mermaid octopus queen with her tentacle legs were so strong in her mind. For a moment, she had forgotten where she was— her bed chamber within the outer lodgings of Atlantea. But she could not recall how she arrived there.

Occurrences flashed by. The darklings were cackling as they swam off. The two fairies—Wildglow and Sunpetal— were met by a fairy cloud of armored fairies. The leader saluted Traveler as she led them all off into the sky.

The caravan's humanoid animal men—frogmen, lizard men, squirrel-like men, fae that looked like raccoons, possums, foxes, rabbits, birds, and mice—marched toward the city together with their animal companions: the frogmen with their giant crabs, the possum men with their giant turtles, the raccoon men with their giant porcupines, the bird men with their large jackalopes (rabbits with antlers as hounds) or enfields (animals with the head of a fox, forelegs like an eagle, and the hindquarters and tail of a wolf). Others guided the group's giant ducks and cranes. Finally was the animal men's own sorcerer, the surly mole-looking fae with his giant carnivorous moose companion.

The animal men began singing with glee in their own races' unique way—squeaks, grunts, chirps, clicks, yelps. They disappeared into the crowds of the ante-city. Song was their way of saying "goodbye."

Lady Aylen felt tears streaming down her cheeks as she recalled the members of the caravan dispersing and each going their own way. The collective euphoria of arriving at Atlantea. Tears of joy. A welcome but bittersweet ending to their quest for unimaginable treasurers for their peoples and kingdoms.

She remembered their human lizard minders letting their giant lizards loose. Traveler conversing with a strange, green-skinned fairy-like fae floating in the air. Their caravan master said their giant lizards would be led back to their natural territories known as Vivaria. For many generations, the lizards would share the stories of their march with Titan's Caravan.

Traveler had arranged for passage back to the human lands for their fae humans, who had been trapped in the magical lands far longer than any man wanted. One hundred men: Tyfer, Oeric and all the others were so happy, crying, smiling, shaking Traveler's hand, and hugging him. They wanted no treasure. They wanted to return to the Lands of Man and live out the last of their days, however long that might be.

The dwelf Bragg, overcome by emotion, and his elfin comrades mounted their carnivorous Diomerian Mares and bid everyone good-bye with tears in their eyes. They galloped into the gates of the first outer settlements of Atlantea. Bragg's eight-foot-tall metal golem, Mr. Glog, ran after them as best it could. The fae berserkers also said goodbye, especially to Pangolin and the Cut-Throats. The fae berserkers would join Bragg and his elves.

She remembered Traveler telling their healer, Mr. Gresham, to join them. Bragg and the fae berserkers would undoubtedly need the services of a healer, even one in training.

"Thank you, Mr. Traveler. I will spend as much time here learning the healing arts as you did. Thank you for giving me the second chance you did with the caravan."

They all felt they would never see any of them again.

All the sprites flew off to the cities of Atlantea—brownies, pech, gnomes, and horned gnomoids. Many of the men had forgotten that all sprites could fly.

The large noble Strag bowed his antlered head as a final gesture and led away the elaphines, rusines, and cervids that had joined their caravan. They moved as a quiet herd into the main gate of Atlantea. Elaphine archers truly were as gifted as elves and centaurs.

"My people will speak about these days and our journey for many centuries, for as long as we can tell the story to our children," he had told them.

Ammon, the chief faun, waved with his daughter, Zefea, at his side. He led his fauns to follow, and now all the hoofed fae of the caravan were gone.

Lady Aylen could not remember Ursi or any of the fae-bloods leaving them, nor the drows.

She felt a wave of sadness because she didn't remember seeing any of the half-elves either. She grew accustomed to them as her guardswomen and the tiny owl griffins they minded, or Mr. Elman, the half-elf whose magic eyes could see further than any elf within the caravan, including her.

For the Elfin Questing Knights, their farewells took some time. Lyre of the Woodland Elf Kingdom of Bravehowl, Taylos of the Desert Elf Kingdom of Falconbright, and Shadu-mun of the Moon Elf Kingdom of Nightshade. King Aereth and Lady Aylen personally bid goodbye to every one of the one-hundred-fifty high elves who saluted with their unicorn swords, one hundred fifty desert elves with their magic falcons perched on a shoulder, one hundred fifty woodland elves with their leopard axes at their side, and one hundred fifty moon elves.

"Where is Chief Ethor?" King Aereth had asked.

"He is already within Atlantea. But he left this." Lyre the high-elf handed King Aereth a folded letter.

"Good journey," King Aereth said. "Your people will be forever welcome in my kingdom of Helm Earldom or any of the Kings' Elder, Strongbridge and Eastmoor."

"The same is true for the kingdom of Sirnegate," Lady Aylen added.

"Then you may see an elf at your gates one day," Shadu-mun said.

The elves marched through the gates into Atlantea. Ahead of them were the great Antaean armored ten-foot giants Grakdar, Barg, Arteus, Aronir, Alceir, and Alebar, laughing loudly as they waved goodbyes with their even longer warhammers triumphantly raised in the air. The human men of King Aereth and Lady Aylen responded with cheers and applause. The humans, with Lady Aylen and Gwyness, were back to their original numbers when they left the Lands of Man, save the three hundred eagle-headed flying hounds of the Cut-Throats. The chamroshes would be with their individual masters for life. She remembered it all clearly, but when her thoughts moved to Traveler...There were words of thanks and praise, but then he seemed to drift away, or was it the memory?

Pangolin said that even if they hadn't fought a single battle on the Trail, the experience, the close bond they had grown between every human and fae on their caravan was stronger than any warrior like himself or any berserker could achieve between war comrades. It was a bond that would last a lifetime. They had walked together to Hades and back. They were forever comrades of Titan's Trail.

Their master-at-arms' words lingered in her mind for a while.

Then Oughtred! His evil face and dark ships upon the waters. But then The Old One appeared. The hulking giant in dark clothes wearing a knight's helmet completely covering his head stood at the base of a white castle and beckoned with a clawed hand.

Lady Aylen awoke and sat up in her bed. She quickly looked around. Only Gwyness was in the royal tent in an adjacent bed, lying fast asleep.

"What is happening? I recollect things, but I'm not sure what is reality from daydreaming," Lady Aylen said to herself. "What of our kirins? I can't remember what became of them."

She lay back down, staring at the ceiling.

"Here we are in the fabled kingdom of Atlantea at long last, happy and relieved. But why do I feel so uneasy? As if something bad is waiting for us."

"Go to sleep, Lady Aylen."

The princess looked over at Gwyness, whose eyes never opened. "You're awake."

"I'm trying to sleep, but you keep talking in yours."

"I was dreaming."

"You can be quiet about it."

"I saw him."

"I know."

"You know? Who? How do you know who I mean?"

"Sleep, Lady Aylen. We can speak about all of it when we wake."

"I will when you tell me who you mean."

"Promise?"

"Yes, I promise."

"The Old One."

Lady Aylen sat up again. "You did see him too? In the dream? Does that mean he's here? Here in Atlantea? He did say that. Where's Mr. Traveler? Why can't I remember where he went? We were saying farewell then...I can't remember."

"Good night, Lady Aylen." Gwyness turned her body away from the princess and covered her head with the covers.

"How did we get in this tent? I don't remember us erecting our tent. And where are we exactly?"

Atlantea's magic permeated every grain of soil, every droplet of water, every particle of air, and all who walked through its realms. Even humans of the most unremarkable ability were imbued with its magic. As Traveler walked from the ante-city to the plains just outside its walls, he could feel the power flowing through him. He moved through the crowds of fae and beasts moving about within, many never before seen by any human or fae of their Titan's Caravan. Even within its special sheath on his back, he could feel the slight heat of magical flames from his sword as the power of inanimate objects of magic were also magnified. His dog walked beside him with the forelimbs of a giant hawk and colored wings folded down his back, but his tail ended in a hardened bony mass much like a flail. The dog would take many griffin hybrid forms while in Atlantea as he had done when they were last in the fabled kingdom.

The party that waited for them were the curmudgeonly väki. Dozens of the frowning, full-bearded little men with pointy hats and dressed in charred dark brown and orange fabric. The sprites were some of the most powerful fire elementals in the Magical Lands. Here in the realms of Atlantea, their bodies radiated with transparent flames without heat, and their eyes glowed with orange.

"What do you want?" one asked. "Our business is done with you. We did our task, protected your treasures, and delivered each to their own party upon arrival in Atlantea."

"How could we part without parting words on my part?" Traveler replied with a grin.

"We do not know why you humans and elves waste time with nonsense. We traveled together. We fought together. We arrived. You paid us. We delivered your treasures. That is all. We never see each other again."

"Oh, that would be a shame not to be in each other's company again."

"Not a shame. We will not be able to return to our lands for some time until we get the smell out of our clothes."

"Then answer something for me."

"What?"

"Why are the Atlanteans closing their kingdom? Do your people know?"

"Why ask us? You know the Atlanteans. You lived in Atlantea. This is our first time here, human. We know nothing."

"Nothing at all. None of haltija-kind?"

"Haltija-kind? Tulen väki do not concern ourselves with any other väki. We are väki of fire, not water, flora, ice, or others."

"What of the väki of precious gems?"

"What of them? The väki of gemstone know nothing of Atlanteans. Atlanteans look like gemstone, but they are not gemstone, human. They are not even of Pan-Earth. You know this."

"Would you tell me if you did know more?"

"No. We're leaving. This realm has heightened our senses. You humans smell worse than the elves."

Traveler grinned. "Then I bid you a long life and farewell and...thank you."

Thanks or praise of any kind incensed these väki. Their perpetual frowns almost creased their faces down to the bottom of their chins in disgust.

"Uggh!" they said in unison, turned, and disappeared into invisibility.

Traveler laughed. He could still see the invisible flames emanating from their bodies as they marched to the edge of the river way and dove in. The water bubbled and boiled for a mere moment. The väki were of fire and at home within the earth, but they could fly and swim too, like all sprites.

Were they not staying in Atlantea for a while?

He probably would never know and likely would never see their spritely, tulan väki friends ever again, as they said. His eyes peered out towards the Colossus of Titan's Point. But the one hundred feet statue likeness of the humanoid Titan known as the Maker of All Mountains was outside their inner realm and not to be seen, especially with the common occurrence of clouds floating just above the waters.

He peered out to where the väki had submerged in the water. Haltija, like leshies, tree people, and fairies, were an ancient race with age-old knowledge. Would they know why Atlantea was closing to all outside their realm? Despite their words, the question was, do väki lie? Yes. Would they lie to him, a mere human? Absolutely, yes, just to be rid of him and answer no more questions.

As she stared up at the high vaulted white ceiling from her bed, Lady Aylen's eyes were pools of swirling water. She could sense all the water around her—in her own body, of Gwyness, rivers beyond sight, the lakes, and the ocean far away. When they battled the elves at Fae'el and the drowess, Dr'amal amplified her power, Lady Aylen was frightened of her true water elemental power. As he lay in her bed, she realized her potential was far greater, but there was no fear at all in her.

She reached out with one hand. Her skin shimmered with a bluish tint. She got out of the bed and stood to look over herself. Was she taller? She definitely felt stronger.

"Amazing, is it not, princess."

Lady Aylen looked across the room. Gwyness watched her, already dressed in her black attire. Her maiden's eyes were no longer light brown but a shade indistinguishable from black.

"You are different too," Lady Aylen said.

"The magic of the place is more powerful than we've ever encountered. Mr. Traveler said we must take things slow until we are fully comfortable with the changes."

"Where is he? Did he really leave without so much as a word?"

"Leave? Don't you remember?"

"I—I think so. Not all. But how can he just leave us?"

"Our caravan master did his deed. He brought us across the Lands of Man and fae to Atlantea. But we will see him and his dog again." Gwyness smiled. "We have our treasure to acquire."

"Yes." Lady Aylen looked at her hands and arms. "I feel strong enough to take on an army by myself."

"Mr. Traveler said you might say that."

"Why can't I remember him leaving? What did he say to you?"

Gwyness laughed as she walked to the princess. "The memories will fully return. The reason you can't remember is because you fainted."

"Fainted?"

"Yes, fainted. And Mr. Traveler caught you and carried you here."

"Carried me? A princess."

"Do not be embarrassed. You were not the only one."

"Who else?"

"King Aereth…"

Lady Aylen laughed. "The king too. Good. Then I do not feel embarrassed. Who else?"

"Mr. Pangolin almost did, but he caught himself. However, many of the Cut-Throats did."

"Very good. Even better. There will be no teasing of the women from them."

Gwyness put her hand on Lady Ayen's shoulder. "Princess, please listen to me carefully. The magic of Atlantea empowers all within it, but there is a price."

"A price?"

"We live under its rules. One must never, ever raise a hand or weapon in violence. If you do, the magic of the realm will send you back to where you came in an instant. Worse than what Oughtred did to us in the Avalonia when he used that teleportation spell. You would be sent back to Sirnegate as you are, as if you never set out on the path to Atlantea to begin with. Even worse, you would never be able to return since Atlantea is closing to all humans and fae for a thousand years. Mr. Traveler gave me the assignment of ensuring you fight no one, no matter how provoked. He even had me secure your war tridents and my war hammers in a locked chest."

"Wise precaution. When do we see our Mr. Traveler then? He remains in the city?"

"He will join us when we have our treasures and see us off back to our kingdoms."

Lady Aylen's attention was drawn to the open balcony of their bedchamber. "Were we not in a tent?"

Gwyness laughed. "Tent? We are in a city. Why would we be in a tent? We're in one of the best inns for newcomers."

A gust of wind moved the curtains wildly as the princess stepped onto the balcony with Gwyness. It had been night, so the maiden hadn't done so before either. Both were equally speechless at the sight.

"We are in the ante-city of the kingdom," Gwyness said, "for newcomers to settle in for a time before moving on."

"Moving on?" Lady Aylen asked.

"Moving onto the real cities of Atlantea," Gwyness replied.

The outer city structures, or the ante-city, were dwellings of one to ten stories with a lake beyond it at the bottom of a row of giant statue heads dozens of feet in the air with a thunderous waterfall flowing from their open mouths. Above the waterfalls was a circular archway whose edges were almost beyond their periphery. On the other side of the archway was another realm with floating white cities resting in the air, and above them were three moons.

"Pan-Earth has only one moon," Gwyness said.

"Where are we? What is this place Atlantea? Realms within realms within realms. But where? Gwyness, do you think these lands of Atlantea where we are going to acquire our treasures may not even be on Pan-Earth at all?"

"Yes, it does seem possible."

"We should have kept our caravan master's services a bit longer as a guide. He did live here."

"We will see him again."

"What else did he say?"

"He said he'd look in on us from time to time."

"What of the others? King Aereth and your Mr. Pangolin?"

"My Mr. Pangolin?"

"Gwyness, your amulet. I've never seen it glow like that."

Gwyness nodded. "I know. It glows in a different color than before. It is not sensing evil or danger, though."

"Your skin has a slight glow too, like mine."

"The magic of this city affects all, whether you are of magic or not."

Lady Aylen's head turned, catching sight of a flying caravan of sylphs and undines on giant flying fish. "Well, well. Our airy and water elemental enemies."

"Lady Aylen, you are already forgetting what I told you. Listen to your former healer."

"Former healer? What do you mean?"

Gwyness took a small gem from her robe pocket, placed it in her hand, and the spell engaged—Traveler's voice spoke from the gem.

"Good day, Lady Aylen. If you hear this, we have arrived in Atlantea at long last. Princess, if you heed nothing else from me, heed this. You cannot lift a physical hand or cast a spell or use any powers in violence against anyone in this kingdom or its lands, for any reason. Your year-long journey will be for naught. You would be returned not just to Avalonia, where we began our trek. You would be standing outside the gates of your royal kingdom of Sirnegate with no more than the clothes on your back. Within Atlantea there can be no violence, so do not even allow a violent thought to enter your mind. No matter what foul creature or enemy you encounter. This Atlantean spell applies to all—to you, to them, to me, all—so do not be provoked or fooled, as there are many a fae that will try."

The voice ceased, and Lady Aylen gave the gem back to Gwyness. "I will heed our former caravan master because nothing on Pan-Earth or beyond will send me back to Sirnegate without our treasure after all this."

Lady Aylen saw the look of a startled Gwyness and turned. In the distance, several celestial nymphs floated in the sky with the three moons behind them, glaring at them.

"How could beings so outwardly beautiful be so wicked and ugly within?" Lady Aylen asked. She didn't know if they could hear her, but when laughter echoed in the air and the nymphs turned and flew away out of sight, her query was answered.

"In a realm where violence is not allowed and applies to all."

"All without exception, Lady Aylen."

"What if I were to throw a glass of water in their face?"

"Lady Aylen!"

While their lodgings were more than adequate, the berserkers, finally within the walls of Atlantea, were not going to spend a minute anywhere other than in the streets and establishments of the ante-city. Yes, some were drowsy, and few were napping but for most, they found the loudest tavern they could find. The one they took over was run by a new race of fae to them—looking like grinning dwarves with arms and legs that seemed to have no bones at all and were as fond of merriment and drinking as they.

When the axe fell, everyone froze. The look on I-wulf's face was of sheer terror. He looked up and all around. When everyone was sure that the realm's magic wasn't going to whisk him away, Pangolin marched over to him and grabbed the axe from the ground.

"I-wulf, I wish you were taken back to Avalonia for being so foolish!"

"It slipped from my hands."

"There was no chance of the Vanishing," an elderly dwarfoid said to them with a toothy grin. "Those who rise to violence vanish, not dropping weapons on tavern floors."

"What does this Vanishing look like?" Nirgund asked. "Does it hurt?"

"One moment you're here, the next you're there."

"There?" Pangolin asked.

"Wherever you came from?"

Pangolin looked at the berserkers shaking his head. "Imagine being sent back to the Lands of Man after all that we have endured over this past year."

"I'd kill myself for sure," I-wulf said.

"They're here!" a berserker yelled.

Everyone's attention turned to the main entrance to the tavern, where two giant dwarves stood with large, stuffed sacks over their shoulders.

"Who purchased food?" one of the dwarf giants said.

The drunken feast had spilled out into the streets around the tavern where the men fed their chamroshes and Nirgund his thirteen alphyns, who were kept occupied with play. The dwarfen giants shook their magic sacks and out fell tables of food: fish, venison, beef, pork, veal, goat, lamb, rabbit, hare, mutton, swans, herons and poultry, chickens, quail, cuckoo, hams, sausages, lamb and veal, turkey, and duck.

While the men and their beasts gorged themselves on the food, Pangolin quietly watched. He had noticed it within himself—his earthen armor was already of magic, but it radiated with a greater power within this realm. But all berserkers were of magic. The rage within that triggered enhanced strength and stamina was of magic. Pangolin could see a glow radiating from all of the men— their eyes and skin. Within the alphyns, their reptilian wolf-hounds, he could see the flames within them flickering and shining through their eyes, ears, nostrils, and mouths. From the chamroshes, the magic made them larger and more powerful.

He knelt down to touch the ground and then grabbed the rich soil into his hand. Clearly, there was an affinity to the earth that he had never felt before. He rubbed the soil on his right gauntlet and stared at it. Metal and earth reacted to each other. He did not know what it meant but knew there was an unrealized power of his armor within the Atlantean realm.

Pangolin thought of the genius to the Atlanteans' "Vanishing" spell of any engaging in violence within the realm. He had seen wars in the Lands of Man. They had encountered a fraction of such in the Lands of Fae. Within the Oceanus Omnis dwelt even more powerful fae and creatures. Without such a prohibition magic spell, any battle within its realms would be of a magnitude powerful enough to destroy its kingdom. He was sure he could not imagine how powerful as he was still only a human and had not seen all that their Mr. Traveler had seen. But the power of the Atlanteans to cast such a spell to encompass any human, fae, or beast within their realms, to be able to teleport any transgressor to wherever they began their journey to Atlantea, was equally beyond comprehension. No wonder they easily defeated the combined armies of fairies, giants, sprites, and elves. The fae never stood a chance.

A drunken I-wulf stumbled out of the tavern to him. "Is my battle-axe secure, Mr. Pangolin?"

"It is as it rests next to my weapon."

"Very good, man. Then it is indeed safe."

"Yes, indeed."

"Doesn't it seem strange to you?"

"How do you mean?"

"We're here. I almost felt we wouldn't make it."

"We had Mr. Traveler."

"We did. If it were not for him, we would not have made it. I don't think any fae caravan master could have done what he did."

"No debate from me."

"The Fates smiled upon us for connecting our paths."

"But for a man to know what he knows, accomplish what he has was at great cost."

"He mentioned he was on caravans where all were horribly lost save him. At the Great Forest, when he knelt down to that spot."

"Land manticore, he said."

"The flying ones are frightening enough."

"I'll miss our caravan and those who journeyed with us. I'll even miss Mr. Bragg, who I wanted to beat his face in repeatedly when we first met." Pangolin chuckled to himself.

I-wulf laughed. "Yes, I'll miss him too."

"You spend a year with people in close quarters in such danger you either kill them or become the best of comrades. Sad that it's likely we'll never see them again in our lives."

"But we'll have a lifetime of stories for children and grandchildren and theirs."

"True."

"Shall we get what we came to this fabled city to get?"

"Aye, treasure. Whenever you and the men sleep off your drink to do an honest day's work, we can depart."

"I always wanted enough coin to buy a kingdom."

"You a king?"

"Yes. Why not? I can be a king."

Pangolin laughed.

"Why the laugh? I'd be a very noble and respectable king. King I-wulf! Isn't that the name of a king?"

"Yes, keep talking, King I-wulf. You are good at talking."

"King I-wulf the Wicked. Or was it Slasher?"

"Or was it Stupid?"

"King I-wulf the Incredible Wicked Slasher and Women Dazzler."

"Now that is stupid."

The greatest of their protection for Titan's Caravan was the crawling trees of their four Tree Shepherds. As human and fae marched on Titan's Trail, they had done so under the constant magical shield of the combined power of the moving trees and the specific clan of leshies who commanded them.

Far from the ante-city and deep within one of the realms of Atlantea proper was a vast land thick with giant blades of grass and brush. The Great Gathering of leshy, tree people, and plant people from all corners of the magical lands, forming a large circle with each of the three main fae races further grouped into separate clans clustered together. Packs of cù-sìth were everywhere, many with one or more rainbow-colored birds on their backs.

As soon as Traveler entered the realm with his dog-griffin hybrid, several of the cù-sìth surrounded them and followed as they approached the Gathering. There was no menace in the "fairy dogs," each the size of a small horse with their shaggy, green coats, pointy green ears, and long curled tails. They instinctively knew Traveler was an ally.

The caravan master smiled as he spotted the four Tree Shepherds among a party of dozens of other Tree Shepherds, each with a crawling tree at rest behind them. They saw him too and were already moving to them. The skin of the other leshies was green, while the Tree Shepherds who protected Titan's Caravan had white skin with green beards. Their hooded robes looked even more like royalty than before. All four of the Tree Shepherds were over six feet, and each carried in his right hand an even taller, thick wooden staff, curved at the top.

"Master Traveler," greeted the tallest one named Greenwig. The other three were Mossberry, Thornbeard, and, the youngest, Little Root. "We did not expect to encounter you again."

"It was important that I personally thanked you for your protection of Titan's Caravan, Master Greenwig," Traveler said.

"No need, Master Traveler. It is we who thank you for guiding us safely to Atlantea to rejoin our brethren."

"It is now the second occurrence in my life that I see more than one Tree Shepherd at a time. You did say to me that it was not uncommon for hundreds of you to be congregated at one time in your lands."

"We call them Great Gatherings."

"I have attended one of the tree people but to see leshy and tree people and plant people combined. I hope it is not a sad omen."

"By no means. With the closing of Atlantea to all for a millennium we must make certain preparations as they are many leshy and allies who live in Atlantea, as you know."

"Yes. May I ask the reason for Atlantea's closing?"

The four Tree Shepherds chuckled.

"Master Traveler, we were about to ask you," said Mossberry."

"It is said that leshies can sometimes pre-tell the future."

"Master Traveler, our gifts are confined to the shepherding of trees," Greenwig said with a smile. "It is said that those dragon-horses you acquired for your humans and the elfess can also sometimes pre-tell the future. What have they told you?"

"They said...they will tell me in the future."

The laugh of a leshy was like chirping birds.

"Then you must wait patiently," Greenwig said.

"Tree shepherding is a high honor enough," Thornberry said, "without the added burden of predestination, especially when such a gift is rarely as for certain as some would pretend. But then you learned that from the cyclopes mages you trained with in Mimir Spring."

"Where are the kirins?" Mossberry asked.

"They explore the realms of Atlantea as this is their first time here too."

"Yes, our magic lands are a treat for the beasts, including Atlantea," Greenwig said.

"Master Traveler," Little Root began, "I wonder if you would share what you suspect as to the reason why the Atlanteans would close their city to all. You have lived here and remain in high regard with them."

"Yes, I did and learned all I could, but I found the Atlanteans to ultimately be more secretive than even ancient leshies.

The leshies laughed again.

"Then good life, Master Traveler," Greenwig said.

"Thank you again for shepherding our Titan's Caravan to its destination. Great Tree Shepherds Greenwig, Mossberry, Thornbeard, and Little Root. If not in life, forever, in great stories."

The four shepherds nodded. They returned to the Great Gathering as Traveler, and his dog left the realm. There were evil and savage leshies on Pan-Earth, but he had the pleasure to meet and live with many different clans of benevolent leshies, some aloof to humankind and most fae-kind, others more like giant imps with their playfulness, but Tree Shepherds were always the most noble and, in their way, most like humans.

The knowledge of leshies was vast. He had been certain he'd learn something from them, if even from their alliance with tree people whose knowledge was even more vast. They were all so calm, which was why he was so worried.

Nodding approvingly, King Aereth sat at a long table staring at them. "The banner of Titan's Caravan," he said. "The white flag featured an iconic representation of the

Titan, the Maker of all Mountains, and seven points of light to represent the seven points along Titan's Trail. The banner of the fairies of Chrysa. The banner of the giants of Antaeus. The banner of the centaurs of Chiron. The elfin banners of Magica, Bravehowl, Nightshade, and Falconbright. Lastly, the banners of Sirnegate, Helm Earldom, Strongbridge, and Eastmoor."

"Very impressive, sire." The steward Hobbs watched the king flip through the flags on the table in deep reflection too. "I dare say, sire, no one else could have assembled such a caravan of humans and fae as our Mr. Traveler."

"Agreed." The king stacked the banners on top of each other neatly, with the Titan's Caravan on the top. "Now that we rest within Atlantea, what will you do with yourself, Mr. Hobbs? It was Mr. Traveler who had hired you, and he is not with us."

"He will return when we are ready to depart for Avalonia."

"When did he say this?" the king looked at him, perplexed.

Hobbs held back a laugh. "He told us—Maiden Gwyness and myself—and you."

"Mr. Hobbs, did I really faint?"

"No shame in it, sire. We caught you with no problem. You and Lady Aylen, and many of the Cut-Throats too. Even Mr. Pangolin caught himself on the way down by taking a knee."

"As long as we're in the company of our master-at-arms, Mr. Pangolin. The sting is not so great. These places of magic."

"I do not know, sire. When we reunite with Mr. Traveler, we can decide the rest of our lives then."

"Yes, we shall."

King Aereth stood from the table, noticing.

"No need to say it, sire. I know. I'm growing hair on my head that hasn't seen hair since I was a young man. And you have far less gray in yours."

"We're getting younger?"

"We are getting stronger too. Mr. Traveler told us that the magic of Atlantea takes hold in those with no magic at all and bestows upon them all manner of benefits."

"Then we should use our new youth and vigor to secure what we came all this way to Atlantea for."

"Yes, sire. The men in wait."

The lodgings they had rented in the ante-city was a quaint two-story cottage in a section populated by humans and fae who looked like humans. They went from having perpetual security when on Titan's Trail to being in a place where security from adversaries or thieves was no concern at all.

"No one steals in Atlantea," a gnomoid had told them. Neither door nor windows had locks on them.

While their lodgings were ordinary, the sights beyond were breathtaking. They could see the roads to Atlantea properly through a circular archway larger than Titan's

Bridge, connecting their realm with one with three moons around the first of many cities of Atlantea.

Immediately adjacent to their section of the city, in the opposite direction, lay a perfectly clear lake with all kinds of aquatic life. Above the lake, flocks of rainbow-colored birds circled, round and round, with an occasional peryton or owl hippogriff flying by.

Outside the cottage, the king and steward found their young Mr. Quillen seated on the ground, sketching more magical animals residing and playing in the lake across. The king glanced at the young scribe's work in his magic sketchbook. Quillen jumped up and ran to the lake's edge.

"Mr. Quillen, do not have those beasts get too accustomed to you," Hobbs said.

Quillen had found new "friends." The creatures were dobhar-chú, known as "water hounds" or "sea dogs" to humans. At first glance, it looked like a giant otter with a tail, much like a fish. In Atlantea, the beasts were tame and playful. In the outer fae lands, the beasts were vicious and carnivorous—a fact the young boy would learn from the berserker Nirgund in great detail as his town had battled an infestation of the creatures and lost men. Quillen sat at the edge of the lake with several of the animals resting next to or curled up around him.

"They like me," a smiling Quillen said.

"Mr. Quillen, will you be taking care of them for your full stay here?" Hobbs asked.

"I think they like humans, Mr. Hobbs."

"Mr. Quillen, you can stay here while we go treasure-hunting," King Aereth announced.

"No, sire." Quillen jumped to his feet, and the friendly but skittish dobhar-chú ran and dove into the lake. "I want to go too."

The men laughed.

"You can dive in after them if you like," one of the men said to him.

Quillen smiled, shaking his head. "Where are the others, sire?"

"Lady Aylen and Maiden Gwyness will join us," the king replied.

"Mr. Pangolin?"

"Perhaps later."

"I can't wait until Mr. Traveler joins us again," Quillen said.

"Here! Here!" men called out in unison.

"Yes, Mr. Quillen, we all do. Mr. Hobbs, now that we retrieved our young scribe, we can prepare to march on."

"Yes, sire."

The shy sprites were overcome by emotion. Traveler had shown them more respect and dignity than any human or fae they had ever met. He had waited for them in a distant part of the city to shake their hand—a human custom—and wished them well. The kilmoulis with their huge noses that covered most of their faces smiled with their eyes.

"Thank you, Master Traveler," one said.

"When we were in the City of Kraken's Wake," Traveler said, "when you were all on sentry duty with the half-elf, Mr. Elman."

"He can see farther than most fae," said one kilmoulis.

"Yes, he can."

"You mean the giants?" asked another kilmoulis.

"Yes."

"One argus and ten fomorians," a kilmoulis said.

"They were headed to Atlantea in their city-ship. Do you still sense them?"

The kilmoulis shook their heads. "We did sense them as we sailed here. We passed near the same path they did, but once we crossed Titan's Gate, the scent was gone. We have not sensed them since."

"If they were here, would you sense them?"

The kilmouils smiled with their eyes again. "Atlantea is a realm of realms. We likely would not, even with our power of smell across great distances."

"Formorians are sea giants. Maybe they entered one of the cities from below the seas, but you would have sensed that."

"Their scent disappeared."

"Not important then."

"You, Master Traveler, believe it to be."

"I am acting like the suspicious caravan master though the quest is over. The Atlanteans care not about goat-headed sea giants or ones with a hundred eyes."

"Argus giants have second sight."

"Atlanteans have similar abilities. I make too much of it. Enjoy yourselves within the walls of Atlantea. You will have many tales to share with your people when you return."

The kilmoulis nodded and filed past the caravan master and his dog for a final time.

One of the kilmoulis stopped and said, "We also sense a group of Klabautermann. The same who captained our ship for a time."

"No. Tunik and his crew? Where?"

"Right behind you."

"Now, now, Captain Traveler." The sea kobold, Tunik, stood with his fellow kobolds, Nifle, and crew. "Not the first time we unexpectedly left a moving ship."

Traveler glared at them, and his hybrid dog growled at them.

"You're not like other humans, Captain Traveler, holding silly grudges. We both made it to Atlantea."

"Master Traveler, why were you cavorting with those ugly sprites?" Nifle said as the sea kobolds cackled.

Larger than the average human, the sea kobolds with their hunched over, thick bodies, ugly faces, and missing teeth, were far from pictures of beauty. But Klabautermann were known as the most able-bodied, hard-working sailors and fishermen by all fae. It was just they couldn't be trusted most of the time.

"I'd say we're even, wouldn't you? You saved me, I saved you. You tried to kill me, and I let it go," Tunik said. "Your dog would try it but too bad he can't here in Atlantea. I heard all about what you did to those star elves. I'm not stupid, human. A bounty is a bounty. We are sorry about it all, truly. Would have saved ourselves a lot of trouble if we simply stuck with our old human healer, Mr. Traveler."

"No, you're not sorry. Might be best not to ever run into me, or my dog, on the outside."

"We won't. My men and I will be spending our last many days right here in Atlantea. Why should the land kobolds have all the luxury? I'd be happy lying on a boat here on the peaceful Atlantean seas rather than out there on the real oceans with all their dangers, especially now—all those krakens about."

"Tunik, finished with sea-life?"

"Why not? Do you know how many years I've been working the seas?"

"How do Klabautermann get to know crab and spider centaurs? I heard they hated fae as much as humans."

"You mean you heard they'd string us up for their next meal. The proposal they made to me was to do what they said or be eaten alive….slowly over very long days. You can appreciate why I thought their proposal was a very fair one at the time. You and your dog are scary, human, but not like that."

"Then I don't blame you. Oughtred, I'm certain, also paid you well."

"You humans and the rest of your caravan are obsessed with this Oughtred king."

"Why wouldn't we be? He tried to kill us on the Trail."

"So did I."

"But not multiple times, with dark creatures we thought extinct."

"Forget, Oughtred. This is far more than Oughtred."

"He's far more than an evil human king."

"Young Traveler, Oughtred did not hire me to betray you. He hired me to hold onto you and your caravan until he could arrive. The creature centaurs were from another. They wanted to kill you."

"Who hired them?"

Tunik cackled. "Oughtred wanted you alive. Did you find out why?"

"He needed me to get into Atlantea."

"How ironic. Perhaps he'll try to kill you again when you leave Atlantea. He has a fleet gathered outside the boundary of Atlantea's waters."

"I know. Who were the centaurs hired by?"

"Is Oughtred the only one who covets the kingdom of Atlantea? Who here doesn't care about its treasures like you? That is who?"

"Tunik, where's your treasure? Seems you're one who doesn't care about treasure either."

"Well, I didn't hire them. Don't have that kind of wealth yet, but I have a lifetime to collect my treasure because we're not leaving."

"You're not going to tell me who, Tunik?"

"You have nothing to barter with since neither of you can harm me here, and I won't be stepping outside of this realm again."

"People always think of shape-shifters becoming deadly, giant creatures, but they can just as easily become harmless tiny creatures, invisible to the naked human or fae eye, crawl down a windpipe into a stomach and...sit there and wait. Like an imp right inside of you. Keeping you from eating. Causing you to vomit or flagellate all the time, not that kobolds mind, but even you have a limit. My favorite is when they simply grow in size and—"

"Okay, human! But what about you and that pretty little water elfess of yours?"

"Mine? What do you mean?"

"Humans." Tunik laughed.

"Tunik, mind your own affairs."

"Struck a nerve, have I? How many men have been fallen by sweet thoughts of..."

"Enough, Tunik. Who?"

"Undines and sylphs."

"That means celestial elves."

"That means star elves, human. They really don't like you."

"I'll just assume you're lying to me as always."

"Then all my work to train you when you were aboard my ship as your captain wasn't a complete waste."

Traveler looked at the smaller second-in-command. "Nifle, I'll say goodbye to you then. You, I liked."

They all cackled. "Who's leaving first?" Tunik asked. "Since we don't trust each other anymore."

"You should go first," Traveler said.

"I can stand here all day, human."

"Too bad you can't do anything to us—you or your dog," another sea kobold said, taunting.

"You'd be whisked away like that," Tunik said, snapping his fingers. "But you know that. You lived here."

"Somehow, I believe we'll meet again, captain."

"I was thinking the same thing, captain," Tunik said with a smirk.

Traveler's dog was getting angrier, wanting to attack them and their laughter only provoked him more. Traveler nudged his dog along, and they walked away into the crowd. But Traveler never took his eye off of his old sea kobold comrades once.

Traveler raced around the corner with the dog following his every step, double backing through another street but all the sea kobolds were already gone.

The King and Hobbs led their party of over three thousand men strong down the busy streets attracting the attention of all who saw them. But it was not their numbers of note but their five musicians—The Brothers Brimm—in their new colorful clothing playing their instruments. The King and Hobbs quickly learned the general disposition of those around by how they reacted to the music. Those who smiled or laughed were good fae; those who did not were dark fae. It was a concept they were still understanding. To Atlanteans, there was no distinction between good fae and evil fae.

As Quillen rushed to the head of the marching columns through the ante-city bustling with people and animals all around, he caught a glimpse of a large black figure at the other end of the street. He couldn't see a face, but he was sure the figure was watching them. He forgot all about it when they turned down another street into more crowds of fae and amazing beasts.

Lady Aylen and Maiden Gwyness joined the men at one of the many merchant quarters. Quillen couldn't wait to share his experiences with them.

"Slow down, Mr. Quillen. You're speaking faster than they can hear," Hobbs said to him.

"Did you draw them in your magic book?" Lady Aylen asked him.

"I did, m'lady," Quillen reached for the sketchbook from the satchel around his neck.

"At dinner tonight then, Mr. Quillen. We're not going anywhere," the princess told him. "We have hard work to do. Our treasure will not jump into our hands just because we will it."

"Lady Aylen, who should be first? Sirnegate or Helm Earldom?" the king asked.

"It should be the kingdom of Sirnegate first, sire. There we acquire treasure for one kingdom. For you, we acquire treasure for three kingdoms. What say you, Mr. Hobbs?"

"Sounds reasonable, m'lady."

"Look, it's the plant people we met earlier," Gwyness said.

"Met earlier?" Lady Aylen asked.

Gwyness looked right at her. "When the royals fainted."

"We are never going to rid ourselves of the indignity, sire," Lady Aylen said.

"I do believe you're right, princess."

The two Atlantean attendants who brought Traveler, with an unconscious Lady Aylen in his arms and Gwyness to their lodgings were part-humanoid, part-flower fae. Gwyness remembered that they smelled so nice.

"Greetings," said one of the plant people.

"Greetings," Gwyness said.

"Our masters wished to invite you to a great feast to honor your arrival at Atlantea after such a long and frightful journey."

"Thank you so kindly," Gwyness said. "Let me confer with my party."

"Yes." The two plant people bowed and stepped away.

Gwyness joined the royals. "We are being invited to a feast."

"But by whom?" Lady Aylen asked.

"We are in Atlantea, so there is no need to worry or be suspicious," Gwyness said.

King Aereth noticed. "Lady Aylen, is she taller?"

"She is, sire, and she feels she is a queen too with all that magic power coursing through her body. Shall we accept?"

"Maybe we should depart for these treasure lands and not delay," Lady Aylen said. "We can feast later. I have seen this sequence of events before. A simple feast. Then all of a sudden, you're in a battle or running from a battle or in the middle of affairs of state, swept away in directions one doesn't wish to go."

"My goodness, m'lady. It is simple food. No battles. No affairs of state. Simple courtesy."

"I agree with the princess. Let us enter these treasured lands and postpone the feasting for afterward. It is what we traveled all this way for."

Gwyness nodded and walked back to the plant people.

"Mr. Hobbs," Lady Aylen called.

"Yes, m'lady?"

"Do we have all that we need to set out?"

"We have our supplies now, and we have plenty of men."

"And plenty of money," Lady Aylen added.

"Which is going fast. There is one other thing we do need, though."

"Which is?" Lady Aylen asked.

"A guide," Hobbs replied.

"Guide? Where is Mr. Traveler when we need him?" Lady Aylen asked.

"We should have hired him for this part when we had the chance," King Aereth said.

"We have to hire strangers now. Mr. Hobbs, what do we need a guide for? We're in Atlantea."

"No, you are not."

The voice echoed through the air, making all of the humans and Lady Aylen stop and turn. A bald blue gem-skinned Atlantean stood before them, dressed in a white robe; his eyes were silver.

"You are in the lands of Atlantea, but all of these structures are the ante-city and are mere settlements that have grown around the direct entrance to Atlantea. A place to rest and revitalize. A place to purchase supplies for the treasured lands. The place one returns from after the treasured lands to set out again for one's own lands."

"Then Atlantea is through the giant circular arch, sir?" Lady Aylen asked.

"What you behold is an outpost to the treasured lands. Atlantea lies beyond."

"Are you saying we haven't yet seen Atlantea?" King Aereth asked.

"No, you have not. But all outsiders call this Atlantea. Atlantea is vast and some distance from here. You will see it when you are ready."

"Thank you for your guidance, sir. Whom do we address, sir?" King Aereth asked.

"I am a Herald of Atlantea. We walk among newcomers and assist where we can."

"Were the ones in the ships of light heralds too?" Gwyness asked.

"The Imperium are guards. Heralds are guides. You may find and hire those you need for the trip at the end of this road."

"Thank you kindly," King Aereth said. "We are eager to travel to the treasured lands."

"How long will the journey take us?" Gwyness asked.

"A week or more."

Everyone looked at each other.

"That is a long time," King Aereth said.

"Your journey here was far longer, and there is no danger here in Atlantea."

"Why do you do this?" Lady Aylen asked the Atlantean. "Allow us newcomers, strangers, to come to your kingdom to and from all corners of Pan–Earth to take your treasures."

"The treasures do not belong to us. They do not belong to anyone until they are claimed. Atlantea is not lands so much as it is doorways to lands beyond."

"Mr. Traveler called it the realm of realms," Hobbs said.

The Atlantean nodded. "Yes, we are the gateway to a realm of realms."

When Traveler arrived in Atlantea for the first time, he was barely a man from years of attempts as a boy. Before he traveled, he spent some time in the fabled city to learn its customs and history, and about its cities and people. He had resided there for quite a while before learning that the ante-city one first came to was actually not Atlantea at all. The fabled ancient city rested in three realms at once—on land, in the sky, and underwater. The ante-city, however, was the best place to get a sense of what was happening in the territories of Atlantea.

Traveler found a nice top-story room in lodgings near the waterways from Titan's Gate to the shore. He knew King Aereth, Lady Aylen, Pangolin, and the others would be weeks getting to the treasured lands and back. With his dog, he watched the ships arrive and depart until the time came when no ships arrived at all. It was true—Atlantea had closed itself off to all outsiders. What concerned him so was that he did know Atlantean history. The only other time Atlantea closed its realm was millennia ago, when all the races of fae made war upon them to seize the fabled city. The legend has it that all memories of where the city lay were removed from the minds of all fae on Pan-Earth. They would have to seek it out, as the newest race on Pan-Earth called human would. Even when they did find it again, they would gain no special favor from Atlantea even though they were merely descendants of those who had attempted to invade. In fact, humans would gain higher status than they. But all that was so long ago that even Atlanteans bore no ill will to fae, and the magic races spent centuries re-establishing their relationships. Though one rule remained—no fae could live in Atlantea forever. All were visitors or traders only. So what would cause the Atlantea to close its kingdom?

His hybrid dog jumped to all fours as they both watched people pour out of the main entrances of the ante-city. Ships emerged from underwater to take sail as laborers jumped or flew aboard their decks to depart.

He saw them! Tunik and his men ran to a ship that had also risen from the deep along the river shore. Tunik's crew of sea kobolds, toad men, and fish men were fleeing. He had crewed with them before, so he knew what their panic looked like.

Traveler saw another and jumped to his feet too. He dashed from the room for the steps, with the dog running after him.

When the caravan master reached the first floor of the lodgings, the streets were now overflowing with fae walking briskly, running, hopping, crawling, or flying to a growing number of ships and boats popping up from underwater.

Traveler's eyes locked on the sea kobold captain. Tunik cackled as he waved goodbye from the bow of the ship. Nifle, standing at Tunik's side, touched his forehead in salute. Their new ship was one of many already on the way out. Then one ship after another vanished.

The mood in the air was one of panic. Traveler had never seen such a thing in Atlantea. But he did not leave his room for the sea kobolds.

"I thought I'd never see you again," Traveler said to the fae sorceress. A slim, tan, and short woman in a red robe but with an imposing demeanor.

She turned, and a look of shock came over it. "The boy is a man!" She ran to him and lifted him straight up, then pulled him close to hug him. "Strong man!" She set him back on the ground. "You have a animal companion." She knelt down before the dog. "You not from Pan-Earth!"

"No, he's not, Mistress Wu."

"What is that on your back? I could see the magic flames from your sword a mile away. You have shape-shifter and Titan sword. You have progressed far since we last saw each other. Sword means you tired of being healer."

"I can be a healer when need be."

"Healer or swordsman. Not both. What do you do? Cut off a man's hand, then say I can sew it back on? Or do you heal the man, then stab him with the sword? Pick one! Not both!"

Traveler grinned. "Sword it is."

"Good. It suits you. You were too curious to remain a healer for long anyway. You are an adventurer at heart. Now you can protect yourself."

"He returns."

Traveler turned to see more of his former teachers from the hidden fae city in the Lands of Man called Last Keep.

"Master Nigelle, and Master Gorb."

He shook their hands. Nigelle was a wizard who could do healing spells. He always wore a dark navy robe and looked like a wizard with his—long white hair combed back past his shoulders, clean-shaven face, and a multi-ringed hand. Gorb was a four-armed cyclopoid fae healer but not a giant. Each of his four arms could move independently as if they had minds of their own.

"Can you still do healing vapors?" Wu asked him.

"It is a favorite of every caravan I lead," Traveler replied.

"A caravan master," Nigelle said to Gorb, impressed.

"There cannot be too many of you on Pan-Earth. A human caravan master for fae," Gorb said.

"And humans."

"Why did you wait so long to find us?" Wu asked.

"My caravan arrived the other day after a year's journey."

"Then you traveled under the guide and luck of the Fates," Nigelle said. "Atlantea closes to all for a thousand years."

"But why?"

"Why?" Wu said. "It is their city. They can close it if they want."

"How many times in their history has this happened?" Traveler asked.

"Three times before," Wu answered. "The war with the fae, the war with the dragons, and the war with the Titans."

"I knew of the first, but not the other two times."

"Why would you. You are human," Wu said. "You should not have waited to find us. We cannot talk now."

"I did not know you were here. Why can't you stay? We haven't seen each other in so many years, Wu. I know you love my stories."

The fae sorceress hated to smile because she had no teeth. But she couldn't help herself. "You are a tempter, human, but no. We must leave."

"Why?"

"You don't have to leave," she said. "Stay as long as you wish."

Traveler looked at the other two fae too. "If three fae wizards I know are leaving a place in haste, is that not a good sign for me to do the same?"

"No, not at all, and we do not leave in haste. We just leave."

"Why?"

"No more talk."

"Why is Atlantea closing this time?"

"Ask the heralds. You lived here."

"How did you know I lived here?"

The fae wizards laughed.

"Were you here when I was?"

"We were, but we had taught you all that you needed from us. Besides, we are healers, and you had already become what you are today," Nigelle said.

"We kept an eye on you from time to time though," Gorb said.

"Please tell me. Master Gorb, you're an oracle too."

"My people are, not I."

"You worry too much," Wu said. "If you don't stop it, you will need a healer for your stomach."

Traveler grinned, but his face became serious again. "My friends are here too. Are we in danger?"

"We are always in danger, human," Wu said. "Life is danger."

"That does not tell me what I need to know."

"Enjoy Atlantea. When you leave this time, though, you will not come back," Wu said. "But too much talk," Wu said. She ran to him and kissed him on the forehead. "You live a long life, human. Have many kids. Don't travel too much though."

"I thought I was about to join not one but three sorcerers," Traveler said.

"Why? Do you need a sorcerer?" Wu asked. "No one can harm you while you're in Atlantea's realms, and you can't harm any either. Besides, you are filled with the magic of Atlantea. That is all you need."

"Please stay. I could use the services of great magic-makers. I've always known you are more than healers."

"Our time is past," Nigelle said.

"You need new blood," Wu said.

"What of him?" Gorb asked, pointing.

He turned to see a lone Frog-Dor watching. The caravan master smiled. "He was my caravan's sorcerer."

"Great conjurer, he is," Wu said.

"I take it that you didn't expect to see him again, either," Gorb said.

"No, I didn't."

"Your sorcerer is shy. Too shy for me. He's elf and something else," Wu said.

"Part-elemental."

"Yes."

"Then I guess this truly is the last time I will see any of you."

"Yes, human. But I'm glad you didn't remain an apprentice," Wu said.

"Very proud of you, Master Traveler," Nigelle said.

"I will give you something, though," Wu said.

"What?"

In her hands appeared a red cloth pouch. "A magic bag of tricks to add to your collection."

He had to say goodbyes to many upon arrival at Atlantea, but this time there were tears in his eyes. He would never see his former trio of fae teachers ever again in his life. And they never told him why they were running away from Atlantea.

The fae trio boarded their rectangular ship and, rather than sail the waters, flew above it. He waved until it too disappeared in the sky.

He turned to a waiting Frog-Dor. He still looked like a royal with his long tunic under his blue cloak and holding a tall wooden staff. He was far from the hobbled, broken man they first met on the Trail and released from his curse.

"I'm so glad to see you, Mr. Traveler. It would have been welcome if we could have continued our caravan within Atlantean walls."

"We arrived, so the services of a caravan master or captain are no longer needed. Our alliance served its purpose."

"True. All good things must come to an end, too, like the cycle of life."

"I am glad to see you. But also, I had to see why so many people are leaving the kingdom all at once."

"Yes, very curious. More curious is that no one will tell us why."

"I see you happened upon my friends of the past."

"Nothing happenstance about it, Mr. Traveler. They wanted to encounter me."

"They did?"

"Without a doubt. Even told me I'd know when to show myself."

Traveler looked in the direction of the trio's ship though gone. "Why pretend?"

"The reasons for ancient magic-makers are not always clear."

"Many reasons are possible, but I'm sure at the end of it all was to give me this red pouch. Sad that I will likely never see them again. I expected you to be enjoying all the sights Atlantea has to offer."

"I realize that I'm not too good around strangers. I miss our caravan more than I expected. It was home. I had gotten accustomed to the faces and the routine."

"Then we must find you new friends and routines. But before that, wait here."

The caravan master realized something. "Atlantea closed three times. War, war, and war," he said to himself.

"Excuse me?" Frog-Dor asked.

"Not important. Give me a moment."

Traveler walked up to an Atlantean herald watching vessels depart, but who turned his full attention to Traveler as he approached.

"May I ask a question, herald?"

"Of course."

"Do you know of a human named King Oughtred?"

"I do. He has traveled to and from our lands many times over the years."

"I once studied under a cyclops mage named Isim."

"Yes, we know of him. A very powerful seer in the Cyclops City of Mimir Spring."

"He told me this Oughtred might arrive. He gave me magic to help Atlantea if danger should descend upon it."

The Atlantean smiled. "Keep hold of the magic."

"You are a great people, but not invincible."

"No one in this vast expanse of realities on Pan-Earth and beyond is. But don't despair. Atlanteans have seers too."

"Is that why you have closed Atlantea?"

"What a seer sees may be only one possibility."

"Yes, all can be changed by sometimes the smallest thing. I wish you had barred him from entering your kingdom."

"That decision was yours."

"I know. But all are barred now."

"Yes."

"And you won't say why."

"Atlantean affairs are our own. You will come and go. We will be here forever."

"Sorry for the offense."

"No offense taken."

"Is Oughtred still in Atlantea?"

"He is. If you wish to see him, attend the Feast of the Gwragedd Annwyn. You have attended in the past."

"I survived the Feast in the past, you mean."

The regal Atlantean smiled. "I understand," he said.

"Then I will attend the Feast."

"It may not be for some time, though."

"Then I will attend whenever it is."

TREASURES OF
ATLANTEA

CARAVAN OF THE ROYALS

Planning for the trek to Atlantea took decades, not years. Lady Aylen remembered the royal court of Sirnegate contemplating the journey when she was a girl. King Aereth remembered his kingdom first speaking of it when he was a young man, and they had attempted it on more than one occasion.

Everyone thought of the wondrous sights and deadly beasts on Titan's Trail. Death was always an ever-present possibility but, however improbable, so was success. In all that contemplation of wonders and terrors, never did it occur to any of them, when arriving in Atlantea, how did one choose which of the treasured lands they would go to? They did not even know there were more choices than they could ever imagine. Did one seek rubies, sapphires, or any of the endless gems of the earth? Did one seek silver, gold, or any number of precious metals, both natural or magical? What of human gold versus elfin gold?

As they explored the streets of the ante-cities, they learned that the shops themselves were also portals to other realms, which meant the ante-cities were far more vast than they would reveal. They understood for the first time that it was true when fae told them that it would take a lifetime to explore every establishment in the ante-cities.

The ordinary of Atlantea was like so many other merchant districts; the streets were packed with fae and animals—well-dressed fae of all shapes, colors, and races. Many were reminded of the fairy kingdom of Faë-Wick, where the fairies were so numerous that the city was more like the inside of an anthill or beehive. People were friendly enough and pointed them to where they needed to inquire further.

The extraordinary of Atlantea was as Mr. Traveler said. Those who made it to Atlantea and lived here were among the most gifted warriors and sorcerers and from kingdoms of the longest honored status and most powerful. They did see fae within Atlantea's wall that they were certain existed nowhere else in the magic lands.

And the magic of the place. Sorcerers, both male and female, walked among them, radiating magic and manifesting it with glowing eyes, special facial tattoos, or from objects, most often a staff but necklaces, rings, neck rings, bracelets, or their animal companion appearing as if they were made of light or a ghost in form.

They reached the section of the merchant quarter they sought and approached the first seated attendant.

"How may I help you, good human," asked a rotund bald fae in speckled garments of purple and yellows. He had only four fingers on each hand, and they realized that he had gills on either side of his neck.

"Thank you, sir," King Aereth said, leading the caravan to him. "We seek a guide to the treasured lands."

"Oh, yes. That wee little question has finally jumped into your mind: which treasured land does one go to and how does one get there?"

"Yes."

"You are humans and an elfess." He said, smiling at Lady Aylen. She did not return the smile.

"Yes, we are, sir."

The fae returned to his table and opened a few of the books resting on them. They appeared to be magic books, with each page turning on its own.

"Human or elfin kingdom do you seek treasure for?"

"Human," King Aereth answered.

"Ah yes, you must be the ones led here by the human caravan master."

"You know of him?" Lady Aylen asked.

The fae chuckled. "There aren't many humans who can command the authority to lead human and fae to Atlantea from the human lands or fae lands. In fact, of all the best caravan masters on Pan-Earth, he is the only human I know of. He is somewhat of a legend."

"Legend?" Lady Aylen was interested. "Our caravan master, Mr. Traveler?"

"A human caravan master. With a sword of magic that can best even elves in battle. There's a little story there. When he first found his sword and realized if he didn't get the proper training, meaning not from another human, lest he cut himself in half and kill himself, he was told only elves could properly train him, but no elf would train a human to equal an elf in battle. He asked if he could get an elf to train him if he said he'd battle goblins. He was told no. Then he asked if goblins could train him if he said he'd battle elves. He was told yes. They can hold their own against elves as their chief arch-enemies. Off he went to the land of the goblins. What a human."

"Are goblins not hated here?" King Aereth asked.

"Hated? Hated by elves. Hated by fae of light. But to the Atlanteans, they are from a time when elves and goblins were the same race, both making war against their kingdom, though both facts you would never know based on how the two races act towards one another in these times. Yes, you are quite fortunate to have hired your human caravan master. If it were not for him, most of you might never have crossed into our fine, fabled kingdom."

"That we know. We are doubly fortunate with Atlantea closing to outsiders."

"Ah yes, doubly so, indeed."

"You even know his name," Lady Aylen said.

"As I said, a legend among those who make caravans and the commerce that surrounds it their vocation. Do you seek treasure for wealth or prestige?"

"Wealth," Lady Aylen answered.

"In the human lands, that means...gold."

The royals looked at each other, smiling.

"That would do fine."

"What other types of treasures of wealth are there?" Lady Aylen asked.

"Depends on the race. There's elfin gold, goblin gold, for the water races, magnificent pearls, for underground races, precious metals, others, gems, seeds, fruits—"

"Seeds and fruits?" Lady Aylen asked, perplexed.

"You're not a fairy or leshy, so it's understandable they would have no value in your eyes."

"How do we find our way to this gold?" King Aereth asked.

"You don't. You hire a guide and bearers, animals, if needed. They will take you." He again opened to a page in one of the magic books. "This is where they can take you. I will write the name for you since you likely don't speak many fae languages."

"Is this the work you do every day, sir?" young Quillen asked.

"Yes, it is, young human. I get to meet people from many different lands right from the comfort of my table and chair."

"How long have you been doing this work, sir?" Quillen asked.

The fae stood up straight and thought for a moment. "Seventy or eighty years. I can't even remember. Long before you were born."

"Long before my father was born."

"Well, yes, that too. You are a human." He scribbled on a piece of paper. "Who takes this, the human or the elfess?"

"I shall take it." King Aereth took the note from the fae and tried to read it, but it was in a tongue he couldn't comprehend and the letters moved on the paper.

"How do you get compensated for your assistance?" Lady Aylen asked.

"You already have," the fae said.

"How do you mean?"

"I receive a portion of what you pay your guide, bearers, and a fee from when you store whatever treasures you obtain. Also, for any laborers in loading said treasures on your vessel."

"My, what a lucrative operation you have here," Lady Aylen said.

"I think so."

"All from your table and chair."

The fae chuckled. "Ah yes, now you see why I've done this job for eighty years and plan to continue for eighty more."

"This is not Atlantea!" said a fae when they were further within the ante-city.

Their guide was a bluecap—a tiny fairy the size of a

human hand with blue skin, blue wings, and clothed in blue. However, she led two columns of giant eight-foot-tall, yellow and white humanoid mushroom men with a large metal bucket in each of their two arms.

Lady Aylen led their new caravan with Gwyness at her side. She felt vulnerable without her tridents, but with her heightened abilities due to Atlantean magic, it was the wisest course not to have them anywhere she could get at them.

King Aereth led their over three-thousand men, with Hobbs and Quillen at his side. Every man, including the king had a large pack strapped to their back. Each pack, as with each bucket of their mushroom men bearers, would magically grow in size as needed when they reached the treasured lands.

They had been marching for hours through the busy streets of the ante-city, had left its last building behind them, and approached the large circular stone arch that literally seemed to be cut into the air itself, touching the ground and at least fifty feet up in the sky. When they crossed its barrier, several feet of stone wide, they stepped into another realm.

Lady Aylen was startled for a moment as the bluecap appeared in front of her face, with fluttering solid blue wings. "We have arrived in one of the treasured lands," she said.

"How far to the mines?" Lady Aylen asked.

"We will arrive tomorrow," she said.

"Surely, in a place of magic, we can get there faster," Lady Aylen said.

The bluecap giggled. "You can always hire a flying caravan."

"And spend all our money? Your proprietor told us the cost. I think not," Lady Aylen said. "We have already decided, Gwyness. If we can march here from the Lands of Man for over a year, one day is of no consequence. And we thought we brought enough money to purchase anything. I say those fae who wanted to rent us those griffin-drawn flying caravans were trying to rob us. We have our bluecap guide and our fae bearers to add to our men. We have what we need."

"Lady Aylen, are you seeing this?" King Aereth asked.

Lady Aylen had but stopped, as had all the caravan.

The mountain ahead looked like it was only a few miles away, but it was an illusion as it was so large that they would not reach it for many hours and probably at night. In its center was carved the perfect likeness of a human mouth with silvery, sparkling water spilling out. But the waterfall didn't create a cloud of mist vapor as they had experienced at the city of Titan's Fall. The water fell and added to the thick billowy clouds that covered all the land before them.

"There is a tunnel under the mountain," the bluecap said. "We travel through it to the open lands there and make camp. We arrive at the mines when the sun is highest in the sky."

They all looked up. There were three suns in the sky.

"Which sun?" Lady Aylen asked.

"The closest one," the fairy said.

"Are we on Pan-Earth?" Gwyness asked, nervously looking up and studying the sky.

"Yes, undoubtedly." The bluecap flew back to point and led them forward again through the land cloud. "I think."

The curious nature of the clouds that engulfed them was as they marched, the thickness would dissipate so that visibility was unimpeded from one end of their caravan to another. The Brothers Brimm played their music, and the men recited one song after the next in merriment. On the Trail, the prospect of being surrounded on all sides by a wall and ceiling of clouds would have terrified them. What creature would pounce on them? But in Atlantea, their safety was assured.

Quillen had his magic sketchbook open, showing his latest additions to the men. The bluecap fairy and the mushroom men. He had also managed to draw all the many fae that could have been their guides—dwarves and elves, or fae that looked like dwarves or elves. The boy Quillen had also sketched all the many kinds of mushroom men who could be bearers into the treasured lands—many sizes, shapes, and colors. Some had only eyes or only mouths, and others had small faces in their stem bodies. The other races to hire for bearer duty were troglodytes, commonly called trogs by most—large dark green-skinned humanoids with lizard-like arms and feet; korricks, small dwarf-like spites, said to love to dance around water; and a race they knew well—the big-forearmed, super-strong pech!

They had the opportunity to secure animals for their treasure hunting—griffins (fore-half of an eagle with wings and hind-half of a lion), griffinoids like opinicuses (full lion's body with eagle head and wings), keythongs (fore-half of a giant eagle, hind-half of a lion and spiky protrusions on its back and head), axex (peacock-like head, wings, wild cat-like body), hieracosphinxes (strong lion body with an eagle head, larger than all). It was at these stables that they were made to realize that the great chests of currency they thought they had were not so great after all. Hiring one of the beasts was equivalent to hiring five hundred bearers. When Lady Aylen heard of the price of a flying caravan to be drawn by one or more of the beasts, she had to be held back from striking the laughing fae by both King Aereth and Gwyness. "We are being robbed!" the princess yelled.

"Princess, you'll be vanished right back to Sirnegate. Is that what you want?" Gwyness said.

They didn't even ask the price of even larger beasts in the stables like a tarasque and a giant creature they had never seen before called a rhinoceros.

"They are actually from the Lands of Man," a fae said. "We brought them here. Don't mind the horn. They're friendly."

So they settled on one fairy guide and a dozen giant mushroom bearers. Unlike most other parties, they had three thousand men so there was no need for animals or wagons. The magic packs were their caravan master's final gift to them with his brilliant talent for preparation.

"Splendid, Mr. Quillen," Hobbs told the boy.

"There are so many types of griffins."

"And don't forget those hippogriffs too."

"The trogs don't seem to like people, Mr. Hobbs."

"But they did say they were good workers, which is all you really need."

"It is so strange not to look up front and not see Mr. Pangolin, our giants, and the elaphines anymore."

"We all miss them, but we'll rejoin with Mr. Pangolin and the Cut-Throats when we secure our treasures and before we return home."

Lady Aylen closed her eyes as she walked, and the water from the falling river high above sprayed the caravan. As a water elfess, she was unaffected. Every human in the caravan was soon drenched.

"Where is the waterfall going?" she asked their bluecap guide.

"Down below, through the ground, to the sea below."

"Through the ground?"

"Yes, you will see."

The bluecap and their giant mushroom men were also unaffected by the torrent of falling water as they moved out from the land clouds into the full mist to step up on a stone bridge. Another opening lay ahead, which was the natural mouth of a cave tunnel.

As they marched across, the men and Gwyness were

soaked to the bone. They peered over the bridge and could see the waterfall crashing on either side of the bridge, disappearing into the earth. Was the earth a mirage? The march across the bridge reminded them all of the terrifying Titan's Bridge at the start of their journey, the first marker of Titan's Trail. The waterfall passing through the ground reminded them of the Mist Plains.

They entered the cave tunnel, and immediately their bluecap fairy became a floating blue flame. The blue light guided them through the darkness. All of them could see the opening at the other end, nothing but a small dot in the distance.

"We will do this twice, Lady Aylen," King Aereth said.

"For the Kingdom of Sirnegate, then for the Kingdom of Helm Earldom," she answered.

"I can't say I'm at ease with the prospect of setting up camp here," Lady Aylen said. "Three moons. Three suns. Where are we really?"

"The place where we'll get all the treasure we can carry," King Aereth answered.

"M'lady, if I may be so bold," Hobbs said, "you are quite negative considering the triumph of our journey."

Lady Aylen sighed loudly. "Yes, Mr. Hobbs. You are quite right. I have no cause to behave this way. We sacrificed much to get here. We should be overjoyed and not critical."

"Maybe, m'lady, we all miss our caravan mates more than we realize," Hobbs said.

"A year is a long time. Marching day by day. In the close quarters of a camp night after night. Protecting each other's lives. Saving each other's lives. Difficult to simply stop. But life does go on. After a good night's rest and the sight of treasure, I will return to my own self."

"Yes, m'lady," Hobbs said.

"Look at our guide," Gwyness said.

Their guide was no longer one blue flame but several, hanging in the air and illuminating their path. It brought smiles to everyone's faces as they were able to better see the interior of the cave. Shiny rocks and...frogs. The entire walls and ceiling of the tunnel were crawling with millions of frogs that all began to glow blue to the amazement of the caravan. One of the frogs chirped, then all the others did so. In moments, the caravan was bathed in the enchanting song of the cave frogs.

Night approached the caravan as they exited the long tunnel. The sights were common for their guide and bearers, but to the caravan, seeing three suns setting and three moons rising was quite stunning. They had been in magical pocket-realms courtesy of their Mr. Traveler, but they knew those realms were of magic, and without that, magic would disappear. The quality of these realms had a reality that all of them wondered more than once that if one of them had collapsed, whether they would find themselves on another world far from Pan-Earth. They already knew they existed, and Traveler's shape-shifter was from one of them.

The men began recalling the Great Forest as their campsite was in a land of giant flowers, mushrooms, brush, and trees but still with vast open green space.

"Sire, it's like our journey on the Trail was to prepare us for Atlantea," Lady Aylen said.

"I thought the same. I've been reminded of more than a few cities and regions we previously visited," the king said.

Lady Aylen jumped again. The small bluecap floated in front of her. "Your caravan can set up camp here. We will be nearby, and the mushroom men will rest at a giant mushroom."

"I always thought elves can't be snuck up on," Lady Aylen said.

"They cannot. You must not have been one for long."

"There is a story there."

"You must tell us sometime. We like stories."

The giggling bluecap flew away.

King Aereth turned to Hobbs.

"Sire, I will see to it," their steward said.

It was like old times. Hobbs was back in his routine, directing the men to set up camp quickly. All of their packs were small-realms—larger inside than appeared outside. They set up the royal tents and the men's, and set up campfires for light, as the air was comfortable with a very slight breeze.

The men laughed when they saw the giant-slippers! They looked like a giant jester's shoe that opened in the top for the man to slide into. Inside it was like sleeping in a giant bed of feathers. For some men, all they preferred was a fur blanket to lie on the bare ground or wrap themselves in.

The smell of cooking food ran through the camp. They could have hired an Atlantean cook too but they had plenty of food leftover from the main trek. The royals sat at the campfire in front of their tents, but unlike the talking and joking men throughout the camp, they were somber. Gwyness joined them as the king flipped through their "book of the dead"—the list of every human and fae killed on the Trail. Quillen had the grim duty of maintaining the book for the caravan.

The king read every name out loud, pausing after each one.

"We were fortunate. They were not. The very least we can do is say their name and reflect upon them. In the morning, we'll have a remembrance with the men."

Servers approached with food and drink. Humans were not Atlantean culinary masters and would never be, but the dinner served was scrumptious.

"I think our Mr. Traveler isn't here because we'd ask him too many questions, ones he wouldn't want to answer," Lady Aylen said as she ate.

"Such as?" Gwyness asked.

"Such as why is Atlantea closing? Is that not a fact of supreme importance to all of Pan-Earth human and fae? But the fae act as if it happens every day. There's almost a willful indifference to things of importance. Like Oughtred's army of undead creatures within their own ports."

"They didn't enter the city," Gwyness said as she instinctively touched her amulet under her dress.

"But why even come here then?" Lady Aylen asked.

"Escorts for when he sails back to wherever he intends to go. For all we know, he always does so for his Kings'

Caravan," King Aereth replied.

"Another question we could have asked Mr. Traveler," Lady Aylen said.

"M'lady, we will see him again," Gwyness said.

"Now that we are here, there is another thing I do not understand. If I were the Atlanteans, I wouldn't allow all these strange races and kingdoms to come to my lands and take my treasure."

"Their lands, but it doesn't seem they care much about wealth. Their own lands are all the wealth they seem to need," King Aereth said.

"Lady Aylen, you are far too suspicious. How long have we wanted to journey to Atlantea? We are here, and you are still unhappy," Gwyness said.

"I am happy, but...maybe I am making more of it than there is. But you cannot deny that Atlantea closing its realms to all of Pan–Earth is a far greater deal than they are revealing."

"Yes, I agree," the king said. "However, it is of no matter to us. We will obtain what we came for and depart for home."

"True, sire. Home. Seems like a faraway dream."

"We might become the stuff of legends ourselves."

"Us? Why, sire?"

"The last caravan from the Lands of Man to travel to Atlantea and return. They'll write fables about us."

"That I could do without."

"We have another destiny, m'lady."

"We may have another destiny, Gwyness."

"Is that what is really troubling you?"

"You both are the descendants of this destroyed Kingdom of Rivermouth," King Aereth said, "where elves and elementals trained their mages and warriors."

"Slayers and seers," Gwyness said.

"Are your abilities enhanced here by Atlantea's magic?"

"Yes, sire, greatly so."

The king nodded. "Then maybe we should add another journey while we're here. Gather treasure for you to rebuild this Rivermouth."

"A new kingdom for the Lands of Man with a history known to fae."

Though it was fully dark, the triple moons illuminated the area. Outside the camp, they noticed that their one bluecap had been joined by several others. The fairies were dancing in a ring, singing. Not too far away, in a patch of giant mushrooms taller than most trees in the Lands of Man, their mushroom bearers stood, asleep, swaying in the breeze.

"We are not alone," the king remarked.

In the distance, they saw several different camps.

"Can you see who they are, Lady Aylen?" he asked.

"Sadly, I'm not like Mr. Elman, sire. Underwater, my eyesight can match his. On land is another matter, but I do believe we have humans, fae, and...something else."

"Something? What do you mean?" the king asked.

"I do wish Mr. Traveler was here."

"Goblins," said a floating bluecap that appeared right above them.

"Mr. Hobbs," King Aereth called out.

The steward was not far as he ate while he moved through the camp, plate in hand. He walked to them. "Yes, sire."

"We have company."

"Yes, sire. The men have been speaking about them. One camp is definitely human. The others we cannot tell, even through binoculars."

"Goblins," Lady Aylen told him.

"Mr. Hobbs, I don't want the men to be alarmed."

"Sire, I'll have sentries posted as a precaution."

Lady Aylen and Gwyness awoke before dawn and sat quietly at their morning campfire. Not soon after, Hobbs ran through the camp, fully dressed.

Most of the men, by now, got up before dawn, but there were always a few, at bliss within their giant-slippers, that needed help waking up.

"Get up, men!" Hobbs yelled as he turned over one giant-slipper after another, dumping men onto the ground.

"Good morning, ladies." King Aereth appeared from his tent, fully dressed in purple.

"We are blue, black, and purple today," Lady Aylen remarked.

"That shade of blue best suits you, m'lady," Gwyness said.

Hobbs neared the royal tents to greet them.

"Anything of note from the sentries, Mr. Hobbs?"

"Nothing at all to report, sire."

When their bluecap guide appeared in an instant, floating in front of them, Lady Aylen was not startled.

"I am ready for you this morning," the princess said.

"I can see. When you are ready, we march to the mines."

"We will be ready shortly," King Aereth said.

"No morning meal? Humans are fond of their morning meals," the bluecap said.

"Believe us when we say that any human, especially after our journey, will gladly forgo food and drink for gold," King Aereth said.

"The mushroom men and I are ready to set out when you wish."

The caravan expected to be led to a mountain where they'd be taken deep within to shovel or pick at their gold. The royals did, but very few of the men knew what unrefined gold looked like. Their bluecap led them over the ridge, and the caravan froze with mouths open. Before them was a mountain range, and each formation was made of glittering gold.

"This cannot be possible," Lady Aylen said.

"Take what you can," the bluecap said.

Over three thousand men were shoveling, carrying, and throwing golden rocks as large as they could manage into their magic packs or the magic buckets of the mushroom men. As the time for the noon meal approached, not one in the caravan wanted to stop.

"Bluebell," Lady Aylen called out, and their guide appeared, floating in front of her. "What were those other camps nearby in the night?"

"Humans, elves, and other fae."

"Elves? I didn't notice any elves."

"Yes, there were many. Further north there are mountains of elfin gold."

"What race of elves?"

"A party of high elves."

"Were there not goblins too?" King Aereth asked.

"Yes."

"Elves and goblins so close to each other?"

"One arriving, one leaving. Far away from each other."

"May I ask a question?" Gwyness said.

"Of course." The bluecap flew to her.

"How does one get back? I mean, the kingdom is closed."

"It matters not. So many risk everything to get to

Atlantea for treasure but so often forget that one must return to whence they came. But you never hear of travelers to Atlantea losing their treasure back along the Trail because the magic of Atlantea can teleport you, your party, and all your treasure to wherever you desire in an instant."

"Like 'vanishing'?" Lady Aylen said.

"The same. Only not against your will and not you alone."

"When we return, how long does the magic of Atlantea stay with us, our enhanced abilities?"

"The moment your foot touches the earth of your land, the magic is gone," the bluecap said.

Three days. Three thousand men with bulging backpacks. Mushroom men who had grown twice their size to carry their oversized buckets. Their bluecap guide led the way, flying back to the giant arch in the sky to cross over to the bath to the ante-city. Immediately behind her were the royals, Gwyness, Hobbs, and Quillen. The caravan was exhausted and hungry but happy. Amongst them, they had more gold than ten kingdoms in their lands could spends in a lifetime.

Lady Aylen had noticed the two plantmen waiting on the other side of the realm. Humanoid plants wearing robes. A curious sight for any human. They had no visible eyes, but she knew they were watching their approach.

"You have greeters," the bluecap announced to them. "I will take you through to the shore where you can find the storehouses for your treasures ahead of your departure. Will you stay within Atlantea for a while to explore?"

"We may for a little while," King Aereth replied.

The two plantmen bowed as soon as they stepped off the stone bridge between the arch connecting the two realms.

They all smelled the plant fae's strong floral aroma!

"You have returned," Gwyness said to them.

"We have a message for you all. You have friends who are waiting for you."

"Friends?" King Aereth asked.

"Which friends?" Lady Aylen asked.

"Sky elves and elementals of air and water."

"Celestial elves?" Lady Aylen asked.

"Yes. You are expecting them too, then."

"How long have they been waiting for us?" Lady Aylen asked.

"We do not know."

"When did they arrive?" King Aereth asked.

"Many weeks before you did."

"Expecting us?" King Aereth asked.

"Yes."

"Where are these friends of ours?"

"It has all been arranged," a plantman said. "At the Feast of the Gwragedd Annwyn."

THE GOBLIN PROPOSAL

Traveler had almost forgotten how mesmerizing the Kingdom at Titan's End was—a vast series of cities on land, sea, and air. Atlantea was not one city but many. He stood with his arms resting on the edge of the observation tower. The drop to the sea below was more than seventy feet. In the distance, another twenty feet above, a massive metallic castle city rested on a ring of clouds. The observation tower was one of twelve that also formed a ringed perimeter encircling the cloud city. Gargoyles, birdmen, and other winged fae filled the sky as the observation towers were also eateries catering to the city dwellers.

He had taken to wearing a thick dark robe and kept his hood over his head to obscure his face, as he was recognizable to many fae. His dog took humanoid form and also wore a dark hooded robe over his stout frame. His shape-shifter had transformed his dog head into the one of a giant hawk.

Traveler came to the observation tower not for sightseeing. He wanted to know who sought him out.

Few races in the magical lands unnerved him like lamias; even their sister race, the gorgons, did not. Gorgons turned people to stone with their evil magic, but lamias devoured their victims alive with deadly speed and efficiency. He and his companion had heard the flapping leathery wings of her guards first—another rare sight: two winged goblins in full armor but with wooden staffs rather than real weapons. The lamia royal was clothed in a brown tunic with elaborate embroidery to cover her upper humanoid half, a necklace of shark teeth. Below her waist was that of a giant, green-scaled snake. Her silk black hair was fashioned in a bun behind her head. She watched with human eyes, though Traveler wondered if it was an illusion spell as every lamia he had seen before had snake eyes.

"May we approach?" she asked with unusual deference for a creature such as she.

"Yes," Traveler replied.

She slithered forward with her goblin guards.

"I was told that winged goblins were extinct," he said.

"They exist in my ancient kingdom. I am Nagisa."

"You already know my name."

"And your reputation."

"What do you want?"

"I am here on behalf of others. We have a proposal for you."

"Proposal? For what?"

"An alliance."

"Strange proposal. I have made a living as a caravan master to Atlantea for some time. My party is here, so no more need for any alliance."

"But I come at an opportune time since you, and every other caravan master to Atlantea must find a new occupation."

"I already know my new occupation."

"Surely, not as a healer again."

"You know that too about me? Why not? It is a noble profession."

"Your talents in another area are more of interest to my allies."

"I will save you the trouble of explaining and myself the time of listening. The answer is no."

"You decide without fully hearing the proposal?"

"I can only imagine who your allies might be."

"Goblins, of course."

"Why would I ally myself with goblins?"

"You allied with them in the past when it was convenient to learn how to fight with your magic sword."

"It was mutually convenient. I wanted to kill certain elves. They wanted certain elves killed. Our goals were aligned at the time."

"They might be aligned again."

"Doubtful."

"My allies and I wish for you to join us against King Oughtred."

He tried to hide his reaction. The lamia did not try to hide her smile. He glanced at the faces of her winged goblin guards. Both watched him with blank expressions.

"I have your attention then, even if for a short time."

"The answer is still no."

"Meet my allies and decide then. King Oughtred is not as helpless as he pretends. Also, you destroyed most of his army of war wizards but far from all."

"Why are you telling me this? Why do you want to destroy Oughtred?"

"He's in our way, and he's human, present company excluded."

"He was a human."

"Human still in our eyes."

"Oughtred has many goblin allies, beast lords, too."

"But none of them are our allies. All you have to do is listen."

"We are in Atlantea, so none of it matters anymore."

"If you listen to our proposal, we will tell you what you want to know."

"Which is?"

"Why Atlantea has closed itself to all for a thousand years."

"How do you know I even care?"

"I know many things. Lamias are very good at sensing the true desires of human men."

Her forked tongue flicked across her lips from her mouth with a smile.

Traveler walked a full day to get to the location, from the highest heights of one city to the depths of another city. They traveled down spiraling stairs of a black mountain city sparsely populated but frequented by underground faring fae. His companion had transformed into another creature.

They had reached their destination at the base of the black mountain city. Its building was well within what was a hollow mountain. Passers-by, from halflings to those twice the size of an average human, moved through the surrounding streets. The common dress here was hooded cloaks to conceal one's identity. Even in Atlantea, such places existed, far from daylight and prying or curious eyes.

Traveler opened the door facade and entered the pocket-realm. The interior was a common, dimly lit tavern packed with goblin patrons. Most were the large, brutish, flat-nosed, very large pointy-eared kind, but at one table were a group of high goblins, with more refined facial features, and body types more elfin than what humans would call goblin. There had been no conversation amongst them. Hands held or nursed large mugs of ale on tables overflowing with empty ones, already drunk. At the very back was the same lamia royal flanked by her winged goblin guards.

"I did offer my magic to you. You could have been teleported here and saved yourself a day's walk," Nagisa said.

From behind Traveler, a creature entered through the same door, squeezing itself into the establishment. A bukavac—a six-legged creature, a monstrous lizard with gnarled horns on its head, and this one had shark-like teeth.

"We like to walk," Traveler said.

"Then let us sit together, at a distance, and discuss our proposal."

CARAVAN OF THE BERSERKERS

"**M**ag-nif-i-cent!" I-wulf yelled at the top of his lungs from the hill's peak.

His fellow berserkers and warriors cheered him on. In the sky above them, their chamroshes, free from their chain leashes, circled their masters as the caravan marched.

They had entered the realm a day ago. In the ante-city, they had asked what treasured lands giants frequent. Here they were. Their centaur guide led them into a realm of storm clouds, which sat on the ground rather than in the sky, massive mountain chains with more gigantic swords thrust into them from the top, and the glow beyond of, what they were told, were lands of gemstones the size of men.

But there was more, and Pangolin glanced at the caravan's weaponsmith, Estus, who had a perpetual smile on his face.

"Treasure and magic," Pangolin said.

"Yes, at long last," Estus replied.

Their large centaur guide was a liontaur—instead of the lower half of a horse, its body was that of a giant golden-fur lion. His name was Narn, an Atlantean guide to the treasured lands for five decades. The hair on his head was that of a golden mane, like a lion. They chose him because he was not dressed in frilly or bright-colored garments of a royal or jester. Berserkers preferred dark colors not colors so bright one needed to shield one's eyes. The liontaur wore a simple leather vest (which they learned was actual tree bark and not leather) on his chest with a ram's horn strapped over it. He held a magic walking stick in his hand, which touched the ground.

Pangolin and Estus marched behind him, leading their nearly twenty-five-hundred men in an unorganized mess, with their four hundred chamroshes above. Nirgund, the berserker, had his hands full tending to his thirteen alphyns. The reptilian hounds were especially playful with their master, playing a type of hide-and-seek behind the men with him. Pangolin glanced at them all with satisfaction. Let the men enjoy themselves, he said to himself. The danger of the Trail was behind them.

"Will we arrive by daylight?" Pangolin asked the centaur.

"We would have, if we traveled without the horseplay, but I understand. For those who survive the journey of the Trail, especially to come as far as you humans have, recreation is both expected and required. We arrive when we arrive. The treasures were there before we were born and will be there long after we are gone from this existence."

"We berserkers simply call it death."

"No belief in an after-life."

"Berserkers do not worry about such things," Pangolin replied. "We live here, not in any after-life. When we get there, we'll concern ourselves with there and not the pre-life."

A smile appeared on the liontaur's face.

"The giant sword we see," Estus began, "is a monument?"

"The sword you see is real. Driven into the mountain millennia ago," Narn replied.

"By whom?" Pangolin asked. "Surely not from the time of the Titans."

"There are other races of giants than the long-dead Titans," the lion centaur said. "This realm is frequented by other caravans of giants because they pay remembrance to the fallen giants when fae-kind warred with Atlantea. There was a huge final battle in this realm. The surviving giants killed themselves rather than surrender to the Atlanteans. That mountain with the sword is known as Blood Concord."

"It is the history of the place, not the treasure, that attracts the giants then," Pangolin said.

"Yes, a very rich history. As warriors yourselves, you can relate to the strong feelings they still hold."

"We can," Pangolin said.

"Atlanteans hold no bitterness?" Nirgund asked.

"No bitterness. They had no bitterness those eons ago either. Other fae races, not only giants, make a type of pilgrimage to realms that have special meaning to them from the past, but you humans do not."

"Because humans did not make war on Atlantea," I-wulf said.

"Because you humans weren't born yet."

"If we were, we still would not have. We'd be too busy making war on each other."

"Yes, Mr. Pangolin, we are all bloodthirsty savages," I-wulf said, slapping his comrade's back with his hand. "All the more reason to visit this Mount Blood Concord."

Under a single blue-white moon, the warrior camp echoed with laughter and conversation as the caravan ate their night meal and consumed ale. They hired no bearers, so their only resident of Atlantea was Narn, who watched them with constant amusement.

"What do you think our six Antean giants are doing?" I-wulf asked as he stuffed more meat into his mouth at their campfire with Pangolin, Estus, and Nirgund.

"Likely they grabbed more treasure than three times what we will get and are already on their way back to their kingdom," Nirgund answered.

"What I want to know is what of the others?" Pangolin asked. "King Aereth, Lady Aylen, Maiden Gwyness."

"We will all be reunited with them once we obtain our treasure," Estus said.

"Watch out," I-wulf said.

Two chamroshes flew just over their heads, one eagle-hound chasing another.

"They miss the crawling trees," Nirgund said. "I miss them too, but we don't have to fear creatures or dark fae here."

"Or so they say," Pangolin said.

In the distance, they could see the campfires of several other camps.

The centaur guide preferred to be alone at his own campfire, but they learned it was not to stay away from them but for meditation. Narn was a member of a fae religious order.

"Humans have religions. Why wouldn't fae have many more," Pangolin said.

"He does seem to have that religious-y look to him," I-wulf said.

"What? Did you make up a word, I-wulf?" Nirgund said.

"You know what I'm saying."

"Can you see them?" Pangolin asked.

Estus peered through his pocket telescope. "Too far away."

The warriors noticed their centaur guide had joined them.

"I imagine that liontaurs are far better at stealth than your equine cousins," Pangolin said.

"All cat centaurs are, but as for the races of centaurs none can surpass spider centaurs, though most, myself included, do not regard them as centaurs at all."

"What are they then?" Nirgund asked.

"Demons." The lion centaur pointed to the camps. "The camps in the distance are different fae caravan. I would tell you their names, but you humans have very limited knowledge of the many races of fae outside of gnomes, brownies, elves, and horse centaurs."

"We have a far more greater knowledge than that," I-wulf said.

"Yes, forgive me. Any human, or fae, who has traveled the Trail has undoubtedly encountered many more fae than the average human on Pan-Earth. I shall return to my meditation. Cat centaurs are naturally dismissive of outsiders. I sometimes fall prey to my nature even after all these decades within Atlantea when I should know better. None of us are the center of all things, and none are either superior or inferior to any other. We are all part of the life in the heavens."

"You are a philosopher too," Pangolin said.

"All centaurs have that trait. Whether they chose to cultivate it or not. We will leave at dawn."

"We will be up before dawn," I-wulf said. "I doubt if any of the men will sleep. If they do, it will be dreams of gems overflowing in their hands, enough to give them the wealth to buy themselves into royalty."

"I bid you a pleasant night."

The liontaur nodded and moved back to his lone campfire without any sound at all.

Every member of their caravan stood along the path without a word or movement of any kind. Even the chamroshes stayed quiet, resting on the ground behind their masters. To their east was another caravan—one of giants. An unknown race of giants to them, every one well over thirty feet. The storm clouds that marked the beginning of the realm when the human entered now seemed to enshroud the giants as they marched. Thunder and lightning rumbled and flashed with an intensity greater than what their caravan had passed through days ago.

"They march along a great river," Narn told them.

"What are they?" Pangolin asked.

"Their race is called fomorians," Narn replied.

"Humanoid giants with the head of goats," I–wulf said.

"Are they not evil giants of chaos and death?" Nirgund asked.

"Atlanteans do not share your views on morality nor us fae for that matter. They judge and act based on deeds. Fomorian giants may be the epitome of evil, but if they lift not a hand or say a word in violence, that is how they are judged by the Atlanteans."

"The monsters are more than just evil. They are said to be demons. Disease and blight follow with them," Nirgund said.

"No such dark magic can take root here in Atlantea," Narn said reassuringly. "No need to trouble yourself with them as they move to another realm deep below in the seas. We shall continue forward."

The caravan of berserkers had left an hour before dawn since all were wide-awake and restless. They never saw the single moon in the night set. It simply faded as the sky grew light but from a source not seen. At first, the sky was cloudless when a ray of sunlight broke through, and they realized that the entire realm was under a single cloud that reached out to the farthest points. The sun was there but kept from sight.

They did as they planned and climbed the mountain of the giant sword. They knew no customs of the giant races, so all they could do in their sacred place was take note of the sword and the land. The rocky surface surrounding the sword had countless markings. Their centaur guide said it was giant caravans leaving their mark over the millennia as part of a tradition.

"I'll leave our mark," Nirgund said. "We are fellow warriors, so the recognition will do no harm."

He carved his own rending of their Titan's Caravan banner, a likeness of the Maker of All Mountains.

"Men, I believe we have wasted enough time! I want treasure!" Pangolin yelled.

The men yelled out the last three words of their master-at-arms. The sounds echoed from the mountain.

"Then go get it and be gone!"

The sight of a giant goat head with red glowing eyes within the raging storm clouds to the east froze every man in the caravan.

"Ignore him," Narn said. "An idle jest on his part."

"It's hard to ignore a thirty-foot goat-headed giant said to be a demon watching you from a thunderstorm," Pangolin said.

"Our entrance is just over the next ridge," Narn said.

Narn, the liontaur, ran for the first time, and the caravan followed. The incline of the land increased and the men realized that they had to run to keep from falling backward. The glow from over the ridge was almost brighter than the sky. Narn stopped right at the edge.

They all reached the spot and stopped in shock. The

head of a serpentine creature rose up and slowly came within inches of Pangolin's face. Then another rose before another man, and another, dozens of serpent heads. Pangolin remained unmoved, and the creature backed away. The dozens of creatures were but a single one—a giant green hydra with dozens of snake-like heads guarding a giant shallow clear lake of gemstones of every color of the rainbow and more.

"No one will believe us, Pangolin, if we tell them," I-wulf said, laughing.

Pangolin watched as the giant hydra's many heads aided the berserkers running through the lake. A serpentine head would dive into the lake, fill its mouth with gems, rise, and expel the gems into an open magic sack of a waiting man. He stood there watching, almost annoyed by the absurdity of what he was beholding. All his life, from the time of a boy, he had read fables of battles against ferocious hydra. Cut one of their heads off, and two would grow in its place.

"Is something wrong?" Narn asked, approaching him in the lake that reached waist-high to the men.

"Is this what the great hydras have become in

Atlantea?"

"I will give a truer account to put your mind at ease. The lake is really a dormant volcano and the hydra's home. The gemstones are churned from within. Too many and the hydra's home is threatened. It is eager to get rid of the gemstones and help any to do so. You see them as precious stones. It sees it as rocks and a nuisance. If you weren't here, it would spit them away."

Pangolin now noticed that the entire area around the lake was littered with gemstones.

"Thank you. My mind is at ease now."

"Good."

"Men, when you feel you have enough! Take even more!" Pangolin yelled.

"Hear! Hear!"

"Is it true about hydras?" Pangolin asked the liontaur. "Cut off one head, and two grow back."

"I would not know. I'm a philosopher, not a warrior. I carry staffs, not swords."

"You're a liontaur."

"I leave the fighting to you and others like you. Our beast here is like me. Content with life, quarrels with no one."

Pangolin chuckled. A liontaur with claws sharper than the metal of most swords in the Lands of Man and a giant hydra were both pacifists.

"If you say so, Mr. Narn. How long can we stay here?"

"Stay as long as you wish and collect as much treasure as you wish. It is, after all, why you traveled so far."

"You will not ever return to your lands, the lands of Chiron or the Centaurian Forests with Atlantea closed to outsiders?"

"You know my lands."

"Yes, we met other cat centaurs on the Trail too and some of my comrades even visited Centaur City."

"Interesting to meet a human who knows of my lands. No, Mr. Pangolin, my existence, when the time comes, will end here in Atlantea. I am never leaving. They are many centaurs who live here now. We have our own Centaurian Fields, Forests, and Jungles here."

"I'm sure they are quite amazing towns and cities."

"They are. If you and your men remain in Atlantea for a time, I may invite you to my town. There are many different races of cat centaurs. Some races never seen by a human."

"We would like that."

"So fae no longer need to leave Atlantea after a time."

"That has not been the case for fae for some time. Humans, however, have always been fragile to the passage of time in such a realm of magic."

"Are you not sad that Atlantea is closing? Who will you guide to the treasured lands?"

"Mr. Pangolin, there will always be visitors to guide to the treasured lands. I know what you ask, but I am a mere guide. I know not of the reasons why the Atlanteans do what they do. I am only grateful that I am fortunate to live happily and productively within their lands and can merely walk to visit other lands, races, and animals whenever I wish."

"No human or fae could ask for anything more."

For five days, the Pangolin Caravan collected treasure. Narn led them back through the circular archway connecting their realm with the ante-city. They were soaked from the downpour of a storm they had passed through only an hour earlier. However, every man had a big smile on his face with their magic sack over one shoulder and their chamroshes also carrying at least half a dozen each.

"Look!" Nirgund yelled. "It's Mr. Elman."

The men ran to the awaiting half-elf who smiled but was unnerved by the sight of thousands of berserkers and warriors running to him.

Pangolin let them all pass him and turned to the liontaur. "Thank you for your service," he said and shook the centaur's hand.

"You are quite welcome. You know where to find me if you should need me again."

"We do."

As the liontaur ran off, the men gestured to Pangolin.

"Pangolin, Mr. Elman has news for us."

"Mr. Elman, it is good to see you."

"Same here, Mr. Pangolin."

"We were afraid we wouldn't see you ever again. Where are your other half-elf comrades?"

"We are all together."

"Very good. What is this news you have?"

"It's Mr. Traveler."

That got everyone's attention.

"What of him? Has something happened?" Pangolin

asked.

"You must come with me, all of you. He told me to fetch you the moment you returned."

CARAVAN OF THE DROWS

In most fae cities, taverns were not just for people but for their animals. Frog-Dor stepped into an establishment filled with a various of fae races deep in conversation with drink and their animal companions at their sides—giant hounds, griffins, hippogriffs, flying unicorns, flying land fish, giant toads, ichneumon (a giant weasel-like beast), and many others.

He walked through the massive cavernous tavern with row after row of tables with patrons. Finally, the wizard saw Traveler at a table under a small tree growing from the wall, but he stopped. The dog was in the form of a six-legged lizard creature.

"It's called a bukavac," Traveler said and gestured. "Have a seat."

"I came as soon as I received your message."

"I need you to find some drows."

"Me, sir? I am a conjuring spell-caster but never had reason for searching spells."

"No spells needed here. You will seek out our drows from the caravan."

"Mr. Traveler, you said yourself that Atlantea is far vaster than imaginable. A realm of realms. How could I possibly find a hundred drows in this land? Drows don't like to be sought after and are hard to find in any land."

Traveler handed Frog-Dor a parchment. "Take this. Atlantea is no different than any city in your land or mine. Cities are a collection of communities, a living network of individuals, and when one knows how to use that network, you can have it do the work for you."

"They can find the drows?"

"They can, and we must find them."

"Are you reassembling Titan's Caravan, sir?"

"Perhaps. But the drows may have special knowledge we need."

"Related to Atlantea closing?"

"Atlantea has only been closed three times in its history of eons. War with the Titans, war with the dragons, and war with the fae."

"What would cause a fourth? Why do you think the

drows could help?"

"I ran into former masters of mine, teachers. Despite their calm demeanor, they were fleeing the city. They are powerful healers and sorcerers. They don't run away."

"We are all afraid of something, Mr. Traveler, no matter how powerful we become or think we are."

"True, but there's something one of them gave me. I need to confer with drows we can trust. Dr'as and Dr'amal are those drows."

"Then I will find them."

"I know you will, Mr. Frog-Dor."

"May I ask something, sir? As an experienced caravan master and previous resident of Atlantea, do you believe we are in danger?"

"Mr. Frog-Dor, sadly, I can't answer that question as confidently as I could have in the past."

"We will be eventually leaving, sir?"

"Yes, but we can never return."

"Atlantea is your kingdom in a way, and you feel a duty to protect it, even in a small way."

"I do, but the Atlanteans can defend their kingdom without us. But I want to know. Perhaps, I'm bored since I'm no longer a guide or captain of a ship and want to pass the time until we return to our lands."

"You are perceptive, not bored. I will find Dr'as and Dr'amal."

Master Traveler had directed him to all the right establishments. Frog-Dor quickly learned of the informal network that existed in the fabled kingdom. Day by day, one contact led to another, and he met with fae from early morning to late hours of the night. Of most help were subterranean elves, also know as nether-elves, with their dark, almost black skin, wearing garments with the appearance of earthen rock.

In Atlantea, there was no distinction between light and dark fae. With the over-magic of Atlantea preventing violence of any kind all races did co-exist freely. But Frog-Dor still struggled with the concept of wandering streets, brushing past an elf or nymph one moment and a goblin or hag witch the next. A puck (a sprite as tall as a human with hunched-over postures, skinny and elastic arms, bushy eyebrows, long noses, large ears, and slim prehensile tails) he met from the day before had referred him to a member of a dark fairy race that in the last encounter of Titan's Caravan tried to kill them.

Lunatishee were the wingless fairies covered in sharp thorns over their entire bodies and were no taller than gnomes.

"I will compensate you for the information," Frog-Dor said to the devilish fairy.

"Yes, you will. A party of drows, newly arrived. Why do you seek them out?"

"Do you know where they are, or should I inquire elsewhere?"

"A drow sorceress? A drow royal—her father."

"You do know them."

"I do."

"Where can I find them?"

"I will tell you if you tell me why."

"The why is easy. They are friends."

"You are from Titan's Caravan yourself?"

"Yes."

"Why do you not know how to find them?"

"You know drows. Quick to disappear."

"I don't believe you."

"That does not matter. I will inquire elsewhere."

"You are not very good at this."

"Am I supposed to barter with you forever?"

"Not forever, but for a time. You know I have the information you seek."

"There."

Shock came over the lunatishee face. Suddenly, the dark fairy had wings.

"How did you do that?"

"Will you give me the information I need, or should I remove your new wings?"

"I will tell you, but remove the wings. Lunatishee hate wings."

The caravan of drows emerged from a realm of dark mountains and gigantic geysers led by a dwarven guide. The drowess, Dr'amal, saw him first standing in the crowd, waiting. Her father, Dr'as, saw him next, and his expression was not a happy one. Drows were a separate elfin race with dark-bluish skin and most often white hair, though sometimes they could have dark hair. Their white eyes often had brightly colored irises. Sometimes their eyes glowed with their colors. These drows all had white hair and purple eyes.

Frog-Dor approached. "Master Dr'as. Good to see you again."

"I did not ever expect to see you again."

"Yes, I know. I am here at the request of our former caravan master."

"Mr. Traveler?" Dr'amal, the sorceress, asked.

"Yes, he needs your help."

Dr'as smiled, surprised. "He needs my help? Why?"

"I can lead you to him."

"Our former caravan master does know how to rouse the interest in a drow. Yes, we will meet with him, of course. We owe him much, a debt we will never be able to fully repay. My drows will store our treasure, and we will follow."

"How long were you looking for us?" Dr'amal asked.

"A few days, but I found you."

Outside their own lands, drows preferred the darkness of night. Frog-Dor arranged the midnight meeting and the drow king, Dr'as, led his daughter and a dozen drows through the tavern's entrance promptly on time. Frog-Dor stood from his secluded table to greet them, but Traveler remained seated with the dog, back in its gray wolf-dog form, at his side.

"This place reminds me of when we first met," Dr'as said to Traveler.

"Not a pleasant meeting for me," Dr'amal said.

Traveler stood and gestured. "Pull up chairs and join us," he said to the other drows. "Good to see you, Dr'as," he said as they all sat.

"I was intrigued to hear you needed my help," Dr'as said.

"Yes, and it's serious."

Traveler recounted his first encounter with the lamia with her winged goblins. Then the meeting with the goblins later that day with their proposal.

Dr'as looked at his daughter and a couple of the drows who were his warrior chiefs.

"Mr. Traveler, it is madness! Goblins, lamias. Surely, even you must see this as utter madness."

"I need your help to assess their proposal."

"None of them can be trusted," a drow said. "Never."

"We both know that not to be true, all the time. We've both dealt with elves who can't be trusted, and I have personally entered into limited pacts with goblins in the past who could, for a time. It is a proposal, not a lifelong treaty. Do you know why Atlantea has closed?"

"What does that have to do with us?" Dr'as asked. "It is not our concern. We obtain treasure for our kingdoms, rest for a short time, and return home with our riches. It is why we came here with you as our caravan master if you recall."

"I do not argue with anything you have said. But I ask for you to join me in assessing their proposal and, further, not to accept."

"To what end? We will not be in Atlantea for too much longer. Besides, you know more of goblins than we do. We know nothing of lamias and care never to know anything of the snake demon race. Winged goblins? We thought them to be long dead."

"Makes one wonder. But to answer your question: there is one race that you know more of than any other."

"No," Dr'amal said. "You are not about to say what we think you are."

"My dog can sense the race of all nearby. There was a night drow in that room of goblins."

"Goblins, lamias, and night drows," Dr'as said.

"All I'm asking is for your counsel, Dr'as," Traveler said.

"They are plotting something. It is what their races do."

"Dr'as, this is not Faë-Land. No one plots anything within Atlantea. Let us not forget Oughtred."

"What could they possibly do, or he? If they engage in any violence, they'll be vanished back to whatever hell they crawled out from. What in your mind could they possibly do? Goblins, lamias, or night drows, or Oughtred. Are you still stuck on the words that he plans to conquer Atlantea? A boast. A lie. Impossible. The combined armies and magic of every fae race on Pan-Earth couldn't defeat the Atlanteans. Oughtred could assemble all the handful of races he wants with his goblin allies and undead creatures. He is a threat to us outside these walls but not to the Atlanteans within their domain. What do you suspect?"

"I don't know, Dr'as. Something is not right. Atlantea is the ultimate kingdom of fantastic treasures. That is why so many risked their lives and died trying to get here, both humans and fae. But as I walk the streets of Atlantea, I notice that there are many around me here who don't seem to be very interested in treasure at all."

"Maybe they are as high and noble as a former caravan master I know."

"I only became so high and noble after I secured my own treasure, Dr'as."

"I do not know what to say."

"Whatever is really happening… the whispering in the shadows is getting louder."

"Atlantea is indeed a great magical kingdom, but its people gossip like all others. Is that not true?"

"It is, but I feel it's different this time."

"Maybe this is how it was when Atlantea closed before. Too bad neither one of us was here to compare those times past to now."

"The previous times had to do with war."

"With whom? Master Traveler, there is nothing for us to do. And whatever we do should not and should never include goblins, lamias, and night drows."

"I say no more other than this: Atlantea has closed its realms to all. They have only done so three times in their long history. I do need to satisfy my suspicions."

"Your curiosity, you mean. A trait you share with most of your humankind. As I told the wizard, I will accompany you, of course, but I am not sure what you believe will come of it.”

“Then consider it a gathering of all the information we need in case their plot extends to our land or mine outside of Atlantea.”

“That makes more sense to me than anything else you have said. When do you wish to meet the goblins and the snake woman?”

MESSENGER

The moment Traveler stepped out the main entrance, he stopped to hold Frog-Dor behind him. Already the dog grew into a larger, bipedal form.

"Is it not I who should be shielding you?" Frog-Dor said, looking around. He noticed that the caravan master was looking up.

The tavern was among many establishments carved into one side of two sheer mountains situated next to each other to form a dark and narrow street. The wizard noticed a figure at the top, standing on the precipice. The figure jumped, and in moments a type of harpy stood before them, smiling.

"How did you sense me so fast, human?" she asked.

Frog-Dor studied her. He had seen harpies before— head of a woman and body of a large bird. But this species was more humanoid. Her human arms were clearly also wings with feathers reaching the ground. Her entire body below her neck was also covered in thick dark feathers.

Her eagle feet ended in menacing claws. Her hair was also feathers but styled to appear as human hair running down her back.

"My dog told me."

The dog growled in a giant humanoid form with clawed hands and feet.

"Tell your shape–shifter I am a messenger, not an assassin. Besides, you know none of us are capable of harming one another here in the fabled kingdom."

Traveler glanced back and noticed the drows behind him, watching.

"What message does a highborn have for us?" Traveler asked the harpy.

"A human who knows my race. How do you know of my kind?"

"Before I was a caravan master, I was a healer. I was a member of a flying caravan that was attacked by trolls. Our caravan master was your kind. She was very displeased with the prospect of a human healer, but it was either me or lose a winged arm."

The harpy stared at him. She had not been expecting his answer. "You will not be able to meet our mutual friends," she finally said.

"Why is that?" Traveler asked.

"Things have changed."

"Changed?"

"Do you know of the Feast of the Gwragedd Annwyn?"

"I do."

"Attend and meet them there. You will recognize them."

"You did not tell me why our meeting place has changed."

"I do not know the full story other than a sky ship was destroyed as it was about to enter Atlantea's lands yesterday."

"Who was on the sky ship?"

"Celestial elves."

"Do we know any of these celestial elves?"

"I do not know anything more, other than it was under the command of a great white elfess of great age."

"Is that all?"

"The sky ship may have also carried night drows," the harpy said, grinning with her sharp teeth, watching for reactions.

"Do you know night drows?" Traveler asked.

"Do I, or do my allies?"

"Both."

"No."

"I don't believe you."

"As you wish. Have you ever encountered shadow elves in your travels?" the harpy asked.

"Why would you ask me that?" Traveler asked.

"No reason."

"Is there more?" Traveler asked the harpy.

"We will see you there. I expect it to be a feast unlike any other with the closing of the kingdom. Fortunate for the magic of Atlantea and the vanishing. If not for it, I am afraid to say what gruesome deaths could occur." The harpy laughed out loud as she crouched down, making a strange cawking sound. "We harpies have such a malevolent sense of humor." She jumped and darted into the sky, flapping her winged arms.

Traveler was about to speak to Dr'as but the drow leader restrained him.

They all looked up to see there was someone else peering down at them from the precipice before suddenly disappearing.

THE FEAST

REUNITED

Griffins were known throughout all lands of fae and humans as legendary guardians of treasure. However, those stories were always of a single beast. The herald led King Aereth's and Lady Aylen's caravan to a floating structure in the sky—the bottom half was an inverted pyramid, and the upper half was a castle. As the castle-pyramid descended to the ground, the castle was overrun by giant griffins three times the size of those used as steeds. A drawbridge lowered and extended to the earth at their feet.

"The griffins will attend to your treasures until you are ready to depart," the Atlantean said to them.

"Thank you, herald," the king said.

"They will not harm you," the herald said. "Store whatever you wish within the castle."

Three thousand men carrying the large packs on their backs marched up the drawbridge. The royals, Gwyness, Hobbs, and Quillen followed, carrying the magic buckets from the mushroom men bearers. The griffins inside reminded them more of playful domesticated cats than the powerful, flying beasts that they truly were. Within the castle walls was a single building storehouse where they placed everything.

The royals looked at the thousands of packs and the buckets, then at each other.

"Here is the official conclusion of our legendary journey along Titan's Trail," the king said. "The treasures for four kingdoms and wealth to last as long as our empires endure."

"I sometimes believe I'm dreaming. We've waited so long and come so far," Lady Aylen said.

"Encountered more danger and horrors than most," King Aereth said.

"But we triumphed," Hobbs said with a smile.

"Yes, we have, Mr. Hobbs," Lady Aylen said.

"All we need to do is get home," King Aereth proclaimed.

"Yes, but we have a feast to attend, sire," Hobbs said.

"Let us...leave. Forget this fairy feast," Lady Aylen said.

"Now, now, Lady Aylen. We must be good royals and

do our duty to our fabled hosts. We have taken riches from their lands, so the least we can do is say thanks by attending their feast."

"Do not mind her, sire. She's been in an awful disposition for days now," Gwyness said. "I have my suspicions as to why, though."

"Do you now?" Lady Aylen asked.

Lady Aylen's ears picked up the commotion first. The royals moved through the men to the entrance of their castle-pyramid. They peered down to the ground and laughed.

A smiling Pangolin stood there with I-wulf and Nirgund, twenty-five hundred men, and their chamrosh and alphyn animals.

"What took you all so long?" the man-at-arms said in his earthen armor that, like most within the realm of Atlantea, glowed with its inherent magical power.

"We have some visitors too," Nirgund said.

Mr. Elman and his half-elf comrades appeared out of invisibility—all seven half-elfesses and eleven half-elfin men.

"You're back!" Lady Aylen yelled.

Without a thought, the princess leaped down from the entrance level, bypassing the drawbridge, and effortlessly landed on the ground.

She hugged the half-elves and soon found herself crawling with tiny owl griffins minded by the half-elfess, Brenn.

Fae residents of the ante-city told them that it was permissible, and that's all Hobbs needed. He had the men strike tents on an empty stretch of land on a green hill with the seashore nearby. The caravan would enjoy each other's company under the nighttime Atlantean sky.

For the young Quillen, he once again could return to the water to play with dobhar-chú. Several of the baby sea dogs followed him wherever he walked. He had already drawn the creatures in his magic book, but he decided to do so again as he sat down on the grass with the animals resting next to him or trying to climb up his arms or shoulders.

The humans were together again, like when they first set out from the Lands of Man. Supper had been served with the men sitting in circles around campfires around the camp. The merriment was shared by their animals with their chamroshes flying above and around the camp and Nirgund's alphyns chased after them. The most enjoyable part of their reunion was recounting the stories.

The caravan leadership sat at the campfire of the royal tents with all of the half-elves, as they had done so often on the Trail.

"I am not at all certain I believe that story, Mr. Pangolin," Lady Aylen said. "A hydra helping you gather precious gems sitting in a lake. This lake wasn't hot or boiling. If it were a volcano, there would be no water. I think they were playing a game on you. No one will believe such a story. Hydras eat people. They don't help you treasure hunt."

"I would not believe it myself, m'lady, if I were not there. Our guide said the creature enjoys the task. We're helping it."

"You said your guide was a lion centaur?" Gwyness asked.

"Yes. A very impressive fae," Pangolin said.

"Our guide was a bluecap. A race of fairies fond of mining, I'm told."

"Your treasures are secure then, too, Mr. Pangolin?" King Aereth asked.

"Yes, sire. In another castle resting on an upside-down pyramid. My people have always believed griffins were solitary beasts. I've never seen so many together in one place."

"Much is different here in Atlantea. The sea dogs that Mr. Quillen has seemed to have adopted. Your hydra. I even saw a one-eyed hag who appeared to have not a trace of malevolence in her body."

"And other dark fae," Lady Aylen added.

"But we know that they do," Pangolin said.

"Yes, we do. Which leads us to this feast," Lady Aylen said.

The king and Gwyness laughed under their breath.

"Why go?" Pangolin asked.

"There! Our master-at-arms agrees with me."

"Because friends are waiting for us," Gwyness replied.

"We have what we came for," Pangoin added.

"We should, at least, explore the fabled kingdom for a bit before we depart. We will never be able to return," King Aereth said. "Our people will expect us to do that."

"I never expected to ever return," Pangolin said, sipping from his mug. "The journey to Atlantea is a once in a lifetime experience, especially if you succeed, which we have."

"We have to also say goodbye to our good 'friend' Oughtred," Lady Aylen said wryly.

"That we can avoid," King Aereth said.

"Have any of you seen this 'vanishing' they speak of?" Estus asked.

"Mr. Traveler!" It was Mr. Elman's voice.

His announcement boomed throughout the camp. Everyone either set their food and drink down or dropped it altogether as they stood to look.

Traveler stood near the entrance to ante-city with his grayish wolf-hound. The air around him wavered, and soon fairies and halfling sprites appeared out of invisibility, all around him, walking to them all.

Estus, the caravan's weapons master, had visited his special pocket-realm with its magic storehouse full of weapons and armor. He had wanted to animate their armor golems, but the automatons did not move. A vast storehouse of weapons that would never be used as long as they remained in Atlantea. Not that he had any quarrel with the situation as they had had plenty of battles along Titan's Trail to last a lifetime.

He was surprised that the halfling sprites, with their long silver mustaches and beards nearly touching the ground, wanted to visit the pocket-realm. They spent some time inspecting the weapons and armor.

"Which is your favorite battle weapon?" one asked, running his finger along the metal.

"I actually prefer a good suit of armor. I forged one for myself—a dreadnought where the gauntlet is as good a weapon as any. I never did get to use it but that was not my purpose. I served the warriors of the caravan, keeping their blades sharp, their shields polished, and kept the metal of their weapons strong. I am not the warrior."

The three sprite halflings looked at each other and nodded.

"That is all we need," one said.

Traveler had told him the three fae weavers would transform each member of the caravan to be worthy to stand in the greatest halls of Atlantea.

Estus stood in front of a floating mirror as the halflings worked. From his undergarments to his clothes to his armor, they "weaved" it from magic fibers they pulled from the air. The clothes seemed painted to his skin, and the armor lighter than elfin metal. His bald head was adorned with an embellished helmet.

"I look like a royal myself," Estus remarked at his reflection in the magic mirror.

"We will design a scabbard for each side to hang along your thigh. Pick matching weapons from the storehouse for each one," one fae said.

"Would it be provocative if I chose an elfin and goblin one?" the weapons master asked.

"We did notice your weapons and armor of goblin metal. At the festival, both races will be in attendance. It would show a wisdom of neutrality for your party or attract wanted gossip."

"Then it is what I shall do. An elfin short sword and a goblin mace."

The sprites nodded and continued their weaving.

"Why can I not command my armor golems as I once did?"

"They are instruments of violence."

"I would not use them for such."

"But others around you could easily seize control of them or your own mind and do violence."

"Could they?"

"Atlantea has some of the most powerful magic casters in all of Pan-Earth. Any one of them could do so with ease. If that were to happen, you would be vanished back to your human lands in the blink of an eye."

"What of they?"

"They would follow."

"We will also place the symbol of your caravan's banner on the chest of your armor," said another spriteling.

Estus watched as the fae drew the symbol on his armor with a finger. In moments, the symbol brightened in intensity and then darkened as if burnt onto the metal. In seconds, the fae did what would take a good forger like himself days to accomplish.

"The wonder of magic," Estus said aloud. "Such fire-staining of metals takes precision and days in my lands."

"We are in the lands of wonderful magic," a fae said.

King Aereth had been to more ceremonies, festivals, and parleys than he'd care to remember. But never did he look as exquisite as he did, staring at his image in the floating magic mirror. The halfling sprite weavers had dressed him in a purple royal attire beyond anything the best of servants could have fashioned for him in Helm Earldom. A dark purple coat with a golden sash as bright as the golden crown that they placed on his head. Black leggings and black boots of a material so soft he felt he stood on air. Lastly, they had weaved a sleeveless cloak down to his ankle with an upright collar. Also, they fitted him with a scabbard on each side of his legs and tied it.

A fully dressed Estus entered the king's tent. "Here you are, sire."

The weapons master handed the sprites two elfin swords.

"I can't say I would even try to use an elfin sword, even in jest," King Aereth said.

"The weapons are for fashion alone," a fae said.

"Of course," the king said. "Mr. Estus, I have never seen you look so..."

"Royal, sire."

"Yes. A true nobleman."

"Thank you, sire."

When done, both men left the tent to see the rest of the caravan being fitted by weavers—three thousand men dressed as noble knights with bright golden plumes sprouting from their helmets. The caravan's twenty-five hundred berserkers and warriors had no armor over their battle dress but instead had a shield with the symbol of Titan's Caravan over each arm.

Their steward joined them in his new purple attire, including a frilly hat.

"Very sharp, Mr. Hobbs," the king said.

"Not sure about the hat, sire."

"It suits you."

"Thank you, sire."

"And have our young Mr. Quillen carry the caravan's banner."

"Yes, sire."

"Where is Mr. Quillen?" the king asked. "Please don't tell me he's at the shore again with those water animals."

Like the many stories of fairies they had heard since childhood, the diminutive fae flew around them with their translucent insect wings weaving their new clothes with strands of light. Lady Aylen and Gwyness stood in the women's tent, each in front of a floating mirror. The princess already felt her new battle dress, courtesy of the caravan's brownies, was perfect. The fairy weavers created something even more impressive—bright ocean blue, all fabric made to look like the scales of a fish, an upright collared cloak, dark blue knee-high boots, and matching gloves. While Lady Aylen's clothes were of the ocean and seas of Fae-Land, Gwyness's attire was of the night—all black with a white metal belt glowing like the moon.

One of the fairies retrieved their weapons. They fastened Lady Aylen's dual war tridents on her back. Gwyness's dual warhammers hung on the right side of her moon belt. Another fairy pulled out the maiden's amulet from her dress.

"Do not hide it from others," she said. "Be proud of what it represents."

"Do I know what it represents?" Gwyness asked.

"Those who should know will."

Another fairy placed a new blue metal crown on Lady Aylen's head. "All is complete," she said.

"Very impressive," Lady Aylen said, admiring her new royal attire in the magic mirror. "The work of your male weavers cannot be all that involved. All they have to do for the men is throw water on their face."

Gwyness and the fairies laughed. "Does that include Mr. Traveler?" Gwyness asked.

"Mr. Traveler is different, of course." She looked at the fairies who continued to float around the women inspecting their work. "For a realm where violence is not allowed, is the display of our weapons wise?"

"It is expected by all for the ceremony you will attend."

"What does this 'vanishing' look like?" Gwyness asked.

"Do not think about it. Keep even the thoughts of violence from your mind no matter who or what you encounter."

"Is that a common occurrence? Trying to provoke others to violence."

"Oh yes," said a fairy. "There are many in this realm who are quite skilled in the practice. Do not fall prey to their words or gestures. If you are vanished from Atlantea, it will be you alone with only the clothes on your body. Nothing else will follow—your comrades, belongings, or treasure."

"No treasure? Why didn't you say that at the start? That's all you had to tell me to behave myself," Lady Aylen said.

At the edge of the camp, Traveler stood with his arms folded. He pulled back the brown hood of his cloak on his head. His dress was the same as when they entered Atlantea with his magic sword sheathed and hanging on his back and his orange-tinted elemental armor glistening over his new battle dress.

Quillen, despite his new attire, was back at the shore to play. He couldn't take his eyes off the magical otter-like animals, a dozen of them waiting for him.

"Mr. Quillen!" Traveler yelled. "Leave them alone unless you want a companion for life, or many of them. You may think them adorable and playful, but they are wild animals. They live in the wilds of Atlantea, not a human abode. So unless you intend to leave Atlantea with them, ignore them this instant. They will soon focus their attention on others."

Quillen gave the three dobhar-chú a last look, then walked away.

"But you have your dog, Mr. Traveler?"

"And?" Traveler asked. "He lives with me, not in the wild."

The dog changed his form to like the cross of a dobhar-chú and dog. Quillen laughed.

"He's making fun of me, Mr. Traveler."

"Your dog is developing a sense of humor, Mr. Traveler. Isn't that right, dog?" Lady Aylen leaned down to pet the dog, but he growled at her. "Or not."

Lady Aylen stood. "Our caravan is reuniting."

Traveler gestured to something over Lady Aylen's shoulder. The princess turned and saw the female half-elves in their new battle dress attire with the owl griffins running on the ground behind them.

"Yes, our royal guardswomen and royal owl griffins. I am no longer sad. Treasure, new clothes, and a reunion. I could not be happier."

Other than Traveler, Pangolin was the only other member of the caravan who did not need the services of the Atlantean weavers. The berserker master-at-arms's earthen metal armor that looked like scales already radiated a newness within the realm. Also, in his eyes and all the berserkers was a tiny sparkle of the berserker rage that lay within each man. Pangolin was glad that he'd be able to carry his giant axe-mace properly—freshly polished by the hands of Estus—strapped on his back.

Pangolin exited his tent to an awaiting I-wulf. His second-in-command looked like a new man in his battle dress and dark elfin armor.

"I-wulf, is that you? Your facial hair is cut and combed? Are you the real I-wulf, or are you a changeling?"

The berserker grinned. "Those fairies even groomed all our animals."

"How do you groom a chamrosh, or an alphyn?"

"The alphyns are going to demand that kind of care from now on, but that's Nirgund's concern, not ours. The chamroshes couldn't care less either way, but they look as majestic as griffins."

"When do we leave?"

"Mr. Traveler is going to speak to the men."

Pangolin had a large smile on his face. "Like we did back on the Trail."

Berserkers were known for their super-human rampages driven by magic rage. But all emotions of the warriors were larger than life. Traveler became the target of a new kind of wrath—joy. Pangolin and the other berserkers and warriors embraced their caravan master.

"You didn't think you'd get away from us without a

proper berserker 'hello'," Pangolin told him.

"I said I'd return when you collected your treasures," Traveler said. "But here now, I'm beginning to reconsider the wisdom of my decision."

The dog watched the reunion with both expressions of annoyance and boredom.

"The dog knows that berserkers can be crazed," Nirgund said.

"Berserkers are crazed, Nirgund!" I-wulf proclaimed.

"Here! Here!" the warriors yelled in unison.

"If you men don't let me go, I'll do something violent so that I can be vanished away in peace from the lot of you," Traveler said to the laughing men.

With King Aereth and Lady Aylen in the lead, the caravan marched back through the ante-city.

"While you need not fear any attacks here, the Atlantean's ultimate magic of instantly vanishing anyone who raises a hand in violence is absolute," the caravan master had told them all hours before within another pocket-realm for a meeting of the entire caravan. "I encountered such magic back in the Lands of Man, in the secret fae city of Last Keep. Whether a resident or visitor, if you ran foul of any of the city's rules, one would be teleported away to the human city of the same name of Last Keep within the snap of a fae finger. The magic of Atlantea is far greater.

"However, as you've already noticed even the weakest human is imbued with a magical strength and prowess possible nowhere else on Pan-Earth or beyond. That is what you must know. Where is Atlantea? What is Atlantea? Atlantea is a city that becomes more Atlantea the further you travel to its center. The lands become more ancient and the magic more powerful. You will also see species of fae more powerful than you have ever imagined. Resist all fear and doubt in your hearts. They may not be able to kill you, but that doesn't make them helpless or any less dangerous."

"What are you saying, Mr. Traveler?" King Aereth asked.

"Surely, the danger that has hung over us from the moment we left the Lands of Man has not followed us right into the heart of Atlantea?" Lady Aylen asked. "We succeeded in our quest, acquired our riches, and will be gone."

"All true, princess. But we have not departed yet. We are here, and so are our enemies. My instincts simply say to take care. Those instincts have served us well and kept us alive through Titan's Trail."

"I would say you kept us alive," Pangolin said, marching behind them.

"Do you speak of Oughtred?" King Aereth asked.

"Sire, you will see for yourselves that Oughtred is only one among many. He may be to us, but he is hardly the most dangerous among them. We will divide the caravan into smaller groups, each with a leader whose sole function will be to keep all its members calm no matter what happens."

"What of our 'friends'?" Lady Aylen asked. "These celestial and star elves are waiting for us."

"Princess, they did tell us we'd see them again," Traveler said. "After the Feast, we will know if we can stay awhile for you to explore as much as possible or if we should depart as quickly as possible."

"How long can we stay, Mr. Traveler? You have always said time doesn't advance as it does in Faë-Land or the Lands of Man."

"Do not concern yourself about that. Humans cannot live in Atlantea forever. We are too short-lived. But we will not be here long."

"What of fae?" Lady Aylen asked.

"There was a time when they could not either, but that

has changed. Though when they do leave such a magic place for home, they can experience the same problems with time as humans. But there are exceptions."

"Sky elves, you mean," Lady Aylen said.

"All fae who can live in the heavens and elementals," Traveler replied.

"We are so glad you're back, Mr. Traveler," Lady Aylen said. "We missed the counsel, and stories."

Traveler grinned. "That is my role now."

"However, are we sure Oughtred isn't the most dangerous one in Atlantea at the moment?" King Aereth asked.

"Pose the question to me again after the Feast, sire."

Nirgund raised his hand. "Mr. Traveler, tell us about these Gwragedd Annwyn. Lake and river fairies, are they not?"

"Mr. Nirgund, these are not the Gwragedd Annwyn of Faë–Land. These are the Gwragedd Annwyn of Atlantea."

The caravan marched on without their caravan master. He told them that he and the dog would rejoin them in the grand hall at the time of the Feast. For now, they would march to a specific castle within one of the realms at the edge of the ante–city and take a flying caravan to, as Traveler had told them, "a walking city with half its grand palace engulfed by a magic vertical lake hanging in the sky."

He did not say why he was separating from them. But he did say he would return, and not alone.

Night had fallen in a way unique to the realm—one moment day, the next night, as if a giant curtain had been pulled over the sky. Frog-Dor climbed the spiral staircase to the top and walked to the lone dark-cloaked wizard on the tower overlooking the outer ante-city. There was no one else on the tower but the two of them. Frog-Dor joined him at the tower and also looked down. Atlantea's ante-city overflowed with fae and their animals as any commerce city would. He could see Titan's Caravan, and at the moment, their own Mr. Traveler was held off the ground in a bear hug by Mr. Pangolin.

"Humans are very emotional creatures," the wizard said to Frog-Dor, his face obscured by his hood.

"They are, indeed."

"Were you so when you traveled with them?"

"I would say I was more emotional than they at the time."

"Yes, you are part human too. I sense more, though. Elfin, perhaps? Elemental too, perhaps?"

"You have the gift. I believe what you say is true. Hopefully, you may be true in your answers to my questions."

The wizard seized Frog-Dor's arm. "Which are? You should not have come here."

"You have been observing our caravan for some time."

"There is no harm in watching newcomers to the kingdom. A favorite pastime of all fae."

"But is this favorite pastime for yourself or another? You took great lengths and much magic to conceal your own comings and goings, but I took greater lengths to trace you to your great flying ship of glass. I am not familiar with its owners and why such a royal house would care anything about treasure-seeking humans from so far away."

Frog-Dor felt the pressure on his arm increase painfully, but then something else was happening.

"Don't struggle; it will all be over soon. It's a shame that you can't use violence against me because you could easily subdue me," the man said.

"You are a midas wizard."

"You know of me."

"I know of the City of Midas—a city of ancient alchemists and those within who practice the craft through potion and magic. I have distant memories of a kingdom, my old kingdom, visiting your secret city of gold."

"The city walls and its structures were originally built of mere wood. We transformed it all to gold as it is today."

"Are you transforming me into gold to kill me?"

"Gold is but many, many things I can turn you into to kill you. A simple stone, perhaps, so that you can blend into this tower."

"Why would you do this? What of the laws of the great magic of Atlantea?" Frog-Dor asked, watching his right arm hardened to rough stone.

"There is no violence here," the wizard said with a black smile. "It is but a spell, and you will be alive, in a way, until you are not."

"Killing is violence, assassin."

"But no one can see us."

"A concealment spell. Almost as appropriate as my seeing-eye spell."

The midas wizard only saw the floating magic eye above him for a split second, as was the look of surprise on his face. He vanished before he could scream. Frog-Dor looked to the sky and noticed a closing hole of light in the heavens.

"Thank you for visiting the fabled kingdom of Atlantea, my wizardly friend," Frog-Dor said as he touched his right arm and closed his eyes for a moment. The spell was reversed, but he felt light-headed.

He opened his eyes to look over the edge of the tower and noticed the half-elf, Mr. Elman looking right at him from the ground. Mr. Traveler would soon know what had transpired. Frog-Dor's eyes moved to the continued commotion of berserkers welcoming Mr. Traveler's return. The dog was also watching him from Traveler's side.

Frog-Dor looked up, and there floated a watching Atlantean in a flowing white robe. "You are warned," the being said, "next time, despite any extrasensory spell you cast to inform us of any infractions to the laws of Atlantea, you will follow the transgressor. Do not involve us in your affairs again, and be sure your master knows this as well."

"It will not happen again," Frog-Dor said.

The Atlantean vanished. Frog-Dor allowed himself to breathe.

LEGENDS

The caravan waited patiently at the edge of a forest. King Aereth held his sword in his hands and slid it back in its golden sheath on his waist.

"Our Mr. Estus does know how to put a fine edge and shine to any blade," the king said to Hobbs.

"He does, sire."

"I've been thinking about the other Kings Elder. Here I stand in Atlantea to represent three kingdoms and all our regions. I do wish they were here, my comrades. We journeyed through Titan's Trail; they returned to fight Oughtred's dark allies."

"They too, sire, were successful in their quest."

"Yes, Mr. Hobbs, they were. I envy you. You have many choices ahead of you. Any of our kingdoms would be honored to have you in our court."

"Thank you, sire."

"It does seem strange to carry our best weapons dressed in armor in a realm where the slightest move of violence vanishes one from their region in an instant. What do you believe will happen at this feast, sire?" Hobbs asked.

"Not a feast, Mr. Hobbs. A public display of the power of one's empire. I know such gatherings well. We do the same in our own lands, do we not?"

"Yes, we do, sire."

A large shadow slowly rolled over the caravan, and everyone looked above.

"So we fly to this great Feast," Lady Aylen said.

A flying ship descended from the sky. The dark mahogany vessel of refined craftsmanship was lined with golden oars that moved on their own. The sky ship had to have been half a mile long but only four human columns wide. It slowly set down at the feet of the royals and Pangolin as a door appeared and opened at the bow, the wooden deck now visible to all.

A lone creature stood before them. A tall, gaunt, almost skeletal, blackened figure with a demonic goat head with long curved horns and empty white eyes. In a brown leather-like robe, its long slender clawed hands held an oar penetrating the floor of the boat.

"Come aboard, all," it said.

"What manner of beast are you?" Lady Aylen asked.

"I am a phooka."

"We have met your kind before, shape-shifter," Lady Aylen said.

"You have never met my kind before."

As the caravan marched onto the boat, wooden pews rose from the deck for seating. Every last one of them and their animals—over five thousand—fit aboard the flying ship. The phooka oarman swung the magic oar back and forth as the vessel rose back into the air and glided forward.

"You know where we are going?" King Aereth asked.

The royals and Gwyness sat behind on one side closest to the oarman. Pangolin, Hobbs, and Nirgund sat on the other.

"There is only one place to go for you. The Feast. You are expected."

"Only us?" Lady Aylen asked suspiciously.

"All who go to the Feast are expected, or they would not be going to the Feast."

"What is the name of the city where the Feast is held?" Pangolin asked.

"The same name as the Feast—Gwragedd Annwyn.

Within the Winged Walking City of Gwragedd Annwyn."

Mr. Traveler had told them that there were many species of phookas—the mischievous and the evil. Though called goblins, the fae shape-shifters were fond of transforming into dogs, foxes, wolves, cats, goats, rabbits, and birds, but more likely hybrids of multiple animals to frighten and shock people. Mr. Traveler's phookas were the benevolent kind, or as benevolent as their nature allowed. But which kind was their oarman? What would he be outside the realms of Atlantea? Even with his majestic robe the black creature looked frightening. A strange choice, they thought, as a guide to a feast of fairies.

Gwyness touched her amulet, but there was no warning from it. If there was any evil within the creature, it was not perceptible by magical means.

The flying ship sailed through the sky with white clouds miles above them. All were reminded of the fairy kingdom of Faë-Wick. A castle city with the mouth-entrance of a giant crowned head of a humanoid insect with large eyes. Fairies always reminded the humans and the elfess of insects with their huge numbers, restless nature, and constant movement. The sky was thick with life as far as could be seen. Griffins, griffinoids of every species, giant birds, flying horses, flying unicorns, flying fish, flying lizards, flying mammals, flying flowers, fireflies, which they knew were real fairies, and, as always, fae creatures they had never seen before.

Men did peer over the side but below them was a sheet of mist. Even Mr. Elman couldn't see to the ground beneath it.

Gwyness pointed their attention above. Smaller clouds moved on their own as a group with clearly visible arms, tails, and black eyes. The cloud creatures looked like wyverns made of clouds. A pack of them disappeared into the real clouds above.

Suddenly, more flying ships with their own oarmen came out of invisibility on either side of them, some at the same level, others higher, others below them. The occupants of the flying boats were many different royal fae leaders with their noble warriors and attendants. Dwarves, leshy, elves, centaurs, brownies, gnomes, nisse, pucks, tree people, fauns and satyrs, sprites. They also saw dark fae such as spriggans, bugbears, gargoyles, hobgoblins, and hags. The sky was thick, not with flying fae and animals, but flying ships all moving through the sky like a giant swarm.

Mr. Elman saw the structure first and he moved closer to the bow of the boat but was careful to stay behind the oarman.

"You can see it, Mr. Elman?" Lady Aylen asked, squinting as if that would increase her sight.

"Yes, m'lady. You'll see it soon."

"And we'll all see it a day later," Pangolin said to laughs.

"All the clouds end in the distance," Lady Aylen said.

"Yes, the city is there in the center," Mr. Elman said.

"Does it truly walk?" Pangolin asked.

"Yes, it's walking now, Mr. Pangolin, and it has huge wings," Mr. Elman said. "But that's not the most amazing thing about it."

"What then, Mr. Elman?" King Aereth asked.

"There's a lake following it, but hanging up and down, sire."

When all humans were able to see the Winged Walking City of Gwragedd Annwyn for themselves, they stared with confusion. A giant white castle covered and entwined with vines and giant flowers. Giant white wings sprouted up from its outer castle walls. Two other features bewildered everyone. Firstly, the castle sat on two legs that seemed to be real flesh and blood of some kind of animal, possibly a horse or bovine, and they were indeed walking. The other curious thing was the giant crystal lake that hung vertically in the air right behind the castle. The giant lake moved with the city as it walked and was filled with giant fish swimming about.

As they neared the city, the aroma of the city's wall fauna overpowered them as they realized that their flying ship and all the others around them were far smaller than everything about the city. What they thought was the tiniest flower on the wall was actually three times the size of their vessel.

The swarm of flying ships crossed over the wall of the castle. Suddenly, giggling fairies were all around them. The men smiled with glee; the berserkers had pained faces. Pangolin and the berserkers, since their journey on the Trail, no longer saw fairies as harmless, tiny females, but the extremely dangerous faes that nearly beat all the races of giants and sprites combined. The phenomenon of a "fairy storm" remained fresh in their minds. However, these fairies were only curious about and flirtatious with the new visitors.

"Where are the male fairies for me?" Lady Aylen asked.

All the flying ships set down on a tall rainbow grass within the city's interior. As Titan's Caravan moved to depart, the phooka oarman raised his clawed hand and then lowered it in front of the king.

"Payment is owed."

The way the creature said the words made them all freeze in mid-step. Men looked at each other in fear. Pangolin simply raised his hand to signal the berserkers to remain calm. King Aereth showed no fear and placed a very large gold coin in the phooka's skeletal hand.

"We will need passage back," the king said.

"I will be here when you are ready," the creature said as it nodded.

Suddenly, they were all standing on the grass as the flying boat rose into the sky.

"What...what just happened?" I-wulf asked.

"We were in the boat, then we weren't," Lady Aylen said.

"We are able to step out of a ship on our own without magic," Pangolin said, annoyed.

All the flying ships rose into the sky and disappeared into the clouds. Their party was the only one still on the grass. All the other fae marched to the many entrances carved into the towering bluish stone wall. More of the fairies appeared around them, fluttering and eager to guide them.

Pangolin took the lead of the caravan again. "How did you know, sire?"

"The coin? Our Mr. Traveler, of course."

"What would have happened if you did not have the currency to pay him?" Pangolin asked. "No need to answer, sire. It is of no importance. We did, and we're here."

The king smiled at him.

"He couldn't have harmed us," Gwyness said.

"Let us all agree that we wouldn't want to anger that creature, even with the protection of Atlantea's magic." Lady Aylen looked up at a nearby fairy. "Will you guide us straight to the Feast itself?"

"We guide you into the palace realm," the fairy said. "Make your way from there."

"What do you mean? The dining hall is not close by?"

The fairies erupted in collective laughter.

"How far do we have to walk?" Lady Aylen asked the fairies.

"You will be quite hungry when you finally arrive," said another fairy.

"Finally? What does that mean?"

The fairies couldn't contain their laughter and began to fly in circles around the caravan.

"What do we expect, m'lady? Fairies and games," Pangolin said.

"But I'm hungry now," I-wulf said.

"You always are," Pangolin said. "Sire, m'lady, I will leave you to take lead. I will join my men at the rear. Mr. I-wulf and Mr. Estus, I leave you here at the front."

"Thank you, Mr. Pangolin," King Aereth said.

"Do you expect trouble, Mr. Pangolin?" Gwyness asked.

"If we are to heed Mr. Traveler's warning of frequent provocations, I expect my berserkers to be foolish. My place is at their side to make sure they don't get 'vanished' back to our lands."

They marched into one of the stone wall entrances and found themselves in another realm.

The fairy's words were true. Ahead of them, their path to the hall was, indeed, miles away. The realm had a bright blue sky and thirteen moons arranged in a horizontal circle. Along the market streets, there were no visible commoners. Every fae seen was of royal blood or a noble of some stature, including their animals.

All King Aereth and Lady Aylen had to do was follow the crowds down the main road to a giant coliseum of a hall where, already, they could hear lively music, dancing, and laughter. Every building around them looked new though they knew all were constructed ages ago.

From a side street, a group of fae came to them.

"Welcome to Atlantea," the delegation greeted in unison.

Two of the men were elegantly dressed in crimson and brown robes with bands around their foreheads, human in every way except one had giant horse hooves for feet, and another humanoid had massive human ears almost like an elephant. The third, in a yellow robe, was a very tall, thick-furred yak man with large ivory horns down his side and pointing out at elbow's level. His royal dress included a yellow scepter in one hand.

"What kingdom are you from, kind strangers?" the yak man asked.

"We are Titan's Caravan," King Aereth answered.

The delegation looked at each other, impressed.

"The last caravan to enter Atlantea for some time to come. The Fates have an important purpose for you if they would shower you with such good fortune."

"Apparently so," Lady Aylen said. "Do you know the reasoning behind this profound decision of the Atlanteans to close the fabled kingdom to all for so long?"

The yak man grinned. "If the Atlanteans have not told you, I cannot say. Regardless, we are citizens of Atlantea, so whether they allow visitors or not is of no real interest to us. Treasure seekers will need to find other lands to satisfy themselves."

"We are so disappointed," King Aereth said with false emotion. "I have all this coin to part with to find one who can give me answers, and I cannot find a soul."

The fae delegation smiled at the king.

"We are certain that you could find many such people if you were to make yourself known," one of the horse-hooved men said. "Sadly, that is not us."

"Though there are many rumors as to the why of the Atlanteans closing of their realm, how would you know truth from falsehood?" the yak man asked. "Maybe the timing has to do with how long it takes for an ocean thick with krakens to calm themselves and return to their normal hunting territories. Maybe, the oceans to Atlantea have been poisoned by magic."

"Who would do that?" Lady Aylen asked.

"Decealia, sirens, who can say. Maybe a jörmungandr has decided to hibernate and wrap its form around all of Atlantea for a thousand years. Many rumors, but which is true? Maybe none. Maybe all."

"I sense a great insight in you," King Aereth said to the yak man.

"Your attempt to heap praise on me and show me special deference might normally have worked on any other day."

"Why not today?" the king asked.

"We know you were guided to Atlantea by the one known as Master Traveler."

"Do you."

"My comrades and I are not here simply to gaze at the latest outsiders to make their way into the kingdom. We were waiting for you," said the fae with gigantic ears.

"Us? Why so?" the king asked.

"Yes. We knew you would pass this way as there is only one road. We have waited day after day and approached every group with humans that have passed."

"Why?" Lady Aylen asked suspiciously.

"Oh, have no fear, water elfess. No violence can be done in the lands of Atlantea. No violence and no dark magic. I might say that makes Atlantea such an uninteresting place."

"Yet you live here," she said.

"We bore easily. If one must live in an uninteresting place, then why not the most beautiful and powerful one in all the magical realms."

"You were saying why you were waiting for us," Lady Aylen said to the large-eared fae.

"The water elfess is not one for the custom of common conversation, is she?" the large-hooved fae said.

"She's actually quite the conversationalist," the king said.

Lady Aylen scoffed.

"You can't get anywhere in this world if you have not mastered the art of simple conversation. The entire cosmos will open up to you, elfess, if you have the patience to simply talk with passion and listen with genuine interest," the yak man said.

"Yes, I was saying," the large-eared fae said, "we waited for you because your friends asked us to tell you when you arrived, that they were waiting for you too."

"Friends?" Lady Aylen asked.

"Do you know a lot of people lost money on you?" the large-hooved fae said.

"We don't understand," King Aereth said.

"Many of the leisurely, non-Atlantean-class pass the time with such activities as wagers," the yak man said.

"Did you bet on us not making it here?" the king asked.

"Many people lost money betting you'd never make it." The yak man grinned. "I was not one of them."

"Why did you bet on Titan's Caravan then?" the king asked. "You know nothing of us."

"No, but when I was told it was led by a boy who had lived in Atlantea and had traveled the Trail many times before, I felt it was a good bet."

"How could you know of our advancement on the Trail?" the king asked.

"Sky elves like to gossip. I like to listen."

Lady Aylen pretended to clear her throat.

"The elfess must learn to hide her emotions better."

"What is your name, elfess?" the yak man asked.

"Lady Aylen of the Kingdom of Sirnegate."

"I was told you were of another kingdom."

"What other kingdom?"

"I would tell you, but you're impatient. You do not partake in the niceties of common conversation."

Lady Aylen changed her tone. "We are guests and new to Atlantea. Surely, you can be more patient with us."

"No need, elfess. All will be answered by others."

The royals realized that they had stopped without even realizing it. In front of them lay the open great doors of the coliseum hall.

"Do you not enter with us?" King Aereth asked. "To continue our pleasant conversation and learn of the friends who had you wait for us and so graciously walk us to the fine hall."

"Only invited guests of the Feast of the Gwragedd Annwyn are allowed entrance," the large-eared fae said.

"May we ask what species of fae you are?" Young Quillen asked. "We have never encountered your people before."

"We are called the Hippopodes," said the humanoid fae with the large horse-hooved feet.

"We are the Panotti," said the fae with large, flapping human ears much like an elephant.

"Call us yak," said the yak man. "Unlike like my brethren-in-life, we need no fancy names."

"Nice to meet you all," the king said.

"We've done our duty and escorted you to where you are eagerly expected. We hope you enjoy the feast, though the food, drink, dance, music, and merriment are far from the point of the event. Think of it as many, many armies on the battlefield staring down each other," the yak man said.

"Not sure how to take that description," the king said.

"Take it with grace," the yak man said. "You have victoriously arrived in Atlantea, human. Few of your kind can make the same declaration. No matter what is said to you in there, even in the rudest and most condescending terms, you can always say back to them: "But today, I stand on the same ground as you.""

The fae trio had already traversed back the way they came down, almost inspecting the men as they went.

"Why did they need to escort us?" I-wulf asked. "Even in a fae city, a straight line is a straight line."

"Notice that they never did answer your question,

sire," Estus said. "About the supposed friends who sent them."

"We know what friends they mean already," Lady Aylen said.

"But do we?" King Aereth asked.

"Yes, sire, you're right. They purposely did not answer."

"We may need Mr. Pangolin and the berserkers up front with us," King Aereth said.

"Agreed," Lady Aylen said.

"But we should maintain our vigil to the rear," the king said.

The king stepped across the threshold into the coliseum hall; the day became night.

"Oh, my—" I-wulf began when he stepped through.

They found themselves under a covered archway miles above them, but it was the sea of giant banners that covered the walls that drew everyone's attention. Some of the fabric and writings looked as ancient as the beginnings of humankind millennia ago.

The king led them forward into the open courtyard of merriment and music that they had heard from outside. Fairies and sprites served from tables overflowing with food and drink. Clearly, it was the custom. All eyes in the vast open court of the coliseum were upon Titan's Caravan. Never had the royals or the men felt such apprehension. Despite the encouraging words of the yak man, they felt out of place.

A fae in full glistening gray armor was wearing a helmet concealing his face above his mouth. He sneered as he watched them. Surrounding him were several eight-foot-tall minotaur guardsmen in battle dress holding nine-foot pike-axes. But the minotaur weapons were dull in comparison to the creatures' sharpened horns that pointed upward. The fae knight continued to watch them as he ate. From his yellowish skin, they knew he was a fae of some species.

The fae knight swallowed the last of his food and approached with his minotaur guardsmen, who used their pike-axes like walking sticks.

"Do you command these humans?" the fae knight asked Lady Aylen.

"King Aereth and I represent four kingdoms from the Lands of Man."

"Why would an elf represent a kingdom in the Lands of Man?"

"Because I grew up in one and am a royal."

"That makes little sense, being a royal in a kingdom of

humans rather than your own elfin kind."

"What race of fae are you, may I ask?" Lady Aylen said.

"None that you would know. I cannot say I am very impressed by what I see."

"What do you mean?" Lady Aylen asked.

"How could a group so weak and pathetic as you reach our fabled Atlantea?"

"I am far from weak and pathetic."

"You, elf, have some skill, some ability. I see none in the rest."

"Our berserker warriors would disagree with you," King Aereth said.

"Berserker humans are still humans. How did you manage to travel across the Trail to get here?"

"We had an able caravan master," King Aereth replied.

"It is you then. Yes, we heard. A human who has lived in Atlantea, with a shape-shifter companion."

"You know of us," Lady Aylen said.

"Everyone here knows of you," the fae knight said. "Some here have even lost money waging on your failure. It must have been the fae within your caravan that did all the work to get you here."

"That is not true either. Everyone in our caravan pulled their weight," Lady Aylen said, starting to grow angry.

"My own minotaur warriors could easily kill every one of your men here with ease."

"We are truly not interested in your fantasizing about something that will never occur," King Aereth said.

The fae knight jumped right in front of the king, startling everyone. "What if I were to slap that crown off your head? I wouldn't be vanished from the kingdom but you would look like the human fool you are."

"I sense you don't like humans," the king said.

"I hate humans!" the fae knight yelled.

His minotaur warriors began to snort air out of their nostrils in an increasing frenzy.

King Aereth raised his hand and looked at everyone in the caravan behind him. "Remain calm, everyone. His words are idle threats. No royal would behave in such an ignoble and lowly way in front of others, especially fae royals from all of Pan-Earth, new and ancient."

The fae thrust his head an inch from King Aereth's. "You are correct, of course. I wanted to see what you'd do. You've called my bluff correctly—this time."

The fae knight jumped back, turned, and marched away with his minotaurs.

King Aereth collected himself. "What a nice greeting."

"Are we going to be endlessly challenged by every fae in this hall?" Lady Aylen asked.

"Sire," one of the men called out.

The royals looked back to see a large group of noblemen and knights briskly walking to them—all were humans.

"Sire," one of them greeted. "You are the Titan's Caravan, are you not?"

"We are," King Aereth answered.

"Then the Fates have heard our pleas. You are of Avalonia?"

"Yes, my kingdom is Helm Earldom, and I personally carry the banners of our allied kingdoms of Strongbridge and Eastmoor."

"We heard your land caravan was fifty-thousand strong and included fae from all the magic lands," said a knight.

"The most our caravan reached in number was a bit over twenty-thousand, but we marched here with ten-thousand," King Aereth said.

"A land caravan to march Titan's Trail from Titan's Bridge to the Great Forest and sail to reach Titan's Gate with only ten-thousand. Impressive. I don't believe we've ever heard a caravan so small make it so far to Atlantea. Caravans traveling by foot are usually no less than a hundred-thousand strong," said another human royal.

"Sire, would you care to join us?" the royal asked. "The fae of the hall revel in taunting humans, but if all of us stay together as one, including, without hesitation, your fair elfess, they will cease. Our own kings would also like to speak with you."

"Of course. In regards to what?" the king asked.

"You allied with many powerful fae. Our kings would wish to speak of forming an alliance of the Seven Empires of the Lands of Man with those fae empires. You, sire, could speak for the Empires. It's already agreed amongst us."

"Me?"

Lady Aylen smiled and gave a slight nod. "Yes, sire, it can't be me. I'm an elf now. And kings outrank princesses."

"All Seven Empires are represented here in Atlantea?" King Aereth asked.

"Yes, sire?"

"When did you arrive?"

"We've been here ten, some more years before that,"

said an older royal.

"Years? So long away from your empires?" King Aereth asked.

"We wished to do the same as King Oughtred of Xenhelm had done. Create a permanent presence for our kingdoms here in fabled Atlantea. But all has changed."

"Atlantea closing kingdom to Pan-Earth?" the king asked.

"Yes, humans cannot remain here forever, so we will have to return to our lands too but will be unable to send replacement representatives any longer."

"Yes, it is unfortunate for all," the king said. "Our kingdoms of the Kings Elders had planned to do the same."

"With this new situation, would this alliance be for our return home?" Lady Aylen asked.

"No, princess, we do not speak of elsewhere or when our parties return to our lands. We speak of right here in Atlantea and right now. An alliance to survive this Feast."

"Survive this Feast?" Lady Aylen asked, confused.

"Yes."

"What is there to survive? What is so ominous about a fairy feast?" Lady Aylen asked.

"Not the Feast. The ancient fae at the Feast."

"We are at the mercy of ancient fae," said another. "They will make their move against us here, likely at the Feast."

"The ancient fae cannot harm us here," King Aereth said.

"They don't need to."

King Aereth felt himself longing for the dangers of Titan's Trail, anything but this. In an instant, he was back in the tedious affairs of state with all its machinations, plots, scheming, moves, and counter-moves. He felt overwhelmed at the realization that the tragic closing of the fabled kingdom would be used by humans and fae to rekindle hatreds and possibly even wars—again.

"Are you okay, sire?" Hobbs asked quietly.

The king managed a smile but said nothing.

The fae knight with his minotaur guardsmen wasn't the only party they kept a watchful eye on them. A dwarfin king adorned in gems surrounded by nine-foot-tall armed guards of ferocious ogres, whose mouths hung open, showing their sharpened black teeth. Winged centaurs dressed in golden armor and one draped in a golden fleece. Many, many different kinds of elfin parties—mountain, forest, underground, river, high noble ones. There were many, many more animal men parties— bird, bullfrog, toad, squirrel, deer, cat, dog, hedgehog, monkey, fish, assorted mammals they were not familiar with. There were eagle-headed humanoids, plant people, tree people, those with large eagle eyes or cat eyes, bird-like beaks instead of mouths, those with lion-like features or cat-like ears, those with green skin, purple skin, or blue. They saw more of panotti, the large-eared people, in colorful tunics and horse-headed ipotanes.

Also, the hall was a menagerie of beasts. Noble keythongs (wingless griffinoid with the body of a lion and the head and forelegs of an eagle), axex (head of a hawk and a body of a very slim, sleek lion), and opinicuses (often mistaken for griffins — all four of its legs are those of a lion with a giant eagle head with or without wings). Flying white horses with rainbow-colored wings. Gigantic golden griffins roaring like lions. Hippogriffs (hind half of a horse and the front half, including head and forelegs, of a giant eagle) shrieking loudly. Many unicorns of different colors, some winged, others not with their elfin, fairy, or other fae masters or riders.

The beasts were all known by humans. However, the many species of hybrid griffin beasts attracted their eye, especially young Quillen. They saw dozens of elefantagriffs (part griffin and elephant with tough grayish skin covered with feathers, mostly around their joints, back, and rear, tusks growing from either side of their beaks, elephant-like ears, elephant-like legs with talons) throughout the hall. They saw other equine-like griffins: zebragriffs (griffins with zebra stripes) and unigriffs (part unicorn, part griffin). There were feline griffins: tigregriff (distinctive stripes of a tiger), leopardalogriff (leopard-like spots), ertoperridogriff (smaller, with distinctive cheetah-like spots), ocegriff (very small, with distinctive, ocelot-like spots), and giant sabergriffs (part griffin, part smilodon, larger and more muscular than any other feline griffin hybrid, with saber-tooth tusks).

They saw lupagriffs (hybrids of griffins and wolves) and ursagriffs (hybrids of griffins and bears with large, stocky builds, bear-like back paws, short tails, and a slightly bear-like face, but still being avian in appearance), taurogriff (hybrids of griffins and bulls with bovine hindquarters, with feathers at the tips of their tails, taloned front legs, and horns on their heads).

They saw beautiful kamilopardalogriffs (hybrids of griffins and giraffes with long necks, long legs, giraffe horns, hoof-like talons, and the distinctive spots of a giraffe) towering above all and tame aloniegriffs (hybrids of griffins and peacocks, with colorful feathers on the front half, and peacock-like tails). Constantly buzzing around all, chasing or being chased by fairies were kolimbregriffs (hybrids of griffins and hummingbirds, with front halves of hummingbirds and leonine hindquarters and tails with feathers on the ends).

"Mr. Quillen," Hobbs scolded, but he knew it was no use.

The boy had pulled his magic book from underneath his chestplate and was feverishly capturing the amazing magical beasts as fast as hand and pen could sketch.

Pangolin had joined the front and smiled at Hobbs. "Mr. Quillen is our chronicler of this fabled quest," he said.

"That he is, many times at the exclusion of his rightful duties," Hobbs said.

"Never could I imagine there are so many different races of griffins," the master-at-arms said.

"Maybe we should acquire some for ourselves," I-wulf said.

"Our chamroshes are plenty for us to handle," Pangolin said.

"They are griffin hybrids. Why not add more? Tell me you're not interested in a griffin-wolf hybrid or that saber-tooth cat griffin hybrid. A dozen of our men could ride one of those."

"And feed them what?" Pangolin asked. "These beasts are for the wilds of the magical lands, not within the walls of a human city in the Lands of Man. They'd eat all the villagers, us, then all the natural wildlife. They stay here, where they belong."

Pangolin carefully studied the layout of the hall. All the tables were arranged in a massive circle, then another closer to the center, and so on. With all the fairy servers flying about, the laughter and the music, he had almost missed it.

"Wait here for a moment," he said to I-wulf and the other berserkers.

Pangolin walked to Lady Aylen's half-elf guardsmen.

"Mr. Elman."

The half-elf turned to him. "Yes, Mr. Pangolin."

"What is in the center of this hall?"

"A floating, circular doorway. The open entrance is not facing us, but rather its small edge. It's why you cannot see it."

"Doorway to another realm?"

"Yes."

"Can you see where?"

"Yes. Another feast."

Lady Aylen had joined them. "I heard, Mr. Elman's

answer. Another feast? Not only is Atlantea a kingdom of realms within realms, next to realms, but so is the case even within their buildings."

"Lady Aylen." Gwyness directed her attention to the crowd.

They noticed the selkie leaders, Nori and Otari, who had traveled with them to Atlantea. Both were dressed as the king and queen and were surrounded by both adult and child selkies in royal attire. The leaders noticed them and nodded to greet them from afar.

"Doesn't seem like they will be joining us," Lady Aylen said to the others as she nodded. "What is this I'm seeing?"

Mr. Quillen had left their party and now stood before the selkies, but that was not his real motivation. He was greeting the selkie girl, who was likely the selkie royals' daughter.

"Mr. Quillen," Hobbs said with a sigh.

Quillen and the selkies were laughing about something; then the selkie girl said something to him. Quillen turned to see everyone in Titan's Caravan watching him and waved.

"That boy," Hobbs said.

"How is that boy finding women and not us?" asked

one of the berserkers.

Even Pangolin had to sniffle a laugh. I-wulf and other berserkers didn't bother.

Music lowered, laughter ceased, and conversation diminished to mere whispers when the creature slithered towards King Aereth and Lady Aylen. They had all heard of the creatures before, but it was the first time they'd seen a lamia in person. Like everyone else in the hall, fear gripped everyone at the sight of the female creature. But she was dressed as a royal in a bright green tunic with purple gems that looked like arrowheads around her neck, covering her green-skinned humanoid form above the torso as her giant snake body moved with scales that looked like metal.

The smiling lamia stopped before the royals. Pangolin, Nirgund, and soon I-wulf were close at their side.

"I am Nagisa."

"I am King—"

"I know who you are, human. Everyone does. We know who all of you are."

"Then Nagisa, what do we owe the pleasure of your

appearance?" King Aereth asked.

The lamia never took her human eyes off of them for a moment. In fact, she never blinked at all. Her silky black hair was fashioned in a bun behind her head. As they stared at her, they realized that if she stretched out her form fully, she would likely tower ten feet or more above them.

"A pleasure? I doubt that. I am here to escort you to the Feast."

"Are we not at the Feast?" the king asked.

The lamia laughed loudly. "This? This is not the Feast. This is where lesser races remain to hide. Is this where you wish to remain? Your human caravan master said otherwise. He said you were ready to stand with legends."

"You spoke to him?" Lady Aylen asked.

"Yes, we spoke for some time, he and I. We were in my bedchamber." She gave the princess a wicked grin.

Lady Aylen wasn't amused. "We know our Mr. Traveler well. He does not like snakes, and neither does his dog."

"I am not a snake."

"That is evident," King Aereth said. "No offense should be taken."

"A place has been set aside for you at the Feast. You

are expected. Do not keep us waiting. Newcomers to Atlantea, especially for the first time, normally do not receive such honored invitations. Respect your good fortune."

"Who did we receive this invitation from?" King Aereth asked. "We thought the invitation—"

"All newcomers receive invitations to this, here, but not the Feast of the Gwragedd Annwyn."

Before King Aereth could say another word, the lamia turned and slithered away faster than the wind of a hurricane, then disappeared at the center of the hall. The creature could fly! Now, all eyes were on them.

"She went through that doorway?" Lady Aylen asked Mr. Elman.

"Yes, m'lady," he replied.

The members of Titan's Caravan glanced at each other.

"No need to postpone what we must do. Mr. Traveler did say we would be attending this Feast of the Gwragedd Annwyn," King Aereth said.

"But he did not say anything about lamias," Lady Aylen said.

"We've been with Mr. Traveler for over a year. He tells us what he needs to," Pangolin said. "How would we have behaved if he had told us we might encounter that evil creature?"

"We would have taken our treasure and departed for our lands as quickly as possible," I-wulf said. "Actually, is there some reason we can't do that now?"

"Everyone, since this is not the Feast and that's where we should be, let us follow after the lamia so we can be where we're expected," the king said.

"Should we do this?" "Why are the other fae so afraid?" "The magic of Atlantea will protect us even there?" The questions plagued the minds of the caravan's leadership.

They stood at the threshold of the floating magic portal to yet another realm, but the view was blurred. They could see the movement of shapes but nothing more.

"Do we take over five-thousand men inside?" King Aereth asked aloud but to no one in particular.

"If only Mr. Traveler were here," Lady Aylen said. "We need guidance. We're following after some snake woman."

The elfess marched from the caravan back to the crowds. Everyone in the hall watched them intently. She reached the two selkie royals.

"Lady Aylen," Nori greeted. Her husband nodded.

"Good to see you both again," Lady Aylen said. "What do you know of what lies beyond that magic doorway? Other than there's at least one lamia inside."

"You should be honored at being invited to join the Gwragedd Annwyn festivities," Otari said. "They are the oldest and most powerful of fairy races in all of Pan-Earth."

"I cannot help noticing the fear in this room, and within you."

"Not fear," Nori said. "Respect for those far more powerful than us."

"Should we take all our men with us inside?" Lady Aylen asked.

"We would counsel against it," Nori said.

"Bring only those that represent the power of your own party," Otari said. "The king, yourself, the berserkers, your necro-seer. No others."

"Necro-seer? You mean Maiden Gwyness?"

"Yes," Nori replied. "We know of her power and yours."

"My half-elves?"

"If you must," Otari said. "But only the one with magic sight."

"Why did we never hear about this aspect of Atlantea?" Lady Aylen asked. "Realms within realms. We thought it to be one great city surrounded by treasured-filled lands."

"Your stories of Atlantea, all stories of Atlantea, were from those who came to the fabled kingdom for treasure alone. No one risks their lives to journey to a magic city to involve themselves in its internal affairs. They can do that from where they live without the journey or the monsters."

"Why do you not go with us?"

"Selkie clans know their place, and our place is outside that realm. We seek a presence within Atlantea for our people, nothing more. Besides, we were not invited," Nori said.

"Thank you for your counsel then."

"You are welcome," Nori said. "We will be here when you return."

Lady Aylen felt there was more to the selkie queen's word but said or asked nothing more. She returned to the leadership of the caravan waiting at the inner realm's doorway. Lady Aylen recited the selkie royal's advice, and they all agreed.

"Mr. Hobbs, I will put you in command, with the aide of Mr. Estus, of the men," King Aereth said.

"Yes, sire."

"You have nothing to concern yourselves with, sire," Estus said. "We will be fine. And we will mind young Mr. Quillen too."

"Mr. Elman, you will accompany us," Lady Aylen said. "Brenn, you will take charge of my royal guards, or I should say, since you have been together longer than we've been together..."

"Don't worry, m'lady. I will take charge," Brenn, the half-elfess, said with the tiny owl griffins calmly waiting around her feet.

The royals and men noticed that the two Selkie royals had joined them at the portal. Nori's hands touched the king's and Lady Aylen's arms. "Think of Atlantea as a roaring fire. The closer you get to it, the greater the heat. The closer to its center, the more powerful are the beings you will encounter. Keep that in mind but never show them fear."

"Mr. Traveler warned us. He said we'd still be overwhelmed," King Aereth said.

"Yes, overwhelmed by fear. But be careful not to give in to the fear or even inadvertently react violently. People can be vanished from any realm within Atlantea."

"We'll be careful, Nori," Lady Aylen said.

"Then we will await your safe return."

The king and princess gave each other one last glance before stepping into the realm. Unlike other portals, they had to walk a few steps to fully pass through, as if they were in some kind of tunnel. They emerged, and their eyes were met with a magnificent night sky littered with stars of many different colors. Dancing waves of light passed over them all.

Lady Aylen was the first to notice movement ahead of them. She looked down and stared. With a night sky so bright, all ahead of them should have been well-lit, but it was a thick blackness. She realized that the movement was the blackness itself. A sinking feeling grew in the pit of her stomach as the creature rose.

"No!" Pangolin grabbed the man next to him from drawing a weapon.

Everyone saw it now. Never had they seen a spider centaur of its size. The spider body towered a dozen feet off the ground on slender legs. However, the human body at its top was of human average size and female. She looked as if she was from the Laurasian region of the Lands of Man, clothed in a dark red garb. Her skin had a slight glow.

"Welcome to Atlantea, new ones," the creature said,

"to the annual Feast of Gwragedd Annwyn. Do not fear. I've already eaten." The arachnid laughed. "Follow me." She crawled away and pierced some kind of barrier.

Noise flooded in, and then their senses were overcome by the sights of a massive banquet as if they had all been transported elsewhere. The starry night sky above them was different.

"Audience!" The beautiful female fae whose voice echoed throughout the festivities came from a fairy, but she had no wings. Her eyes were red but flickered as if behind them were candles, and her hair was white. The men could feel the magnetism of the fae as if she were some kind of nymph or siren, as though her limbs and bare feet were dry, her clothes were dripping wet. "Of those called Titan's Caravan, King Aereth, human royal of the Avalonian Kingdom of Helm Earldom in the Lands of Man. Lady Aylen, elfin princess of the Avalonian Kingdom of Sirnegate in the Lands of Man!"

"At least she said nothing more," Lady Aylen said to Gwyness.

"Prince Pangolin, human royal of the Laurasian Kingdom of Gonwanda in the Lands of Man!"

"How does she know that?" Pangolin asked.

"Maiden Gwyness, human noble of the Avalonian Kingdom of Sirnegate in the Lands of Man!

Gwyness also did not like that the fae knew all of them.

"Nirgund, berserker warrior of the Avalonian Kingdom of Chariot's Cross in the Lands of Man!

"How does she know that?" Nirgund said angrily. He held the chain leashes of his alphyns tight as they reacted to his anger by jumping up and down.

"I-wulf, berserker warrior of the Baltican Kingdom of Repent in the Lands of Man!"

"Why did she announce you before me?" I-wulf asked.

They expected the fae to cease her announcement, but as she continued, they realized that she would announce every last Cut-throat and warrior. The fae announced all two thousand men, which seemed like hours but also seemed like no time at all. What they all noticed was different groups nearing them from outside their view as if enshrouded by magic cloaks of invisibility. People, groups, then whole armies all seemed to appear from nowhere.

"And their animals of thirteen alphyns and four hundred chamroshes!"

"My, she is quite thorough, isn't she," Lady Aylen said.

The fae approached them and nodded. "Welcome, Titan's Caravan."

"Good day," King Aereth said. "We have never seen a fae such as you before."

"I am a korrigan. We are cousins to fairies and sirens. Step forward with me to join the others. It is the custom of the feast to walk and eat as you converse."

"Then that is what we shall do," King Aereth said.

Again, it seemed as if they were teleported away as they followed the barefoot fae into the feast. Lush grass was beneath their feet, tall trees with lanterns stood nearby, and wooden tables flowed with food and drink for the taking.

They found themselves in front of another party. Nemean lions were not new to them, but before them was one with fur so golden that it glowed like the sun. The beast was twice the size of the one they had encountered in the Great Forest, with claws and teeth sharper than any human or fae metal. Its eyes glowed but with white flames.

The beast's master was a nine-foot cyclops in royal attire and crown and a thick wooden staff in one hand. "Welcome," he said.

The royals nodded.

The Nemean tilted its head back, barred its teeth, and roared. The air all around them shook so hard they were almost lifted from the ground. Nirgund struggled to keep his alphyns calm, as did the Cut-Throats with their chamroshes.

"My ancient companion bids you greetings, as well," the cyclops said. "He is friendly, so you and your animals have nothing to fear."

"Friendly, indeed," King Aereth said. "I imagine friendly as long as you are here."

The cyclops nodded. "You are perceptively correct. You have come far."

"We have. As far as the Lands of Man," King Aereth said.

"Faë-Land Minor. Faë-Land Major. Faë-Wick. Arion's Spire. Fae'el. I passed along the Trail so many moons ago; I doubt very little is the same. I envy your journey."

"We had the honor to visit Mímir-Spring," the king said.

"A great and noble kingdom. The cyclopes of Mímir-Spring are great seers. The cyclopes of Agaitha, my people, are great builders. Our forefathers constructed Titan's Point as a gift to the Atlanteans."

"Impressive," Lady Aylen said.

"We are their descendants and remain highly proud of their achievement to this day."

The Nemean lion locked eyes on Pangolin. The berserker wondered why.

"He can sense warriors of a similar temperament to his own," the cyclopes said.

"I will not roar a greeting, but you can tell him that I wish him a fond hello too," Pangolin said.

"He knows. I will let you meet others in the Feast. It has been some time since we had true newcomers."

As the cyclops moved past with his Nemean lion, he seemed to evaporate, and other parts of the area around them became alive with other parties, deep in conversation, debate, or laughter.

They struck up a conversation with a party led by a stag centaur king. His antlers sprouted horizontally from his head and were as wide as his horse body was long. Clad in brown armor that appeared to be the texture of wood bark, though they knew it was as strong as any metal. He was attended by an army of armored ipotanes—horse-headed fae with a hand on the hilt of their swords at all times.

"At one point we had over twenty-thousand in our caravan—human and fae," the king told the centaur.

"I would not attempt such a journey with any less than

one-hundred-fifty thousand fae and beasts."

"We had a good caravan master," Lady Aylen said.

"That is what we have been told. He is well-known and well-respected...for a human. Take no offense."

"We do not," King Aereth said.

"Any centaurs in your caravan?"

"No, but we had fauns, a race called elaphines traveling with rusines and cervids."

The centaur king was visibly unimpressed.

"Amazing archers, the elaphines," Lady Aylen said.

"But worthless warriors. They faint when afraid. Fauns are too civilized. It is their cousins, the satyrs, that are the more decent warriors."

"We had four Tree Shepherds in our caravan," Gwyness said.

"Four?"

"Yes, with their magic crawling trees."

The centaur king seemed moderately impressed.

"Oh, I did neglect to mention we did fly the fae banner of many, including the Centaurs of Chiron," King Aereth added.

Now, the centaur king was impressed.

As they moved from party to party in conversation,

every fae and every animal glowed with power.

"What a battle it would be, here, if it were possible," Pangolin said, smiling.

A humanoid approached them wearing a hooded cloak, his cape fluttering as he moved.

"How many land caravans have reached Atlantea with far greater numbers? Very few. Impressive, I would say with such a small number. And with the Great Four Kings as your adversary the whole time," he said.

"There is nothing great about the Four Kings," Lady Aylen said. "Or should we not say the Two Kings of Xenhelm."

"Yes, I stand corrected." The man stared at her with yellowish eyes. Everyone in the caravan knew the man to be a wizard and who his master was.

"A lesser caravan would have found themselves food for the beasts of the Trail."

"Titan's Caravan had a motto to feed its own beasts generously so as to not be the food of the creatures of the Trail," Pangolin said to the wizard, clasping his hands together to calm the temptation of wanting to strike him.

"You achieved your goal. You had a true caravan master. A true sailor too, from what I hear."

"Yes, indeed," King Aereth said. "Never did we experience such sailing such as his in our lives—on water, underneath, and flying in the sky."

"Diving, crashing, racing at the speed of a hurricane," Lady Aylen added.

"Now you are in Atlantea at last," the wizard said. "May I kindly offer some advice?"

"Please do," King Aereth said.

"You are here only because you were invited. Like those outside this realm, you are nothing more than minor races. You are an amusement, an item for gossip. The ancient races who annually attend this honored feast—the Great Feast of the Gwragedd Annwyn—have little patience for lesser races. They may not be able to hurt you here in the realm, but they can do so outside of Atlantea, and you will be outside of Atlantea soon. You humans, elves, and giants, so love your treasure. So hold your tongue. Eat, drink, and stay out of the matters that do not concern you."

"Is this your advice, or your master's?" King Aereth asked.

"It is mine. A kindness on my part to welcome you to the fabled kingdom. If I were you, I'd leave now."

"We prefer to stay," Lady Aylen said, "since we were invited."

A blue rose magically appeared in his hand. "May I give you a pretty rose? For a pretty elfess."

"I would not reach your hand anywhere near my person, wizard," Lady Aylen said with gritted teeth.

The rose vanished from the wizard's hand. "Sorry to make you uncomfortable with only a mere rose. If you are afraid of a mere rose, what will you do when you encounter the rest of us here."

"Lord Odyssean, human caravan master of the former kingdom of Iona in the Lands of Man, adopted son of Atlantea, known as Traveler," the booming voice of the korrigan announcer echoed.

Titan's Caravan glanced back to the entrance with collective amazement.

Traveler approached them, in his hooded cloak and elemental armor, his sword in the sheath hanging on his back. The dog marched at his side in the form of a giant dog-headed griffin hybrid. The wizard, Frog-Dor, followed on one side, and the drowess, Dr'amal, on the other. However, they marched with their own army. Dozens and dozens of drows, and on the other side, dozens of elves. Surrounding them all were many more black humanoids with the heads of locusts with swaying large antennas rising from their heads and smiling with white teeth in their human mouths.

"Spiders and snakes, snakes and spiders!" the darklings sang.

"No!" Lady Aylen said in disgust. "It cannot be."

The yellow-eyed wizard was gone and already forgotten.

The korrigan's announcements continued.

"King Dr'as of the Drow Kingdom of Nightfire in Faë-Land Major! His daughter, Princess sorceress Dr'amal." Every drow warrior was announced, nearly a hundred in number.

The royals and Pangolin, however, were surprised by the elfin leaders—their elfin comrades from the caravan left behind in Faë-Land Major. "Duke Druil, high-elfin wizard, of the Elfin Kingdom of Magica; Duke Galadaer of the Woodland Elfin Kingdom of Bravehowl; Duke Taylon of the desert elfin of Falconbright; and Duke Staric of the Moon Elfin Kingdom of Nightshade in Faë-Land Major!"

Every one of their Elfin Questing Knights were announced—high elves with unicorn swords, desert elfin falconaires carrying their magic falcons, perched on their right shoulders, woodland elves in green armor, each with a leopard axex, and moon elves with their moon swords.

"I must say, Duke Druil," King Aereth said. "We never thought we'd see you again, but glad we are wrong. How did you get to Atlantea?"

"Please, sire. Mister suffices, not duke. Never did like that royal title. We actually arrived before you did."

"Before? How?" Lady Aylen asked.

"When the matter of Fae'el was in hand, elfin wizards greater than I teleported us here in a sky vessel just outside Titan's Point," Druil said. "It is far more involved than that, but that is the short story. We've been waiting for you."

"How did you know we'd arrive?" King Aereth asked.

"We had no doubt of it," Staric said.

"If we only knew we were traveling with a lord," King Aereth said, grinning at Traveler. "We were right all along. Lord Odyssean."

Traveler shook his head as the royals, Pangolin, and everyone else smiled at him. "A granted nobility, sire, by a caravan I guided to Atlantea. A caravan of kings."

"Lord Odyssean," Lady Aylen said with a smile.

"Lord Odyssean," Pangolin said, patting their caravan master on the shoulder.

"Dr'as, we are glad to see you and your drows, too," King Aereth said. "May I assume this is the beginning of a true elfin-drow alliance?"

"A needed alliance, king," Dr'as said.

The drow leader glanced at the elves. Drow and elves were intentionally silent.

"Will we see our Elfin Questing Knight comrades, Lyre, Taylos, and Shadu-mun?" Pangolin asked.

"You will see them again," Druil replied. "We are here. They remain in charge of our elfin forces at our camp."

The ears of royals and humans perked up. The korrigan's announcements were in a different language.

"What is she saying?" Lady Aylen asked.

Traveler smiled. "Nice of you to ask, princess. She's announcing my darkling comrades."

"You must be joking."

"All are announced who arrive at the Feast of the Gwragedd Annwyn," Traveler said.

The black shape-shifters in the form of humanoid locusts with swaying large antennas and smiling human mouths danced around them.

"Is this a new alliance, Mr. Traveler?" Druil, the elf, asked. "Elves, drows, humans, and phookas. We are eager to take the treasures we obtained and return to our lands. But you've coaxed us into staying longer than we intended to find out the true reason for the fabled kingdom closing to all for ten centuries and ascertain if the sky elves have secured any special favors from the Atlanteans."

"I know you're far more perceptive of things than that," Dr'as said.

"Equally curious is all," Lyre said to the drow king. "Our human knows the words they say to get our attention. If sky elves are involved, we want to know."

"Frog-Dor, the wizard of the Lost City of Elora," the korrigan's voice boomed throughout the hall.

Everyone in Titan's Caravan turned to look at him. The expression on the man's face was one of confusion.

Traveler walked over to the man.

"I thought I had convinced her not to announce me," Frog-Dor said to him. "But why did she say that? I am not of Elora. I do not know of such a kingdom. Do I know of an Elora?"

"As Atlantea is not one kingdom but many, so is the case of other cities," Traveler told him.

"I don't understand. Did you know she would announce me so?"

"When we were on the Trail, I had others seek out your identity."

"You didn't tell me."

"You were cursed by a powerful elfin sorcerer for many decades to suffer. That curse wiped away your memory, your past, all that you were. None of it matters anymore."

"Then you know what I did."

"I do not, and it matters not."

"Tell me of this, Elora."

"No need. We will all find out together."

"Find out what?" Dr'as asked.

"Is this a feast, or will there be fighting?" the elves asked. "What's about to happen here, Mr. Traveler?"

"I am sorry for what you are about to see," Traveler said with an ominous tone. "There is a reason those outside the Feast are frightened by what's within. Keep your emotions in check, show no fear, and keep still. If you move, you might inadvertently raise your hand in violence and be vanished from Atlantea, or run, which is almost the same as you'll find yourself in another realm that will take you forever to find your way back."

"Mr. Traveler, I don't like anything of what you just said," Pangolin said.

"I am the one responsible for our invitation," Traveler said.

"You, Mr. Traveler? Then why are we here?" King Aereth asked.

"We are safer here as one. If my suspicions have no merit, we will endure this feast of ancient fae today, and tomorrow all of us will set off to return to our lands with our considerable treasure. But as I've convinced the drows and elves, we must know why Atlantea is closing before we depart. As those waiting outside the feast are already pondering, the closing has consequences for all our kingdoms. It would be a gross disservice to our kingdoms and people to be here and not find these answers. As once we leave, we can never return, but those consequences could affect our lands for many years, centuries, or more to come."

"Those outside the feast are frightened of their own shadows," Druil said. "I do not share their panic. We were all part of our Titan's Caravan. We know each other now, even if we may or may not like each other. Our alliance will endure even outside of Atlantea."

"I wish I shared your optimism, Druil," King Aereth said. "I listened to my fellow humans for only a few moments, and their minds were not of bettering our lands and people with our new riches, but fear of what fae may or may not do with Atlantea closed. From their words, I trust you more than them."

"At last, you can relate to us in our animosity towards the sky elves," Druil said.

"I do. Mr. Traveler, I had not expected this. I had expected a golden age of man with the aid of our Atlantean treasure. It has been the dream of mine and the other Kings Elders all our lives. I feel a cloud over us. That I may have deceived myself, all because this fabled kingdom, the desire of kingdoms for centuries, closing its doors the very day we arrive."

"We must find out why, sire, if we can," Traveler said. "There is also another, more immediate concern. Atlantea has been the main home for ancient fae for many, many centuries."

"Who are these ancient fae?" Lady Aylen asked. "Are fairies, sprites, and elves not ancient fae?"

"We are not," Dr'as said. "Humans are new races. We are the middle races. Then there are the ancient fae."

"Ask yourself would you want this creature of the ancient fae marching to us, this moment, to remain here in Atlantea or to encounter her in our own lands?" Traveler said.

His dog hybrid growled as Nirgund reptilian hounds

and the Cut-Throats chamroshes became agitated.

She had returned. The arachnoid creature stood fully visible before them. They looked up to see her humanoid upper torso. But at her giant spider feet, giant tarantulas the size of dogs gathered.

Nirgund's alphyns violently barked at the ground spiders. He strained to keep them at bay, holding their chains. "Calm yourselves, lads."

"They have eaten already, too," the arachnoid creature said, "but not dessert."

The korrigan flew to them. "Ignore her jests. She plays the same tricks on all newcomers."

"How presumptuous for ones so weak to call yourselves Titan's Caravan," the spider centaur queen said.

"It was a name we chose for the benefit of those outside Atlantea's realms," Traveler responded.

"May I ask what kingdom you are from?" King Aereth said.

"You know not of the great kingdom of Nuwa, its empire, its people, its ancient history and power. I pronounce its great name in a way your human ears and minds can comprehend."

"Your form appears as female from Laurasia in our

lands," Pangolin said.

"They are the descendants of our realms, as you humans are the descendants of realms of your elves, fairies, and dwarves," the ancient spider centauress said.

"That is a description we have never heard before," Lady Aylen said. "Humans descendants of fae."

"Yes. Fae with no magic. That is what you humans are to us."

"It was a pleasure to meet you, empress," Traveler said. "We will visit with others."

"Yes, thank you," King Aereth said with a nod.

The arachnoid did the same. She was content to say no more.

The caravan carefully and nervously walked away from the arachnoid and her spider pets to a banquet table where slender fairies with very large eyes in white dresses, floating on air, served them food and drink.

Some of the Cut-Throats kept their eyes on the spider woman. As they moved further away from her and her spiders, the image of her changed. The arachnoid was not alone. She was surrounded by many dozens of red-armored spider centaur, with humanoid Laurasian-looking upper male torsos, not the blue-skinned drows that they had encountered on the oceans outside Atlantea before. In their humanoid hands, they carried thick golden spears.

"How much of our conversation do you think she heard?" Dr'as asked Traveler.

"All of it, I'm certain," he replied.

Chatting echoed throughout the banquet in a tongue unfamiliar to human, elf, and drow alike.

Winged creatures fluttered down from the dark sky into visibility. The hybrid humanoid beasts had heads of jackals, eagle bodies the size of men, black wings that moved without noise, and razor-sharp talons. Leather quivers with golden arrows draped their backs, and they carried long golden bows. Marrashi rained down to the ground and formed up in battle column after another.

Several serpopards also descended from the sky. The creatures had heads of falcons on snake-like necks and bodies of winged leopards.

Finally, several winged bulls, called tauruses, descended with their flying queen. A giant creature with the head of a woman, crowned with a golden and jeweled helmet, and body of a lion with the wings of a giant falcon—a sphinx.

Once landed, she leaped forward and ran to them.

Traveler placed himself in front of the caravan with his dog at his side. Every man and woman in the caravan held their own fear at bay. The giant creature stopped below him; she had muscles upon muscles under her feline body.

"I have not tasted human flesh in countless years," she said, staring into Traveler's eyes, then scanning the rest of the caravan.

"And it will be many more years until you do," Traveler told her.

"Perhaps I should lead a caravan to the Lands of Man, but rather than for treasure for food and sport," the sphinx said. "If Atlantea is closed to all, then I must have some amusement."

"Sphinx, do not venture into our lands," Traveler said.

"Why, human? Do you feel because you can stumble along a path from your insignificant regions to Atlantea that you are worthy of anything more than ridicule and disregard?"

Traveler stepped up to the face of the sphinx. "Perhaps you should inquire with the star elves what happens when a fae or beast crosses me."

Laughter rolled through his army of darklings in their

insectoid form.

"You may be capable, human, but you are mere food to my kind, as are your elves and drows. My kind has ruled for many millennia before your races ever crawled from the earth."

"Yes, your dark fae races once ruled Gondwana and Laurasia. Should I tell my caravan here why that is no longer the case despite your claims of being so powerful, or will you?" Traveler asked.

The sphinx glared at him.

"You almost suffered the same fate as the dragons. That was at the hands of the elves, sprites, and giants. But your dark races were at the hands of humans. All that remains are your temples in the isolated sands where no one lives anymore. Do you wish to battle us again?"

The she-sphinx laughed. "There are many more of us than then, and we have many more able servants than then."

"Do not venture into our lands, sphinx."

"I would listen to him, sphinx," the elfin duke said. "Even the presence of one gorgon, basilisk, lycanthrope, or undead fiend in the human lands summons all fae-kind to hunt and destroy them. We can add your name to the grand list."

From both flanks of the sphinx queen and her army came many more parties. Waves of lamias formed up in columns around them, their human upper torsos more serpentine than the ones they encountered before.

A cloud of creatures descended above the sphinx queen and her lamias. Flocks of hieracosphinxes (heads hawks and bodies of a lion) and ram-headed sphinx creatures (criosphinxes).

The snake moved faster than the blink of an eye and snapped its jaw shut an inch in front of Traveler's face. But he hadn't flinched. Traveler raised his hand and looked back at the caravan with a look of calm.

Pangolin held his Cut-Throats and both elves and drows had to summon all their inner strength not to fight. The sphinx queen had a tail. The snake was her tail.

"You have met sphinxes before," the sphinx said.

"I have, and your childish game to scare us, sadly for you, will not work."

"We were looking forward to seeing all of you vanished back to where you come from."

Sphinxes appeared from all sides—androsphinxes with heads of men. Traveler was the only one among them that realized the significance. "Sphinx-kind has its own alliance after centuries of war, separation, and distrust."

"Yes, human, we can create alliances too. All of sphinx-kind is unified under one queen—me."

"What happened to the over-king of the androsphinxes?"

"I ate him, and all his subjects gave their allegiance to me."

"You killed their king, and they simply swore their allegiance to you."

"I didn't kill him. I ate him. He lives within my belly, imprisoned forever. That was was the fate of the final battle between us to decide who would rule us all."

A sickening feeling came over everyone in the caravan who heard her words.

"If there were a war between sphinx and lamias against human, elf, and drow, which alliance would win to rule us all?"

"Human, elf, drow, and giant, and sprite, and leshy, and cyclopes, and centaur, and mermaid, and fairy...." Traveler went on as the sphinx queen turned with a huff and led her growing army away from them.

When out of earshot, King Aereth walked up to their former caravan master when he stopped reciting the races. "Mr. Traveler, it would seem the fear of the others outside the feast is more than justified."

"Possibly, sire. We will know when the Feast is over. It has not begun yet."

"We came to Atlantea for treasure, and we may leave with more than we bargained for," the high-elf, Druil, said.

"The danger of this day is still ahead for you," Traveler said.

"More are coming," said Mr. Elman, running to their caravan master.

"Stay calm, Mr. Elman," Traveler said. "We are fine if we simply stay calm."

First ancient fae of spiders, snakes, and sand. Marching towards them were ancient fae of oceans, seas, and lakes.

The Melusina queen reminded the caravan of a male triton as she neared them. Her legs were the tails of fish below the waist with bluish-green scales that also had the dense texture of metal rather than flesh. Her upper torso was clothed in a garment of silky kelp, pearls, and seashells. A tall white gold crown sat on her head; she was already taller than their tallest man in the caravan. Like a nymph, her fair skin and refined features enchanted all men, her dark hair ran down one side of her body. She extended her bat-like wings from her back and flapped them only once, ever so slightly, but the gush from them nearly blew the caravan back.

Her attendants were beautiful nereids in battle dresses with white golden spears. The sea nymphs all had blue-green skin and fiery red hair. Following them were sea dryads in battle dress and a single water tree crawling after them on its roots. The trees were thick with leaves and many, many tiny fairies sitting on the branches.

The queen stopped before them and stared as if she had not seen humans or younger fae before.

Traveler said nothing but nodded with a courteous smile. The melusina queen did the same, turned, and led her army away from them.

Many more nymphs appeared for the Feast of an endless variety of sub-races of all colors. Some were dressed in such sheer attire as to be almost naked, and others were in full armor. Those with weapons carried spears and shields mostly.

"We no longer have the charms around our necks for protection from the nymphs," the king said to Traveler.

"The magic herbs, vines, and crystals are sewn into your clothes, sire," Traveler said. "It is the real reason she came to us."

"What would have happened if we were not protected from their enchantment?" Pangolin asked.

"You'd likely never see your lands again as you'd be under their spell for life."

Suddenly, siren song filled the air. Traveler quickly reached into his cloak. The caravan never saw the fae or creature singing, but the magic of its melody was at first soothing, then trance-like, but then painful in their ears and finally disappeared altogether. Traveler removed his hand from his cloak.

"What manner of siren was that, Mr. Traveler?" Lady Aylen asked.

"Not certain, princess. Could have been an ancient mermaid or cecaelia or decaelia."

"Those mermaid octopi or mermaid squid?" Pangolin asked.

"Yes."

"Why don't we see her?" Pangolin asked. "Or our Mr. Elman?"

"I don't know. They don't want us to for some reason," Traveler answered.

"Maybe they're shy," I-wulf said.

"Maybe they're not," Pangolin said, pointing into the sky.

Tentacles floated away in the night sky and disappeared behind some clouds high up. They were as large as a giant octopus, the size of a large ship.

Traveler did not wait for anyone to say anything. He could see the growing apprehension in their eyes. "Stay calm. We wait for our honored hosts, the Gwragedd Annwyn. After that, our ordeal will soon be over."

The caravan continued watching the night sky. Not because of any other flying creatures, but the stars were falling. The dots of light drifted down and began to circle the hall. As they did, the dots grew in size and became humanoid. The caravan found themselves in the eye of a fairy storm. More fairies came out of invisibility, flying around them from the ground to the night sky.

Titan's Caravan had met many different races of fairies on the Trail and two of them had been valued members of their party. The cyclone of fairies filling the air were not fair-skinned with translucent wings glowing with daylight. These fairies looked moth-like with two furry antennae sprouting from their foreheads and had skin like the earth and thick, dark wings. But their eyes were not insectoid. Their human eyes sparkled with light.

The fairy queen appeared. She was taller than all others and had four arms rather than two. Her royal attire was a bluish robe over her exo–skeleton armor. She floated to the front of the caravan.

"Master Traveler?" the moth fairy queen asked.

"I am."

"We are the moth fairies of Frena. Congratulations on your arrival to Atlantea."

"Thank you."

"Queen Chrysa bids you salutations again at the completion of your journey. She thinks highly of you, for a human."

Traveler nodded. "We thank her for acting on our behalf in regard to the Four Kings of Xenhelm."

The fair queen nodded. "We will take charge of the princesses, but we do not see them among the others."

Traveler looked down at his own cloak. "Wildglow! Sunpetal! Come out this instant! No one is moving from this spot until you do."

"We don't want to!" the voice of the older fairy said somewhere on his person. Traveler's dog jumped back, trying to see them too.

"This instant!"

"Princess Wildglow! Princess Sunpetal!" the moth fairy queen yelled.

"We don't want to be a princess!"

"Now! I will tell your mother about your behavior."

"Alright," Traveler said. "One last time before you go."

He pulled a yellow fruit from his cloak. Two fireflies appeared in front of him, and then the fairy sisters appeared in full form. A two-feet-tall fairy, Wildglow, and her younger sister, Sunpetal, half her size. Both had two antennae poking out from their heads, the taller one with her short blondish hair, translucent insect wings from her back, and a muted ivory frock, the smaller one in her brown half-jacket that had the texture of a woolly caterpillar.

The two fairies landed on the ground as the one fruit became two. As they ate, the fairy sisters smiled.

"Good journeys, Master Traveler and your caravan," the moth fairy queen said as she picked up the fairy sisters in her arms.

She turned and flew into the air. The cyclone of fairies continued for a time, then faded away as if it were never there.

"They were with you all this time, Mr. Traveler?" Lady Aylen asked rhetorically.

"When one makes a promise to the fairy queen of all queens, then it's wise to keep that promise. But Titan's Caravan delivered them safely to Atlantea."

The beast announced her name as Arabia and afterward hummed an enchanting tune that moved through their bodies. The alkonost queen had flown to them from the sky after her own living cyclone appeared around them. Her race was a woman-headed bird the size of a human but Traveler would later tell them that alkonosts existed before harpies. The feathers on her body were black, tipped with white.

Her army that flew in its own formation to mimic a cyclone were ancient gargoyles. When they stopped in flight and floated in the air, their skin appeared more stone-like than any previous gargoyle they had encountered.

At her side was a beast Traveler's dog had taken the form of before on the Trail—a giant phoenix. The splendid orange bird looked at them with squinted eyes of curiosity rather than any malice. That was not the case with her other animal that landed on her other side—a ferocious winged orthurus. The giant two-headed wolf stood taller than ten feet.

She called out and the night sky became filled with a war-flock of stymphalian birds. Pangolin quickly looked at his berserkers, who had already grabbed their chamroshes, and Nirgund held the leashes of his alphyns tight. Stymphalian birds were carnivorous giant birds with beaks and feathers of metal.

"Your caravan truly was under the banner of the Queen Mother of the fairies of Chrysa. We should let you alone then and find others to molest."

The alkonost queen turned and flew away with her party.

"The realms are merging," the elfin wizard, Druil, told them.

The magnitude of the hall came into focus and the many different parties, or armies, were becoming visible, whether close by or far away in the distance. They were still under the same nighttime sky with grassy plain, but trees, brush, and a variety of plant life encircled them.

The armies of the arachnoid queen, the sphinx queen, the melusina queen, and the alkonost queen were larger than they first appeared.

Then new parties appeared. Columns of giant scorpion men, or scorpion centaurs—head, torso, and arms of a man and the body of a scorpion—marched to their place on the field and were twice the size of an average man. Their king, with his black beard, almost to his waist and tall silver crown, watched them. None of the dark fae had weapons, but then their scorpion tails were deadly enough to be all the weapon they needed.

An army of traditional centaurs arrived to also situate themselves on the plains. The giant centaurs were larger than the scorpion men, clad in dark grey armor, armed with tridents and bows, quivers stocked with metal arrows on their backs. Their crowned centaur king had fangs and a forked tail.

The giant centaur army had their own beasts. Packs of wild cerberuses—three-headed demon dogs with snake-like tails—followed all around their masters. Though smaller than the centaurs, each cerberus, was as large as a horse.

"Why do they bring such armies to a feast, Mr. Traveler?" Pangolin asked.

"The first Gwragedd Annwyn feast took place on a battlefield eons ago, and the tradition remains."

Stars from above descended again and Traveler pointed the caravan's attention to them.

When the fairies came down from the sky, they were in the form of dots of light. The new stars that descended were many times larger and transformed into flying ships of light.

While the attention of most were fixed on the sky ships, some saw the dark fae already on the ground appear from invisibility. Night drows, too, had many sub-races. They had seen the dark purple-skinned ones before but never those with skin as dark as night.

One after another, the night drows kept appearing until the fullness of their numbers was visible to all. They were a combined army with the purple drows as the swordsmen, and the black drows (shadow drows) carried bows and arrows of shimmering black metal.

When their eyes of pure white saw their blue-skinned drow brethren, they began laughing. Drows once were elves until clans tried to use dark magic for benevolent purposes. The practice blacked their skin with the dark magic. While drows abandoned the practice and forbade the use of dark magic ever again, night drows did not. The war between the two was centuries-old, and hatred was deeper than between elves and drows or elves and goblins.

"Why are they laughing?" King Aereth asked.

"Provocation," Traveler said and turned to Pangolin. "Have your Cut-Throats keep them back, far back."

When the night drow king appeared with a black crown with a skull on top of it, he raised his clawed hands. His eyes glowed red, and he roared. Every night drow did the same.

The rage within the glowing white eyes of the drow leader, Dr'as, and his sorceress daughter Dr'amal grew. Soon every drow among the caravan was ready to draw their throwing blades. Pangolin's men held them back from their approach as the taunts from the night drows grew.

"Ignore them!" Traveler said to the drows.

The elves found the lack of control of the drows amusing until the first sky ship landed and its passengers came down the magic gangplank.

When they descended from the light ships, people called out, "Angels!" The contingent of winged elves in golden armor from head to toe stepped down from the sky ship.

The joy of the caravan's elves at seeing their long-lost elfin brethren was replaced by expressions of anger when they saw the other elfin races spilling out from the ship: wind elves in yellow gold armor and winged helmets and cloud elves in blue armor floating forward on small clouds.

Rising from the ship to follow, were flocks of anzu—lion-headed hawks the size of dogs. Though in the Great Forest they had encountered larger, more ferocious versions of the beasts. The elfin anzu were trained, noble beasts who landed around the winged elves and walked on their flanks.

The elfin armies continued marching from the ship: archers, falconaires with their birds perched on their right forearms, shieldmen, warriors bearing pikes, battles-axes, and maces.

A final sky elf emerged from the ship in white golden armor. He glanced at Titan's Caravan, smirked, walked away, stopped, then turned. He stared at them as if arguing internally with himself.

The elfin king in white golden armor slowly walked to them with guards of winged elves, wind elves, and cloud elves at his sides.

"The legendary Titan's Caravan," he said when he reached them, staring face-to-face with Traveler. "I would leave if I were you."

"Why?" Traveler asked.

"Do I need to say it?"

"Yes, you do."

"The star elves have a bounty on your life to this very day. I have never seen the celestial elves show emotion, yet they show much of it, all anger, when they think of you."

"They enslaved another world."

"They conquered a world of creatures to be domesticated."

"The creatures disagreed."

"You disagreed and took it upon yourself to rile up the animals against their masters. I see you have one of them at your side. Was that your true purpose? Acquire a shape-shifter for yourself?"

"I rescued my animal companion, unlike the great star and celestial elfin empires."

"I am glad you remain so passionate about your cause. You will have the chance to say it to their faces."

"I am more than ready to send more star elves to their

Maker."

"Yes, I heard about that too. A human who can best an elf with a blade. But have you ever vanquished a celestial elf? I think not."

Traveler felt the king's hand on his forearm.

"Maybe we should save this conversation for another time," King Aereth said.

"What other time?" the elfin king asked. "We will never see each other again in our lives after this day. What do we have here?"

The sky elfin king walked to the Elfin Questing Knights.

"Your own pet elves," he said angrily. "You disgust me!"

Druil, the high-elf wizard, Galadaer, the woodland elf, Taylon, the desert elf, and Staric, the moon elf, all trembled with a rage ready to boil over.

"Strike me!" the elfin sky king yelled. "Strike me! Or do you need permission from your human masters! Or is the drows commanding your action? Or maybe it's one of the pathetic creatures I heard your great caravan took into its arms. Strike me! Unlike you, I have the courage of my convictions!"

The elfin sky king swung. A sword of light appeared in

his hand from thin air. Pangolin bear-hugged Druil to restrain him and the other berserkers pushed back the other elfin questing knight leaders. The elfin sky king yelled and swung his light blade. The Elfin Questing Knights yelled back to attack.

Too late for any of them. The elfin sky king vanished, his voice still screaming in rage. Druil, Galadaer, and Taylon vanished.

"Stop!" Traveler yelled.

Staric could not, and neither could the other sky elves, now enraged that their king was gone. The faces of the winged elves were crazed with rage, and the wind and cloud elves yelled out. Staric fired his moon arrows at them. The sky elves attacked, throwing weapons and magic at the other elfin questing knights. Staric disappeared. Then the sky elves disappeared.

All the elves were gone in the blink of an eye. With all their masters gone, the anzu, one by one, leaped from the ground into the sky and flew away into the heavens.

Titan's Caravan stood silent in shock. Pangolin looked at his arms that he used to try to restrain Druil.

Above them all in the night sky, everyone could see a myriad of holes of light closing.

"Mr. Pangolin," Traveler said, tears in his eyes. "Assign a group of your men to get the drows out of here this instant."

Pangolin moved quickly and was in no mood to tolerate any resistance from the drows but there was none. Berserkers escorted the drows from the hall.

Already they could hear the laughter and taunts of the night and shadow drows in the distance.

The ancient fae in the hall watched with complete indifference or amusement. The points of light in the night sky were gone. Titan's Caravan had been so curious about the "vanishing" but now wished they had never witnessed this cosmic magic of Atlantea.

King Aereth approached Traveler. For a moment, he realized that the caravan master's dog had been completely calm the entire time. In fact, the darklings, still in their insectoid form, were remarkably well behaved. Except for their smiling and chuckling under their breaths, they watched it all quietly.

"Mr. Traveler, should we not all leave too? We are not in control of this situation," the king said.

"We are in control as long as we stay calm, sire. What happened should not have happened, but there is nothing to do about it now."

"Mr. Traveler," Lady Aylen said frantically. "Shouldn't you leave if these star and celestial elves will be here soon?"

"No need, princess. Star elves can be impulsive, but they will try nothing here. They will not risk it. Their great power means nothing here. The same goes for my sword and the dog."

"Why are we here?" she asked. "This is not worth it."

"I agree completely, Mr. Traveler," the king said, "we should go, take our treasure, and depart."

"I know how you feel and why you believe it wise to do so. All I ask is for you to trust me. Sire, both you and the princess have to remain to the end. Trust me."

The royals grudgingly nodded.

"We stay to the end then," the king said.

Three more sky ships of light descended. Surprising all was the center ship landing straight on top of the vanished sky elfin king's vessel. The previous ship of light disintegrated, then disappeared. A trio of ships landed and their bows swung open like mouths.

For a moment, they saw nothing, and then the star

elves appeared out of invisibility.

The caravan found themselves surrounded by an army of star elves in glowing yellow armor.

One of the star elves walked right to Traveler, cocked his arm back as he clenched his fist, and punched. But his fist stopped in front of the caravan master's face. The star elf smirked.

"No such luck in rousing you to violence like your lesser elves," he said.

"Or yours," Traveler said.

"No insult to me. Wind and cloud elves are lesser elves to us, like those of land and water."

"The winged elves?"

"That is unfortunate. But we really just keep them around for display. Everyone is so mesmerized by their white feathered wings, even other elves. I don't understand it myself. Wings are wings." The star elf put his face in Traveler's face. "Sol-ren was of my clan."

"Sol-ren was a disgrace to elfinkind, and I am proud I ended his evil ways and his life."

"He will be avenged."

"Perhaps, but not here, and not today."

The star elf stepped back. A celestial elfin king

appeared from invisibility in front of Traveler. The elf was in a long-robed tunic of black material, his skin was almost white and his eyes and hair were black. The nails on his hands were blackened and as long as his fingers, likely as sharp as any blade. There was no anger in his face, no emotion at all. He looked Traveler over and then Lady Aylen, then everyone else in the caravan.

"Unimpressive. Why were they invited to our Feast?" he asked the star elfin leader.

"Maybe the Gwragedd Annwyn wanted something for amusement this year, m'lord."

"We have animals for that," the celestial elf said, sighing heavily.

He turned away from the caravan.

"He is the one who lost us our world of shape-shifters," the star elf said to his lord, trying to provoke a conflict.

"There are others," the celestial elf said without a care.

The star elf angrily glared at Traveler. "There will be star elves in the Lands of Man soon."

"I look forward to it," Traveler said. "So all humans will grow to know the true nature of star elves as I and all land and water elves already know."

The anger left the star elf's face.

"Do not speak to the human," the celestial elf said. "We have no time for petty revenge against such an insignificant race. Ignore him; ignore them all. They are of no importance to us or our empires."

As the single celestial elfin king and the star elfin warriors marched in formation behind their lord to their space on the plains, the caravan realized that all the parties, or armies, formed a giant circle.

With the appearance of the trooping fairies, Traveler told them the Feast would indeed begin soon. A long procession of fairies in multi-colored dresses, no taller than two feet, winded down to the ground from the sky. Laughter and singing from the fairies filled the air. However, all of Titan's Caravan was still shaken by their elfin comrades being vanished. To all others in the hall, the event was already forgotten.

From high above, in the heavens, the end of the trooping fairies could not be seen, but they kept coming as if moving down an invisible spiral staircase the very diameter of the great circle all the parties sat in.

The first of the elementals arrived in their own flying ships. The caravan recognized the ones who flew from the first ship. Endless waves of sylphs, the beautiful nymphs with pale, almost-transparent skin and long, flowing blue-white hair. Air elementals were said to be the most powerful of elementals.

All around them flew tinier versions of the nymphs like swarms of bees. The sylphids followed their individual mistresses as they all floated to their place in front of their sky ship that had already begun to rise back into space.

Undines exited the second translucent sky ship. These nymphs seemed to be made of water but clothed in sheer, flowing dresses of nature. The elementals of water floated to their place.

The third ship was filled with humanoid beings of nearly invisible fire. Walking with them were orange amphibians emitting their own flames. Like the phoenix, the bright orange salamanders were creatures that thrived in fire. The fire elementals, known by many different names in many different tongues, had eyes that could be seen if one stared at them for a time. Humans had mistakenly thought that salamanders were the fire elementals when they were actually their lizard-like companions. The magic of the hall kept the fiery touch of the vulcans from setting the grass on fire.

Humanoids of rock, stone, and earth exited the last ship. Their "skin" was of no uniform color or type of rock. The earth elementals were large, bulky, and slow moving.

They marched to their place, and their ship, too, as with the others, rose back into space.

The ancient four elemental races of Pan-Earth were rarely ever seen together and were rumored to be the oldest of fae from the time of the Titans, which made them more knowledgeable than all other races.

"You said that the air elementals, the sylphs, are allied with the celestial and star elves?" Lady Aylen asked Traveler.

"Yes, and, through them, the water elementals."

The trooping fairies continued to walk and dance down from the sky as more parties arrived.

Giant flying chariots appeared filled with armored and armed fairies pulled by winged horses with thick muscles and legs. A winged humanoid sat at the back of each chariot in their royal attire and simple crowns. Strong gusts of winds swept through the halls, first warm, then cold, then filled with rain droplets. It was only when the chariots landed that they could see that the ten-foot-tall humanoids were the source. They ceased blowing the winds from their lungs and laughed amongst themselves.

The winged ancient fae were Anemoi, who could blow hurricanes, rainstorms, or snowstorms from their very lungs. When their winged horses finally set down on the ground, bolts of lightning erupted into the sky from their bodies.

The trooping fairies ignored all as finally, all attendees of the Feast could see the last of them coming.

"There is only space for one more party in their great circle," Traveler said.

The royals nervously looked at the caravan master. He anticipated their question.

"Yes, it must be him," Traveler said.

They all recognized the robed iguana man wizard as he appeared, floating close to the ground. A row of elongated yellow scales that ran from the top of his forehead to his back seemed longer and brighter. His bright-yellow streaked green tail snaked out from the back of his robe as he moved.

King Aereth's body trembled, and Lady Aylen's stepped back. Where did he come from? King Oughtred of Xenhelm, all of a sudden. The iguana man wizard and his elfin sorceress appeared at his side.

"We meet again," Oughtred said with no emotion. His Xenhelm crown on his head, clad in full knight's armor with a red cloak, his hair, mustache, and beard blood red.

But for the first time, his appearance was more of something undead. His pale skin was translucent enough that one could almost see his bones underneath. "I see that your elves are no longer with you."

"How does one become an undead creature?" King Aereth asked. "Was it worth it all?"

"Two questions," Oughtred said. "Which do you wish for me to answer? I will answer both with the same sentence. I am here, am I not? And far, far from alone."

Oughtred's army was a goblin horde. Never had any of them seen the races of goblins that the human lich had assembled. They knew of the common goblin—green skin, stout and muscular frame, flat nose, and large pointy ears. They knew of high goblins—more like elves in appearance than goblin with their green skin. But here they beheld red goblins with bright red skin instead of green and charcoal-skinned shadow goblins, with packs of black-furred koerakoonlased—half-human, half-dog cyclops creatures clustered around their legs.

Many more common goblins appeared, riding giant dire wolves, both in thick armor of brown goblin metal. The riders were attended by the murderous Redcaps, a kind of goblin that looked like short, old-looking humanoid males with coarse, graying hair down their shoulder, long prominent teeth, skinny fingers ending in talons like eagles, large fiery red eyes, and grisly hair streaming down their shoulders. They wore their iron boots, carried pikestaff weapons, and, more prominently, wore red caps on their heads, said to be red from soaking it in the blood of their victims.

Oughtred whispered to Traveler and the royals. "Do know that there will be retribution for what was done to my sons, Wuldricar and Renfry?" There was not a hint of either anger or hate in his words.

His goblin army was joined by lampads, the race of dark nymphs from the Nether-Lands, with glowing blue skin and the enchanting power to drive men mad. But in Atlantea, their evil magic had no power.

Two of them noticed Lady Aylen and Gwyness and floated to them.

"You both do not recognize me," the lampad said.

"Recognize you?" Lady Aylen said with disgust. "Why would we?"

"You should. I was the midwife to your mothers."

Suddenly, there was a familiarity to her face—flashes of memories.

"She lies! Do not listen to her," Traveler said.

Lady Aylen screamed. "You are trying to bewitch us."

"Why do you suppose the great kingdom of Rivermouth would have Nether-Land nymphs within their walls?" the lampad asked.

"Why do you live there, and they do not?" Gwyness asked angrily as she moved closer to the lampad.

"Because others made me an offer I could not refuse."

"We would never have allowed your kind in our kingdom."

"You can't defeat dark magic if you do not understand it."

The lampad laughed and joined her sisters.

Oughtred was joined by another high goblin wizard, a beast lord. They knew because the high goblin said it to their faces as he greeted them. Gargoyle warriors guarded him. More sylphs and undines appeared, sitting on white-eyed, large winged black horses.

How did a human lich assemble such an evil alliance?

Oughtred led them all away.

"How is Prince-King Gervase?" Traveler said.

Oughtred stopped in his tracks, but he did not turn around. He continued on with his army following.

"Brave but not wise," said one lampad to the caravan master.

Oughtred and his army took their place in the

remaining spot of the great circle. The troop fairies had all arrived on the ground, gathered in their own circle within.

"That was not wise," King Aereth whispered to Traveler.

"It was worth the attempt, sire. Drive him to anger. Get vanished away."

"That would have been too easy," Lady Aylen said. "But I'm glad you tried anyway, Mr. Traveler. I am not enjoying myself. Something I did not expect within the walls of the fabled kingdom of Atlantea."

"Not much longer, princess. We stay to the end."

The full breadth of the hall was clear to all in Titan's Caravan. The sky changed again to reveal the open void of a star-filled space. The walls and ceiling were gone. In the distance, a small light slowly descended towards them. The stars above increased in intensity to replace the illumination from the ceiling candles that had disappeared.

Pangolin was not the only one in the caravan to view the gathering not as a banquet but as a battlefield with some of the most formidable beings of Pan-Earth in one place. This Feast of the Gwragedd Annwyn happened every year in Atlantea, they were told.

A giant golden ram standing ten feet high peered at them from across the field at the lead of a dozen other creatures. A giant bull with black fur at the same height with glowing white eyes. A siamese giant stood on the other side, with two bodies attached at the torso, clothed in dark robes and hoods draped down, covering their faces above their mouths. A giant ten-foot crab made of some sand-colored stone, its legs and pincers erratically moving about. A giant lion of glowing fur visibly more powerful and ferocious than any Nemean lion. A giant woman covered from head to toe in a silk-like robe, most of her face covered. The next giant being looked like some kind of automaton in the form of a walking set of scales. The humans of the crowd could not tell if the arms of the creature were real or sewn onto the metal. A monstrous ten-foot centaur stepped forward, each arm part bow with an arrow, each seemingly protruding from the palm of its hands. A giant red scorpion with a golden stinger tail. A giant horned humanoid goat with the lower torso of a giant fish, as a mermaid, sitting and propped up on its bottom half like a lamia. A blue-skinned giant with webbed hands, carrying a golden urn, its eyes blindfolded. The final creature was a giant fish floating in the air with large, crazy eyes darting all around.

"The Zodiac welcomes you all to the Feast of the Gwragedd Annwyn," said the Aries ram beast. "Our noble hosts arrive."

Stars above intensified in brightness, then beautiful dancing waves of light, first orange, then yellow, green, and blue, washed over the night sky.

The Gwragedd Annwyn was indeed among the most ancient female fairies of Pan-Earth, and hundreds of them fell from the sky, landing softly on the ground. Their realm cities were beneath the largest lakes and rivers in the Magical Lands. Like the nymphs, undines, or sylphs, they had enchanting beauty and a mesmerizing presence. Their porcelain skin glowed, as did their long, light-colored hair flowing down to their bare feet. Their sheer dresses were covered in flowers, and they wore crowns made of roses. They ignored everyone else but Titan's Caravan. Large transparent wings appeared on their backs as they flew to them.

"It is an honor to have someone new to our Feast after so many years," several of them spoke in unison.

"We are honored to have been invited," King Aereth responded.

"We were most fascinated when we were told that you were invited and would be here," several of them said.

"I thought you had invited us," the king said.

All the Gwragedd Annwyn playfully laughed.

"That would not be possible since we have never met you," they said. "Do you not know who invited you to our feast?"

"We have so many friends," Traveler said. "Who can know?"

"Yes, you do have many, and many enemies for someone so young in this world."

A herd of white stags appeared and walked up to all of them and the Gwragedd Annwyn. The beasts looked like white-colored antlered deers of the Lands of Man, but they could feel the magic in them as they stroked their foreheads or patted their backs. The stags sniffed and rubbed their noses on the bodies of those in the caravan.

"Our companions are very curious of new ones," several of the fairies said in unison.

"Their skin is impervious to all weapons, and their touch can heal all wounds," Traveler said, patting one. His dog sniffed back at another. "Like a Caladrious bird."

"A Caladrius bird with the hide of a Nemean Lion," the fairies said.

"Point out the banner of your Titan's Caravan," said another group of the fairies in unison.

King Aereth pointed and was surprised that the banner moved on its own. For all to see, their caravan hung in the air. A white flag with an iconic representation of the Titan, the Maker of all Mountains, and seven points of light to represent the seven points along Titan's Trail boldly in the center.

"Great Fairies Gwragedd Annwyn," the celestial elfin king began. "I can understand the curiosity, but should we not excuse this Titan's Caravan to join their kind outside our realm. They do not belong here."

"Do you speak for yourself or Oughtred?" Traveler asked.

"I speak, always, for myself," the celestial elf said.

"He is to be addressed as King Oughtred of Xenhelm," the iguana man lizard said loudly at Oughtred's side.

"Why do you allow them here when Oughtred has armies of draugr outside Atlantea's gates?" Traveler asked the Gwragedd Annwyn.

"I sail back to my lands with more treasures than all my previous caravans combined, and no one will take it from me," Oughtred said. "It is not as you have falsely reported to all. Attacking Atlantea is not possible, which all the races here know intimately."

"Then why did you say it to me when you thought I would die?"

"You imagined it all. None of it took place. All lies."

"Says the king and kingdom of lies and evil."

"Do know we will meet again outside Atlantea."

"When we meet again, we will do to New Xenhelm to you."

"I cannot die."

"Even the undead can die; ask your two sons, Wuldricar and Renfrey."

"No, I can't. I will appear when you are an elderly old man barely able to lift himself from the ground, let alone wield a sword of Titan."

"The only way someone as dishonorable and low as you could defeat him," Pangolin said to Oughtred angrily.

"Who invited these humans to Feast?" the celestial elf demanded.

"I did."

The elderly elfess with her white hair flowing down her shoulders and back, nearly touching the ground, in her glowing white-collared robe, her white crown upon her head approached.

"You," the celestial elfin king said. "The Queen Mother Anelle of the Celestial Elves of Nimbus. How far your great house has fallen. To see one once so great go mad from extreme age. Aren't you supposed to be dead?"

The white elfess smiled. The Old One came out of invisibility to her side. The giant in black shredded clothes, his head concealed by a knight's helmet, had his clawed hands resting on his sheathed broadsword at his belt.

"You were misinformed by your spies, dear son," the white elfess said.

"Then let the Feast of Gwragedd Annwyn begin at last!" the fairies said in unison.

THE LAMIA GAMBIT

They'd have no food at the Feast of Gwragedd Annwyn when it did officially commence. Titan's Caravan was under elfin queen Anelle's direction, and the impatient white elfess led them straight for the hall's exit—closed metal doors in the distance hanging in the air.

"We are honored to have known you, Queen Mother," the Gwragedd Annwyn said in unison. "Sadly, we believe that we may not see you ever again."

The white elfess stopped and turned. She walked back to the fairies. Ignoring all others, with tears in her eyes, she hugged one of them. Hundreds of the Gwragedd Annwyn were overcome by sadness themselves too.

"If not here, we will meet in the next life, where evil does not dwell," she said to them all, wiping the tears from her eyes.

She turned back to the caravan and pointed to the exit again. Her ancient guardian, the Old One, didn't walk; he glided along the ground. Traveler and the royals led the caravan after them.

All the attendees of the Feast silently watched the white elfess lead the caravan through the exit and disappear.

"I thought you told us that she was dead," the celestial elf yelled at the night drows.

"Don't scream at us," a night drow yelled back.

"She will tell them everything," the celestial elf yelled.

"Calm yourself, brother. They can do nothing," Oughtred said to them calmly.

"We will not condone any use of the Feast to plot against others," the Gwragedd Annwyn said in unison. "Be elsewhere."

"Then we shall," Oughtred said to them.

"Enjoy your Feast," the celestial elf said to the fairies with contempt. "Enjoy your oblivion to all that unfolds around you."

"Go now, so our joy can begin at never having to see any of you again," the fairies said. "Or must you be persuaded?"

Every party of the great circle, all the ancient races present, stood to attention. Gwragedd Annwyn began to grow in size and their alluring appearance and fair-skinned complexion grew dark and menacing, eyes black, fingernails became claws, and two arms became many, many slender black ones. Towering at twelve feet and continuing to grow.

"Go!"

When they emerged through the floating magic portal back to the massive open court of the coliseum outer realm, the white elfess and the Old One continued forward but Traveler stopped the caravan with the raising of his hand, as they were rejoined by their other members.

"Good to see you all," a waiting Hobbs said to them.

The darklings appeared and immediately ran off, chasing each other. It was as if Traveler had goaded them somehow to behave themselves until they re-emerged. Back in the outer-realm, their mischievousness wildness had returned.

"Queen Anelle," Traveler called out.

"Do what you need to do here, Master Traveler. You know where to find me afterward," she said without ever turning or stopping. She and the Old One passed through the next entrance.

"Do you know where to find her, Mr. Traveler?" Lady Aylen asked.

"No, but if she said so then I must know how somehow."

Their berserkers with their eagle-headed hound stood with the still-enraged drows.

"Are you calm yet?" Traveler asked the drow king, Dr'as.

"I will be."

Traveler turned to his daughter. "Ordinarily, I'd welcome drow rage, but not here."

"Drows are best when they are angry," Dr'as said.

"But not here. We lost the Elfin Questing Knight lords."

"Why is it so important for us to be here?" Dr'amal, the drow sorceress, asked.

"It is important because you are part of Titan's Caravan, and as long as we are within Atlantea, that alliance is of utmost importance. That's why," Traveler said.

While they were gone, the merriment and music of the

hall hadn't ceased, nor did the fairies and sprites serving from tables of food and drink.

"At least we lost none of our men," Lady Aylen said to the king.

"Five thousand humans mean nothing in Atlantea," Dr'as said. "You saw the ancient fae inside that realm. If we had met any one of those parties along Titan's Trail, we would not be here."

"I doubt that, Mr. Dr'as," the king said. "Our caravan master would have found the way."

"Yes, of course." He looked at him. "None of them frightened you?"

"When I first came to Atlantea, yes, many things frightened me. But I grew used to them, as with all the fae within Atlantea. The primary thing to keep in mind is that they consider us insignificant. Do not bother them and they'll likely never notice you."

"That I doubt," Dr'as said.

"We never saw that lamia," Pangolin said to Traveler.

"Nagisa."

"She was the reason we even went in there to begin with."

"She was there."

"You saw her?"

"Yes, because I knew where to look. I've been to the Feast before. What you saw were the parties of the great circle. There were many, many more invisible to the human eye but observing and listening to everything. She was there. I suspect she did not wish to be seen by Oughtred's alliance."

"An annual feast to show off armies," the king said.

"Yes, sire, for those in Atlantea that do not seek treasure or live here, they live for the events to amuse themselves, show off their wealth and power, plot endlessly what their empires will do with that wealth, and forever seek knowledge and secrets."

"Knowledge and secrets of what?" King Aereth asked.

"Everything, sire."

"Then let us speak with this celestial elfin queen mother," the king said.

"Yes, and she was the true reason we were at the Feast, not the lamia. Queen Anelle must have sent the lamia to seek us out. But I don't know what Oughtred's allies meant when they expected Queen Anelle was dead."

"Doubtful anyone or anything could harm her, let alone kill her, with her ancient giant spell-talker as a companion, even with his mouth sealed shut," Lady Aylen said.

"An alliance of a celestial elf with a lamia?" King Aereth asked.

"No stranger than anything else we have seen, sire."

"This is not the Atlantea you remember, is it?" King Aereth asked.

"No, sire, it is not. The fabled kingdom was far above all this machinations of empires. The fabled kingdom is not so fabled anymore. It is a common place like all the other empires of humans and fae," Traveler said, a hint of sadness in his voice.

The king put a hand on the caravan master's shoulder in reassurance. "You promised to get us to the fabled kingdom, Mr. Traveler, and you did. No more was expected, especially any promise that the kingdom would remain as-is when we arrived."

The attitude of the outer-realm parties had changed to Titan's Caravan. Titan's Caravan had been among the ancient fae, invited by name and in the company of an ancient celestial elfess and an Old One. None of the outer parties could boast the same.

The caravan marched from the outer feast to the entrances to leave and return to their lodgings. While the men conversed with those who had been at the Feast,

Traveler turned to Frog-Dor and said, "Tell me."

Frog-Dor told him about the encounter with the midas wizard at the tower the night before and his vanishing.

"The Atlantean mentioned my name directly?"

"Yes."

Traveler remained quiet.

"Is that significant to you in some way?" Frog-Dor asked.

"It is."

"You have lived here."

"They know of me. Some may have met me directly, but with millions upon millions of humans and fae here within their realms, why know of my activities. I am but a human caravan master. Unique but no more. Atlantea's concerns include Pan-Earth and many other worlds and many more magic realms."

"What does it all mean?"

"I wish I knew."

"All we came to Atlantea for was riches."

"Yes, that was our original plan."

The two selkie royals, Nori and Otari, waited, but so did the same contingent of humans representing the Seven Empires in the Lands of Man—Avalonia and Baltica, Laurasia and Gondwana, and even those furthest away with Larentia and Oceania. The uninhabited land of Borea was claimed by the other six empires, but no human lived on the ice continent.

One of the royals rushed to King Aereth. "It was fortuitous that we have met here in Atlantea," he said. "Not only are you allied with powerful fae, but you are recognized by the most powerful of the ancient fae. Will you extend your alliance to all the Seven Empires of the Lands of Man? Be our voice?"

King Aereth found himself surrounded by the human royals, knights, and attendants.

"King Aereth, may I introduce our own king?" said another royal. "He has led us all these past years here in Atlantea."

"King Aereth, an honor to meet you. I am King Theor of the Baltican kingdom of Armathia." The men shook hands.

"King Theor, I know your kingdom well, but you left for Atlantea..."

"Ten years ago. We've been here since. The Kings Elder are held in high regard throughout Avalonia. We had expected to see King Eothelm the Blessed and King Sigbard the Humble with you."

"Sadly, they had to return to our lands with our chief sorcerers to lead our army in battle," King Aereth said.

"Against whom?"

"King Oughtred's forces."

"We know more of that evil man than we care to. It is why we remained here as long as we did."

"Do you know a Queen Issaleth of Armathain?" King Aereth asked.

"Yes, but the queen collected her treasures and set sail back to her kingdom days ago."

"We were hoping to see them again. We traveled here to Atlantea together for the final leg of the journey."

"Queen Issaleth gave a full account as a member of your Titan's Caravan. But do remember, for humans, the allure of Atlantea is wealth for our kingdoms in whatever form of treasure one can acquire. Few humans ever are invited to this Feast, which I'm sure you have already surmised is far more."

"Once we conclude our affairs, we should return to our lands together," King Aereth said.

Traveler put his hand on the king's arm to get his attention. "Sire, as the elfin queen said to us, do what you need to do. You speak to them. We can speak to her. Both are of equal value to us."

"But when do we depart, Mr. Traveler?"

"We can depart as a great fleet," a royal interjected. "A fleet of the Seven Empires."

Traveler and king nodded. "Sire, I believe that would be a good thing for all of us," Traveler said.

"Yes, I agree."

"Mr. Pangolin should remain with you."

"No, I prefer he stay with you."

Lady Aylen looked at Pangolin. "Our fate is being decided by those right before our eyes. Do you think we will have a say, Mr. Pangolin?"

"Doesn't seem like they're interested, m'lady."

Traveler's attention turned to the two selkie royals waiting nearby. "There is one thing I need to do first before we visit our white celestial elfin queen," Traveler said to Lady Aylen.

Traveler and the dog reached another secluded part of the ante-city. Very similar in appearance to their last rendezvous, down a spiraling staircase of rock carved out of a black mountain. They had reached another tavern.

The fae on the streets were few, and they were unfriendly or secretive. Traveler pushed the door open and entered the tavern's pocket-realm with his dog, in the form of the same six-legged bukavac with gnarled horns on its head and shark-like teeth as their previous meeting.

Inside, the lamia snake sat with high goblins on each side of her, the winged goblin guards behind them, and common goblins around them and throughout the tavern. Traveler approached them, but his creature remained at the entrance after he allowed it to close.

"Why would you be afraid of us when you have encountered far more deadly than us?" the smiling Nagisa asked. "You did well among the ancient fae."

Traveler ignored her and sat with his back to the entrance, and his shape-shifter's view.

"I am here as you requested."

"Are you ready to accept our proposal?" she asked.

"Why did you not show yourselves at the Feast?"

"Why did I need to? You saw me there, and I did fetch you."

"Who else is here? Perhaps night drows?"

Night drows appeared from the shadows. Five of them, with dark purple skin and long, pointed ears, approached them and stood at their table.

"His shape-shifter can detect other races nearby, visible or not," Nagisa said to the night drows.

"Queen Nagisa asked you a question," the lead night drow asked.

"Why would you wish to ally with me?" Traveler asked.

"Titan's Caravan," Nagisa corrected. "Why not?"

"Lamias stay to themselves, and you are allies to the sphinxes. From what I saw, the sphinxes have ended their ancient civil war amongst themselves, so you already have an alliance greater than us."

"Two races is not an alliance," Nagisa said. "It is two races."

"Night drows are especially adverse to other alliances with others. Today, I saw shadow drows. More rare than even winged goblins," Traveler said.

"Every race here is forming greater alliances," the night drow said. "It would be foolish to do otherwise as Atlantea will be closed to all for ten centuries."

"Why not join your alliance with Oughtred? He has goblins and night drows and shadow drows."

Nagisa became deadly serious as she said, "No."

"Why?"

"He has races in his alliance that we do not care for," the night drow said.

"The alliance we propose is for convenience," Nagisa said. "It is for here while we remain in Atlantea's realms. When we return to our lands, all can return to the normal distrust and hatred."

"Remain? We will soon depart Atlantea."

"Perhaps. If so, then the alliance will be a short one, but important nonetheless," Nagisa said.

"What are you afraid of?" Traveler asked.

"Nothing," Nagisa said. "We are afraid of nothing."

"He is not going to join us, even against Oughtred," the night drow said. "We waste our time."

"He is here to listen," Nagisa said.

"He is here to gather knowledge at our expense. Human, we reveal nothing to you," the night drow said.

"What would this alliance mean, practically?" Traveler asked.

Nagisa leaned her snakish body forward. "If there is any danger that overwhelms either of us, we would come to the aid of the other."

"A lamia and goblins and night drows coming to the aid of humans, elves, and drows?"

"I hear you lost your elves," the night drow said.

"We lost some, not all," Traveler said.

"Or humans, elves, and drows coming to the aid of us," Nagisa said.

"Against Oughtred?"

"Yes," Nagisa replied.

"But he cannot harm you or us while in Atlantea."

"True," Nagisa said. "An alliance of show. Let them all believe it is more and lasting beyond Atlantea. The ruse benefits us all."

"Who else is in your alliance?" Traveler asked.

"Our races are enough," the night drow said.

"What is your name?" Traveler asked the night drow.

"Vral."

Traveler stood. "Agreed." He reached out to shake the night drow's hand.

The night drow was both incredulous and suspicious, but he shook the human's hand. Traveler expected a cold touch, but the night drow's hand was warm like any elf or drow. In fact, a drow's touch probably was colder.

He shook the lamia's hand. Her eyes squinted as she stared into his eyes. He was under no illusion—every dark fae in the room would not and would never be considered on the side of goodness. However, nothing of what was unfolding in the fabled kingdom he had lived in was the natural state of things.

"I expect your side to live up to the agreement of the alliance," he said.

Nagisa, the night drows, and goblins just stood there.

"Of course," Nagisa finally said.

"Is there anything else?" Traveler asked.

Nagisa and the night drow looked at each other for a moment.

"No," Nagisa said.

"Then my dog and I will leave you."

Traveler moved to the door.

"Wait, human," Vral said.

Traveler turned. Vral held up an open palm. A ball of purple fire transformed into a parchment. He threw it to

Traveler, who caught it in one hand.

"Do not leave without the agreement. We prefer written parchment to human handshakes and words."

"I'll have a wizard or two review it, but I assume all is as we said since we said it so simply and vaguely."

"This is not a jest," Nagisa said.

"I consider nothing a jest when it comes to Oughtred. How does one human have such a grip on even Atlantea?" Traveler shook his head.

"It is not him alone," Vral said. "He is but one of many."

"His time was occupied with his Kings' Caravan to and from Atlantea. With the fabled kingdom closed, he will focus all his attention elsewhere. The members of Titan's Caravan will not allow him to walk free outside of Atlantea and plague our lands. I cannot."

"Not just your lands," the night drow said.

"And not just Pan-Earth," Nagisa said.

Traveler nodded. "Then we do understand."

The caravan master left the tavern with his beast.

THE DYING CELESTIAL ELFIN QUEEN

Pangolin had the duty of guarding Traveler, Lady Aylen, and Gwyness as they traveled to the castle of the white elfess. But with the dog, he knew his real duty was to protect the princess's half-elfin royal guards. The half-elves had the title but, by the nature of their youth, had many more years of real training before they could live up to that title, even with their mixed elfin heritage.

Traveler learned of the location from the Gwragedd Annwyn. The Queen Mother Anelle of the Celestial Elves of Nimbus did reside in the palatial quarter of Atlantea among the celestial elfin population and other sky elves unaffiliated with her son or Oughtred. The sole castle floated in the sky away from every other structure nearby in Atlantea. Tiny fairies ferried them to the castle on a large winged flying chariot, and when they arrived, they stepped onto the ground and surveyed the castle.

The fairies rode off in their chariot. For a moment, they all looked over the edge to see they were hundreds of feet in the air above even the clouds. Pangolin was about to ask how they would get back but said nothing.

The grounds of the castle seemed empty of all life. They glanced at the half-elf, Mr. Elman, who carefully scanned the grounds and the castle to its pinnacle and saw nothing either. The female half-elves had left their tiny owl griffins behind, so Traveler's dog was their only animal with them. The dog explored the immediate grounds in its gray wolf-dog form but of a much larger size.

"Follow me!"

The words echoed in all their minds. A strange experience to hear words but not by one's ears.

None of them saw where he appeared from, but the Old One stood before them in front of a now open, raised gate.

Lady Aylen stepped to him. "I do not like people invading my dreams. That was you, was it not? When we first arrived at Atlantea."

The Old One turned and floated through the gate. Traveler led them in, and, unsurprisingly, they entered another realm where the inside of the castle was far more massive than was apparent from the outside structure. Inside was not empty—elfin knights clad in white silver armor, armed with curved-bladed spears in hand, stood at attention in formation throughout the massive chamber, with white stone walls and ceilings and a black marble floor. An army waiting for an army, or so it seemed to them.

"Why does the celestial queen not reside with the other sky elves within Atlantea?" Traveler asked.

The queen is dead.

"Dead?" Gwyness asked with shock on her face.

Lady Aylen stopped. "We saw her. I know that was her."

You saw her because it was her. My magic sustained her, and it has since the murder.

"Murder?" Traveler asked.

Her house had her killed. She shall explain, and more.

The sitting room was smaller than they would have expected for a royal of her stature, with barely enough room for their small party. The Old One had left them and none of them knew what to expect as they waited in the empty room. Two celestial elfin knights carried what at first they thought was a clothed skeleton and carefully lay her on a chair. It was the white elfess.

Gwyness approached her first as the two elfin knights left the room. Lady Aylen joined her. The celestial elfin queen they had seen just the previous day and months ago was a strong, powerful fae. What sat before them was an elfess that, for the first time, showed the centuries of age. But it was more that she was gaunt; her very bones were visible beneath her white skin. Half her body was black but not from flames.

"The black magic flames of shadow elf," she said to them. "It is not painful but a fitting end to this elfess. I look like what you humans call undead of a sort."

"The warrior clerics. The water elemental and sin-seer," she said, looking at the woman and smiling.

Traveler and Pangolin stood behind them, with all the half-elves peeking in from the back.

"Have your half-elves wait outside," she said. "I don't want such young ones, so full of life, to see me like this, reeking of death."

Lady Aylen looked at them, and Mr. Elman led them from the room.

"Shadow elves still exist?" Traveler asked.

"And others. There are kingdoms of them beyond Pan-

Earth. They are among the fae who have left this world for others and have never returned."

"They tried to kill you?"

"They tried to stop me."

"When did this happen?" Lady Aylen asked.

"Weeks, weeks ago," she replied.

"The magic of your guardian must be powerful indeed," Traveler said.

"No, it was my magic primarily, but he did assist me. I can still cast a good spell or two."

"You did not need to risk going to the Feast to see us," Traveler said. "We would have come to you."

"It was not for you. I want my murderers to see me and know they failed."

"They did fail," Traveler said. "We are all here."

"That we are. Please sit. My neck grows weary."

Pangolin grabbed the chairs from against the walls for everyone. When all were seated, the white elfess smiled.

"You made it to the fabled kingdom," she said.

"Did you have doubts?" Lady Aylen asked.

"I wagered that you would arrive, but I did have

doubts. Nothing is certain until it becomes the past. You will never know how many adversaries were sent to stop you, nor all that a network of allies in the shadows we assembled to ensure your success."

"We thank you all," Traveler said. "I suspected you would watch over us."

"But ultimately, your human caravan master with his knowledge of the Trail and its lands that made it all possible. You have made quite a few powerful allies, human caravan master, in your short life. Others were watching over you without us because you carried their banners and had their people within your caravan."

Pangolin noticed first, then the others turned. The Old One stood at the back. Though most of his body was covered, what living being would not be unnerved by his presence? His large, pale, clawed hands were clasped in front of his body.

"Ignore my guardian. He guards me, even when he does not have to. I would say we have come full circle in the relationship. He was my servant, and I, his queen. I am now the servant, for he is more powerful than me. The centuries have been good. Though we were far from that most of our life."

"Queen Anelle, will you tell us, at last, what we need to hear. We are in Atlantea, and Lady Aylen and Maiden Gwyness sit at your side."

"Yes, we have waited so long for this day. Like a dream to end my nightmare."

"When we arrived, queen, others told us that friends were expecting us," Lady Aylen said. "The celestial elves and elementals of air and water."

"The celestial elves is me alone. The sylphs and undines of my alliance are few. They will not publicly reveal themselves."

"Why?" Gwyness asked.

The white elfess smiled. "You know why, young one. Their queendoms have been enchanted by the allure of immortality and power as my house was centuries ago."

"We met a group of dark nymphs at the Feast," Lady Aylen said. "They claimed they were mid-wives to our mothers. Not sure if they were suggesting they helped in our births or that they had helped birth our mothers. Why would lampads have even been part of our lost kingdom of Rivermouth?"

"You believe them?"

"We don't know what to believe. So I ask."

"They were not being truthful. Rivermouth did not and would not ally with evil races."

"Why did they say that then?" Gwyness asked.

"They are evil nymphs. They said it to upset you, and it worked. But I don't blame you. You would not know either way. I see your human caravan master grows impatient with me to tell the tale. So long I have waited, but the day is here, and I hesitate."

"You could have told us back when we were in Faë-Land Major," Lady Aylen said.

"You hadn't crossed into Atlantea yet. You had to arrive here first."

"Tell us about Rivermouth, or do you wish to begin with Oughtred?" Traveler asked.

"They are the same story. It's all my fault," the white elfess said with visible tears in her eyes.

"The drows were punished for their dabbling in the practice of dark magic, but it was not them alone. The reason the kingdom of Rivermouth was destroyed, the kingdom that trained the great warrior clerics of all lands of fae and humans, was because none of us wanted our forbidden practices to be revealed to Faë-Land. We were the greatest kingdoms, noble, honored, respected, worshiped. We elves of the heavens. We could do no wrong. Never would we engage in practices punishable by vanishment or even death. That's what we told all fae. Rivermouth would have discovered the truth eventually.

"The lower elves that practiced dark magic became the

drows. The higher elves that did... We all wanted immortality. That's all that we sought, to do good. To live as long as Pan-Earth did, to live as long as the stars. That was all we would do. We were not engaging in dark magic for evil...but we created evil nonetheless."

"What did you do?" Traveler asked.

"Fiends," the queen replied.

"Undead creatures?" Lady Aylen asked.

"Yes. That was the result. The very first of them, the first ones were us, beings once elves and other fae, their noble ears falling from their heads in decay, those who had failed. We found immortality...as undead beings.

"I help you because they are doing it again."

"Now I understand what I saw at the Feast," Traveler said. "The celestial elf. His skin had an almost transparent quality as if one could see through it to his bones, like Oughtred."

"A lich too," the queen said.

"An elfin lich?" Lady Ayen asked.

"Yes. That is what Oughtred discovered. That is why he has the status he does. He gave us, what he calls, immortality. But for those of us ancient enough to remember, we know it for the evil it is. I will not allow my race of celestial elves to be destroyed by this, or any of those called sky elves. Conquest among the stars has already stripped my kind of the compassion and concern for life that we once had, like the younger races. It has darkened the hearts of star elves. I knew their race when star elves were as peaceful and caring as woodland fairies of light. We have destroyed ourselves, are destroying ourselves, and for what? To be immortal, immortal without a soul, a beating heart, without blood running through one's veins. If that is our fate, then we do not deserve to exist. Fiend, undead, an abomination to life."

"Do all sky elves agree to this path that has been chosen for their races?" Traveler asked.

"Elfin kingdoms are no different than those in your human lands. One secures the support of key major kingdoms, and others follow. They all know why I am a queen mother in name only. To be made an example of what can happen to any who oppose this path, with the accompanying lies spread about you through gossip."

"How do the night drows play into this drama?" Traveler asked.

"Oughtred discovered the way that they've been searching for all these many centuries. They view him as some kind of deity. They would do anything he says. They've helped him acquire his darkest creatures for his evil deeds.

"This is why I help you at the risk of my own life. I was

responsible, my people, for the destruction of Rivermouth and your people, your families. Me. I deserve my fate. But I will set it all right before I die."

"Why does Atlantea close?" Traveler asked.

"I do not know, which I know to you seems impossible, but it's true. What I do know, what I sense, is that a great evil marches to Atlantea. Atlanteans have always kept their secrets hidden from even us ancient fae."

"Does Oughtred know why?" Lady Aylen asked.

She paused. "Perhaps, perhaps not. Atlanteans are good at keeping secrets. They did, after all, defeat all of fae-kind in our great war. Oughtred has no power with the Atlanteans."

"Then should we leave Atlantea?" Lady Aylen said to Traveler.

"No," the white elfess shouted. "You must promise me. You cannot leave until you know why the Atlanteans are closing their gateway to Pan-Earth. Promise me. If you do, we might all be lost. Every elf, human, fairy, giant, sprite, every beast of land, air, sea, or the earth. You cannot go and leave Oughtred and his allies here."

"Your son is one of his allies," Pangolin said quietly.

The white elfess nodded. "My son, my clan, my house,

all. Only my guardian remains. That is why you must listen. Oughtred's alliance is far greater than you know."

"What could we possibly do that the Atlanteans cannot?" Traveler asked.

"Promise me. Maybe you cannot do anything, ultimately. But know before you depart. Promise."

"I feel a special bond to Atlantea, so I do promise, but none in the caravan should be bound to us," Traveler said.

"No. All of you must promise. You, human caravan master, cannot do this alone. You must have all your allies and more, and we must create many more." She squinted. "What do you wish to tell me?"

"Can you read thoughts too, queen?" Traveler asked.

"You would like my answer."

"I may have secured other unlikely allies against my better judgment," Traveler said and told her of the lamia, goblins, and night drows.

The women and Pangolin were visibly appalled but were surprised by the queen's reaction.

"Good."

"Good?" Traveler asked.

"They hate Oughtred and his alliance more than you."

"What are their true motives, though?" Traveler asked.

"Their real reason is because he has created an alliance they wished they could have. They despise that a human, not a goblin or dark fae, heads this alliance. They feel that they can use a human to defeat a human. They feel that the elves of his alliance are using him to ultimately take control of his alliance, once again leaving goblins and dark fae behind. I could go on endlessly. But, yes, they have truer motives that they revealed, and helping you defeat Oughtred beyond Atlantea is far from the only one."

"Is this ignoring of morality the reason you are in this state?" Lady Aylen said boldly.

Traveler was a bit taken aback by the princess's caustic question. For a moment, the white elfess reflected on her words. "Your words are true, but you are not practicing in dark magic. You are allying with enemies to defeat a greater one and threat to you both. It has been done in wars before any of us were born and will be done elsewhere after either of us cease to exist. I am glad you did so. Besides, better to have these enemies close. I told you back in Faë–Land Major you would need to build an army. You mistakenly thought I meant for Titan's Trail. I meant here in Atlantea." She looked at Lady Aylen with annoyance. "Would you prefer they join Oughtred?" she asked her directly.

"No."

"Then it is settled."

"Do you know of a highborn messenger?" Traveler asked.

"Beautiful bird faes. I know their race."

"She sought me out and also invited me to the Feast Gwragedd Annwyn on behalf of friends," Traveler said.

"Not from me or any of my allies. I did say you have many allies that you will never know of. Perhaps others will seek you out. But enough of that. I did say we must create more alliances. That is where the women come in."

"Us?" Gwyness asked.

"I helped destroy Rivermouth. I shall help in its rebirth."

"How?" Lady Aylen asked.

"Do you have the volumes of works remaining from Rivermouth?"

"Yes, within a library in a small realm that never leaves our person."

"Good. Always remember they contain all the secrets of Rivermouth's training of mages and warrior clerics, the weapons, methods, and magic. We will reassemble the warrior clerics of Rivermouth. Did you not meet its followers in the Great Forest?"

"We did," Gwyness said.

"But sent them away," the queen said. "One of the few mistakes you made on the Trail, and from your faces, you realize as such. Do not fret. I found them and they are here."

"Here?" Lady Aylen stood to her feet.

"Here and waiting for you both. They will be your warriors and mages. Rivermouth was a kingdom of both land and water, so you must have races of both. You must begin here in Atlantea, where this kingdom's magic will shield you from even Oughtred's allies. The perfect place for rebirth. That is why I had to wait until you all arrived."

"Queen Anelle, besides the question of why Atlantea is closing..."

"Which you will not leave until you find out why," she interjected.

"Yes. But there is a greater question," Traveler said. "No living being within Atlantea can engage in any act of violence lest they be vanished from its lands."

"Yes, that is true. Is there a question?"

"Do you have an answer?"

"I was once told as a little girl that no wizard could be so powerful that they could kill by simply speaking magic words. But there, my guardian stands behind you; we have known each other for centuries. Do you know what the human King Oughtred's full title is?"

Traveler stood. "King Oughtred the All Knowing."

"When I first encountered the human king Oughtred—I did tell you all I met him—he was a typical pompous royal with that mark of evil, no allegiance to any if he perceived them as a threat to his ambitions, including his own blood relatives, willing to do anything for the sake of power. He was in good company in those traits as I have met countless other humans, elves, and other fae equally lustful of power and immoral to the core. He traveled beyond where any other human or fae would dare go and, through sheer will or happenstance, made his boastful title far from conceit."

"Luck, or was it the help of others?" Traveler asked.

"Who can say? We are where we are in this game, and there is no room for weakness or doubt. I hear your question, human caravan master. I share your suspicion. But Atlantea's magic remains all around us. My guardian and I would know if that changes, not you. No more questions. Shall we begin?" the white elfess said.

RIVERMOUTH REBORN

SUN AND SNOW

"Aereth! Aereth! Aereth!" crowds of men shouted in growing intensity as King Aereth was hoisted above the ground and carried by them triumphantly through the streets.

The king expected a dignified parley when he bid Traveler, Lady Aylen, Pangolin, Gwyness, and the half-elves farewell on their journey. Instead, he found himself swept up in an impromptu rally. Neither Hobbs, Nirgund, I-wulf, nor any of the berserkers could save him, but they had tried. All they could do was keep up with the procession as best they could as more and more men assembled in the streets in front of what they learned was the main castle within Atlantea that served as the seat of power for the Seven Empires in the Lands of Man. Royals, nobles, knights, warriors, ruffians, barbarians, and mercenaries from all of Avalonia, Baltica, Laurasia, Gondwana, Larentia, and Oceania gathered.

As the king rested on the shoulders of the lead men carrying him to the castle's main gates, keeping a blank, dignified expression on his face, he intuitively knew what the source of their joy at the alliance of the Seven Empires with Titan's Caravan was. These men, these kingdoms, were frightened.

"We thought we lost!" yelled one king from Baltica. "But the Fates have smiled upon us and all the Seven Empires to bring our salvation to us at the moment when the fabled kingdom closed its realms without warning to all of Pan-Earth for a thousand years."

"King Aereth the Wise of the Kingdom of the Helm Earldom and representing the Kings Elder and their ally kingdoms of Strongbridge and Eastmoor will be the voice of the Seven Empires and the great alliance of his Titan's Caravan!" shouted another man.

"We leave Atlantea soon, never to return in our lives, but we bring those alliances with us. Atlantea has been a great benefactor to humankind for centuries, and will be again to our descendants. We thank them for their friendship with all our hearts. We look forward to when Atlanteans and humankind will be reunited again!"

The applause thundered and echoed. King Aereth once again stood on his own two feet. Hobbs and the berserkers were at his side and close.

"Look!" a knight shouted. Soon others noticed. The attention of the gathering fixed on a circular vessel that descended from the bright sky high above them. Men quickly moved away or ran from where it was settling down. It made no sound at all when it did, and its drawbridge fell to the ground. The vessel transformed into its own castle of crystal.

Two different races of elves exited. One looked like star elves, but their skin was almost golden. The other elves looked like moon elves, but their skin was blue-white, and their clothes were white.

"Good humans," said one of the golden elves. "The sun elves and snow elves had returned to Pan-Earth to rekindle our own alliance of centuries' past when elves and humans sat together at the great round table of Faë-Man."

One moment King Aereth commanded the center of attention of all the men of the Seven Empires, but no more. King Theor of Armathia and all the representative kings of the Seven Empires surrounded and greeted the contingent of ancient sun and snow elves that most humans thought were extinct or a myth.

"How quickly one is discarded," Nirgund said aloud.

"Actually, Mr. Nirgund, I am relieved," the king said. "If the elves wish to be carried through the streets by yelling men, they have my blessing."

"Sire, you will be the attention again," Hobbs said.

"Yes, Mr. Hobbs, I suspect you are right. But the attention belongs on these elves."

The conversations between elves and human royals lasted for some time. King Theor finally looked in their direction and raised a hand. He and the other kings led two of the elves—one sun elf and the other a snow elf to them.

"King Aereth, this is Inarian of the Sun Elf Kingdom of Ljósálfar and Foldruin of the Snow Elfin Kingdom of Ice Niflheim."

"King Aereth, is it?" the sun elf asked.

Like most elves, they were taller than the average man. Both had the bearing of royals.

"Yes. It is a great honor to meet such ancient elfin races. We encountered another of your races we thought lost. Winged elves."

"Yes, our angel brethren."

"We have heard much about you and your caravan," the sun elf said. "When we all dine together, we very much would like an account of your long journey from your lands to Atlantea. You have already done what we will do with the alliance you formed for fae and humans for your Titan's Caravan."

"All the praise goes to our able caravan master."

"A human called Traveler," the snow elf said.

"Lived in Atlantea too, we hear," the sun elf said. "We have so much to speak about when we dine."

"It will be our pleasure. Tell me more about this alliance you propose."

"The closing of Atlantea should not be regarded with sadness but as a great opportunity. My snow elfin brother and I have much work to be done. We not only propose to rebuild the alliance of elves and humans, but we have an even greater undertaking at the direction of our own kingdoms. Reunification."

"Reunification?"

"Of all elfinkind. Sky elves, land elves, elves of the seas and oceans. We must all be unified so when Atlantea returns in a millennium, we can rejoin them as equals."

"We even plan to re-embrace our ancient brethren you call drows," said the snow elf.

King Theor had tears in his eyes, overcome with so much joy. "King Aereth, we had spoken of departing Atlantea as one great fleet. But now, the magnitude of what could be. All of the Lands of Man and the Magic Lands following in the footsteps of your Titan's Caravan to create the greatest alliance Pan-Earth has ever known."

Theor could not help himself. He jumped and hugged King Aereth. "Thank you, King Aereth and Titan's Caravan. You brought this dream to reality."

The two elves laughed. King Aereth smiled.

"The Great Alliance of Faë-Man reborn!" the sun elf proclaimed.

Day became night when King Aereth found the opportunity to excuse himself from the conversations of humans and the new elfin races—or ancient elfin races. The royals of the Seven Empires did not want him to leave, but Hobbs did his duty and had the Cut-Throats drag their king away to retire.

They returned to their lodgings quickly. The men noticed that King Aereth did not say a word as they marched through the ante-city to their two-story cottage. The men had lodgings in all the cottages surrounding those belonging to the king.

"Mr. Hobbs, I want—" The king stopped mid-sentence.

Traveler, the women, and Pangolin sat in front of his cottage, waiting. They did not see their caravan master's dog.

"I hope you were not waiting long," the king said.

"Not long, sire," Traveler said. "We did not want to disturb your kingly duties."

"You saw us?" I-wulf asked.

"We did," Pangolin replied.

"Your visit was a success?" the king asked.

"It was," Lady Aylen answered. "She told us all that we needed to know and do."

King Aereth crouched down close.

"Mr. Traveler, we must leave. I have such a strong sense of foreboding that it's doubtful I will be able to sleep at ease as long as we remain in Atlantea. Oh, Mr. Hobbs, I want sentries on watch for all our lodgings."

"Don't bother, sire. The fae of Atlantea could slip past us to and fro no matter how many sentries we had on guard. My dog can do a far better job than any of us."

"So you have him on watch, which means you feel the same as me."

"I felt the same the moment we arrived in Atlantea."

"That you did. When can we leave?"

"We cannot leave, sire," Lady Aylen said. "The queen made us promise."

"I appreciate what she has done for us. However..."

"She has done a lot more for us than you know, sire, than we know."

"I do not doubt it. Were you really watching us?"

"Winged goblins, winged elves, shadow elves, shadow drows, sun elves, snow elves, so many lost races arriving in Atlantea at the same time the fabled kingdom closes itself off to all," Traveler said.

"Who would know of these sun and snow elves?" the king asked.

"Is this not a great thing, sire?" Nirgund asked.

The king stood. "Reunification among all elfin races and the drows? Madness."

"Madness, sire?"

"It's a ruse," the king said. "I feel it in my bones. Do you not agree, Mr. Traveler?"

"It obviously is. The world is not Titan's Caravan. The hatred that exists is not going to vanish simply because some sun elves and snow elves announce it to kingdoms of desperate humans."

"You saw it too. They're afraid. That's why they want me as their figurehead and the alliances we hold."

The men had not attended the Feast Gwragedd Annwyn, and the caravan master saw their questioning looks.

"The Seven Empires are afraid that our lands will be overrun by dark fae and their creatures. Without Atlantea, they fear they are losing a key ally and do not believe good fae will come to their aid," Traveler said.

"I still disagree, Mr. Traveler," Gwyness said. "What of the alliances with dark fae we have entered into here?"

"What alliances with dark fae?" the king asked.

"That is a conversation we should have privately, sire," Traveler said. "A conversation I will have to have with our drow allies too, which I'm not looking forward to."

"Go on, Maiden Gwyness," King Aereth said.

"Why not give these new elves, the sun and star elves the benefit of the doubt. No one thought Mr. Traveler could have formed our caravan with races that had long been enemies of each other, but he did. We all depended on each other, had our lives in each other's hands, and fought for the collective caravan, for a year. Why would a great alliance these new elves want, be any different? It is simply of a greater magnitude."

"Your arguments are sound, but I do not believe them. I believe they appeared to stop our own alliance of the Seven Empires," the king said.

"But that will still be, sire," Gwyness said.

"A great alliance of humans and elves means humans are not in control," the king said. "Present company excluded."

"No need to qualify your comments, sire. We know what you mean and agree with you there," Lady Aylen said.

"Gwyness, there is a way we can know."

"How, Mr. Traveler?"

"We know two who would know."

"Surely, we can't visit them tonight?" Lady Aylen said.

"We don't need to, princess. Gwyness, you can call out to him."

Gwyness stared at him. "What do you mean? Who?"

"Gwyness, you know. The Old One."

"I am not calling out to that creature. He scares me."

"He is the celestial elf queen's guardian, and they have helped us along the Trail and are helping you and the princess rebuild your lost kingdom. It is safe to say they are allies."

"Yes, but...I can't. How?"

"If he called out to you and the princess in your dreams, then you can do the same."

"No, Mr. Traveler. I have no such ability."

"He has the ability to hear you."

"How do you know this?"

"He told me in my dream. We don't have to revisit their castle because they will not be there. But if we have a question or wish to summon them, she said to have the human sin-seer do so. When she is alone and quiet in her room, all she has to do is call out."

The moons were at their highest in the night. Gwyness had stared at them for hours. Finally, she sat up in her bed and grabbed her knees. Her eyes closed to concentrate.

Can you hear me, Old One?

Yes, I can.

Gwyness was unnerved by how fast the guardian had responded and how clear his voice was in her mind.

Tell me of these sun and snow elves.

Why do you trouble me with the trivial? Has my queen misplaced her faith in you young ones? Are you so easily deceived? Celestial elves did not walk the path of darkness first. They followed the sun, shadow, ice, and aeriel elves into the heavens, and the darkness. All are allies to the human lich king of Xenhelm and seek to kill you and all the humans, elves, and drows of Atlantea. We sacrificed all for you. Do not disappoint my queen, as I have no mercy in me. Fulfill her wish before she dies, or I will seek vengeance upon you worse than any imaginable even by the human lich.

THE LOST WARRIORS

Traveler stood at the bow of their long yellow boat. He paddled with a long oar on one side, moving forward on blue waters, but their view ahead was obstructed by fog. Both Lady Aylen and Gwyness sat on the deck. Behind them, the dog stood watch on all fours in his dog-headed griffin form, with two tentacle-like tails.

"Atlantea was supposed to be this wonderful city of riches and wonder, Mr. Traveler," Lady Aylen said. "Why would these star and snow elves engage in such treachery? The Old One called them ice elves."

"They could be the same elfin race or were two different ones in the past," the caravan master said. "We will call them as they announced themselves to us."

"Why would they wish to kill humans, drows, and their own kind. Those they have never met have done them no harm?" Lady Aylen asked.

"We must tell the others," Gwyness said.

"No, we mustn't," Traveler said. "King Aereth knows."

"He was right; I was wrong," Gwyness said.

"There is nothing to blame yourself for. Let the king handle the Seven Empires. He has ably done so many times in the past. He is a royal of the Kings Elder. You focus on your destiny."

"Destiny, Mr. Traveler?" Lady Aylen asked.

"Rebuild the kingdom of Rivermouth."

"Caravan master. Captain. What is this role you're taking upon yourself within the walls of Atlantea? Builder of kingdoms?"

"Guardian."

"This is a journey of destinies for all of us, is it not?" Lady Aylen said.

"It is, princess."

"Cannot say I relish being threatened by The Old One," she said.

"He did threaten us," Mr. Traveler said.

"Sounded like a deadly threat to me," Gwyness said.

"Words of annoyance, nothing more. The white elfess would hardly harm us or allow him to harm us after doing so much on our behalf. She is dying."

"Should we not accomplish this task before she does die like The Old One said? He is after all a spell-talker and could easily remove his metal helmet," Gwyness said.

"Yes, I agree it would be wise to heed those words."

"He threatened us, Mr. Traveler. Do not defend him."

Traveler grinned. "He is a creature that does not need my defense."

A single white flag jutted through the mist ahead. As the women watched, land became visible, then shadows of people waiting on the shore.

Lady Aylen's elfin eyes could already see them clearly. The same humans and fae that sought them out when Titan's Caravan was in the Great Forest. She pulled her war tridents from a magic pouch within her cloak, took a deep breath, and jumped from the boat to the shore in one leap. She could hear Gwyness sloshing in the water behind her and glanced back. In Gwyness's hands were her slender war hammers.

The band of elves, humans, and humanoids approached. At the head were the same trio that had greeted them then.

"Aylen and Gwyness, we are honored to see you again," an elfess said. Lady Aylen hadn't been sure before, but the female was a water elf too, though of a different species than her.

The other two in the welcoming trio were a human male and a humanoid female with an antenna sprouting from her head. Behind them were about two dozen humans or humanoids, almost evenly split, male and female.

"Is this your entire party?" Lady Aylen asked.

"More of us await in the Lands of Man and Faë-Land. They can be summoned when we return," the young elfess replied.

The trio had their eyes on Lady Aylen's and Gwyness's weapons.

"Your war tridents and soul-strikers were forged at Rivermouth itself," the human said.

Lady Aylen looked at her tridents again and nodded. "That is what we assume."

"Among many things, they are instruments of great history," the elfess said. "A history of a great kingdom of warrior clerics."

"I feel you may know more about it than I do," Lady Aylen said.

"I hardly believe so. We are finally united after searching for you for so long," the elfess said with a big smile.

"Where are my manners? Introductions," Lady Aylen said. "You know me and my maiden. In the boat is Mr. Traveler, the caravan master who guided us straight from the Lands of Man to Atlantea. But, you know that, since you tracked us to the Great Forest."

"We would have joined you and traveled with you. That was always the intention," the man said.

"The dog is Mr. Traveler's, but take care."

"A shape-shifter," the man said.

"Yes."

"I am one too."

"You a shape-shifter?" Lady Aylen asked.

"Yes."

"Tell me your names and introduce your party," Lady Aylen said.

"I am Raine," the elfess said.

"A water elf?" Lady Aylen asked.

"A river elf."

"Do you know what type of water elf I am?"

"You are an ocean elf with water elemental powers. We heard of your battles."

"I am Ossarian," the human said. "I am of the Faoladh."

Gwyness stepped closer. The young man looked at her. "Your amulet will not glow in my presence because we are not of evil."

"But aren't you—?" Gwyness began.

"Would you not want a Faoladh at your side if you came across a lycanthrope, especially the most evil of them—werewolves?"

"Don't mind, Gwyness," Lady Aylen said. "Once she warms to you, you will not be able to find a more loyal friend. And you? I have not seen your race of fae before."

"We are fae who live in great tree kingdoms and converse with the trees, birds, bees, and fairies. I am Rya."

"You speak to the trees, birds, bees, and fairies. That would make you more powerful than us all because you would know the goings-on all around us from the network of flora, fauna, and tiny fae."

Rya smiled and nodded.

"And the others?" Lady Aylen asked.

"Humans, elves, and faoladh," Raine replied. "All sworn to be the new warrior clerics of a new kingdom of Rivermouth with their lives."

"Please, don't swear allegiance and your lives to a cause until you understand it fully. Gwyness and I have barely become aware of our heritage. We have the weapons and some knowledge."

"We have the full library, Lady Aylen," Gwyness reminded.

The lost warriors looked at each other, excited.

"You have the libraries of Rivermouth?" Raine asked.

"We do," Lady Aylen replied.

Traveler joined them. "Lady Aylen, gather your 'lost warriors' together here in this realm and begin building."

"Building?" Lady Aylen asked. "Building what?"

"The kingdom of Rivermouth, princess."

Lady Aylen and Gwyness look at him with bewilderment, but the lost warriors erupted in joy, laughing and clapping.

"How can we build what we have never seen?" Lady Aylen asked.

"You don't need to because you are building the new kingdom. It will look however you wish it to, but if that's your excuse for delay, I will help."

Traveler opened a small pouch in his hand, and out came a giant book that fell to the ground. He leaned down and opened to a page that had a detailed color-painted picture of a city—palaces, walls, buildings, waterfalls, open fields, stables, walking paths, a dock for ships, a port for sky ships.

"Princess, Gwyness, this is where you were born."

"Then that is what we will build then," Lady Aylen said.

SELKIES AND DROWS

Traveler had lived in Atlantea for years as a young man, and, though it was not decades or a century of experience like some fae, it was long enough to understand the "feel" of the place. The fabled kingdom was a destination and city like no other—full of wonder and joy. However, these streets had an air of uncertainty and even fear. After all his many inquiries, he still had not discovered the true reason for the kingdom's closing.

He had tried to get into the elfin section of the city, but it too was closed to all, after the vanishing of so many elves at the Feast Gwragedd Annwyn. Fortunately, those elves that had traveled with Titan's Caravan were not among them, but they were still inaccessible to him. He would try again.

His dog walked ahead of him in its griffin hybrid form. The streets to the drow part of the city—colored in many different shades of blue—were more sparse than usual despite daylight hours. Drows were people of the night, but even so, there would be other fae on their blue streets, but there were not.

Traveler found Dr'as sat at a table by himself with a single mug in the center near his outstretched hand. His daughter, Dr'amal, and other drow warriors sat in the open outdoor tavern at their own tables. The drow king's face went sour as his eyes watched the caravan master approach, as if they were strangers, or even enemies, and not comrades on a deadly year–long trek.

"Are you still upset with me?" Traveler asked him, standing with his arms folded at his table.

Dr'as did not answer.

"The elves are in a panic because their leaders are gone. Would you have preferred if I let you join them?"

Dr'as still did not speak. He just stared at his drink.

"Since you hate me at the moment, I did not think I could do much more to damage our alliance, so I wanted to tell you what I did directly. You may try to strike me, which is why my dog's tail is a tentacle to restrain you if you do."

Traveler sighed heavily. "I practiced what I was going to say, but I don't think I should say it."

"You allied with the goblins," Dr'as said.

"The alliance is a temporary one, while we remain in Atlantea only."

"Why would you need such an alliance? No one can fight or attack another lest they be magically snatched and deposited far away."

"The goblins have allies too, in addition to the lamia. Dr'as, do not rise from your chair to hit me. Night drows too."

Dr'as sipped from his drink, not looking at him.

"At least you cannot say I hide it from you," Traveler said. "I told you face-to-face. I cannot control what you do, but I did it. Maybe it is a ploy of some kind on their part. Maybe they truly do hate Oughtred and his goblins and drows more than we do. I do not know. For one who lived in Atlantea, I do not know much anymore when it comes to Atlantea. I will let you be."

Traveler left the tavern with his dog without ever turning. He didn't have to. Every drow eye was on him, but not a word was spoken.

News had spread throughout the ante-city of the sun and snow elves. Some fae saw it as a sign of great things to come; others, a dark omen. Regardless of the stir caused by the ancient, now new again, elves to Atlantea more races prepared to depart for the last time in their lives.

Traveler had found the selkie clan at a ship docked at the Atlantea port. Both leaders greeted the caravan master and his dog.

"Do you depart already?" Traveler asked.

"We have secured our treasures for our people," Nori said. "We have no more reason to stay now that you are in contact with the celestial elfin queen."

"I have a request but feel no pressure to accept."

"You have done much for us, Mr. Traveler. If we can, we will accept, of course," Otari said.

"It is to aid, Lady Aylen."

"The rebuilding of Rivermouth," Nori said.

"You know of this?"

"Queen Anelle is known to the selkies in Atlantea. They made us aware of the history of the kingdom."

"The construction will begin here."

"Here?" Nori said with surprise.

"Yes, wise," Otari said. "You would be protected by Atlantea's magic."

"We need laborers."

"It was a kingdom of warriors against darkness, not just dark fae?" Nori asked.

"Yes, an island kingdom."

The selkie leaders looked at each other as if communicating without words.

"Would you be interested in joining our water elfess and maiden in this calling?"

"Selkies are not warriors as such," Otari said. "But a kingdom, any kingdom, has many roles that are equally important to the city and its people."

"True, all cannot be warrior clerics."

"We would help her," Otari said. "Also, we can talk to other selkie clans in Atlantea to aid with the labor."

"Thank you. Lady Aylen and Maiden Gwyness will be happy to see you again."

"Their kingdom Rivermouth was destroyed by necromancers?"

Necromancers came in two main varieties: those who practiced dark magic by convening with the dead and those who were the undead and capable of great dark magic.

"Yes, in a way that's true," Traveler replied.

"You mean to say elves were involved," Otari said.

"Elves here in Atlantea."

"Others as well."

"Selkies are viewed as a quiet and peaceful race, but we have had to contend with fiends," Otari said.

"Especially when some would think we are some kind of lycanthropes of the sea."

"Yes, I understand. But for now, we merely construct a beautiful palace."

The wizard Frog-Dor did a variety of errands for Traveler day and night. Since their caravan master felt he was being watched and was known among the kingdom's fae, he didn't feel comfortable doing them himself. Frog-Dor preferred to work alone, and the tasks gave him purpose. He had purchased or traded for many objects and spells for sale. He had located those members from their caravan too, who were busy acquiring their own treasures, exploring the fabled kingdom, or preparing to depart. Of paramount importance was that he was Traveler's eyes and ears within the city.

Frog-Dor was a great conjurer and spell-slinger, able to create things of magic or shoot magic in any form from his hands. From his fae lineage, the wizard could sense the presence of other magic-casters and their abilities.

Another wizard brushed past him in a bright tan robe, tapping his walking staff on the ground as he moved. Frog-Dor knew at once. The wizard was a necromancer. Dark wizards that cast their magic by communicating with the dead, apparitions of the undead, or demons. So vile were they, even most dark fae wizards avoided them. There were also necromancers who did not need to communicate with the dead because they had changed or turned themselves into the undead. The human quickly walked away down the street. Why would such a practitioner of dark magic be within the ultimate kingdom of light? He was the fifth one Frog-Dor had seen in so many days.

Pangolin had charge of making preparations for Titan's Caravan's departure from Atlantea. For that, the Cut-Throats purchased a warship. One could do no violence in the fabled kingdom, but that did not mean one couldn't acquire weapons, beasts, and vessels of extreme violence from the right sellers.

Twenty-five hundred men, four hundred eagle-headed chamroshes, and thirteen alphyns—all hard at work aboard stocking supplies, fortifying masts and sails, and painting the entire ship with a substance that would turn its wooden hull to a material identical to elfin steel without increasing the weight of the ship. Pangolin put Estus in charge of readying all the ship's cannons, all twenty of them. Though they would be transported back to the Lands of Man, it didn't mean they could not be attacked there.

On the shore, Pangolin could hear and see the growing gathering of humans of the Seven Empires to meet with sun and snow elfin kings. No other elves had been seen yet, but rumors were that all land and water elves in Atlantea were also planning to attend the gathering.

"Do you think there will be trouble, Mr. Pangolin?" I-wulf, his second, asked.

"I do, but we're berserkers. We expect trouble all the time because we thirst for it. However, this is trouble I do not want."

"Not what we expected in the fabled kingdom."

"Not at all."

"But we have our treasure."

"I want us to start training again."

"Battle exercises? But the Atlantean magic."

"Training, not engaging in real violence. We must be

ready for anything."

"I think the king and Mr. Traveler know something," I-wulf said.

"I think so too."

"I'll find those pocket-realms we used when we were on the Trail. We'll be ready. Weapons?"

"Wait on that. But have them close."

They had sailed right away. Traveler stood at the bow of the lead selkie ship with his dog at his side. Nori and Otari assembled dozens of other selkie clans on several other small ships.

"Continue on," Traveler said to the selkie leaders, seeing the drows onshore. "My dog will fly me back to catch up."

"Very well," Nori said.

Traveler jumped from the ship to the shore. Dr'as approached him with his daughter and hundreds of drow warriors.

"I didn't think you would ever speak to me again."

"I wasn't, but my daughter made me reconsider. But if you hadn't lived among drows, she wouldn't have bothered. Since, human, you shared something with me that you didn't have to, I will return the favor. Drows hate being in debt to any, especially non-drows like humans."

"Tell me then."

"What is your true purpose with your alliance with goblins, night drows, and a lamia? You cannot possibly trust them," Dr'as said.

"Strangely, I do."

"We cannot fight here, so what does it matter?" Dr'amal, the sorceress, asked.

"Unless you or they know something," Dr'as said.

"What do you want to tell me?" Traveler asked, ignoring the question.

"The night drows of Baneshade have formally requested a gathering of all drows, night drows, and shadow drows!"

"Reunification?"

"Yes, it's like a mad disease spreading through Atlantea. First humans, elves, and now drows. Fortunately, I am immune to such diseases."

"So am I."

"Have you heard from your elves?" Dr'amal asked.

"They are not my elves, and you're not my drows, which is what I say to them. I have been unable to enter their section of the city. It remains closed, but we can assume they will be caught up in all this talk of a great alliance soon enough."

"Yes, a great alliance, and then all these smaller great alliances will all meet together in one spot in Atlantea."

"Is that what you heard?" Traveler asked.

"That is what I was told."

"Will you be there?"

"No. I am a proud drow, but I cannot embrace stupidity as my brethren have."

"It is like they are enchanted," Dr'amal said.

"Are they?" Traveler asked.

"No. It isn't possible to enchant so many. Drows, we would feel such trickery."

"But not immune to enchantment spells. This is Atlantea."

"We are not humans," Dr'amal said. "It's not possible to enchant so many without our knowing."

"When I return, I'll see the elves, and push my way

past their guards if I have to, but stay away from the great gathering."

"Whatever you and the seal people are doing, I would hurry," Dr'as said.

"What are you doing?" Dr'amal asked.

"Rebuilding a kingdom that used to battle the darkness for humans and fae alike."

"You are building the lost kingdom of Rivermouth here?" Dr'as asked. "You do know that some of the very races responsible for its total destruction are here."

"You do know of it, then. Any drows involved?"

"Whom do you think? Certainly, night and shadow drows. They have never ceased the practice of dark magic and were enemies to all who opposed any use of it. This past, you have no idea, human. All elves, including the races that became drows, could have been destroyed."

"I know this, Dr'as. I have sympathy for your race because I know elves made you the scapegoat for things they did in secret."

"Yes, they did," Dr'amal said. "We don't hide what we did, but they hide their role. After all, we were all of ancient elfinkind back in those ages."

"That is why I say what you do is madness. You only remind them and provoke them.

"What can any of them do?"

"Here, nothing. Outside of Atlantea, the exact same thing."

"But we will have all these great alliances to stop such a thing."

"This is not a laughing matter."

"I know."

"We see that your people are preparing to leave."

"We are preparing, that is all. Dr'as, you can dock your ships next to us."

"I think not this time."

"Then let's promise each other here. If we do prepare to depart, I will have Frog-Dor send you a message, so we have the opportunity to join you. If you do, have Dr'amal send a message to us for the same."

"Agreed."

Traveler sat on the back of his giant hawk and was far enough away in the sky. The drows continued watching the sky from the shore of the docks. Others watched fae passersby in the streets and vessels in the sea.

"Watch him. Tell me everyone he sees," Dr'as said to his daughter.

"Father, Traveler is no fool," Dr'amal said. "He lived with drowkind. He knows how we behave. I am sure he'd be expecting me. If not, I am unlikely to evade his dog sensing me."

"You are a sorceress in a magic city. Use your magic and evade detection!"

"Father, I do not wish to leave our area and go off on my own. This may be Atlantea, but I do not feel at ease. Too much is happening. Too many of our enemies are here."

"I will make it worth your while. I'll have the drows re-enter the Treasured Lands."

"I can do so on my own, which I asked you from the start."

"Your father isn't good enough to gather precious gems for his own daughter? He does know what she fancies."

"No, he does not."

"I did raise you if you recall."

"Father, that was a long time ago. I'm not a child

when I thought gemstones were colored rocks to be thrown against the wall to play games."

"You did do that. What of Traveler?"

"This a city of magic. If I can't cast the spell myself to watch him, I can purchase one at one of the stores."

"Buy magic?"

"Yes, father. This is a city of magic. You can buy and barter for spells at the shop."

CITY OF FAYLEN

Lady Aylen relaxed on a green hill, slightly reclined on its slope. Since becoming a full elf, she did not sweat as she once did at doing hard labor. After days of hard work, the beginnings of their kingdom rose at the center of the island. Much of the work was done magically, but there remained plenty of manual work to do.

A great sea gate marked the beginning of the path to the palace, a simple but pristine footpath to a bridge. Three towers comprised the great gatehouse, the center taller than the others. Within the walls were the guard towers, a great hall, the kitchen, storehouses, and meeting chambers. All were created on the first day.

On the second day, their workers of humans, elves, and fae concentrated on the residential quarters, training palaces and fields, great libraries, land and water stables, and chapel.

This day they constructed fortified towers at the four corners of the island.

Gwyness strolled up the hill to Lady Aylen. "Will you join us for the noon meal?"

"Look how much we've completed in these few days," the princess said.

"We are in realms of magic. Anything is possible."

"Yes, it is."

"They are asking what we will name this new Rivermouth."

"We should choose another. Honor the old but choose another. How about the city of Faylen? Queen Faylen was the mage mother of Rivermouth. It should be in her memory."

"Yes, that will be the name then."

The announcement to the lost warriors and selkies was met with approval and cheers.

"Queen Faylen, the mage mother of Rivermouth, would be so honored. A fitting name for our kingdom," Nori said to them.

"What will we build tomorrow?" Ossarian asked.

Lady Aylen looked at the palace. "The City of Faylen is as much a kingdom of water as it is land. Tomorrow, I will use my own magic."

Lady Aylen and Gwyness walked the grounds of the palace. From mountain peaks alongside either side of the palace, water fell into open pools. Besides the sparkling waterfall, throughout the open courtyards were fountains, both large and small.

The two selkie royals followed them, doing their own inspection.

"What do you think?" Lady Aylen asked.

"Splendid," Nori said.

"My wife and I have discussed it, and we would be greatly interested in having our city of Therian join with your city of Faylen. My wife and I are respected teachers in our rite—she of academics, debate, and diplomacy, I of hunting, food gathering, farming of fish, and fauna of the ocean. Our people lead a simple life but are hard, diligent workers. All which might be welcome in a city of warriors and mages," Otari said.

"Very welcome, indeed. It is we who would be honored."

"The faoladh are an interesting people," Nori said. "They are shape-shifters such as us but have such a benevolent nature for warriors."

"Very true, but are said to be the best against lycanthropes of evil," Lady Aylen said.

"The dark creatures are very rare, though," Otari said. "There are many kinds, and the lupines may be the deadliest but are the rarest of them all."

"Will the celestial elfin queen visit us?" Nori asked.

"That is a fine question. I do not know," Lady Aylen said.

"Does any of this bring back memories of Rivermouth for you?" Otari asked.

"Gwyness and I were taken away as infants. She remembers more than I," the princess said.

"Flashes of faces and people but nothing more or significant," Gwyness said.

"Supposedly, I am the last surviving member of its royal clan," Lady Aylen said.

"What is the name of the kingdom you were raised?" Otari asked.

"The kingdom of Sirnegate."

"What are your plans?" Nori asked. "Will you maintain a relationship with your old kingdom?"

"We will."

"Who will train your mages and warriors?" Nori asked.

Lady Aylen and Gwyness looked at each other.

"An excellent question. One we have not thought much of, but must," Lady Aylen said.

"Mr. Traveler will know."

"I should hope so. If he can find all the many gifted warriors and beasts and fae he did for our caravan, he should be able to find us the best trainers on Pan-Earth. Gwyness! We must set out on another caravan to the treasured lands."

"Another?"

"We must acquire more treasure for Faylen. It is a new city, and we will need to acquire much when we depart."

"Where will Faylen be?" Otari asked. "The Lands of Man or Faë-Land."

"What is your counsel on the matter?"

"The city should be in Faë-Land. Near the threshold to the Lands of Man but the magical lands. All of us, the city, including the humans of the city, are all of magic. We should remain connected to it," Nori said.

Lady Aylen nodded. "Agreed."

Traveler held on tight as his dog, in the form of a giant hawk, descended through the clouds to the Faylen island. The contrast between the dual fifty-foot waterfalls and the shooting fountains of the large center courtyards added to the uniqueness of the white palace.

From below, people waved to them. Traveler waved back as his giant hawk set down in the main courtyard. Already his name was called out, and Lady Aylen and Gwyness summoned.

"A full city in five days," the caravan master said, looking around, as did his gray wolf-dog, transformed from the giant hawk seconds before.

"Impressed, Mr. Traveler?" the princess asked.

She appeared with Gwyness, her female half-elves, a trio he had seen before, and the two selkie leaders.

"Already you act like a royal with your own procession," he said.

"We are here to greet our caravan master. Well? Impressed?"

"Very."

"Good."

"When will you be done?"

"The third palace and the docks will be done tomorrow. We can keep making additions."

"Have you begun your routine?"

"Routine?"

"Training, you mean," Otari said.

"Yes."

"All of our energy has been focused on building the city," Lady Aylen said.

"Who will be the steward of the city? Your own version of our able Mr. Hobbs."

Lady Aylen glanced at Gwyness.

"Don't look at me," Gwyness said.

"Not Gwyness," Traveler said. "You and she are a fighting team."

"We can fill that role presently," Nori said. "It would be an honor."

"Gwyness and I discussed the trainers we will need. We had planned to visit the treasured lands again to hire those that we needed."

"Wise. Do it immediately."

"Why immediately? Is something happening?"

"Much is happening, princess. I will have Mr. Pangolin lend you some of his Cut-Throats to begin training your warriors." He looked at the trio. "What are your names?"

"I am Raine."

"I am Ossarian," the human said. "I am of the Faoladh."

"I am Rya."

"How are your fighting skills?" Traveler asked.

"They are exceptional," Raine answered. "We have practiced for years."

"Our berserkers will test you on the field. What weapons are you best at?"

"Trident," Raine replied.

"Do you fight with a trident because you can or because you think a water elf should fight with one?"

Lady Aylen whispered to them, "Our Mr. Traveler has beaten elves not only with a sword, but once I recall that all you needed in one battle was a dagger."

The trio looked at him with a bit of fear.

"A human who can beat an elf?" Rya said.

"Mr. Traveler, we need look no further. You can train Faylen's warriors. Who better?" Lady Aylen said.

"I definitely set my own trap on that one," Traveler said.

Lady Aylen smiled, and Gwyness laughed.

"What of you?"

"Blade or axe," Ossarian said. "But prefer my hands when I change."

"And you?"

"Archer," Rya said.

"Good. As good as an elf or centaur?"

"No, but one day I will be."

"We have elfin archers among us," Raine said.

"Princess, I will train them in close-quarter fighting with the blade. But Pangolin's men will assist. Besides your faoladh, what other magic can your people do?"

"We all can cast spells," Raine answered.

"Who's the best?"

The lost warriors looked at each other. Raine raised a hand and a few others. "I am the most powerful spellcaster. I started as a child."

"We need someone for magic, a gifted teacher," Traveler said.

"We have a question," Raine asked. "When will Lady Aylen and Maiden Gwyness begin our training in the ways of Rivermouth?"

"I say there is no time like the present," Traveler said. "When do you wish to go to the treasured lands?" he asked the princess and Gwyness.

"I was going to do that today," Lady Aylen answered. "Will Mr. Pangolin and the Cut-Throats accompany us?"

"They are watching over King Aereth at the moment. I want them to stay close to him. I will accompany you with my dog."

"Then Gwyness and I will prepare to depart for more treasure hunting, but only after Mr. Traveler gives us a full account of what is happening outside this realm."

"Do you know, princess, that you are about to be reunified with all of elfinkind? Sky elves, land elves, water elves, maybe even drows, all as one. Then you will become part of a great, grand alliance with all the Seven Empires of humans."

"Mr. Traveler, what nonsense are you talking about?" Lady Aylen asked.

For Frog-Dor, a quiet meal in the new city of Faylen after a long but productive day was a welcome respite. Most in the palace were asleep, but there was a minimal contingent of sentries on duty.

The caravan master had joined him and sat opposite him at the table. Just the two of them in the kitchen. His dog lay in the corner of the room, half done with the meat his master had given but always watchful of the surroundings.

"Dr'amal," the caravan master said, swallowing more of his meal.

"Dr'amal?"

"I can ask her to train our mages."

"She is not that kind of sorceress."

"I believe she can guide them for the time being."

"Her father hates me."

"Why do you say that?"

"I can tell."

"He's a drow. Ignore him. You and Dr'amal work well together."

"It's hard to ignore an angry drow father who thinks you are after his only daughter, and it's not true."

"You're a non-drow, but he'll get used to you. Besides you're a conjurer and he's not."

"He doesn't need to be a sorcerer to throw a two-blade into my chest and kill me."

"He'll get used to you."

"If they or I are around long enough."

"I want them to remain in Atlantea as long as possible too. If Dr'amal is here, they are here. Besides, I still cannot get entry into the elfin cities. Still closed, and none of their elfin guards will tell me, or anyone else, when they will open again."

"Where are your darklings?"

"I am taking no chances. People and beasts have been vanished for mischievous activities that the Atlanteans viewed as violence."

"Explains why many of the races keep their beasts from the public streets."

Traveler knew Frog-Dor was still getting used to being free, free from his curse, free to go and do whatever he wished. He also knew that Frog-Dor remained uncomfortable being among people. But the new city of Faylen, the caravan master thought, would be perfect for the sorcerer and allow the man his space.

"A provocative thing you and Lady Aylen engage in, this new Rivermouth called Faylen. I heard gossip about it."

"People are talking about it already?"

"Yes. About the city, you, the princess and the maiden, Titan's Caravan."

"What are they saying?"

"That you're asking for violence. That you're putting people in danger. But you know that. You wish to be provocative. Not Lady Aylen or Maiden Gwyness. It is you."

"Not me. We follow the instructions of the white elfess, and I agree with her reasoning."

"What are you both trying to provoke, Mr. Traveler?"

"A response."

"You should know there are necromancers in Atlantea."

Traveler stopped eating. "How many?"

"I counted almost a dozen so far."

"A dozen? In the same or different areas of the city?"

"Different parts. All traveling alone and separately. If they gather somewhere, we would never know unless they wanted us to. Do you wish for me to remain here, in the new Faylen?"

"Is that acceptable?"

"A city of three palaces and hardly any people at all. I would welcome it."

"Then you will have your own room in a castle as you deserve."

"A room anywhere is fine; it does not have to be in a castle. You should also know that the gossip about the new sun and snow elves has also been intense. Was Atlantea like this when you lived here?"

"No."

"The fabled kingdom's attraction has waned considerably for me. When I arrived, it was a magical place those first few weeks. But after...the Feast Gwragedd Annwyn, everything has changed. As if the city isn't as magical as it once was."

"What you say is so true. I'd like for you to get a message to Dr'amal."

"Meet her here?"

"If she will. Likely, I will have to meet her in one of the drow cities of Atlantea. They remain there knowing that night and shadow drows are about."

"I would like to observe this gathering of men and elves."

"Is it curiosity alone?"

"Mostly."

"Do as you wish but do not suffer the same fate as our elfin friends. You and I are both under the Atlantean's watchful eyes."

"Would they truly vanish us for defending someone? That is the only reason you would engage in any violence within their kingdom."

"We should take no chances. The fact that they warned us should speak volumes. We are being watched."

"Is that normal to Atlantea too?"

"The Atlanteans are not foolish. When you have this many fae, including ancient ones, in a realm that does to all what Dr'amal's magic touch can, making all more magical and more powerful, then you must. What follows more power is also more power hungry."

"Very true. I sought out oracles in the city."

Traveler chuckled.

"You laugh at me. Did you know I would do so?"

"I knew some in our party would."

"I could not find one."

"Mr. Frog-Dor do you really want to see the future."

"I thought it wise to consult with an oracle, yes?"

"Mr. Frog-Dor, all the oracles in Atlantea left the same day we arrived."

For the moment, the structure that would be Faylen's library of ancient works was a simple lecture hall. Lady Aylen had given speeches before as a princess to the royal house of Sirnegate but never was she a teacher.

Every single one of the lost warriors sat on the floor, eagerly listening to her every word. Some even scribbled on their own parchments with magic quills. Gwyness and the selkie royals sat, crouched, in front of the crowd.

"Yes, Rivermouth was destroyed. I am told the battle was long and fierce, but details remain obscure. That is the true reason Gwyness and I wanted to risk our lives to journey to Atlantea. It was not treasure alone. We sought the details of Rivermouth's destruction, both of us were taken away as infants to save us. There are many who do know those details, but they remain silent either out of fear or their own complicity. The lesson of Rivermouth, a kingdom as powerful in magic as it was, is if it could be destroyed, so could we. That is the risk I take, Gwyness, and all of you.

"We will know as much of our past as we can and are able, the knowledge is not completely lost, and we will eventually uncover it all, but we must also chart a different path from our noble predecessors, or we will suffer their same fate. No one came to the aid of mage queen Faylen and Rivermouth in their time of need. We must be stronger than they were and, not to be disrespectful in any way, must have better allies than they. Rivermouth protected many who ultimately did not return the favor when it mattered most."

"Do the Atlanteans know of Rivermouth's fate?" Raine asked.

"Possibly," Lady Aylen replied. "But Gwyness and I will worry about that. You must worry about your studies and training."

All of them heard a commotion outside the walls of the hall. Then screams. Everyone jumped to their feet, but only Lady Aylen and Gwyness had their weapons. The princess burst out of the room into the exterior courtyard. The half-elves stood outside the doors, swords in hand, terrified.

The Old One stood at the gatehouse.

The white elfess walked around him from the gatehouse, looking as if she were reborn.

"Close your mouths, Aylen and Gwyness. I am not dead yet. I told you I am still able to cast a decent spell to allow me to disguise my decaying form to appear vibrant and walk amongst young ones. I want to see what you have accomplished." She clapped her hands and said to the crowd, "My guardian is more powerful than all of us will ever be, so pay him no mind. Come back in the hall and hear from an ancient elfess involved in the complicity that destroyed Faylen."

Now, the mouths of everyone hung open as they looked around at each other.

"Firstly, Rivermouth was the given name of the city by the humans. I never did care for it. The city was always called Faylen. Actually, the mage queen Faylen was named after the city. She was born there."

The celestial elfin queen held court at the head of the hall with everyone, including Lady Aylen, seated on the ground before her. The half-elves and everyone else from the city had joined the gathering, all seated on the floor.

Queen Anelle reached out her hand, and both of Lady Aylen's war tridents flew out of her cloak to her hand. She reached out her other hand, and Gwyness's slender war hammers flew to it.

"Faylen trained warriors and mages. The war trident and soul-strikers were the weapons and the symbols of those two noble clans. Slayers and seers."

The white elfess threw the weapons back to the women. Both caught them in their hands with ease.

"I would have been very, very, very upset if either one of you had dropped them."

The room laughed.

"Mr. Traveler and your dog. And who is the wizard?"

Everyone turned to see Traveler, his dog, and Frog-Dor at the back.

"Frog-Dor is his name. He was one of the sorcerers for our caravan," Traveler replied.

"I would say he was the only real sorcerer you had on your caravan. Where was I?" The celestial elfess rubbed her chin, thinking. "I forgot my place."

"You threw our weapons back to us," Lady Aylen said.

"You were talking about how war tridents and soul strikers were the weapons and symbols of Faylen," Gwyness said.

The white elfess smiled. "You were paying attention. Maiden Gwyness's parents were both strong sorcerers, but she is not one. Lady Aylen's parents had no magic powers but she is a powerful water elemental. The point is, mage or not, of parents who were mages or not, all played a vital role in Faylen.

"Lady Aylen is not just a water elemental. She is a Faylen warrioress. She has the magic and the weapon to kill any living thing. Maiden Gwyness is not just a human. She is a sin-seer. Her amulet detects evil creatures and, with her soul-strikers, can kill anything, whether living or already dead."

Gwyness felt light-headed remembering the minotaur ghoul she vanquished on the Trail.

"The Old Faylen was a sacred kingdom led by elves and elementals who trained warrior mages and warrior clerics as it was the only city of its kind in all of Pan-Earth that specialized in the defense against darkness. You are their descendants, all of you, whether fae or human.

"What is the word you humans say that makes no sense to us fae?"

"Undead," Gwyness said in almost a whisper, but everyone heard.

"Undead, yes. Fiends. Faylen was an elfin city in its founding but became one of the water elves and water elementals who harnessed the kingdom's streams of sacred water as a weapon to defend against, fight, and kill evil creatures. Later, they would add humans and other fae races to their ranks.

"Your Lady Aylen and Maiden Gwyness already have

the original libraries from the city with all its history and spells from the day Faylen was born to Pan-Earth."

"But the libraries were not rescued," Lady Aylen said.

The two elfin females stared at each other for a long time. The fear came over everyone again, some expecting to see The Old One break through the main entrance.

"You are correct, Aylen. They were not rescued. They were taken so that no other could rebuild Faylen or any city could do again what they had done. The library was given to me to destroy. I obviously did not do what I was told," the white elfess said.

The celestial elfess stayed quite a while before she spoke again. Everyone watched her not knowing what to think of her destroyer and now resurrectionist, and conspirator and now ally.

"You will, one day know the full account of Faylen's last days, you and Gwyness. By then, I will be dead, and there will be nothing to do about it, as there is nothing I can do to undo what I did in under my house's edict. When you do, you will have to decide on whether to be filled with hate, or to recognize you are one of Faylen's leaders and its future, not past, is in your hands. When that inevitable day comes, I will spend much time with your human named Traveler in the back. Learn his lessons on how he let go of his hatred of fairies, elves, and goblins to become the man he is today, respected by all three of those races and more. A respect that if it did not exist, you would have died on the Trail, and neither you young ones nor I would be here in this room today."

FAE-MAN

King Aereth gazed out over all the kingdoms representative of the Seven Empires in a half-circle formation awaiting the return of the ancient elves. He stood at the center, as the newly elected speaker for the Seven Empires. Even in Atlantea, he could not escape the politicking of men and apparently elves.

Hobbs was at his side as he had been for Traveler. Pangolin and his Cut-Throats stood right behind them ready to protect at all costs. Quillen now had his own telescope which poked through between Pangolin and I-wulf to see what was descending from the sky.

A fiery yellow globe slowly fell from the sky to the mouth of their formation. The king thought to himself how the magic performance of these elves was to convey superiority rather than be the legitimate way they traveled.

The globe opened, and for a moment, they all saw a portal. Several silhouettes approached into the light.

Inarian of the sun elf kingdom of Ljósálfar, with a few sun elfin knights in solid golden armor stepped through. King Aereth kept his eye on the portal and the shadows of elves who did not depart. The portal closed, and the fiery globe flew back to the heavens at incredible speed. Then a wintry cyclone appeared nearby, then disappeared. In its place, Foldruin of the snow elfin kingdom of Ice Niflheim approached with his own quartet of snow elfin knights.

Men cheered, and the talks began. King Theor of Armathia was always the most enthusiastic of all the other royals and greeted both elfin royals first. Hours would pass after much discussion and debate before King Aereth would say his first word.

"To that end, we will make our base on your continent of Borea," Inarian said.

For the first time, the gathering of men did not cheer.

"Why would you need a region of our human lands for your base?" King Aereth asked.

"You call yourself the Seven Empires when it is only six. It is a frozen continent where humans cannot readily survive. We believe it to be the perfect location for our sister kingdoms on Pan-Earth. My brother Foldrun will have his land kingdom upon its icy mantle. My new kingdom will float above in the sky. Humans would have an ally in their own lands to join them against any threats from the magical lands, but none will dare."

"Will your dual kingdoms require anything else from the Seven Empires for this protection?" King Aereth asked.

"Nothing more. Our races have existed without Pan‑Earth, humans, or other elves for many centuries. None of that will change. We will be here only to protect the Lands of Man."

Inarian's seemingly genuine words and earnest manner quickly won over the human royals.

"I see doubt in your eyes," Foldruin, the snow elf said to Aereth.

"No doubt. It is much to happen all at once. To stand among elves thought long extinct. Then to have their offer of protection and talk of an alliance of all elves, humans, and others. We do in days what should take centuries."

"Yes, indeed, King Aereth," Inarian the sun elf said. "But if we can strike an agreement here in Atlantea, we can sail together to the Lands of Man."

"Hear! Hear!" shouted the humans, except for King Aereth and his men.

How quickly things shifted, King Aereth thought to

himself. Before, he was a hero and savior to the Seven Empires. Now, with the arrival of sun and snow elves, he was becoming a pariah. He could see it in their eyes and the whispering under their breaths. He smiled when they smiled, laughed at their jests, nodded to everything they said, like the rest of the royals and nobles of the Empires. But all false. Not long from now, he would be cast aside as the speaker for the Empires.

"I had forgotten the suspicions of some humans," Inarian, the sun elf, said to him. The new elfin leaders came to him the first chance they had with King Theor and other human royals close at their sides, looking at Aereth disapprovingly.

"Not suspicion. Simple caution. Before making grand decisions, I believe in thoroughness and knowing all the facts, not some or little. Is that not the way of things in your elfin kingdoms?"

"It is, but there is a line between thoroughness and deliberate obstruction," Inarian said, with a hint of annoyance in his voice. Humans around him hung on his every word and nodded in agreement.

"I do have an honored reputation for deliberation and diplomacy, sir. The Kings Elders are known for wise decisions without fail."

"Very good."

"I say we make the decision as quickly as is able," King Theor said.

"Why not before the night falls?" Inarian said to Theor.

"Yes, we quite agree."

"Then we will take our leave and allow you to discuss it amongst yourselves and bring along those who are more uncertain and timid to join with the majority," Inarian said.

The king gave a false smile.

"Yes, indeed," Theor said, glancing at Aereth.

"We will return at dusk."

The ancient elves departed, walking through the cheering crowds to where they had landed. Above, their fiery globe of magic descended on cue. The snow elves were instantly swept away by an ice cyclone of magic and were gone. So too were the sun elves into the sky.

Theor angrily marched back to Aereth with a contingent of royals and knights.

"Are you trying to sabotage this momentous event?" Theor asked Aereth.

"Sabotage what? We haven't agreed to anything. We are simply conversing with the elves."

"In case you do not know what is happening, Atlantea will close its gates, and every fae and their beasts will be turned back upon the world. They could be at the doors of our kingdoms and palaces, and we would be helpless to stop them. We need this alliance more than anything else," Theor yelled.

"We have good relations with Faë-Land."

"But not all. You saw the ancient fae at the Feast."

"Yes, I did, but you did not."

"We know who they are. What malevolent beings they are. Do you wish to have them at the gates of Helm Earldom?"

"We will have this alliance, King Aereth," said a royal in wizardly clothing and also wearing a crown. "We say to you what will say to all others of your same mind: oppose this alliance, and we oppose you. You will sail to your lands alone, and you will be alone, if you should need our aide."

"What a threat to make," King Aereth said, for the first time angry. "You speak of great alliances, but here you so casually and recklessly cast aside the alliances we have made within the Lands of Man for decades and centuries. You gaze upon elves gone from this very world before our kingdoms were born for only a moment, and you throw all that we humans have accomplished and built on our own as if our own alliances never existed. They built nothing for us and fought no battles at our sides."

The men were quiet.

"We are sorry," Theor finally said.

"You are correct, of course, King Aereth," the wizardly human royal said. "But our fear is real. The need is real."

"I know," Aereth said. "But let us be intelligent in our decisions. The elves could be taking advantage of us. They could be true to heart. We need to know more. Here is what I propose. Let us take counsel with the elves we know. See what they say. They must know their ancient brothers have returned. Why did they not come out to greet them?"

"Fair point, King Aereth," the wizardly royal said. "We should consult with the elves immediately. They were part of your Titan's Caravan. Shall you take the lead?"

"I would be honored," King Aereth said.

He turned, but the men were already following.

Pangolin shook his head and said under his breath to Hobbs, "Foolish politics."

The section of Atlantea where elves resided were large castle structures of stone, gemstone, and metal. Elfin knights and wizards stood watch at every possible entrance. They had ignored all pleas from the human royals for an audience, but King Aereth told them they would not leave this time. They waited at the same palace gate for hours. The men were restless, scared the sun and snow elves would return as dusk without a unified decision of the Seven Empires. King Aereth remained calm as he sat right at the feet of the largest elfin guards at the gate. The elves were not happy, and King Aereth was glad he did not speak elvish. He knew they uttered every profanity at him.

The gate swung open, and the elfin guards moved aside. King Aereth rose to his feet and was overjoyed. However, his elfin friends showed no emotion.

The Elfin Questing Knights of their Titan's Caravan met them with more elfin knights spilling out of the palace. Lyre, the high–elf of the woodland elf kingdom of Bravehowl, Taylos of the desert elf kingdom of Falconbright, and Shadu–mun of the moon elf kingdom of Nightshade stood opposite the humans with a growing number of elfin knights behind them.

"You wish to know about the sun and snow elves?" Lyre asked.

"Yes. They wish to form an alliance with us, but we do not know anything of them."

"Neither do we. They haven't been in contact with any elfin kingdom of Faë-Land Minor in three or more centuries. You know as much as we do."

"I see."

"They sent a message to us. We too will be gathering. Land elves and water elves meet with the sky elves. A bit of excitement about the prospect from many elves."

"Seems all of a sudden, though, does it not?"

"So is Atlantea closing its gates."

"I know why my fellow humans would want such an alliance. Why would great elves such as yourselves want this alliance?"

"Alliances are good, I am told. Were we not in one ourselves along Titan's Trail? It keeps people safe. I, for one, do not wish to see sphinxes or spider centaurs or scorpion men or red goblins at the gates of my kingdom. Do you?"

"The same as us humans then. Fear."

"Elves have fear, human. Fear can be a healthy emotion when the danger is real."

"If you are meeting with the sun and snow elves, then we should not be concerned with meeting them again."

"Anything else?" Lyre asked.

"I am sorry your brethren were vanished from Atlantea."

"If they could return, they still could not enter. No one can enter into Atlantea's domain without their permission."

"They all knew the penalty," Shadu-mun said. "But it does not matter. We will be leaving Atlantea soon ourselves."

"Never to return in our lives, or those of our children," Lyre said.

King Aereth wondered if the elfin knight was drunk. He did not have his normal bearing and didn't seem to care about anything. Do elves get drunk?

"May I ask one more question?" King Aereth said.

"Why? Do you think we would meet with them if they were in league with Oughtred? They don't even know who he is."

Lyre was done. He swung around and marched back into their palace, and his two comrades followed. Their knights closed the metal gates behind them, leaving many more elfin knights outside to stand guard.

"If he doesn't know anything about these sun and snow elves, how would he know if they were or were not in league with Oughtred?" Pangolin asked the king.

King Aereth had wanted reassurance for the Seven Empires but instead felt sadness and had only more questions. His elfin friends were not themselves, and he didn't know why. However, he would have to ponder it all later.

The men of the Seven Empires and the humans of Titan's Caravan stood silent as hundreds of drows and night drows marched across them, away into the distance.

Then came the goblins: common ones led by high goblins, marching with packs of dire wolves held tight with metal chains. Humans jumped when they saw goblins flying giant bats above towards wherever the drows and goblins were heading.

"King Aereth, I am starting to come to your way of thinking," King Theor said. "There is something not right about all this. A grand alliance of humans, all elves, all drows, all goblins simply because the notion is spoken from two races of elves that not even the elves have set eyes of for three or more centuries."

Hobbs never showed his emotions. He had been trained as a noble steward to serve and did so ably and honorably. One never made one's personal wishes known to royals or noble knights without prompting. But King Aereth saw the distress in his face. He wanted them to leave Atlantea.

CARAVAN OF THE LOST KINGDOM

Lady Aylen and Gwyness escorted Queen Anelle outside to the main gate while everyone else remained behind in the hall.

The white elfess had ended her talk to the group with the following: "When you are able to defeat these creatures of ghouls, draugr, lich, then you can defeat any on Pan-Earth. Rocs and jörmungandr would be exceptions. You don't defeat the largest bird and snake creatures in the magical lands the size of mountains. You run from them."

"Sorry I lashed out at you," Lady Aylen said.

"Why? Your reaction was not unexpected, and it's completely justified. I'd expect nothing less from someone who felt I had a hand in the death of her parents and her kingdom."

"Did you know our parents?" Gwyness asked.

"I will just tell you since you will find out but promise never to repeat it, at least for some years."

"Repeat what?" Lady Aylen asked.

"Queen Mage Faylen was likely your grandmother."

"But she was human."

"She was an elf who appeared human. When Faylen was created, it wasn't controversial only because of its work against practitioners of dark magic. Faylen was one of the few cities where humans and elves lived and worked together at a time when humans and elves were warring against each other. The only reason it ceased wasn't that humans and elves became allies, but because we elves decided to make war against each other, and then there were the goblins to occupy our time. Do they not teach history in school anymore?"

"Queen Anelle, you have helped us from the first time we met," Lady Aylen began, "and we thank you."

"Yes, I have." She stopped to admire the fountains shooting high up in the air. "I always support winners. My problem is not picking the right winners. I was short-sighted and weak when I should have taken the long view and been strong. No matter what people say, it is always hard and terrifying to be all alone with your convictions, no matter how right you are, especially as a royal. The patrons of Faylen no longer felt it worthy of support anymore at that time."

"The original city of Faylen was not worthy of support anymore?" Gwyness asked.

"We were the ones not worthy."

They had traversed the courtyard and reached the gatehouse where The Old One waited.

"I hope you post sentries at night," Queen Anelle said.

"Yes, we do. Per Mr. Traveler's direction," Lady Aylen answered.

"Always remember, if we can enter this realm without your knowledge so can others."

"Who would want to?" Lady Aylen asked.

"You are only safe because most don't know what you're doing, and with everything happening?"

"What is happening out there? Mr. Traveler was not very coherent."

"Don't worry about what is happening out there. Continue with your work here and without hesitation."

"We must go out," Lady Aylen said. "We have more treasure to secure."

"Good, but I would do so now."

"Why?" Lady Aylen asked.

"I did say to you when we first met that Faylen's allies became their enemies and are yours. Go now."

Do so now.

The Old One's voice echoed in their minds causing their bodies to shake. But not just Lady Aylen and Gwyness. Every human, elf, and other fae race in the palace felt his words.

Elfin gold, rocks of its ore piled high on the deck of their five flat barges. Lady Aylen sat at the back of the lead boat; Gwyness, the selkie leaders, and lost warriors sat aft on the other four, respectively. But none of the barges sailed themselves. Lady Aylen reflected upon the many sights and races she had beheld in the realms of Atlantea. It was as Traveler had told them—wonderful and terrifying. She would add another description—absurd. Again, they used the services of the dark oarmen they had before when they traveled to the Great Feast aboard flying ships. Here she had five of them to ferry them across dark waters and thunderous skies threatening rain.

The treasured land was further away than most, one day to, and a day back. Mr. Traveler had hired the dark fae—black phookas in majestic robes over skeletal humanoids. Their caravan master told them that the creatures knew how to get to their destination without the knowledge or interference of others. But Traveler gave them one firm warning, do not engage them in conversation. Resist any urges of courtesy or curiosity to speak to them. As the princess watched the one at the bow of her barge, swinging a long, black oar in the water back and forth, she thought of the fable of the skeleton ferryman of Styx, the land of the dead. Were these oarman an omen of things to come?

She pushed the comparison out of her mind. They acquired more elfin gold than the vaults of ten elfin kingdoms. They would need it, for it was unlikely they would ever be allowed to mine any from the lands of elves when they returned. Their elfin gold came to them from a giant volcano that spat out the rocks of ore that covered its land for miles around. The rocks were hot enough to burn flesh or set fire to anything flammable, but they could shovel them up into the barge. The volcano was not only the giver of elfin rocks of ore, but it was also the source of the thunder and storm clouds of the magical realm.

The thunder shook the realm again, and finally, the heavy rain fell just as their five barges passed from the realm into the clear waters and sun-drenched sky of another.

Lady Aylen stepped from the barge onto the docks as Mr. Elman waved to her from on top of one of the island towers.

"I wonder how many miles away we were when you first saw us," the princess said to herself.

In their absence, she had left the half-elves in charge of Faylen, which meant the three palaces and the grounds. At the moment, the new city of Faylen was only these structures, but there would be a day when it would become a great city.

As lost warriors ran past her to the barges, everyone stopping to greet her with "G'day, m'lady," she saw the half-elfess Brenn slowly walking toward her with a sheepish grin.

"How did you and Mr. Elman enjoy being in command of Faylen in our absence?"

"We enjoyed it. Thank you, m'lady. Nothing to report, with one exception," her royal guardswoman said as she pointed.

Across the bridge, waiting at the entrance of the gatehouse to the main castle was the drow sorceress, Dr'amal.

"Has Mr. Traveler returned?"

"Not as of yet, m'lady."

"Brenn. Where are your owl griffins?"

The half–elfess laughed at the question and pointed.

Lady Aylen looked above, and the tiny griffins peered down from the roof of the sea gate.

"You are training them to be stealthy in their growing age. Good."

"One of the female fae said they will grow a bit once they become adults."

"I hope not too big."

"The size of a large cat."

"I will see what our drowess has to say."

"Before you go, m'lady, we have been talking about it amongst ourselves."

"Yes."

"We have decided that, well, could we become warrior mages too?"

"You'd want that?"

"Yes, m'lady. We're fighters. We are already accustomed to magic. With the things we've seen on the

Trail."

"You are not scared of these things, the evil things we may have to fight?"

"We have faced down many evil things in our lives."

"I have no doubt that you have. So you no longer want to be my royal guardswoman?"

"M'lady, it's not that—"

"Brenn, I am joking. Tell the others that you all will be warrior mages of Faylen. I already know your previous employer, which is me, of course. Gather up all your belongings and you will lodge with the others."

"The lost warriors, yes."

"I don't like that term. They aren't lost anymore. We need a new term."

"Warrior mages of Faylen, m'lady?"

"Yes, why did I not think of that? Mage warriors?"

"Warrior clerics?"

"We could do this for some time. Go give your fellow half-elves the news."

Brenn began to run off.

"After! ...all our gold is safely stored away within the

palace."

"Gold, m'lady."

"Yes, on the barges."

"Yes, m'lady. Right away."

The half-elf touched her temple and then ran to the barges. From the gatehouse and across the bridge came her four other half-elfin sisters. Each greeted the princess as they ran past.

"Why can't I speak to other elves without speaking like they can?" Lady Aylen asked herself.

"Dr'amal, there is not a single thing you could possibly say to put me in a foul mood. We have boatfuls of gold. I have a new city. My former half-elvin guardswomen and their male counterparts, who made their living as kind of mercenaries, all are joining my growing clan of warrior mages."

Lady Aylen strolled across the bridge to the waiting drowess.

"I am here to decline Mr. Traveler's request."

"Dr'amal, you did not need to come all this way to tell me that. You simply needed not to appear."

"I wanted to see your elfin city for myself."

"It's not an elfin city. We have humans and other fae too. I would even accept drows."

"Would you?"

"I would. Why, Dr'amal, are you in such a foul mood? I thought we were friends. We are fellow travelers of the Trail."

"We don't care for goblins and night drows."

"So Mr. Traveler told you?"

"He did."

"I can't say I understand it either, and a lamia of all creatures too, but our caravan master does know what he's doing. We saw so for ourselves for a year. Is there anything I can say to make you reconsider?"

"Reconsider?"

"Meet these young ones. They could use guidance from a sorceress."

"My magic of illusions?"

"Dr'amal, you laid your hand on me, and my inner power was increased ten-fold. You are far more of a sorceress than a mere illusionist. Meet them. Do it for them, if not for me."

The drowess sighed. Her opposition was weakening.

"Besides, Mr. Traveler told me your clan in particular has much experience in dealing with practitioners of dark magic. Here's my proposal. You stay, and I'll tell you what the celestial elfin queen told me."

"Why would I care?"

"That all of drowkind was made to suffer for things that others engaged in too."

"What do you mean?"

"That is my proposal, Dr'amal. In fact, now that I see you, why don't we have drows as part of Faylen. Your clan is the..."

"D'Shar."

"You did form an alliance with elves already, with me and the Elfin Questing Knights of our caravan."

"That was different. A unique situation."

"Are you staying or not? You said you wanted to see the city for yourself, then let's take you to see it."

Lady Aylen marched into the castle. Dr'amal grudgingly followed.

The wizard rose from the waters encircling Faylen. He saw no others on the grounds with his eyes that were like fish. Dressed in a black tunic and pants, he reached out with his webbed hands but did not touch the bridge. He floated on it and walked across to the open gatehouse.

He ran through the outdoor courtyard, then into the palaces. The city was abandoned. He found the library vault, and it too was left open. Stepping inside, he waved his index finger in small circles in the air. A ball of fire snapped into existence and hung above his head so he could see. Mounds of black ore of elfin gold filled the storehouse.

Where were they all?

He ran back out of the vault and moved further into the island. He saw nothing. Frantically, he ran to its tallest tower, the one in the center of the trio of towers of the gatehouse. He burst onto the roof and gazed all around, across the island. There was not a soul on the magic island besides himself. His body trembled as he began to cry, falling to the ground.

Did you fail in your task?

The wizard looked up. The words echoed in his mind.

"Who is there?"

Who sent you, necromancer?

The wizard jumped to his feet. "Reveal him!" As his eyes turned, black apparitions appeared around him.

The Old One slapped the air, and the apparitions screamed as they dissipated. The wizard dove over the roof, but The Old One's giant clawed hands had grabbed him.

Who sent you, necromancer?

"No, I cannot tell you.

You have already failed in your task. Your punishment is assured. You do not need to add my punishment to your fate.

"Where are they?"

This is not the realm of Faylen. A mere illusion for its enemies to seek out and find. Shall I show you where you be?

"No, please don't."

Who sent you, necromancer? I shall not ask again.

THINGS OF NIGHT

The sun and snow elves had told them they'd return before dusk to enter into the final agreement with the Seven Empires of Man. But instead, a fairy elf flew down from the sky and told them the ancient elves had to "meet with the goblins and drows instead as their races favored the night as humans favored the day." The fairy elf flew away, and the men decided to set up camp where they waited rather than trek back to their section of the Atlantean ante-city.

Conversation was almost nonexistent as they consumed their dinner meal. King Aereth had no appetite but did sip a hot brew with the other royals of the Seven Empires, all seated together in a massive tent. More guards stood watch outside it than they would have had on Titan's Trail but they were in Atlantea. The men became uneasy and frightened as the howls and growls grew in the distance. The goblin and drow hordes that marched past them were not all that far away.

King Aereth and the Titan's Caravan men were

reminded of when they first set out on their journey through Titan's Trail when they were in the Lands Between. He recalled the cold valley of the Howling Mountains. The winds were fierce and freezing, and the men couldn't tell if it were the winds that howled or the mountains.

The howling in the distance was not the winds. They were goblins. How many, none could say, but enough to be an army many times the size any of the humans could assemble.

King Aereth recognized the ploy of the ancient elves. Deliberately sow fear among the humans so the next morning, they would agree to anything. His resolve strengthened against any alliance with such elves. But if the Elfin Questing Knight allies entered into an alliance with them, they might have no choice.

Men jumped as the howls of many dire wolves echoed, the chosen giant black beasts of the goblins in battle. The howls grew into a wild frenzy.

King Aereth stood calmly and said, "We should move about the men outside to reassure them."

"Agreed," Theor said as he stood.

"But have we reassured ourselves?" the wizardly king asked.

"We must act as if we are," Aereth answered.

The sun elves landed in their glowing globe of fire as they had done with the humans. But with the night, the vessel lit up the entire area along the shore revealing the massive numbers of goblins. Inarian and his knights exited and the vessel vanished. Though the air was plunged back into the night, the sun elves glowed like lanterns. The snow elves were set down on the ground by their icy cyclone of magic, and they glowed a white blue.

Goblins gathered in the formation of a half-circle, then multitudes of drows stepped from invisibility to make up a matching half-circle formation to greet the ancient elves. Laughter erupted as goblin and drow royals made their way to the sun and snow elfin lords. Blue-skinned drow and purple-skinned night drows, refined high goblins, and ferocious green goblins. The packs of dire wolves were held at bay with metal chains by the largest goblins amongst them.

Conversation went on for many hours, but the agreement was reached. The ancient elves had their alliance with the drow and goblin races signified by raising cups of drink in unison into the night and then drinking with much laughter and howling to follow. From invisibility, new fae joined them.

Many fae had watched the entire gathering from a

distance, whether standing from the shore or seated in the street or taverns overlooking it all. As Traveler stared at the gathering, it dawned on him. Shadow elves, shadow drows, and black goblins. The sub-races were indistinguishable to the eye because they were no longer truly different races anymore. All began as one race, and through whatever magic they engaged in over the centuries, these fae had become one again.

"You truly see it, don't you," the sun elf Inarian said to him. The sun elf suddenly appeared next to him. "We started as one, and we will be one again. What I propose for us has already occurred for them. They are our future, and we are the past. The union of all fae as when Pan-Earth created us."

"What dark magic or practices allowed them to become what they are?"

"No dark magic. We are not Oughtred and his accomplices. We practice magic, but there is nothing dark about it. A different kind of magic that transcends light and darkness. Power greater than magic itself."

"Greater than magic of light or dark magic?"

"The magic that created everything that exists. Magic of the cosmos. Greater than Atlantea even. With it, I could become as bright as the sun and destroy Atlantea."

"Your consistent talking tells me you are as fearful of

the over-magic of Atlantea as every other ancient fae and demon I have ever met."

"Demons, you say?"

"You genuinely are interested in that."

"I am. We will all one day be one, as we began."

"I would say, sun elf, that you are quite insane."

Inarian laughed out loud and almost barreled over and fell to the ground. What concerned Traveler was that as the sun elf finally fell to the ground laughing hysterically that bright yellow flames of light emitted from his mouth and nostrils.

Traveler grabbed his dog and ran. The dog transformed into a griffinoid form as Traveler flipped onto his back. Both man and beast rode as fast as they could away from the gathering.

The king had to get away. He had chosen a tavern of brownies to relax in and finally eat something, his first bite of anything for the day. He figured his men would not let him slip away—and he was right.

Pangolin seemed like a giant when he stepped in for a

moment. "Sire, I'll be outside the entrance should you need us," he said and walked back out.

As an establishment for sprites, it was made for halflings, not humans, elves, or any fae of their size. But he was happy to get away to be alone with his thoughts.

The time did not last long as Traveler joined him at his table. His dog curled up nearby, watching. The caravan master brought his simple meal and drink with him to the table, tossed a piece to his dog, who snatched the pheasant in mid-throw and swallowed it down.

"You would have loved the Atlantea I knew," Traveler said. "There were always the busybody ancient fae and the sky elves, but they kept to themselves, and everyone ignored them. People were about treasure-hunting and exploring Atlantea's lands and realms and trade and establishing business partnerships within and beyond the fabled kingdom. No violence. No dark magic. No danger. You might see dark fae but no more. They were like any other, doing the same things.

"When I first arrived, I had to get accustomed to the magic of the place. As you know already, it invigorates all who dwell here—stronger, healthier, happier. People forget all that troubles them. Such contentment with the place. That is why we humans were always warned because, like Faë-Land, time does pass the same as it does in our lands. You could spend a year here, go back to the Lands of Man and find out that decades or a century has passed. You may remain as you were or grow old yourself and die.

"Always there was that hint of danger alongside all the beauty and wonder and magic.

"What has happened then to this fabled kingdom?" King Aereth asked.

"I wish I knew, sire. I am trying to convince the drows of our caravan to remain for a bit longer. I don't know if I'll succeed, but I'll keep trying."

"I tried to speak to the elves of our caravan. We finally got an audience with them. Lyre, Taylon, and Shadu-mun. But it was for naught. It was as if they did not know me. The distress in their faces. It must be more than their royals who were vanished. What it could be...I have pondered all day and night and have not reasoned an answer."

"There is good news, though, sire. Lady Aylen and Gwyness have constructed the new city of Faylen."

"I am happy then."

"Our princess will soon find herself a queen if she isn't careful. Regardless, she and Gwyness will be good leaders for the city and the warrior mages they will train."

"Is this Faylen that important? If it were wiped from the earth by creatures of darkness."

"Creatures directed by others."

"Others, as residing in Atlantea at the moment."

"That is what our celestial elfin queen had told us."

"What keeps us here, Mr. Traveler? Is this question on why Atlantea is closing even of any concern to us anymore? We are faced with the aftermath of its closing. The Seven Empires wait here as if waiting for an impending death sentence. We came all this way for treasure. We will leave with that treasure and return to our lands, but what will follow after us there? That is the only question for me and the Seven Empires."

"Both questions are of equal importance, sire."

"What do you make of these sun elves and snow elves?"

"That is where I was before the dog, and I came to join you. I saw them."

"With the drow army and the goblins?"

"I believe this sun elfin royal—"

"Inarian is his name."

"I believe him to be mad."

"Mad?" King Aereth asked.

"I have seen it with the celestial elves. With the star

elves too. Removed from Pan-Earth for so long, away from the planet's soul. A fairy had told me that once. I believe her now. Away from the soul of our world, its animals and beasts of the air, land, and sea, insects and flora, people, and our own magic lands beyond Atlantea and within. They live in the emptiness of the dark heavens. They see their own wonders—stars, other worlds, other creatures beyond our imagination, but it is still the coldness and emptiness of a void so vast they could never see its end if such a border even exists. I believe that coldness becomes a madness within them—celestial elves, star elves, all of them. If the sun and snow elves have been out there for centuries longer than even the celestial elves who we all thought were the first to leave our world, then I dare not contemplate the state of their minds."

King Aereth touched his forehead in distress. "We are supposed to form an alliance with them in the morning. They ask us to hand over the ice continent of Borea to them. No human lives there, so all have agreed it is a small price to exchange for their protection, but you say there will be no protection."

"I saw shadow elves and shadow drows and shadow goblins, sire. To the human eye I could not tell which was which. I don't believe our Mr. Elman or any elf could either."

"What does it signify?"

"There were no shadow elves, shadow drows, and black goblins in the beginning. Drow were split from elfinkind because of their dabbling in dark magic. Something else, possibly as evil, certainly more powerful, caused this. Shadow elves are a new race, as are shadow drows and these shadow or black goblins. Whatever the cause, they are all equally involved."

"We should set a timetable. As you said, humans cannot remain here forever. We must pick a date certain to depart, whether our questions are answered or not. For me, my mind is consumed with preparing for war. I am so upset. Our journey to Atlantea was to secure wealth for our people. Expand and improve kingdoms, from the cities to the tiniest of villages. Am I really to return with all this wealth and tell them we may have to prepare for war with fae none have ever seen or thought long extinct from the time of the Titans? I am angry, Mr. Traveler, angry. I feel the Atlanteans have done this to us. They have called humans their friends. One does not do this to friends."

"Sire, you should tell them that?"

"Excuse me."

"Do just that. Lead the Seven Empires to the first Atlantean you find and make your case to them. You risk nothing in doing so and could gain much."

"You said they would never change their minds about closing the city."

"True, but maybe they would help in another way. Atlanteans are intelligent and merciful. Make your case."

"Yes, I will. I will tell the Empires that we will do just that before our meeting with the ancient elves. Maybe we will postpone the meeting as they did to us to meet with the goblins and dark drows."

King Aereth rose from his table. His distress gone. They had a new plan.

LADY IN THE LAKE

Mr. Traveler had convinced Lady Aylen and Gwyness not to keep the hidden magic vault of the libraries of Rivermouth in their new city of Faylen. But the princess brought in a few of the large books for the warrior mages-to-be. She waltzed into the hall where Nori the selkie had begun her classes. The youth had jumped up from the wooden desks and one-person pews.

"Can we study the kinds of creatures we'll encounter?" Ossarian asked as they all looked at the large, ancient volumes in Lady Aylen's arms.

"Creatures you may encounter. What are your lessons currently?" she asked.

"Elvish?" Raine replied with a displeased look.

"You speak elvish, Nori?"

The selkie leader nodded. "Since I was a little girl. It is one of many languages they will need to master."

"But when will we get to fight?" another of the students asked.

"Or do magic?" said another.

"Listen to your teacher," Lady Aylen said. "I certainly cannot teach you any elvish."

"Maiden Gwyness said your own studies have been progressing well," Nori said.

"If she says." To the class, she said, "You don't learn elvish merely to speak with elves. The language is magic. You are learning magic now."

"Thank you, Lady Aylen, but I cannot teach anymore here when they eagerly await to read about monsters," Nori said. "Perhaps in the books in your arms?"

One of the students cast a simple spell, and each one of them had a duplicate copy in front of them.

"The weakest of the undead creatures is the ghoul, the one on the page in front of you," Lady Aylen said, reading.

Traveler had joined the class and looked over the shoulders of half-elves seated at the rear. He walked up one of the aisles to Nori and Lady Aylen at the head.

"Mr. Traveler, welcome to the class," the princess said.

"Unlike the zombie, they are intelligent and

calculating," Traveler said, getting the class's attention. "They are extremely strong, and only special magic or physical force that can destroy their entire physical form at once can kill them. They can also turn another into a ghoul with physical contacts, such as with a scratch or bite. Ghouls serve dark masters and live to commit acts of evil."

"What about zombies?" a student asked.

"What of them?" Traveler asked.

"No pictures of them in the books."

"Don't you know what they look like?"

"Yes, but—"

"There's a young man in our caravan named Mr. Quillen. If you need a picture, he can draw it for you. If you can defeat a smart ghoul, why do you worry yourself with a dumb zombie? Just ensure they don't bite you, is all."

"These are in the ships outside Atlantea," a student said, showing Traveler his book.

"Draugrs are undead creatures of incredible strength and power. They are blackened, gaunt, frightened, walking corpses with the sickening stench of death and decay. They are intelligent and cunning like ghouls, but never forget they are warriors and, as such, wear armor and fight with hand weapons. They live to terrorize and kill the living. Like ghouls, they are attracted to graves or the dead. They can increase their size, like sprites, to become giants, solid enough to rumble the earth. They can also pass through walls and rock like an apparition."

The students looked at each other.

"They can kill with our weapons; however they prefer to crush victims to death in enlarged form, eat them, or even devour them whole. They possess the magic to drive living things insane, people or even animals in proximity to them. Further, the undead creatures are shape-shifters."

"Shape-shifters?" Ossarian asked. "I never heard that."

"Yes, grow to giants and shrink and shape-shift into another form to sneak away."
The class looked at each other.
"Finally, there is the creature far more powerful than the draugr and often controls them in numbers."

"The lich," Raine said.

"The undead wizard of dark magic. One who is a necromancer. They appear as decaying corpses, completely skeleton-like, or..." Traveler stopped.

"They look like King Oughtred of Xenhelm," Lady Aylen said.

"Liches are powerful wizards and, besides controlling armies of draugr, they can control hordes of the lesser undead creatures. Any questions, students?"

"That is the name," Lady Aylen said. "No more of this 'lost warriors.' You are the pupils of the new city of Faylen until you become full warrior mages."

"Mr. Traveler, can we discuss more of draugr being shape-shifters?" Ossarian said.

"When do we train to defeat these creatures?" the fae, Rya, asked. "Mr. Traveler, have you battled these creatures with your magic sword before?"

Before he could answer, they heard voices outside the hall calling out, getting everyone's attention. Lady Aylen grabbed her war tridents.

"Princess, put those away. We don't need to see you vanished," Traveler said.

He rushed out the hall with his dog. Lady Aylen and class followed them.

The white elfess had returned with The Old One.

For the first time, the white elfess looked old with

wrinkled skin. She walked slowly as if hard to exert herself in any way. While she seemed smaller in form, her guardian was taller, and his frightful pale clawed arms hung almost to the ground.

"Time grows short, young ones," she said to all, then looked up to Lady Aylen. "I found it."

"Found what?"

"You need to trust me. Once you obtain the object, decide where the new Faylen will be—Faë-Land or the Lands of Man. Decide quickly but go now."

"Why? What are you talking of?" Lady Aylen asked.

"Leave now while it is safe to do so. I had thought you had more time, but others know you are in Atlantea. They have necromancers everywhere searching for you."

"Necromancers, in Atlantea?" Gwyness asked.

"You know of the Cyclops City of Mímir-Spring where their magic nullifies the magic of all within, except its own cyclops mages. The new Faylen will have the same protective power for its kingdom. It is an object of incredible power that will also cloak your kingdom in its shield of magic, like the leshy Tree Shepherds did for your Titan's Caravan. But you must leave at once."

"But what is this object?" Lady Aylen asked.

"The Bident of Faylen. A dual representation of its

warrior slayers and magic seers of Faylen. A giant two-pronged weapon that you will place in the center of your city. It was stolen from the original Faylen by those they thought were allies. It was the beginning of the end of the city. You must take it back," the white elfess said.

"Go where?" Lady Aylen asked.

"The water realms of Atlantea," she answered.

"We should wait for Mr. Traveler," Gwyness said.

"Why? This is your task, not his. If he were here, and his shape-shifter, yes. But he is not, and you have your own shape-shifters."

"We can transform into wolves alone, nothing else," Ossarian said quickly.

"I did not say you were powerful shape-shifters as his. Your abilities are sufficient for what you must do. All has been arranged. You will seek out the one called the Lady of the Lake for your magic object.

"You have sailed across the Oceans of Faë-Land Omnis, resided in water kingdoms of the City of Kraken's Wake, and visited the Elfin City of White Waters. Where you go will not be unfamiliar."

"Is this a task for a few or many?" Lady Aylen asked.

"You are not going into battle. Again you are told you must remove all thoughts of aggression from your minds, even if you are provoked. If you are vanished from the lands of Atlantea at this time, all our plans might be defeated. Take only those with you that are even-tempered and can control their fears. The ability to swim and hold one's breath for extended periods wouldn't hurt either."

"Is this Lady of the Lake a friend or foe?" Lady Aylen asked.

"She's a monster," the white elfess replied.

"Swim to the bottom of the sea," the white elfess had told them, then she and The Old One walked out of the palace and disappeared.

Lady Aylen selected who would go among the Faylen students, assembling a small group. At their new port at the rear of the island, they boarded one of their yellow boats, remade magically from the long flat barges they had used before, and sailed. Once they crossed out of their realm, as instructed by the white elfess, she dove into the cold sea.

As a water elf, Lady Aylen could breathe as freely as on land. Gwyness, Raine, Ossarian, Brenn, and Elman followed her down in a straight line. A spell placed a bubble of air over the heads of Gwyness, Brenn, and Elman. Ossarian was a gifted diver and forgoed the spell. Two large gold-furred seals swam past them all to take the lead.

Soon they passed into another realm and were overcome initially by the intensity of aquatic life, mostly thick schools of fish of every color and size, swimming right up to them, even in their faces. Lady Aylen and Gwyness were reminded of the Great Forest. Here one moment was a fish the size of one's hand, and then the next was one so large its eye was three times the size of one's body.

Down they swam. Never did it grow darker, nor did the pressure of the depths change. It actually got brighter, and the pressure decreased the deeper they dove.

The two seals disappeared first through the barrier. When Lady Aylen passed through, she felt as if the entire world flipped from upside-down to right-side-up. She had dove up through the surface and came out in the exact duplicate of the Atlantean ante-city. Gwyness and the others popped up too, and they were equally disoriented for a moment. When Ossarian emerged and went to gulp in fresh air, all he got was water and began choking. What looked like air in this realm was also water. Lady Aylen realized it herself and didn't know what to do as she locked eyes with Gwyness.

Raine laughed and threw a ball of white magic at

Osarrian's head and then at Gwyness. Both had air bubbles for helmets. They walked out of the sea onto the shore to join Lady Aylen. Nori and Otari had already transformed from seal to human form, waiting on the shore of crystal sand.

The land city of Atlantea had hues of brown, yellow, and red; this underwater version was of blues, green, and orange. White and gold were universal to both.

"Is that not Titan's Gate?" Lady Aylen asked, confused.

Titan's Gate was the final marker of the ancient Titan's Trail to Atlantea, but that was above. However, the circular structure, a thick ring of stone, fifty or so feet in width, and three-fourths of the Gate above the water line towered in the distance.

"Lady Aylen, it is Titan's Gate too. But for the watery realms below," Nori said.

"We are told there is a third Titan's Gate high above in the distant sky for those fae entering Atlantea by the heavens," Otari added.

"Three Titan's Gates? Does that mean three Titan's Trails?" Lady Aylen asked.

"If it helps, your Titan's Trail is the true one," Nori said.

The Titan's Gate was also over a mile high. Vessels that

passed through it looked like giant fish or whales made of metal. As they looked above, the "sky," or the threshold back where they came, was thick with fish flying together very similar to flocks of birds. Though no perytons, as in the land version, the fish made the same birdsong. In the distance, they saw many mountain cliffs.

"Lady Aylen, we still have a little ways to swim," Nori said.

"Why swim when we can get a ride?" Raine said and summoned a group of giant fish slowly passing by.

"You can enchant the fauna of the sea," Lady Aylen remarked.

"You can too, Lady Aylen."

"No, not like other water elves. That ability was forsaken for my water elemental magic."

"Then you got the better trade," Raine said.

They rode the giant fish through the city. The selkies simply held one of the fins of the giant fish to be pulled along. Raine, Ossarian, Brenn, and Elman rode theirs like horses. Lady Aylen and Gwyness sat side-saddle on theirs.

Again, just as above, they passed a network of large white stone piers where the fish and whale vessels anchored. Lime green grass covered the seafloor, swaying in the currents. Beyond, an identical smaller version of

Titan's Bridge, which was the first official marker of Titan's Trail in the Lands of Man. At the other end of the bridge was the same open entrance of a castle wall of towering keeps.

"So strange to see a duplicate of the same Atlantea of land," Lady Aylen said. "Why not make it different?"

"The people are different," Mr. Elman said.

"Yes, I notice now," Lady Aylen said.

Mermaids, merman, merrows, sea centaurs, tritons, water elves, and an endless variety of water fae, such as fish men, frog men, toad men, sea kobold, water fairies, water gnomes. Sea lions, sea horses, dolphins, fished-tailed hippos, swimming griffins, and an endless variety of aquatic beasts.

"Mr. Traveler did say Atlantea had underwater docks for water fae, but I didn't know he also meant a duplicate city," Lady Aylen said.

"I wonder what the others are doing," Gwyness said. "We haven't seen them."

"Their time is occupied as us, but we may indeed leave when we finish this task."

"Leave without them?"

"Gwyness, we need to leave. I grow more uneasy with each day. Not the fabled kingdom as expected with a cloud of danger over us at all times. No, we need to go as soon as we can."

"Lady Aylen," Nori called out. "We'll lead. We know where we must go."

The selkies dropped away from the fish and for the first time, they all directly saw them transform into seals and swim to the merchant area of the ante-city. The rest left their giant fish steeds. Raine waved to the giant fish and seemed to be speaking to them with her mind. They followed Lady Aylen after the selkies.

Fae and animals in all shapes, colors, and aquatic races packed the shops along the streets within the ante-cities as the ones above. Here, too, were sorcerers, both male and female, glowing with magic and manifesting their power with their glowing, skin tattoos or jewelry, objects, staffs, or animal companions like a sea horse, eel, large fish, or swimming lizard.

"Impossible," Lady Aylen yelled out.

In the center of the merchant section sat a rotund bald fae in speckled garments of purple and yellows. He had four fingers and gills on either side of his neck.

"Do you work here and in the land Atlantea, or are you able to be in two places at the same time?"

The fae laughed as he stood. "No magic, elfess. You speak of my brother."

"Brother?"

"Yes, and my other brother offers our services at the Titan's Gate on the cloud city of the stars."

"Another brother?"

"Yes. You are the first party in a long time to visit more of the main elemental realms of Atlantea," he said. "How may I help you, good elfess?"

"Your brother on land talks in the exact same way and tone. Says the same words."

Lady Aylen was fascinated by the man, who chuckled. "Duplicate city, duplicate merchant man," she said.

"You seek a guide to the treasured lands then?"

"Yes, obviously. If your services are the same as your brother," Lady Aylen said.

"Which treasured land do you seek, or do you know?"

"The one of the Lady of the Lake," Nori replied.

The male fae lost his smile and laugh. "There? Whom told you of there?"

"It is where we were told to go. Is that a problem?"

"I would choose elsewhere. It is not the treasured land that is of issue. It is the path you must cross to get there. There is much unrest in Atlantea."

"There is in the Atlantea above too."

"Is there?" the fae asked. "My brothers and I don't speak as often as we should. Our unrest began with the arrival of ancient elves—elves of ice and the sun. Elves no fae or human has seen or heard of in centuries."

"I never expected to ever see you again in life."

So many mermaids, sea nymphs, sea centaurs, and tritons floated in front of the section of Atlantea's shore that they appeared as a thick black cloud from afar. When the Mermaid Queen Geneva of Kraken's Wake saw Lady Aylen and her party swimming to them, she was visibly shocked and swam to them.

"Why are you down here?" she asked.

"We had to acquire something that is only here in the water realms," Lady Aylen replied.

"You should return to the surface. Ancient elves have

arrived—"

"Yes, they have appeared above too," the princess said. "What is this gathering for?" she asked.

"To determine the treachery for ourselves. The ancient elves want the water elves to leave our alliance to join with the land and sky elves. We believe it is a prelude to war. The ancient elves will be here shortly. They have arrived!"

The mermaid moved faster than the humans and half-elves could see, except for Mr. Elman. The elves and selkies saw her streak away.

Above, he was called a snow elf, and below, his skin was whiter and more like crystal. The elf Foldruin, of the Snow Elfin Kingdom of Ice Niflheim, descended into the center of the floating fae with his own quartet of ice elfin knights. Lady Aylen noticed immediately that the snow elf saw and recognized her. He looked away, but she noticed the smirk on his face.

"We go," Lady Aylen said to her party and swam quickly away, leading them back to the merchant markets where their guides waited.

"Honored nymphs, mermaids, ichthyocentaurs, tritons, and all water fae of Atlantea, do not fear. We are at the dawn of a great alliance of all fae. For if we are successful when Atlantea re-opens its doors, we of Pan-

Earth will be able to join them as equal brethren and sisters," they heard Foldruin the ice elf pronounce.

The translucent fish men who had guided them to the realm refused to follow them in and quickly swam away into the darkness as they entered. A vertical portal of blackness. When they stepped through, no longer were they underwater. The bubbles of air around the air breathers among them vanished. They all stood upon a great plateau mountain with only the stars of space all around them. All of them walked to the glowing blue lake that made up the surface of the plateau with the small rim of land encircling it.

"Who approaches me?" a voice echoed around them.

"We are here for the Lady of the Lake," Lady Aylen answered.

"I am not the Lady of the Lake. I am one of many. We exist in the oceans, on land, in cities, and in high mountains in the clouds. We guard great things."

"Treasures," Lady Aylen said.

"No, we are not griffins of the good nor draugr of the evil. We do not keep treasures, but we do keep treasured things."

"We are here for the Bident of Faylen," the princess said.

"Who are you to be worthy to receive it?"

"I am the heir of the lost kingdom of Faylen."

"Then Lady Aylen Brytthony of the adopted human Avalonian Kingdom of Sirnegate, adopted daughter of King Beothor and Queen Meri, of the lost elfin Kingdom of Rivermouth under the mage mother Queen Faylen; you are worthy to receive it."

A figure rose from the center of the lake. Draped in a white shroud, the lady of the lake rose as a giant two-pronged staff of gold rose with her. She appeared human as she moved to where they stood.

"Receive," she said.

The staff flew from the lake to Lady Aylen. The princess thought she would simply catch the object in her hand. The moment it touched her skin, she fell back as its length, width, and weight rapidly increased. The others ran to her aid, and they all struggled to keep the giant bident from tumbling off the plateau, taking them with it.

The lady of the lake continued to rise. The white shawl lay over her white robe. She pulled back her shawl with her two human hands. The air echoed with mesmerizing humming.

"May I help you, worthy one?" she sneered.

There were mermaids with giant fish tails in place of legs. There were cecealia, often called mermaid octopi, who had eight tentacles instead of legs. The Lady of the Lake, this lake, was a decaelia but not just with the ten tentacles of a squid. She was unlike any other for, in place of human hair, many squirming tentacles dangled from her skull.

"You cannot harm us," Lady Aylen said.

"Who sent you?" the decaelia asked.

The bident had grown so large that it was about to tip over the plateau. They could not hold it for much longer.

"May I help you, worthy ones, to die?"

Her two squid-like tentacles shot out to strike them. Lady Aylen pushed the others away and jumped over the tentacles.

"You cannot harm us!" Lady Aylen yelled. "No!"

The princess watched the bident tumble over the edge, falling to the depths below to the pained faces of her group.

Laughing, then the humming again.

"Whoever sent you sent you to die," the creature said.

"You strike at us, and you will be gone!" Lady Aylen yelled.

The tentacle hit her faster than the blink of an eye. Lady Aylen lay on the patch of ground, stunned, coughing blood. The tentacle that had smashed her rose up into the air, ready to strike again.

Ossarrian yelled out as he transformed into a giant wolf and ran to Aylen's aid. He was snatched by another tentacle and yanked into the lake. The others frantically and desperately charged the decaelia. The selkies turned into ferocious seals, and Raine threw magic daggers at the creature. They all met the same fate as tentacles grabbed and pulled them into the water.

"Is this the object you sought?"

The creature raised another golden bident with the tentacles of her head.

"This is a kingdom of magic. But in this realm, my realm, I can do anything. The over-magic of the Atlantea has no power here."

Good!

The Old One appeared, rising up from the darkness to step onto the plateau. So did the white elfess.

"I was the one who sent them, Gorgana. The trap was for you, not them," Anelle said. She looked at a broken

Aylen. "I am sorry, but this was the only way for us to know. You have your answers."

The white elfess caught the tentacles that struck at her with lightning speed. Anelle screamed and yanked the tentacle from the decaelia's body.

"Queen Anelle, you will never trouble me again!" the Lady of the Lake yelled.

Celestial fire erupted from the palms of white elfess, and the decaelia's many tentacles erupted in black flames. The white elfess was ensnared by dozens of the burning tentacles and soon caught fire herself. The Old One was upon the decaelia and ripped her upper torso from the rest of her body.

The realm began to shatter. The screaming Lady of the Lake vanished. The burning body of Queen Anelle. The Old One's body began to disintegrate as it too vanished. Three points of light closed in the ocean above.

Lady Aylen lay floating on top of the sea. Gwyness and Brenna emerged from the surface. The selkies and the lost warriors appeared too.

"Look," Mr. Elman said.

The golden bident floated to the surface—the true one, not the false one that fell from the plateau. They grabbed it and all of them hung on in a watery realm of blackness. The only source of light was the glowing Bident of Faylen.

Traveler dove into the waters to Atlantea Aquatic. His dog transformed into a version with a giant fish tail for his lower torso. Man and beast reached the mirror city as quickly as possible; both had visited it many times in the past. A bubble appeared around both their heads as they passed through the threshold, and their center of gravity reversed.

They swam through one lake into another realm to dive into another lake realm. The way was solitary but quicker to the destination. The last lake they needed to pass was vertical, and they stopped.

Floating in the water at the threshold of the lake portal were three cecaelia of blue-green skin. Traveler recognized their warrioress clan.

"You seek passage into the realm of the Lady of the Lake, human?"

"I do."

"We cannot allow you passage."

"Why?"

"Our mistress commands so."

"Have my friends entered her realm?"

"The elves, selkies, fae, and the human female? Yes, they are there."

"Then I must join them."

"We heard of a fable, human, that you were so brilliantly skilled that you were able to best even an elf in battle with the blade."

"It is a good fable."

"I believe the fable to be false."

"We will never know here in Atlantea."

"Do not worry about being vanished from its realms, human. We are in the domain of the Lady of the Lake. The magic of the Atlanteans has no power here."

"Their magic has power in all the realms of Atlantea."

"No longer, human. I will show you."

The mermaid octopus held a sword in one of her tentacles.

"I am a land dweller—"

"Give our magic just a moment."

All the water in the realm drained up to the sky. Only the vertical lake remained. The main mermaid octopus crawled to him as her two sisters sat on the ground to watch.

"No one can say that we cecaelia had an unfair advantage. Shall we play, human?"

"You will not trick me, witch."

"I am no witch, human. I have killed many fae with the blade, elves among them. If you can best them, then I must best you. Draw your weapon."

"I will not."

Traveler motioned his dog, now on all fours but with spiky quills like a sea porcupine, growled as it stepped back.

"Well trained," she said of the dog.

Her blade struck fast but his sword caught the thrust that would have slit his neck open had it landed.

"Impossible!" the mermaid octopus yelled.

She swung again. A translucent flame enveloped Traveler's blade as he cut her blade of obsidian metal in half. She slapped him with two of her tentacles. He rolled onto the ground but got to his feet quickly. Her two sisters threw her another sword.

The cecaelia cackled. "The stories are true, and I am a witch!" Her one sword became eight. Her human hands were free, but every tentacle swung a sword.

His dog dodged the arrows from more cecaelia from

above as it transformed.

The cecaelia witch screamed, expecting his eardrums to shatter, but no effect. Her movements were a dizzying flash of tentacles and swords in front of her.

"No land fae or human of two hands can best a cecaelia who has ten!" Swords also appeared in her two human hands.

"Your words are so true."

He threw his sword at her. She swung all eight of her swords with her tentacles at it. The scream exploded in the realm. Her swords and tentacles were severed by the spinning sword of Titan metal. It landed in her chest, and her entire body erupted in flames.

The dog transformed into a land kraken and grew quickly. Though not as colossal as its sea-faring cousin, its massive tentacles snatched and crushed every attacking cecaelia in the realm. So wild and powerful its frenzied attack was that not even the mermaid octopi could dodge the shape-shifter's grayish tentacles.

The witch was right. The over-magic of Atlantea to prevent any violence did not exist in the realm. Atlantea's magic that protected its kingdom and territories, held together and connected all its realms and punished any who engaged in violence within had lasted for millennia. Races that did care for each other like fairies and giants, or races that hated each other and were in constant war beyond like elves and goblins, and those that lived to destroy each other like sorcerers of light and witches and warlocks, all co-existed within Atlantea because of that over-magic. Atlanteans did not see races or clans or fae of light versus dark fae; they saw behaviors and actions. The Atlantean's code had tempered all the races of Pan-Earth. If they wished to enter the fabled kingdom, their wars and hatreds on the outside could never be so unbridled as they would meet their blood enemies within Atlantea's walls and would have to behave. But without Atlantea's magic to enforce this code, what would the races within do if this new knowledge was known? Would they continue to co-exist without incident, or would Atlantea erupt in violence not seen since their ancient war with the Titans?

Traveler ran as fast as he could and dove into the vertical lake. He had to warn them. The witch said the magic was gone from this realm, but if here, why not elsewhere? Lady Aylen and the others were walking into a trap known as the Lady of the Lake.

WHEN MAGIC
TURNS TO DUST

WHERE'S OUGHTRED?

ady Aylen opened her eyes. From the ceiling, she recognized that she was in her room in Faylen. From the corner of her eye, she noticed him and turned her head.

Traveler got on a knee at the side of the bed. "You awake, princess?"

"Don't say like sleeping beauty."

"If you say."

"How long was I asleep?"

"Not too long. A few hours, but you are recovering."

"So, I thank you again for your healing skills."

"Not me this time. In a realm of magic, one can cheat or find the proper spell from the local merchant wizard."

"How bad was it?"

"Why does it matter? You're healed. It's in the past

and the creature will never be able to do it again."

"They told you."

"Yes. They carried you here to your room."

"What evil creature was that? Aren't ladies of the lake supposed to be benevolent beings?"

"In the Lands of Man, they are. Often wingless fairies from ancient fae times."

"What was this one? She was one of those squid mermaids. But she also had tentacles for hair."

"She must have been an ancient decaelia of extreme power and magic."

"Did not help her against The Old One?"

"No, it did not."

"They are dead?"

"From what your students told me, yes."

"She did save us at the end. Both of them did. We will honor their sacrifice."

"Princess, what did she say to you there?"

"That...we had all the answers. That she was the one who set the trap for that creature. She knew it and called her Gorgana. What does it all mean?"

"What was this object she sent you to fetch?"

"The original Bident of Faylen. She said the object was magic and did the same as the magic of Cyclops City of Mímir-Spring."

"Nullifies the magic of all within, except its own cyclops mages."

"Yes, and we would have the same protective power for our kingdom. It would cloak our kingdom in its shield of magic. What answers did she mean?"

"The creature said that the over-magic of Atlantea had no power in her realm."

"Yes."

"They killed each other, princess, before they vanished."

"Yes."

"Princess, the magic of Atlantea permeates every realm within it. I must leave and make inquiries. If one ancient face can harm or even kill before being vanished, then we are all truly in danger, every human and fae in the fabled kingdom. I must find the Atlanteans."

"I can come, too." The moment Lady Aylen sat and turned her body to stand up, she clenched her teeth and closed her eyes tightly. Her hands on the bed were also clenched. Never had she felt pain of such magnitude. She felt Traveler's hand on her shoulder and opened her teary eyes.

"You, princess, are going nowhere." He turned to the door. "Brenn!"

Another of the female half-elves opened the door and rushed in. Another followed.

"I need you all to carry Lady Aylen to the water outside, and that is where she will remain. If you need a water elf to heal fastest, you keep her in water."

"I can walk on my own," Lady Aylen said.

"No, you can't. Let your female comrades help their friend."

Brenn and the other female half-elves entered the room.

"She is to be placed in the water surrounding the city and not be allowed on land for any reason," Traveler said.

"Mr. Traveler, the first Faylen was destroyed, and I will not let that happen to the second," she said.

"Princess, any more destruction will wait during your rest."

"Mr. Traveler, you did not tell us that the other Atlantea of the water realms was a mirror copy of ours up here."

Traveler directed the half-elves to pick the princess up from the bed.

"Princess, I wanted it to be a surprise because I know how much you like surprises."

"I don't want to stay in water like a fish and do nothing."

"You will hardly be doing nothing, Lady Aylen. The bad news is that your entire upper torso was crushed by the tentacles of a decaelia more powerful than any we have ever encountered. The good news is when you recover, your upper torso will be stronger than it ever was."

"Able to withstand the crushing tentacles of a decaelia twice that creature's size, perhaps three times, or four times."

Traveler moved out of the way as the half-elves carried her through the door. "Yes, princess. Four times or even more."

"Oh, there's one more thing, Mr. Traveler. That's why I asked about the water Atlantea below. I saw him."

"Who?"

"The ice elf?"

"They call themselves snow elves."

"There, they call themselves ice elves, and they look

like ice. He knew me. I'm certain of it. He saw me and grinned a little. He tried to hide it, but I saw that he knew me."

"You alone?"

"I think so. I was looking right into his eyes. He was floating in the center of a massive crowd of water fae. They are doing the same thing there as here. This great alliance of theirs."

"Thank you, princess. You have revealed volumes to me."

The drow sorceress strolled through the courtyard and saw the family half-elves carry Lady Aylen to the largest of the fountains of the palace. Dr'amal found the sight amusing but continued in.

"Leaving us, Dr'amal?"

The drowess recognized Gwyness's voice but stopped because she did not know how the human was able to approach her so stealthily.

"I go to see my father," Dr'amal replied.

"Have you seen and heard all that you needed?"

Dr'amal stopped to look at the maiden. "I see you are wearing your amulet above your clothes. Should it not be kept hidden from view?"

"It is."

The image of Gwyness evaporated.

Dr'amal could sense the real human female ahead, waiting at the arched entrance to the gatehouse and outside the palace.

"An illusion spell," Dr'amal said as she approached the real Gwyness. "You have actually impressed this drow illusionist."

"I must practice."

"You did fool me, so it is working whatever you are doing."

"I asked if you had seen and heard all you needed."

"And I answered."

"Why not do as Lady Aylen asked and stay with us just to guide us for a time?"

"I would say you could fill that role."

"I am a novice stumbling around in the dark with occasional success. I am not a sorceress."

"What happened to you and her, the others?"

"We were in a battle."

"Battle? Here, in Atlantea?"

Both women stepped aside as Nori and Otari led a large party of selkies into the palace—adults and children.

"More students for the new city," Dr'amal said. "The selkies are teachers."

"Instructors in languages and academics but not the magic arts."

"Gwyness, I am not a teacher. I am quite bad at it because I have no patience. If my drow sorceress instructor were here, she would tell you. I was also a bad student, and I'd be a worse teacher. Surely, you can find better."

Dr'amal looked out through the gatehouse chamber to the front of the palace. They both recognized the same celestial king who Queen Anelle had referred to as her "dear son."

With skin like hardened glass of a slight blue tone, the celestial elf king watched them in his royal battle dress. He had the same crown upon his head as they had seen him with at the Feast, but that was all. He came with no others.

Gwyness met him at the entrance with no fear. Dr'amal stayed close to her side.

"Is it true?" he asked. "My mother is dead."

"She was vanished by Atlantea's magic," Gwyness replied. "Where would she have been transported?"

"She is dead. All that arrived on our celestial city were ashes and melted jewelry. Her guardian?"

"Dead."

"Fortunate. Without her, who can say what he would have done? He never liked me. Might have killed me out of spite. Who killed her?"

Before Gwyness could answer, the celestial son said, "I should thank them."

The maiden glared at him.

"She disobeyed our house, and she got the death she deserved. I would say you have lost mighty guardians yourselves today," he said, noticing something behind them.

"I do not think so." Traveler stepped from the entrance to join them with his dog in a blackened vicious form.

"The human who can kill elves."

"I dealt with your kind at Mímir-Spring. Should I deal with you too?"

"You could try."

"You know of the fate of your mother. Now you can go. You likely were among the ones who tried to murder her before."

"As I said, it is fortunate her guardian did not survive. He might have said the same. Though I had nothing to do with it."

"Why are you here?" Gwyness asked.

"I take my leave. I only wanted you to know that I know where your city of Rivermouth is. If I know, others do too."

"I am sure," Traveler said.

"Sure of what?" the celestial elf asked.

"Celestial elves are more detestable than star elves. Your mother was the sole exception."

"If you only knew all that my mother did in her many centuries, you would not praise her so freely."

"What kind of royal would even entertain speaking ill of his own blood family. No human house. Even goblins would not," Traveler said.

"We celestials do not care about the customs and morals of this world. We have our own."

"You have none."

"You know nothing, human. She was weak. Her

guardian was weak for siding with you. Looking at your white palace, your elves, humans, and in-breeds, and a pack of selkies, you have some ways to go before you become what the original Rivermouth was. And they were wiped from the earth. Do not listen to lies from my late mother. The mage queen Faylen was a lazy, weak tart. She alone brought about the demise of her kingdom."

"Why do you try so hard to anger us?" Traveler asked. "No one will strike you or do anything other than stare at you with amusement and contempt. Why did you really come here? You didn't need Maiden Gwyness to tell you your mother was dead. You knew. You didn't need to tell us you knew where the new Faylen was. Your mother told us your house knew."

"You humans are far too smart for me. I'll leave before I embarrass myself more. I am an accomplished swordsman myself, human. Perhaps, we will meet in your lands, and we can see for all who is the better."

"Doubtful. I expect you'll be dead long before then," Traveler said.

"An elf-killer and an oracle. A human of many talents. I will tell King Oughtred hello for you."

"You need not bother. I'd like to do so myself, in person. Where is your master Oughtred anyway?"

"He is not my master. You know nothing." The

celestial elfin king laughed to himself. Up he went, magically flying into the sky. He reached high above and stepped through a portal that appeared and disappeared.

Traveler looked around. "He was here for a reason."

"You believe he did something?" Dr'amal asked.

"What do you think he did?" Gwyness asked.

"To be safe, inspect every room, every inch of the city," Traveler said. "He was truthful about one thing. We no longer have the protection of the white elfess or The Old One anymore."

The latter is not true.

"Are they injured? Should I take some of the Cut-Throats to this Faylen city of theirs?" Pangolin asked.

The king could see the sparkle of the berserker's inner rage in their master-at-arms' eyes. Traveler had given him instructions as telling the king of ferrying a gravely wounded Lady Aylen and her pupils to the hidden realm of the new city of Faylen. He assured the king that the princess would recover.

"Mr. Traveler would have said so if he needed our aid.

He told us we should remain here with the Seven Empires," King Aereth said.

"The celestial elfin queen is dead. Her giant is dead. She was a powerful celestial elf. He was more powerful."

"Mr. Pangolin, you ask questions I have no answers for. Mr. Traveler will tell us. Or Lady Aylen will tell us, knowing her. For now, we wait."

"Sire. Nothing good will come from this. You know it as well as I do."

"We must play our noble roles and graciously attend the parley of humans, elves, drows, and goblins as the guests of the sun and snow elves."

"We will be ready, sire."

"We have only to listen, Mr. Pangolin."

"Listen. I have been engaged in many a battle that began with talking and listening. One side not liking what the other side said."

"We must remain calm at all times and let others get themselves taken away from the fabled kingdom forever."

"The kingdom has not been very fabled these days, sire," Nirgund added.

The men waited in their own royal tent. One side open so they could keep a close watch on the other royal tents of the Seven Empires, all waiting for the great parley to begin again. Hobbs sat quietly in his chair, smoking his pipe, something he had not had a chance to do in a while. Pangolin paced the ground. Nirgund sat on the ground playing with his reptilian hounds to keep them occupied, most of them lying next to him.

Outside the tent, I-wulf stood guard with other Cut-Throats. None had their weapons, but all were in armor, as were every human of the Seven Empires. For the berserkers being without one's weapon was the same as being naked.

When it began, it was its own form of violence. Representatives of the Seven Empires yelled one after another making their case loudly in favor or against the great alliance proposal of the ancient elves. None opposed an alliance with the elves, some were open to one with the drows, but most were strongly against any alliance with the goblins.

King Aereth rose from his seat and stepped from the tent; Hobbs and Pangolin followed behind him. The king scanned the vast gathering of humans in a huge circle. But he was not looking at the humans; his eyes searched for other races. He saw a few cloaked figures, but he could not see any of them clearly. He thought it odd that there were no birds, perytons, or other beasts in the sky as they had been accustomed to in Atlantea. For as loud as the debate was on the shores of the ante-city, the king felt a creeping loneliness for all the humans present.

Traveler had left the new city of Faylen for the cities of Atlantea. Something told him where to go as if he were enchanted by a nymph or mermaid from afar. But it was neither; it was The Old One.

The fear within him was not at the prospect of meeting the giant again, for the first time freed of any obligation or direction of his queen. He had to keep the knowledge of what he had learned buried deep. There were fae said to be able to read one's thoughts from afar, but even a simple spell from a novice wizard could defeat his resolve with the words: "Tell me anything you don't want anyone to know." The knowledge could destroy Atlantea if any of its fae learned of it. You can kill within the fabled kingdom, and all that will now happen is that you will be whisked away after the deed. Compared to that, even The Old One was of no importance.

His dog growled at something. As Traveler turned his head, he immediately saw the black-robed giant in the distance. Though there were many fae in the streets, the Old One stood out. Neither his size nor his dress made him unique in such a city. The nature of who he was made him unique. Traveler wondered if even the power of a true spell-talker had any power in Atlantea. One fae had retained some power. Why not another?

Traveler didn't have to see The Old One's face behind his helmet to know he was watched. He approached the creature while his dog barely contained his frenzy. Traveler had to think "happy thoughts" to reassure his animal companion.

"I must completely and sincerely thank you and your late queen for intervening on our behalf," Traveler said.

We have invested much in this path, and you. We will see it to the end. The ancient one's voice sounded in his head.

"So certain we'd be successful in our quest to Atlantea?"

Was there any doubt in your mind?

"We could have been killed many times, including from a creature more powerful than even you—a landvættir."

I have encountered the beasts, though not as gargantuan.

"You did not think to warn us."

The question is irrelevant since I knew we'd be standing across from one another as we are.

"You knew we would make it. Through the Great Forest. Survive the landvættir. Survive the siren storm."

You have made the journey more times than most fae caravan masters with success. Your feigned surprise at your achievement bores me.

"Then say what you wish. Is this the last time we meet?"

It is our third last time but not for the reasons you believe. I was vanished too but I will always remain in Atlantea for my last days since here I was born.

"Atlantean magic could not foresee a being that was born in its own lands."

You shall return to your lands, alive or dead, as I promised my queen. A thousand years will pass, and neither one of us will exist anymore—only our descendants.

"Yes, you were not always the being you are."

Will you assist your elfess in her quest?

"I will assist her with the rebirth of Faylen if she wishes it and if that is what you mean."

The rebirth may begin sooner than either of you believe. Was it your words that sent her followers away?

"It was. I thought it wise at the time with the dangers

of the Great Forest."

Very unwise. We made the decision for you and sent them here to await your arrival. We make right our wrongs, human. That is what a royal does. Here.

The key flew from the creature's clawed hand. It was made of corroded black, pocked metal.

It contains a magic bag of tricks.

"For what?"

There will be no answer to your question. You have the key. If the barrier to Atlantea is to be breached by any outside forces, then the package will be of value. But take care. Only those within the barrier of Atlantea could survive.

"What are you telling me, Old One? Atlantea is in danger."

My queen told you young ones, and you saw for yourselves. You have all your answers.

"Yes, I believe we do. But is there more? Why not say all rather than leave me guessing?"

It may not occur, so discussion of it is pointless. You will know.

"How will I know? What will I see?"

If it happens, you will be the only one who will know

besides the Atlanteans.

The Old One turned to walk away without another word.

"Old One, what of the draugr outside the Void Between? Can they breach the barrier?"

You focus much on the obvious but not the most significant. The two are not the same. Heed my words carefully, human, and safeguard that key. My queen and I have done all that we can. You young ones will have to do the remainder.

"Why not remain with us? Your queen's son visited us at the new city."

I know and do not care. He is and always has, along with allies, been insignificant compared to what comes.

"Help the Atlanteans, if that is what's needed. You are probably the most powerful sorcerer in Atlantea."

The ancient giant cackled. Flattery will not sway me, young one. Atlanteans will not listen. They are arrogant in their invincibility as the elfess queen mage of Rivermouth. No one is invincible. The moment you believe so is when your end rises from the ground and seeks you out.

Traveler felt desperate. "We are not invincible either. If not help, what will you do?" It was an ironic situation to want a spell-talker to talk, whose mouth was welded shut to keep it from using its tongue. A creature who could kill with a spoken word.

Sleep and never wake again.

The Old One was a giant but managed to fade into the crowd of fae and animals around him and vanish.

When Lady Aylen opened her eyes, she had forgotten she was resting at the bottom of a pool. The selkies had fashioned a bed for her with sheets made of fiber so like silk that she still did not believe they were strands of white kelp. Her eyes stared not at a ceiling or the top of a pool but the smiling faces of baby seals. Lady Aylen frowned.

The seals swam away. They dove out of the pool to transform into giggling little children. Soon after, the princess rose to the surface and moved to the edge of the pool. A distressed Nori ran to her.

"Lady Aylen, the children, did they disturb you?"

"Not at all. I am myself again. Mr. Traveler was right. All I needed was to be submerged in water for a time."

"Are you healed?"

Lady Aylen slapped the sides of her chest. "You would never know I was crushed by some squid mermaid creature. These magical lands, so many creatures, so much violence. Am I not a friendly water elf, Nori?"

Nori laughed. "Yes, m'lady, you are. Should I get Maiden Gwyness?"

"I'll find her. Tell me about you. Are you all settled into your rooms?"

"Yes, we are. My husband had taken charge of the docks and finishing its construction. The rest of my clan is working well with the students. The children are...playing."

"The original Faylen had water elves and water elementals."

"I do not believe undines will ever join our new city."

"I wonder if it were they who first betrayed Faylen."

"We do not know and might never know. But what we do know is they are in league with the current enemies of the city."

"Since I am a new elf and new to the magic lands, tell me the meaning yourself in the difference in the words of our warriors to be. Warrior clerics and warrior mages."

"Lady Aylen, elves, especially the older and ancient clans, are very religious. Clerics are the religious mages of their clans. Mages may or may not be, and it's the term most often used by younger elves and fae. The original Faylen, or Rivermouth as called by humans, was ultimately a religious city as they saw their faith as another weapon against the particular dark creatures and forces they fought."

"Never thought much about it myself, to be honest."

"I would recommend you keep the old traditions and cultivate them. Ancient fairies, cyclopes, tree people, elves and humans are not the only races with religious clans."

"There was only darkness, then there was Pan-Earth and all the races of fae, then humans and the rest."

"Yes. My own mother used to tell us children that we were created to be the light within that endless dark void."

"And that darkness is always trying to destroy us all to return to the time-before. Why would elementals ally with Oughtred?"

"He is allied with celestial elves. With that comes the alliance with undines and sylphs."

"Are there different clans among them like elves and drows? The moon elves were once part of the sky elves but chose to leave to join land elves. If we could only find water elementals who reject this alliance with Oughtred."

"Lady Aylen, I do not wish to discourage you, but the elementals are unified in their own races. If there were separate clans within each in the ancient past, like all other fae, they left that all behind."

"Do we need elementals? I cannot be the only one."

"True, but we do not need to solve all our problems today."

Lady Aylen jumped from the pool onto the marble ground. "That is a relief. What do you make of our encounter with the Lady of the Lake creature?"

"The magic of Atlantea is not as absolute as we had thought. If one can be killed before being vanished, then there are many within the kingdom who would believe that to be a fair trade."

"Yes, that is what I fear too."

"But we should not arm our people. The temptation would be too great."

"Are more of your people coming?"

"The other clans will not be joining us."

"Why?" Lady Aylen asked with concern.

"They are afraid. Much uncertainty grips the cities throughout Atlantea. My clan came here to establish relationships with those who have resided here for many,

many years, but with that possibility gone with Atlantea's closing, they plan to leave. No selkie clan would be cut off from its people or lands for ten centuries."

"Nor would I accept that if I were they, or you. Then we make do with who we have."

"You will be pleased to know that the Bident of Faylen is in place."

Lady Aylen looked up. The magic two-pronged staff rose from the tallest center tower of the gatehouse. Lady Aylen smiled as she could see with her own eyes the barely visible barrier of magic domed over their island city.

"I did not know we had a sorcerer of our own," Nori said, looking past the princess.

"Who?" Lady Aylen asked.

The man Frog-Dor appeared behind them.

"Mr. Frog-Dor. Where did you come from?"

"Mr. Traveler wanted me here to watch over the city." He looked up at the bident. "Security for Faylen will no longer be the concern that it was for us. No one can enter unless we allow them in."

In the king's experience, rumors could be both good and bad. But most often, they could be a terrible thing, especially to create panic. King Aereth watched the men of the Seven Empires spread the latest one like wildfire.

"The water fae are attempting to shut out all land and sky fae and humans from Atlantea!"

The king saw Theor and other leaders look at him. King Aereth shook his head.

"What are we to make of it, sire?" Hobbs said.

"Mr. Pangolin, have your Cut-Throats grab those men and bring them here. Not only does this latest rumor make no sense, it is certainly untrue and deliberately false."

"Let me take on the task, sire." I-wulf gestured to other Cut-Throats, and they ran to the warrior running from group to group with the rumor. They tackled the unsuspecting man.

"The sun and snow elves' doing, sire?" Pangolin asked.

"I think so too, Mr. Pangolin."

"What power do these sun and snow elves have? Do any of us know?" Pangolin asked.

"Sun elves are a kind of elemental," the wizardly king said from nearby. "Their power is not from fire, but far greater—the flames of the sun. They can shoot beams of light from their hands or flames of sun fire. Snow elves are cousins to wind elves, but their gusts of wind are icy cold and can freeze anything, living or object, to solid ice. Neither are to be trifled with."

"I'm not interested in trifling with them. I want to know if I can kill them if the need arises," Pangolin said.

"The magic of Atlantea aside, preventing violence, we would be no match for them," the human wizard said.

"The knowledge is to know, not to act upon it, of course," Pangolin said.

"Our Mr. Pangolin would be their match," Nirgund said. "His armor and weapon have the magic shell of an earth elemental."

"Our conversation is pointless. Thankfully the only battle between us will be of words," the human wizard king said.

Traveler watched the gathering of humans from afar in crowds of onlooking fae. His dog stood beside him as a hulking wolf-dog-headed humanoid. The caravan master had draped a cloak around him. Crowds were watching the humans and gossiping.

"Hello, Dr'amal," Traveler said without ever turning his head.

The drow sorceress was at his other side. "How long ago did you see me?"

"I lived with drows, if you remember. You've left Faylen."

"I didn't know Frog-Dor was in the palace."

"Is that a problem?"

"If you have a real sorcerer, what do you need me for? Besides, are you trying to get me in trouble with my father?"

"I have no idea what you are talking about."

"You do, but that's not why I had to find you."

"Then what do you have to tell me?"

"You can imagine that seers are in high demand within Atlantea at the moment."

"Seers can see possible future, not always the real future."

"I am glad you know that distinction, but most fae and humans do not. But knowing possibilities of the future is still an advantage to knowing nothing of what lies ahead."

"The elfin rogue I killed, a wicked noble, had a wizard

seer. After his master was dead, I told the seer that his magic could not be very impressive if his master lay dead on the floor. He told me he did see me killing his master in a vision, but he and his master both agreed it was laughable."

"Nice fable. You have met your share of wicked elves. More so than the average drow."

"Yet I don't hate all of elfinkind as drows do."

"You know why and seers do have value, or they would not be sought after."

"One takes whatever comes."

"A philosopher human, too. My father had me try to hire one for us."

"And?"

"I cannot find even one. How can one not find a seer in all the lands and realms of the fabled kingdom? You lived here. Is this normal for Atlantea?"

"I have some contacts. I'll look for you."

"For us or for you?"

"I told you my view of seers, so it would be for you."

"In exchange for what favor?"

"Dr'amal, you know what I want. It hasn't changed.

Stay in Atlantea until we are all ready to leave."

"Sail off together as one happy alliance?"

"Haven't you heard? There's going to be a great alliance of humans, elves, drows, and goblins."

The drowess scoffed and stormed off.

"I'll find you when I hire one."

He did not think it wise to tell her that all the kingdom's oracles left the very day they arrived in Atlantea.

Estus, the caravan's weapons master, was back in their special pocket-realm with its magic storehouse full of weapons and armor. He made it a point to visit the realm every day or so. Like any weapons master, he loved the look, feel and smell of weapons and always found one to polish.

He led Pangolin down the spiral staircase to the open storehouse. In formation was their army of armor golems.

"What did you have to show me?" Pangolin asked as they stepped down onto the stone floor.

Estus simply raised his arm, and automatons stepped forward in formation and stopped.

"When we first arrived in Atlantea, I tried but never could I get them to move. Mr. Traveler said it was the magic of Atlantea that prevented it as they are inherently weapons of violence. But today, I can command them to move as easily as when on the Trail."

Pangolin thought for a moment. "Was any other in our armory besides you or the men?"

"There were those halfling sprites who dressed me for the Feast we attended, but that was it. I hardly believe they'd cast some spell to allow me to animate the golems. They had no interest in any of our weapons or them. They were interested in what armor and weapons would look best on me."

"I will discuss with Mr. Traveler."

"I hope it's not a bad sign of some kind."

"Do you still have the magic gauntlets?"

"With the magic shields to extend out? Of course."

"Secretly, fit the men with them. A few at a time. Have the men say nothing to anyone, though, not even each other."

"Mr. Pangolin, you are worrying me. We are in Atlantea. We are supposed to be safe from all danger."

"We are safe, but do it nonetheless."

Traveler visited the wizards' shop in one of the remote areas of the city. He had last been there many years ago, but the ownership had changed. Rarely were establishments of business sold. They stayed within families forever, but even in magical lands fae died who had no children or heirs. He sought out a looking glass and made his request to the shop's new owner.

As with many shops in the kingdom they often contained portals to other realms. Traveler paid for the use of the wizard shopkeeper's sole looking glass. The shop had a vast interior filled with endless shelves of objects, potions, trinkets, and books. Traveler pulled back a red curtain on the wall to open a simple, weathered door. The new realm was an octagonal chamber with majestic rugs covering the walls and a long oval glass mirror hung above a statued hand rising from the ground as if to catch or grab the bottom. After he moved closer, he pulled the curtain back for privacy with his dog standing guard.

Traveler had tried before to contact the cyclopes of Mímir–Spring without success. He assumed it had to do with the city restoring its magic or, perhaps, the power of the surrounding territory of the sirens. However, he had a greater need to communicate with them. Lady Aylen's encounter with the Lady of the Lake revealed a very troubling reality that endangered all within Atlantea. The magic of Mímir-Spring's mountain city nullified the magic of all, except its cyclops mages, but he had seen that magic breached by both star and celestial elves.

Furthermore, the two elfin races had used a spell to conceal their flying caravans from Mímir-Spring's all-seeing argus giant with his one hundred eyes. It reminded him of the old Rivermouth, a city of warrior mages, protected by a giant magic bident staff, which purportedly did the same thing, yet it was breached by armies of fiends who utterly destroyed the city. Was the same happening to Atlantea?

"Master Isim," he called.

The face of the chief mage and leader of Mímir-Spring appeared.

"I was expecting you, Master Traveler."

"Master Isim, I need your counsel. I tried to reach out to you before but could not. I surmised it may be because you were restoring the magic of your city or, after our encounter with a siren storm, that their dark power still enveloped your island."

"No, Master Traveler. A darker power prevented it but not the sirens."

"Then who? Oughtred?"

"Master Traveler, there is much we still do not see. I had told you that I saw many possibilities of the evil conquest of Atlantea by Oughtred and his dark forces."

"In one possibility, he succeeded."

"In most others, he did not, but there is more now."

"What do you see?"

"Even the great seers of Mímir–Spring cannot answer you."

"Master Isim, I believe what the celestial and star elves did to Mímir–Spring is happening here in Atlantea."

"What makes you say that, Master Traveler?"

Traveler quickly recounted the battle of Lady Aylen, her people, the white elfess, and The Old One against the Lady of the Lake."

"The creature could have killed them before being vanished. That is not supposed to be possible, Master Isim, even within her own magical realm."

"Master Traveler, leave Atlantea."

"Abandon the fabled kingdom? You thought I was about to say something else. Master Isim, what did you think I called you for?"

"We know a great merman seer who lives in Oceanus Omnis. He was not far from Krakens Wake. He had departed the fabled kingdom some weeks ago to explore the ocean depths."

"He saw the krakens."

"Master Traveler, he saw something far greater and deadlier than krakens. He swears he saw a *demi-titan* on the way to Atlantea."

A look of shock came over the caravan master's face. "Are they not dead?"

"The Titans are dead. These would be their descendants."

"Demi-Titans? Where?"

"They originated far from Pan-Earth where the ancestral burial grounds of their Titan forefathers rest in these realms far, far away."

"Then how could one arrive back on Pan-Earth? With all the many fae races here, we would know. We would feel it."

"Would we?" Isim asked.

"Would the Atlanteans hide such a thing from everyone?"

"I am unsure. The merman seer also said the giant traveled with great evil, which is why he could not see it until it was right upon him."

"Master Isim, you would see such a thing. Your argus sentinel would see such a giant."

"When you were in our noble city, you witnessed that none of us saw the celestial and star elves invading."

"Could it, this demi-titan..?"

"Destroy Atlantea? We had to consult the old scrolls because they existed before the ancient fae. The consensus is that we do not know."

"The Atlanteans defeated far greater than one demi-titan. They withstood the Titans. Master Isim, hiding such a thing is not the Atlanteans we know."

"I agree. But they have closed the city for a thousand years."

"Is this why?"

"All in Mímir-Spring believe so. The Atlanteans would be preparing for it."

"Does Oughtred have a hand in this evil?"

"This is something far beyond his scheming but not beyond his ability to take the advantage."

"What of his allies—sky elves, drows, goblins, elementals? Do you know there are sun and snow elves in Atlantea, newly arrived?"

The cyclops was surprised. "Like the demi-titans, they too were said to be long since extinct."

"If a demi-titan were in Krakens Wake, it would have arrived weeks ago."

"Master Traveler, the void one must cross to get to the realm of Atlantea can be as short or as long as the Atlanteans wish it to be. Their magic remains greater than all on Pan-Earth."

"Is that truly what you recommend as a course of action?"

"Yes, Master Traveler, leave Atlantea as quickly as you are able."

Traveler walked down the aisle of bookshelves followed by the dog and stopped when he saw the humanoid fae wizard shop owner.

"Do you know of the one named Oughtred? A human royal, or was born human."

"I know of him. He has come to Atlantea for many years. The King's Caravan every three years. What of him?"

"I want to know where he is. Seems that seers are scarce in Atlantea these days.

The man laughed. "They left Atlantea months ago."

"I know. Are there any left?"

"That you could hire, human? Not sure. There's a goblin seer I know of. Have problems with goblins?"

"Yes, but that will not stop me."

"To find this fiend of a human, Oughtred?"

"Yes."

"You don't need a goblin seer for that."

"Why not?"

"I saw him."

"Oughtred? Where?"

"At Titan's Gate."

"Which one?"

The shopkeeper grinned. "You do know Atlantea, human. The one you can't go to. The fourth one."

"There are only three entrances to Atlantea: land-bound, underwater, and the cloud city in the sky."

"The one you can't go to. You don't know Atlantea as much as you do, human."

"How much do you want, or should my dog speak with you?"

"Your shape-shifter doesn't scare me, human. It touches me, and you both disappear."

"Why bother with you then? I'll ask the Atlanteans themselves."

"You might have trouble there."

"Why?"

"Another question for you."

Traveler realized that he hadn't seen one Atlantean on the streets, the sky, any of their light ships in days, possibly weeks.

Why didn't he become aware of this before, he asked himself.

"The magic of Atlantea, human. Makes one forget all sorts of things and fall prey to so many other distractions," the fae said to him. "No one is completely immune to it, including those of us, human, who live here or have lived here in the past."

THE GREAT ALLIANCE

Estus fitted the gauntlet over King Aereth's forearm. The king noticed the nervous expression on the weapons master's face.

"Thank you, Mr. Estus. My wardrobe feels complete," the king said.

The camps of the Seven Empires extended miles in all directions between the ante-city and the seashore. No one felt at ease despite there being so many people, and King Aereth had hardly slept during the night.

King Theor and other royals marched into his tent. "The ancient elves have returned," Theor said, "and they are not alone."

King Aereth and the men, as with all the humans of the Seven Empires, couldn't believe the numbers of fae around them. The waiting humans represented were only half the sea of elves to the west of them and goblins to the east. Anchored in the waters were ships of drows.

Above them all arrived the sun elves in golden flying chariots floating in the sky.

"The Great Alliance is born!" Inarian, the sun elf yelled. "From this day forward, the Sun Kingdom of Ljósálfar and the Snow Elfin Kingdom of Ice Niflheim will come to the aid of your kingdoms—human, elf, drow, goblin—against any and all your enemies! After our long absence, we are here for Pan-Earth!"

Above them, giant flying vessels appeared in the sky. Sun elfin knights filled golden glowing sky skips, and ice elfin knights appeared in blue ice sky ships. Soon the sky was thick with the ancient elfin fleet.

"Gather your men and your treasures; we sail as one from Atlantea to your lands. None of the ancient fae of lamias, sphinx, spider nor scorpion nor crab centaurs, or their dark beasts or their daemon allies or their dark magic will harm you, defeat you, kill you, or seize Pan-Earth from you!"

The sun elf's words were met with cheers but not by all.

"Daemons?" Pangolin whispered to King Aereth.

"Gather our treasure, sire?" Nirgund said, "so it can be stolen from us by them."

"Sire, I do not trust them either," I-wulf said.

"Even in these realms of magic, I am certain the fae also say that if something seems too good to be true, it likely is," King Aereth said.

All eyes watched the two ancient elves float in the sky, speaking to a glowing female of light that joined them. Whether it was a fairy, air elemental (sylph), or some other kind of fae, she had six butterfly-like wings and two antennae drooping down from her head, and long hair down her back past her feet. While every man, elf, drow, or goblin stared at the three—time crawled by.

"Sire!"

King Aereth and other men turned, and there was Traveler at the entrance to Aereth's royal tent, the dog at his side. The men smiled as the king moved quickly to him.

"Mr. Traveler," the king greeted.

"Lead the men away from here immediately," Traveler said quickly.

"What's wrong, Mr. Traveler?" Pangolin asked.

"Do you know how long you all have been waiting here?"

The men looked at each other. None could answer.

"Were we bewitched?" the king asked.

"Return to the city immediately. This great alliance can be great with you elsewhere. Spread the word among the other empires to do the same," Traveler said.

King Theor and the human wizard king were listening.

"What do you know, Mr. Traveler?" Theor asked.

"Only a precaution."

King Aereth gave him a look to urge him to say more. The caravan master shook his head. "Their elfin ears can hear us even now. Mr. Hobbs, have the men strike camp and follow King Aereth," Traveler said.

Their steward loudly called out to the men. They knew the routine with their eyes closed. As Titan's Caravan prepared to march back to the city, the men of the other empires moved their gaze from the ancient elves and female fae in the sky to Hobbs' men. Humans asked each other why they were leaving. In the distance, elves wondered the same as they watched. So too were the goblins and the drows on their ships on the sea.

Traveler's eyes were locked on the two ancient elf leaders, especially Inarian, the sun elf. Both elves watched him, and their affable demeanor and smiles turned to frowning disgust as the moments went by.

Lady Aylen walked the grounds with Gwyness. She knew it would be some time before the warrior mages of Faylen could reclaim the noble reputation of its predecessor.

"The 'lost warriors' say there are many others waiting in the Lands of Man for our return, in the secret city of Last Keep," Gwyness said.

"Yes, I remember. The fae city hidden from all human eyes. One of my first ordeals with Mr. Traveler before I became my true elfin form. How many, though?"

"Over fifty, Raine told me."

"More elves, humanoid fae, and 'good' werewolves. All of them, children."

"We are children, too, in a way. They knew what they were long before we did."

"We always knew, in a way. We only needed a full history of it all."

"We will be reunited with them."

"But they are there, and we are here. We need all of them training as one."

The two women reached the gatehouse where Frog-Dor, the wizard, stood guard. He saw them and held up his hand.

"Sorry, Lady Aylen, but you and the maiden must remain here."

"By whose authority?"

"Mr. Traveler's, naturally."

"Our former caravan master may indeed be noble, but he doesn't command me in that capacity. This is our city. I am leaving it to join King Aereth and the others. How can we remain here when so much takes place there? A great alliance of humans, elves, drows, and goblins. A great trap is what I say, and we know of what we speak."

"You going there will not help. Mr. Traveler said you must stay here and protect your city."

"We have the Bident of Faylen for that. Its magic protects our entire island city from all enemies and outsiders."

"But not out there."

"What is about to happen?"

"I am not certain, m'lady."

"But something is about to happen?"

"We cannot risk losing either of you to an attack or the vanishing," Frog-Dor said.

"If he is concerned, why not take the Bident with us?" Gwyness said.

Lady Aylen smiled. "Yes! Excellent, Gwyness. There Mr. Frog-Dor, you can satisfy Mr. Traveler and me without upsetting either. We take the object with us. The city of Faylen can survive empty for a little while."

All three of them looked up at the sky.

"What's wrong with the air?" Gwyness said, her amulet around her neck glowing brightly.

The sky rippled as if it were the surface of water.

"Something is wrong?" Frog-Dor said.

Lady Aylen grabbed her ears first and hunched over with her eyes closed as the sky began to shatter like glass. Gwyness kept her eyes on the sky, eyes that widened in shock. Above them, a whole city was crashing down towards them.

Then their realm began to fall—the island city and the magic sea. The castles and buildings of the city above them impacted the magic protective dome of the Bident, breaking apart, bodies of screaming fae everywhere, most flying upwards for their lives. The city of Faylen began to tip over as its island broke apart and its seas drained away through the crumbling and twisting earth below.

The human wizard king informed the royals of the Seven Empires of the revered company around them. The humans had their Seven Empires. Elves had the Thirteen Great Houses. The drows had the Three Kingdoms. The goblins had the Towers of Ten. All waited on the ancient elves in the sky.

The snow elves had flown high into the sky above their sun elfin comrades just before they released their magic attack. Drows dove for their lives into the sea as their ships erupted in red flames. The cyclone of sunfire created by the sun elves was yellow at first, then orange, but now radiated red and shot intense flames at all on the ground. The men of Titan's Caravan had the magic shields of their gauntlets engaged and shielded themselves from the wave of fire. The men of other human parties were not so lucky—men on fire screamed, others were instantly burnt to ash. The air all around them radiated red with the relentless intensity of heat.

Pangolin watched as one sun elf after another vanished. He could see in their faces that they did not care. His body was protected by his earth elemental armor, and the berserker shielded other humans.

"Stand behind me!" he yelled.

Other berserker Cut-Throats stood shoulder-to-shoulder with him to create a live wall to protect the many humans behind them. They heard the screams of dying elves and goblins burning alive.

Behind them, King Aereth and the other royals of the Seven Empires yanked the crowns and bands from their hands, the metal searing their skin. Some of them collapsed from the red heat.

"They kill us with the power of the sun!" Theor yelled and collapsed.

The red sun cyclone increased in size and intensity. Pangolin could see that even with their magic shields, his Cut-Throats, dripping wet with sweat, were being roasted alive, many about to pass out.

"I have no choice!" Pangolin said, his berserker rage welling up within. "I'll kill their leaders."

"No! Pangolin, don't!"

The air, in a flash, went from deathly boiling to cool. The giant tsunami crashed over both the sun elves and snow elves from above. The sun cyclone was gone, and the air around them returned to its natural state.

"There!" I-wulf pointed.

The men turned to see Lady Aylen in the distance. Gwyness and the man Frog-Dor were next to her. However, what shocked them all was a virtual mountain range of whole cities, or their rumble, resting on top of each other, extending from one section of the Atlantean ante-city to the sky.

The air felt so cold. The men turned their attention back to the sky ahead of them. The snow elves again floated in the sky and began to create their own cyclone of icy destruction. A flurry of arrows ripped through their bodies from both the elves on the ground from the west and goblins on the east side of the shore. Sun elves took to the air in defense and fired their sunfire from their palms at them. Some burned the arrows racing in mid-air and hit the attacking archers; others were riddled with arrows and killed. Giant bats dove from the sky to devour or rip the bodies of sun or snow elves. The creatures either succeeded and vanished or were frozen or burnt alive, plunging into the sea.

A myriad of dots of light crowded the heavens above them. All the sun elves and snow elves, and on the ground any elfin archers, goblin archers, or human that had fired their bows vanished. But the magical effect was not quick. Each vanishing took moments. Each dot of light in the sky lingered longer.

Sun elf globe vessels of fire and icy blue sky ships came out of invisibility to rain down fire and ice on the entire land but for only a moment. The ships stopped in their descent as if giant invisible hands grabbed them, and the violent lurch forward ripped the hulls apart. Elves fell from inside to the ground below. Then the elves and all the sky ships slowly vanished.

Realms on the ground, on the water, and in the air appeared and merged into theirs. Invisible barriers shattered everywhere. Whole sky cities fell to the earth. Everyone on the ground—humans, elves, drows, and goblins—had to run into the Atlantean land cities or risk diving into the sea for the bottom as fast as they could.

"The magic is gone!" yelled Nagisa. Traveler noticed an exhilaration in the lamia's face at the death and destruction around them.

But she was right. The great magic of Atlantea that had protected the fabled kingdom, the realm of realms, for eons was fading away.

LETTERS

Traveler sat quietly at a small desk. He finished the next letter on a magic parchment. Thirteen letters he wrote with one magical pen of yellow, a blue pen for three parchments, a purple pen for ten parchments, twenty parchments with a pen of green, a golden pen for three parchments, and he continued on until late night became early dawn.

His dog had watched him through the night. Their small-realm overlooked a busy street of passers-by, and the caravan master had gotten used to the sound of voices and footsteps. The view was one-way and, having lived in Atlantea, the mood of the crowds was not of joy of exploration and commerce or the contentment of the daily duties of life. A sense of panic and fear existed among the fae. At dawn, Traveler stood from his chair and knelt before his dog.

"I have a very important mission for you. You will have to go alone, but I know you can do it." He smiled as he rubbed his forehead. "You and I have been together a long time. I don't think we've been apart since I found you, or did you find me? But I have to stay here, and you are the only one I trust who can do this. You will even get a chance to pretend to be me."

FROM THE
DEVOURING
DARKNESS

ESCAPE FROM ATLANTEA

Traveler never flinched during the entire attack. He needed to stay calm for his dog to remain so. His dog had transformed into a fearsome griffin hybrid but had not moved from his side. Both remained in the circle of magic from Traveler's bag of tricks—the hidden pouch, or small realm, used by fae and others to keep spells, objects, provisions, etcetera—to shield them from the intense heat.

He watched the vast shore with sadness. The purpose was clear. The ancient elves had gathered all the parties to slaughter them. He suspected it but to see it unfold before him was another matter. He had truly met elves more malicious than the sky elves, even towards other elfinkind.

Healers of all parties were overwhelmed. Death among them was not as great as it could have been without the intervention and forewarning of Traveler and Titan's

Caravan, but the numbers of wounded, including those severely burned, was high.

The human wizard king used his magic to heal the skin of the humans of the Seven Empires. Elves had their own magic healers. Goblins would undoubtedly have theirs. Drows were the most fortunate of them all as their numbers of wounded and dead were few since they so quickly swam deep to the sea's floor. They emerged from the depths to form up on the shore.

Hours passed as all parties attended to their wounded and made preparations to bury the dead.

Lady Aylen and Gwyness joined King Aereth at the center of the tents of the Seven Empires.

"You gave us all the time we needed," Pangolin said to the princess.

"I actually did little, Mr. Pangolin, other than directing the water. We all were falling from the sky, and the water had to go somewhere."

"They meant to kill all of us," one of the human kings said.

"Sacrificing themselves in the process," King Aereth said.

"Why would they do such an evil thing?" Theor said.

"The true question is why the Atlanteans would allow

such a thing!" an elf yelled.

The elves arrived, stepping from invisibility. The Thirteen Great Houses of Elfinkind. There were many sub-races of elves but they recognized the Elfin Questing Knights, Lyre of the Woodland Elves, Taylos of the Desert Elves, and Shadu-mun of the Moon Elves. There were forest elves, jungle elves, savage elves, mountain elves, subterranean elves, and high elves. River elves were the only water elves present. Water elves had their own numerous sub-clans.

"We can't seem to be rid of you," Lyre, the woodland elf, said to the humans.

"We did share our concerns with you directly about these ancient elves," King Aereth said.

"Yes, that you did, and we have our own elfin brethren that will need to be buried," Lyre said.

"We did what we could. Our own Lady Aylen gave us our chance," King Aereth said.

"Yes, your elf," Lyre said.

"I'm no one's elf," Lady Aylen said.

"Elf?" one of the hulky wild elves said. "Who is this child elfess?"

"I am not a child!"

"You're barely an elf from the smell of human from your skin."

The Faylen students and half-elves moved to the elf, but Gwyness raised her hand to hold them back.

"I was raised by humans, and I am not ashamed of that in the least, but if we must play childish games, then we elfin adults should leave you here," Lady Aylen said.

"Where is Mr. Traveler?" Shadu-man asked.

"Good question," King Aereth said.

Lyre turned to the wild elf and said, "The human who led us here. Look who comes."

Members of the Three Kingdoms of Drowkind moved through the crowds of humans to them. Dr'as the drow king, approached them with his drow warriors. He seemed to be in the same role as King Aereth was to the Seven Empires; Dr'as spoke for the Three Kingdoms.

"Dr'as," Lyre said.

"Elf," Dr'as said.

"We do all know each other," King Aereth said. "We traveled the Trail together. Lived on the Trail together."

"Fought the same enemies on the Trail together," Pangolin added.

Angry yelling erupted among the elves and drows.

Traveler appeared, marched to them with the lamia queen, and a party of goblin representing the Towers of Ten—brutish common goblins were the majority and most vocal of the group's leaders, but high goblins were among them.

"I did what I knew none of you would," Traveler said as he reached them with his dog in griffin-hybrid form.

"Why are they here?" the elves and drows yelled.

"Their arrows felled as many of the ancient elves as yours," King Aereth said.

"Goblins, you must be laughing to yourselves. Another chance to kill more elves," Lyre said.

"You elves killed my goblins!" one of the goblin kings yelled.

"Who is the lamia witch?" the savage elf asked.

"Silence!" Traveler yelled so loud that everyone was startled.

Moments passed before he began to speak. "Look around you. Atlantea, where we stand, the fabled kingdom, is in shambles. The magic that prevented any violence within its realms is gone. The magic that held its realms apart wanes. Before you kill one another, consider this: Where's Oughtred?"

All the parties looked at each other. No one knew the answer. No one knew what to say.

The caravan master's eyes were fixed on Gwyness's glowing amulet. "How long?" he asked her.

"When we were in Faylen, when it was in its own realm, before the realms collapsed," Gwyness asked.

"Thus is your answer, human," Nagisa, the lamia, said. "Oughtred comes. Do you not hear them?"

"Hear what?" Lady Aylen asked, but she did hear them.

Elves, drows, and goblins. The humans looked at them nervously.

"Mr. Estus," Traveler said to their weapons master. "Empty the weapon's storehouse. Every man in Titan's Caravan is to have the best weapon, Mr. Pangolin, his axe-mace, Lady Aylen, and Maiden Gwyness their Faylen weapons, equip her Faylen students and half-elves with whatever they choose. The magic of Atlantea is not here to protect us anymore."

"The armor golems," Pangolin reminded.

"Yes, assemble them."

"We are in Atlantea, the ancient fabled city from the time of the Titans," Theor said sadly. "We were supposed to be safe here from any violence or darkness of magic."

"Many things in Atlantea are not as they're supposed to be," Traveler said.

"The ancient sun and snow elves got their great alliance after all in their short time in Atlantea," Pangolin said. "We did to them what they planned to do to us and sent them to their maker, or far away from whence they came not to return."

Swarms of perytons filled the blue skies, flying away. The fantastic deer birds were said to have lived in the mountain cliffs around the fabled kingdom from its birth. Yet the beasts were flying away from their home. Would they ever return? Could they ever return, or were they too fated never to cross back into the kingdom for a thousand years?

Everyone noticed that Traveler seemed to be waiting for something. Fae took to the skies and marched from the cities with their animal companions, provisions, and treasures.

"What is happening, Mr. Traveler?" Lady Aylen asked.

"They are leaving Atlantea," the caravan master answered with sadness.

The elves, drows, and goblins were fully armed themselves as the humans of the Seven Empires.

"I say we follow," the wild elfin leader said to the

other elfin royals.

"No," Traveler said to them sharply.

"Why should we not?" Lyre asked. "I no longer view our great journey through Titan's Trail to Atlantea as rewarding as I first thought. My king vanished along with many others, many dead, killed within the fabled kingdom where such was supposed impossible. My elves have lost more in lives here within Atlantea than our entire march on the Trail."

"Where are the sky elves?" another elfin lord asked. "This ruse of reunification and murder was their creation. Of that, we have no doubt. My arrow will pierce the heart of the first wind, cloud, star, or celestial elf who appears."

"Why did we think anything would change? The sky elves do not believe us land elves or water elves are equals. They feel they are superior to us since they walk among the stars, and we crawl on the earth. Their words are of insult and hatred."

Lady Aylen watched the elves, and they took notice.

"Do you have something to say, elfess?" the desert elf asked.

"Mr. Traveler is right. We are all the same. Humans and elves. I don't know enough about drows and goblins."

"Please don't place drows in the same breath as

goblins," Dr'as said.

"You begin to understand, princess," Traveler said. "We must all remain, assuming we can refrain from killing each other. I, for one, feel an allegiance to Atlantea for all that it has given me."

"All are fleeing the city," an elf said. "We should follow."

"Mr. Traveler, if the magic of Atlantea is gone or weakened, then to encounter Oughtred and his forces would be a far greater battle than what we just engaged in or have engaged in, even on the Trail," Pangolin said.

"Why should we stay, human," the wild elf asked. "You never did answer me."

"The sun and snow elves were right." Traveler's words made everyone stop and watch him closely. "A great alliance," Traveler said. "But not as they had planned. Oughtred's boast of conquering Atlantea seems to be a certainty now unless we intervene."

"Why should we?" a human royal said. "Where are the Atlanteans? This is their kingdom, their responsibility, not ours."

"The Atlanteans are not here, so I will wait until they return wherever they may be."

"Where do you believe they are, Mr. Traveler?" KIng

Aereth asked.

"I think I know where they are. But with the warning glow of Maiden Gwyness's element, we, or you, have a decision to make."

"I am not going to war with Oughtred," Dr'as said to Traveler directly.

"And the elves, this time, agree with the drows," Lyre said.

Traveler looked at the lamia and the goblins.

Nagisa laughed. "I am already part of your alliance, human. We will stay."

"Why snake woman?" an elf yelled. "Traveler, do you truly mean to ally with goblins?"

"If you go, go," Traveler said to the elves and drows, and looked at the Seven Empire human royals. "Nagisa knows because her race is among the ancient fae who have lived in Atlantea for tens of centuries. I have told you all this before. Atlantea is not one realm; it is the gateway to many. If Oughtred and his dark forces gained control of Atlantea, he would have unobstructed access to magical lands throughout Pan-Earth and beyond. That cannot happen and must be prevented at all costs. If you wish to abandon the kingdom, my dog and I will make our stand with the goblins."

"I stay then," Lady Aylen said. Her lost warriors formed up around her.

"I stay," King Aereth said.

"Then you'll need my services," Hobbs said.

"I as well," Mr. Estus said.

"My weapon and the Cut-Throats live for battle," Pangolin said.

"Good, and the goblins will represent Faë-Land Major and not elves," Traveler said.

"I can see them," Shadu-mun, the moon elf, looked out in the distance.

"Oughtred?" Lyre asked.

"Yes," Shadu-mun.

"How could we ever show our face in our kingdoms again, any of the Elfin Questing Knights, if it were learned we fled the fabled city to leave humans to protect the Atlanteans and their fabled city. And to rub more salt into the wound aided by goblins. We would be vanished by all of elfinkind. With great duress, our clever former caravan master, we remain for your Titan's Army."

"You elves, with your arrogance, have spoken for Faë-Land Major for too long," a goblin royal said. "The noble goblin empires should represent Faë-Land Major to defend Atlantea."

"Noble goblin empires?" one of the elfin royals said, laughing.

"Forgive me, but there is nothing noble about goblins," said another elf.

A high goblin yelled, "Were we all not attacked by elfinkind. Elves who tried to kill you as well without cause. The narrow, limited view of an elf. There are many goblins in the magic lands—some barbaric, no doubt, but then there are those who also walk among the stars and build worlds rather than ravaging simple villages like animals. We are not all the same, which is why we are here to represent goblinkind. You elves falsely wish to brand all goblins as evil when we all are not."

"Nice words for a beast-lord. Are the dire wolves you enslave outside the mark of a noble goblin?" a forest elf said.

"The beasts are not enslaved, any more than your animals."

"The drows say they are. I believe them."

"Drows?" the high goblin said. "Stained for eternity for their transgressions with dark magic."

"Then, my noble goblin friend, is that the standard? Only those races that have not dabbled in dark magic should be the voice of Faë-Land Major to Atlantea. I agree completely then," Lyre, the high-elf, said.

"Is that all?" a goblin said to the high goblin. "Maybe we should not be part of their alliance."

"No," the lamia said. "No words or insults will drag us from our great alliance. Master Traveler, we will be at your side."

"No more arguments," Lyre said to the other elves. "A new elfin alliance with the humans it is."

"As long as our new elfin alliance does not include the sky elves," said another elf.

Dr'as shook his head. "The Atlanteans will owe all of drowkind much after this."

"Atlanteans are fair people, Dr'as," Traveler said. "They are very generous to everyone by nature but especially to those they find favor with. I am one who can speak to this directly."

"Then where are they? Why did they allow the attack of the sun and sky elves to happen?" the wild elf asked, whose eyes glowed with a flicker of yellow. The elf was also a berserker like Pangolin and the Cut-Throats.

"Do not concern yourself, Mister elf. When the Atlanteans return, it will be I, not you, who will be yelling the questions at them the loudest," Traveler said.

Traveler held his magic sword in his hand. Its star magic blade was a piece of a true ancient Titan sword, said to be the combined power and essence of a real star itself. The translucent flame of the sword rippled around it. The power of the sword remained, but the amplified magic of Atlantea no longer existed.

Lady Aylen joined him with her dual war tridents. "Its flame is not as bright here as before, is it?"

"The power of the sword has not changed. Being in Atlantea gave it more."

"That more is no longer?"

"It is not important, princess."

Gwyness led the other Faylen warriors. The maiden had her dual war hammers. Raine, the younger water elf, and Rya, the humanoid, both carried silver tridents fashioned by elves. The female half-elves carried swords and crossbows. The male half-elves were armed with long bows and daggers. All the archers had quivers draped over their backs with the most powerful magic arrows from Estus's armory. Ossarrian carried a silver mace in one hand and a gold shield over the other arm.

"We have company," Lady Aylen said with disgust.

Nagisa the lamia slithered to their caravan master. "The sun and snow elves birthed our great alliance. The irony of things. I wonder which one of them conceived such a ruthless idea."

"My alliance is not such a bad thing to you anymore," Nagisa said.

"I think it's still a bad thing," Lady Aylen said.

"Nagisa, will the other ancient fae attack us?" Traveler asked.

"Why would they? They care nothing about humans, less about your lands."

"I wish I could believe that."

"If it would put your mind at ease, I could speak to them," Nagisa said.

"I'd prefer you here. Nagisa, I know you do this only because you have a rivalry with Oughtred."

"No, human. If Atlantea is to be conquered, it will not be by a human, lich or no."

He sensed the lamia was far from being truthful but changed his mind about saying something.

"No threats?" she asked.

"No."

"You know something, human," she said. "More than this. More than suspecting the ancient elves had planned to attack us from the start."

"I suspected nothing that you didn't also."

"You know more still."

"If we are to go to war with his armies, I expect you to fight as fiercely with us to the end as I know you are capable of."

"You are such an interesting human. No fear of my kind. Freely moving between humans and elves and drows and goblins. I should hire you as a caravan master. There are many races that would turn my stomach to speak to, but you could do that for us."

"Nagisa, let us postpone any adventures until we are sure that we won't be dead by nightfall."

"We could always be resurrected as fiends."

"I have no interest in being of the undead."

"Personally, I enjoy sunlight too much, so it wouldn't be desirable for me either."

Lady Aylen sensed something as she knelt down onto the ground. Water was seeping from the ground and rising fast.

The river elves made their way to the front of the elfin

royals of the Thirteen Houses.

"The water fae are here," one of the river elves said.

"Why do you not say that with joy?" Lyre, the woodland elf, asked.

Lady Aylen recognized the water elfin royals: Kings Finlor, Elfred, and Agis, Queens Amphitrite, Leena, and Eriana, as they stepped out of invisibility. Anger showed in their faces, and weapons in their hands—tridents, battle spears, and water crossbows. Staring at the drows and goblins, their rage visibly increased.

"Lady Aylen, take charge," Traveler whispered to her quickly.

"So the evil alliance of the sun and snow elves is here!" one of the elfin kings yelled.

"No more violence amongst us," Lady Aylen yelled. "We dealt with the sun and snow elves. Their dark plot failed. We were victims, not accomplices, if you are making accusations."

Queen Geneva of the Mermaids and Queen Oluania of the Oceanids appeared from invisibility too. King Centauro of the Sea Centaurs, King Traerio of the Tritons, and Queen Atopia crawling along with her tentacles appeared next, following. More and more water fae appeared, seemingly ready for battle.

"They tried to murder us!" Queen Geneva yelled.

"The snow elves tried to freeze the very sea waters about us," Queen Oluania said, "but we were ready. Our sister, Queen Atopia, warned us beforehand of their possible treachery."

"Dear sister, I must confess that another warned me," the mermaid octopus queen said.

"Who?" the mermaid queen asked.

"Our former human captain, of course," she replied.

Queen Geneva stepped in front of Traveler. His dog growled, and every mermaid and water nymph trained their weapon on it. Lady Aylen placed one of her tridents between them. Traveler put a restraining hand on the shape-shifter.

"Move your weapon, water elfess," Queen Geneva commanded.

Traveler nodded, and the princess complied.

"How did you know?"

"I suspected. The Lady of the Lake tried to murder Lady Aylen and her followers. The vanishing happened only after her attack."

"That's how you knew the Atlantean magic had gone."

"Yes."

"You could have done more, said more."

"Such as what? The sun and snow elves would have changed their plans. We had to know for certain."

"I have mermaids who died in the attack."

"We have humans and fae who died too in the attack. It is a dangerous world, mermaid queen."

"But it is not supposed to be so in Atlantea."

"The Atlanteans were not on hand to stop it either."

"They have disappeared," the triton king said. "Where are they?"

"I suspect outside the realm of Titan's Gate, but what should concern us all is the real meaning of all of this," Traveler said.

"Human, we do not care. We leave you, the land elves, your dark fae, your goblins, and your lich king Oughtred to embrace yourselves in battle without us," Geneva said.

"We are not dark fae, mermaid!" Dr'as said.

"All this smells of dark magic, which your race is quite familiar with. No more words. Atlantea is yours."

"Why do you look at us so?" Lyre asked the water elfin royals. "Land elves have always been allies with water elves against the treachery of the sky elves."

"You have your great alliance here on land, but we chose to join the great alliance of oceans and seas," Finlor the water elf said. He looked directly at the river elves. "Do you remain with them, or do you leave with us?"

The river elves glanced at each other before one spoke. "We remain with our land brethren as we always have."

"Understood."

"May I make a proposal?" Lady Aylen asked.

"The answer is no, water elfess. We know your question is the human's. We heard you speaking before we appeared."

"Cowards then," one of the goblins said with a smirk.

The mermaid queen glared at him.

"Please do not fight here. I am using all my mental might to keep my animal calm," Traveler said. "Or do you want him to transform into a kraken?"

"If you heard our words, then stay and fight not on our behalf but on behalf of Atlantea," Lady Aylen said.

"Do you know how ludicrous what you say is?" Queen Atopia, the mermaid octopus, said. "The Atlanteans defeated the Titans, the dragons, the combined armies of all fae of Pan-Earth—sea, land, and air. Why would such beings need us to defend them against a human lich and his dark armies?"

"The Atlanteans are not here. The magic of Atlantea has gone. If they are gone and their magic, then we will not stand in the way of the end of the Kingdom at Titan's End," Geneva said. "You want to keep Atlantea from Oughtred? Fight for it and kill him. We take our treasures and go to the seas and oceans of the magical lands. We care not of the affairs of the land."

"What if these events of the land spill into the ocean's depths below?" Traveler asked.

"Then your great alliance of land will have our great alliance of water fae at your side. Until that time, farewell, Master Traveler."

King Centauro of the Sea Centaurs floated to him. "You did help us get to Atlantea as an ally and flew the banner of our land allies, the Centaurs of Chiron—"

"And flew under the banner of our allies, the fairies of Chrysa," the water nymph queen chimed in.

"So we take our treasures, armies, and people back to our territories, knowing we may not be able to return to the fabled city for ten centuries, should the city survive. But there is no reason we cannot leave our magic here to you," King Centauro said.

"Leave most of it with Lady Aylen," Traveler said. "She and Maiden Gwyness will be resurrecting the lost kingdom of Rivermouth."

"A kingdom of land and the ocean against the darkness," Queen Geneva said. "We are not troubled by fiends in the deep."

"But if their kind were to rise, you would have to deal with demons of the deep," Traveler said.

"You know too much for a human," Queen Atopia said.

"Then it is settled," Centauro said, "and if you return your lost kingdom of Rivermouth to Faë-Land or your human lands, we may send you a sorcerer, sorceress, or more to aid you."

"Farewell, Titan's Alliance," Queen Geneva, the mermaid queen, said.

"Farewell, great Alliance of the Oceanus Omnis," Traveler said.

LICH LORD

The threshold to Atlantea remained sealed, but the magic was weakening. On the serene surface of Oceanus Omini outside, it appeared as if Atlantea, its colossal markers, and all its lands had vanished. From inside the realm, invisible to all, looking out was like peering through softly color-tinted glass. The sounds of gusts of wind slapping against the barrier were amplified.

Three Atlanteans stood on disks of light resting on the dark waters, waiting, watching in the cosmic realm between the world of the humans and fae with their now hidden Atlantean realm. A dark sky filled with stars and moons. The abomination could not see them but knew they were there. A giant skeletal warrior clad in rusted metal pushed its one decaying leg through the portal at the top of the dark waterfall. The draugr passed through into their realm and let itself fall down the massive waterfall of dark water to crash at the bottom of the cosmic watery realm, breaking apart to pieces and nothingness. Another undead warrior had grown more as it extended a leg to step through the final portal into the Atlantean realm.

The three Atlanteans were concerned but not frightened. As its leg passed through the final barrier into Atlantean territory, with the bright sky and warm air, in direct contrast to the in-between realm outside, the magic of their true realm did what it had done from the beginning of time. The giant draugr's body began to wither away. With an unwavering single-mindedness, it marched forward even in face of the magical disintegration of its body, the wind carrying the dust of what it was back across the realm to land in the dark cosmic waters. No dark magic, or a creature empowered by it, such as the draugr, could exist in Atlantea. Soon the abomination and its armor were gone.

The Atlanteans looked on. Another giant draugr lumbered toward the threshold, and another followed behind.

A blockade of hundreds of thousands of giant Atlantean vessels of light hung in the sky from the surface of the water into the heavens, from one end of the horizon to another. One by one, they began to fade away.

Estus, clad in his own special armor, commanded the

hundreds of the caravan's armor golems to form a wall facing the sea. Each moving suit of armor armed with a sword or axe stood at attention.

The human royals of each of the Seven Empires of the Lands of Man would command the men of their own regions—Avalonia and Baltica, Laurasia, Gondwana, Larentia, and Oceania. Different banners flew high within each formation of knights and other warriors. King Aereth ceded Avalonia's command to the eldest king so as to exclusively command the men of Titan's Caravan who were not berserkers. Nirgund would remain at King Aereth's side at all times with his thirteen reptilian hounds. Hobbs insisted, though not a warrior by training, that he would remain at the king's side too.

Between Estus and his armor golems at the front and the humans were the Cut-Throats. They were under Pangolin's command with I-wulf at his side. In his earthen elemental armor, the master-at-arms held his massive ax-mace weapon made of the same magical material. The Cut-Throats carried heavy double-axes and war maces, and their three hundred eagle-headed winged dog beasts (chamroshes) impatiently waited with them.

The elfin armies of the Thirteen Great Houses had columns of swordsmen at the front. Their knights wore ornate helmets—plumed, winged, spiked, horned, antlered, and feathered. Elfin archers with long bows and arrows of magic in the center. With their royals at the rear were so many sorcerers, male and female. Entrancers to mesmerize and control others with their spells, conjurers to create things of magic, enchanters to animate and control inanimate objects, magic slingers who could throw balls or rays of magic, and those who wielded magic scepters and staffs with their own magical properties.

Whatever the woodland elves, desert elves, moon elves, forest elves, jungle elves, savage elves, mountain elves, subterranean elves, high elves, and river elves had, the armies of goblins had the equivalent in their own wizards and witches. At the front of their columns were their own royals, with the most fearsome of their warriors with bludgeoning and crushing weapons. Their goblins with cutting weapons had bladed pikes and scythes with blades as long as a man.

The drows formed up all as one, warriors, sorcerers, and archers. None speaking, all watching. Dr'as and a few other drow kings waited in the center.

Traveler had given a command to his dog, and the shape-shifter shot up into the sky as a fiery bird and disappeared. Human, elf, drow, and goblin could only wonder what horrible creature the dog would transform to when they saw it again in battle.

"Where are your winged goblins and night drows?" Traveler asked the Nagisa.

"I felt it best to wait before showing them to our elfin

and drow allies. We have a good alliance, but a fragile one. I will await Oughtred's appearance. One can direct pure hatred at only one party at a time."

Behind all the armies were Lady Aylen and Gwyness. For the first time, the human maiden was in her battle armor, all–black and constructed by Estus for her with the aide of fairies. Gwyness had her amulet visibly around her neck.

"The Old One said it was a weapon," Lady Aylen said. "Do you know how yet?"

Gwyness shook her head. "Not for certain, but I believe I can shoot magic from it."

"Really? You should practice."

"I can't practice, m'lady. It will work in battle, when I need it to."

Behind them, Lady Aylen had given archer duty to all her half-elves, save Mr. Elman, who was the spotter with his incredible magic eyes of sight. Under Traveler's direction, the three "lost warrior" leaders had the task of guarding the two women.

"Are you going to turn to a werewolf in battle?" Gwyness asked Ossarian.

The young man only smiled with his slightly fanged teeth.

"What's wrong with that, Gwyness? He's a good werewolf," Lady Aylen said.

"Not a werewolf, m'lady," Ossarian corrected. "Faoladh are humanoid wolves of light magic. We remain human at all times within ourselves. Never do we succumb to the primal evil of a beast."

"I hope that doesn't mean you'll be weak in the face of danger," Lady Aylen said.

"Far from it, m'lady."

Traveler walked to them with his magic sword already drawn and held it close to his side, but he was looking up.

The wizard Frog-Dor descended from the sky with the drow sorceress touching his shoulder and flying down too.

"You found her," Traveler said.

"Why did you have him find me?" Dr'amal asked.

"We need you both. Oughtred has his chief wizards. Then we must have ours."

"I am hardly a chief sorceress," Dr'amal said.

"Frog-Dor, I have a spell for you to cast. I think it may require more of your magic power than any other you have ever cast or will ever in your life," Traveler said.

"Where did you get the spell?"

"One of my mage trainers of the past. The day we first arrived in Atlantea. They were leaving. You met them."

"Yes, they had me wait for you."

"Yes."

"She was an oracle, was she not?"

"She would say, no, but yes."

"She knew we'd be here at battle."

"She knew that there likely would be a battle."

"Why am I here?"

"Dr'amal, drows always tell me how experienced they are with fighting practitioners of dark magic. You are D'Shar."

"I am an illusionist."

"And more, and we need you here. Let your father, Dr'as, know that he and I with Lady Aylen and Maiden Gwyness will be the ones to greet Oughtred."

"Greet Oughtred?" Lady Aylen said.

"Yes, princess. You are the leaders of the new Faylen. Time to go to work."

"Likely, he will refuse to command our drows and send me in his place," Dr'amal said to Traveler.

So many of the fae had seen the image of the approaching Oughtred army, but they never got closer. The illusion spell kept repeating. No one knew why, though they knew there was a reason. Finally, the illusion was gone, and Oughtred's humanoid iguana wizard appeared as he came out invisibility, with his elongated yellow scales from the top of his forehead to his back. The wizard rode on dark hippogriff past their armies close to the shores edge, then across the sea and stopped on the surface, floating above it.

"King Oughtred of Xenhelm and his armies will claim the great fabled kingdom of Atlantea as his own! Leave now, submit to him as your true and only king, or die!"

A magic arrow caught the wizard in the forehead, passing through the skull before he ever had a chance to react. The iguana man's body fell into the sea, and his hippogriff steed flew off.

Pangolin didn't see who fired the arrow. Likely an elf, possibly a goblin, by the lightning speed. "There's your answer!" Pangolin yelled.

The sky all around began to shatter like glass but not because of the berserker's call.

Fae had left all the ante-cities nearby by foot, steed, air, or sea. The actual cities of Atlantea were miles away, but they assumed the same occurred there. Atlantea was an empty kingdom except for their armies at sea.

Birds had long since left the skies of Atlantea along with all the winged and flying beasts of air, including Mr. Quillen's favorite deer bird perytons. The boy was put under the care of the selkies, who remained behind the battle formations with all the families and children of the humans and elves, and miscellaneous fae.

After the skies shattered like glass, the scream literally shook their bodies. The magic from living beings, whether light or dark, did not have a feel. However, magic of fiends chilled the atmosphere and was perceptible to one's soul. They did not see the shriekers yet but they could feel them approaching. The amulet around Gwyness's neck had a steady bright white glow. They had never seen it with such intensity before.

The very sea that they had sailed into Atlantea now loomed far away in the distance. In its place where they stood was land of a dark, ancient, and well-trodden sand. Beyond, Oughtred slowly rode to them upon a golden griffin with dark feathers. Oughtred, crown on his head, clad in a full knight's armor with a red cloak, had a slight smile. His facial hair was so red that it had to be dyed. As with the last time they had seen him at the Feast, his appearance resembled one who was of the undead or practiced in its dark magic. The pale skin of his face truly was translucent enough to see the bones underneath.

Oughtred was far from alone, each stepping from the concealment of invisibility magic. First was a single giant knight in armor carrying the orange-and-white flag of Xenhelm with the symbol of their kingdom in the center—the majestic griffin. From its gait, build, and size of its arms, the knight had to have been some ogre-like creature. On his own golden griffin sat King Prince Gervase, his remaining son, in black armor with no part of his face or skin showing. After the terrible price he paid at the hand of Traveler's dog and knowing that Oughtred and his sons were all, in fact, liches also, all wondered if the man beneath the armor had any human form at all. The elfin sorceress they had also seen previously floated in the air beside Gervase. Many, many hooded humanoid wizards with strange yellowish eyes followed behind her, riding hippogriffs.

Then came Oughtred's goblin horde army—common goblins, high goblins, red goblins, and the even rarer shadow goblins with packs of black-furred koerakoonlaseds—half-human, half-dog cyclops creatures. Every goblin rode a giant dire wolf in the toughest brown goblin metal. On foot marched beast men covered in thick black fur with pale monkey-like faces and razor teeth, part-baboon, part-reptile, in formation behind them. Then waves of Redcaps, a murderous kind of goblin that looked like short, old-looking humanoid males with coarse, graying, grisly hair down their shoulders, long prominent teeth, skinny fingers ending in talons like eagles, and large fiery red eyes. They wore iron boots, carried pikestaff weapons, and, more prominently, wore red caps on their heads, said to be red from soaking it in the blood of their victims.

The new sky around was not the bright, warm, cloud-filled one that existed. A dreary blue, cold sky surrounded the lands. Soon lampads, the race of dark nymphs from the Nether-Lands, with glowing blue skin, filled the dark sky like black swarms. A single lampad floated above Oughtred in a dark dress more ornate than the others, thorned vines hanging. She was clearly the lampad queen.

A trio of goblins—one high goblin, a red one, a shadow goblin—rode forward on their frightening dire wolves to form up near Oughtred.

Traveler moved to the front of the great alliance armies on foot to face Oughtred. Lady Aylen, Maiden Gwyness, Frog-Dor, and Dr'amal joined him, standing behind their caravan master.

"Whosoever killed our herald will walk forward and die," King Prince Gervase said. They had not heard the man's voice in almost a year, the man who was once known as Gervase the Fair.

Commotion erupted from the ranks of the goblin armies of the alliance. A single goblin archer pushed through the goblin shieldmen formed up and walked a dozen or so paces. Gervase snapped his metal gloved fingers of his right hand, and something ripped apart the sole goblin from the inside in the distance. The goblin's bloodied body collapsed to the dark ground.

Everyone waited, but Gervase did not vanish.

"Whosever kills one of us; then one thousand will die," Gervase said and pointed at Traveler.

"I said to you, Master Traveler, that there would be retribution for what was done to my sons," Oughtred said.

"No, father, let it be my right," Gervase said. "I will avenge my brothers, Wuldricar and Renfrey. I will avenge what was done to me."

"Then it shall be so," Oughtred said. "We fulfill a destiny that I shared with the so-called Titan's Caravan. To conquer the fabled kingdom of Atlantea. We sacrificed so much, so many years, but the day is at hand."

Oughtred watched Traveler and the four behind him suspiciously. He must have wondered why there was no fear, not even the faintest, in their eyes.

"The great magic barrier of the Atlanteans that prevented my assembled armies and all my allies entry is no more. The final path to Titan's Gate and here where we stand is open to them all," Oughtred said.

The screams of darkness shook the land again, and all could hear the rumbling as the unseen giants approached.

From directly above, came the sky elfin armies surrounded by flocks of gargoyle warriors. Celestial elves, star elves, cloud, and wind elves. Air elements (sylphs) and water elementals (undines). Shadow elves and winged elves.

"Oughtred, we have dealt with the ancient fae who plotted against us," said the celestial elfin king, Queen Anelle's son. The elf's skin was more translucent than from the Feast. His bones beneath appeared to be of crystal. "None will trouble us anymore. The demon creatures we set upon them will occupy them for some time."

The other celestial elfin king floated near Oughtred, calm and serene in his manner. "Atlantea is ours," he said.

"Who is in charge?" Traveler asked. "There can only be one in charge of the fabled kingdom of Atlantea and its power. I've been given the authority by all in our alliance to surrender."

"Surrender?" Oughtred asked, genuinely surprised.

"Yes, surrender, King Oughtred," Traveler said.

"I expected you to use the magic of the mermaids and water fae, a variety of a myriad of ancient spells to use against darkness."

"We cannot defeat a force more powerful than even Atlantean's magic as is yours. Which of the four lich kings, or queen, shall Titan's Army surrender to?"

"Do not fall prey to his ploy," Oughtred said to his people. "There are enough realms in the realm of realms for us all to satisfy our lusts for power. It was decided long ago. My son and I would have the realms of lands. The sylphs the skies. The undines, the seas and oceans. The sky elves would have the heavens. The lampads the realms of under-earth."

"We have a young lad in our caravan, a Mr. Quillen," Traveler began. "He asks endless questions about the natures and history of fae, fantastic beasts, and frightening creatures. I told him once that there are three beings where you never see more than one. A doppelgänger cannot exist in the presence of another for any length of time. They must flee because their changeling magic is counteracted by the other and their true hideous forms are revealed for all to see. Ogres are so territorial that they would rather kill and devour another than share their food and territory. Liches are the other. There is never more than one. Their evil is never quenched and the only being more knowing of that is another lich. The moment they are aware of another, they must seek them out and destroy them. That is why liches are so very rare. But all that I say, you already know. You formed your dark armies because each one of you said at the start: if we succeed together, I can just kill the others to rule alone.

"The answer to the question that I've been asked about the human lich named Oughtred: how did he assemble such an evil alliance? By finding those as evil and single-minded in their quest for immortality and power as he."

Oughtred smiled, then laughed loudly.

"Sorry, my son, but your vengeance will have to fall to another," Oughtred said to Gervase.

Gervase snapped his fingers and black arms burst out of Oughtred's body, but the lich king did not react as the slippery black hands from his stomach clawed at his face. The king grabbed the arms and yanked them from his chest, tossing them on the ground. The black arms writhed on the ground until they dissolved to nothing but dust.

The elfin sorceress transformed into a ghoulish giantess with dark eyes and a round mouth of silver razor teeth and clawed arms that extended down to the ground. She devoured the king prince whole and the top part of his griffin steed.

The celestial elfin king and lich burst into celestial flames but laughed as his skeleton remained in motion and fired back at Oughtred with his own magical flames. Star elves from above fired their star fire at the celestial elfin lich, wind elves encircled him in cyclones, and other celestial elves rained more fire down on the elfin lich. The combined magic of the sky elves pulled him apart.

Red goblins jumped the one high goblin on his giant dire wolf. The high goblin lich face grew more skeletal as his rage grew. He commanded all the dire wolves of the land to kill his attackers. Dire wolves succeeded in killing many of the red goblins, but the shadow goblins passed right through them, three grabbed the throats of the goblin lich, and with a violent explosive exchange of dark magic, the goblin lich was dead.

Above, Oughtred's elementals attacked the sole dark nymph lich with lightning and ice. Hurricane winds from the sylphs and spears of water from the sea commanded by the undines hit her from all sides. The lampads showered her with endless arrows. The lampad queen lich evaporated.

"When I was alive, I made it a point to destroy any who threatened Xenhelm, including my own blood, as my father learned. Nothing changed in my new incarnation."

Oughtred smugly sat on his griffin.

"Show yourselves, or I will destroy the entire

kingdom!" he yelled.

His draugr army had reached the shores. The undead creatures wearing rusting armor that had filled ships outside the border of Atlantea. Each stood as giants, fifteen feet or so tall. Skeletons with dead white eyes or empty eye sockets either skinless or draped with dead skin. Their foul stench now saturated the cold air.

Oughtred's warrior army of living dead, worse than ghouls, assembled in their own formation among his living army.

A portal opened in front of the empty Atlantea ante-city. An Atlantean of green gemstone skin clothed in a white robe and tall ceremonial hat floated out. He held a long crystal staff.

"I claim Atlantea, overseer," Oughtred said.

The Atlantean reached him. "We acknowledge our defeat, King Oughtred. Do you accept the rulership of Atlantea, the land of realms within realms?"

"How arrogant you Atlanteans were to think you were forever invincible. How foolish not to recognize goodness and evil. You could placate the former with your trivial treasures, but the latter always coveted your kingdom and would do anything to seize it no matter how long the time, no matter what had to be sacrificed. You in Atlantea gave me all that I needed to do so. The treasures, the wealth, the magic."

"Then Atlantea is yours." The Atlantean handed Oughtred the crystal staff.

"This trifle is the symbol of your power?"

"In a land of treasures, and beings whose very skin resembles precious stones, in realms of magic, the ordinary trifle is what we designate as our symbol of power."

Oughtred raised the staff. "Then all who wish to live further bow down before me!"

Oughtred's armies—the striga back in her elfess form, his elves, goblins, nymphs, gargoyles, beast men, elementals, even the giant draugr, all took a knee to bow. So did Traveler's Alliance—Traveler, Titan's Caravan, those of the new city of Faylen, the representatives of the Seven Empires of humans, the Thirteen Great Houses of elves, the Three Kingdoms of drows, and the goblins' Towers of Ten, even Pangolin and all of the berserker Cut-Throats. Finally, the sole Atlantean floated down to the ground to bow on both knees.

"Come forth, or I will command the celestial and star elves to incinerate you all!" Oughtred yelled.

Nagisa the lamia and her alliance of goblins and night drows came out of invisibility. Nagisa could not hide her fear, nor could any of her party. They immediately took a knee, and Nagisa lowered herself to the ground and bowed her head.

"Did you think the human and his forces would destroy me? Was that the wager you made, as the ancient celestial elfin queen and other traitors in the shadows?"

"No," Nagisa answered.

"Do you wish to join my forces then, creature?" Oughtred asked her. "Your winged goblins and night drows? Now that I destroyed all your ancient fae hiding in the shadows with my demons."

Nagisa looked up. "We prefer to remain here."

"Did you know she and her allies meant to kill you all," Oughtred said to Traveler. "After they killed us, or so they intended." He looked at the lamia and said coldly, "Remain with the weak then. Don't be afraid. I won't kill you. The other ancient fae, with your secret armies, those who survived my demons, said the same. I knew what you were plotting, lamia, all of you, hiding in your hidden realm. You are so predictable. You were not here to fight alongside your false alliance with the humans, elves, drows, and goblins. You were here to alert your ancient fae army when I appeared with my armies."

Oughtred laughed. "All of you were as arrogant as the Atlanteans. The Gwragedd Annwyn, the greatest and oldest of the ancient fairies, hide in fear. But if they do not submit, we will find them. I know their hidden realms too. I always know. I am King Oughtred the All-Knowing.

"Did you think the Atlanteans would be your champions against my armies? My draugr army simply walked across their barriers. Their ships of light, an armada of thousands and thousands, flew as fast away as they could travel, away without even casting a single spell to defend their kingdom. I can see the magic spell around all you, aside from the Atlantean," Oughtred said to Traveler. "Is it a spell to erase fear, erase ego, submit to those you hate so without care? No other soul brought me so much destruction as you. I could have killed you, all of you, at any time. But as I said then, that time has passed. You are beneath my concerns. You failed in preventing me from conquering Atlantea as you were always destined to fail."

"No!" a star elfin warrior yelled as he flew to Oughtred's side. "Let me have the human, Traveler, King Oughtred. He is wanted for many crimes against the star elfin empires, the loss of our worlds, the loss of our sky vessels, many lives of star elves, including killing my brother, Lord Sol-ren."

"He killed my sons, destroyed my war wizard army, destroyed New Xenhelm, and none of it matters. Revenge brought us to this point in time, but we are immortal, all-powerful. Revenge is for the mortal weak."

King Oughtred waved his hand, and the star elf yelled

as he vanished.

"Atlantean," Oughtred said, "you had but one final chance to have stopped me. You could have kept me from entering Atlantea this final time. You should have listened to the human called Traveler. He warned you. Unable to see friend and foe, good and evil. You should have fallen a long time ago. I have succeeded where the Titans, dragons, and all the armies of living fae failed!

"One day, Traveler, I will have the power to resurrect all my sons. I will send them after you when I do, burning with the fury of revenge in a quest to do unspeakable murder. Your new city of Rivermouth and its warrior clerics will not save you either. They will suffer the same death as their founders. That is the horror you have to look forward to. That is the only reason why I let any of you live. For in the Kingdom of Atlantea, as has always been the ways of things, even one of such evil must show mercy. So you live, but you will never set foot here in Atlantea again in one thousand years, or ever. I will be here on its throne, but not you. Leave! We have conquered but one small corner of a vast realm of realms. It will take us an eternity to conquer the rest, but that is why I became the most powerful of the undead, so I would have all the time I needed. As its new ruler, I will allow you Atlanteans to remain as caretakers for the physical cities as you have done for eons. There, another gesture of mercy."

The Atlantean raised his head. "Thank you, King Oughtred, for your kindness. You will rule the kingdom of Atlantea and defend against all its enemies forever."

"Is this your futile attempt to cast a final magic spell upon me?" Oughtred asked.

"Do you not wish to rule Atlantea forever? To remain its ruler, defend and defeat all its enemies forever?"

"Yes, I shall, forever!"

"You are Oughtred of Atlantea now. The one who speaks for the fabled kingdom for all," the Atlantean said.

Oughtred stood in a celestial hall similar to the one of the Feast of the Gwragedd Annwyn. A sky for its ceiling, open to the void of a star-filled space.

The Zodiac appeared. The giant golden ram standing ten feet tall peered at them as he approached, leading the procession of his comrades. The giant bull with black fur at the same height with glowing white eyes. The siamese giant, two bodies attached at the torso, clothed in dark robes and hoods draped down, covering their faces above their mouths. The giant ten-foot crab, its legs and pincers erratically moving from moment to moment. The giant lion of glowing fur—visibly more powerful and ferocious than any Nemean lion. The giant woman was covered from head to toe in a silky-like robe, most of her face covered. The metal giant, its body a walking set of measuring scales. The monstrous ten-foot centaur, each arm part bow with an arrow, each seeming to protrude from the palm of its hands. The giant red scorpion with a golden stinger tail. The giant horned humanoid goat with the lower torso of a giant fish. The blue-skinned giant with webbed hands, carrying a golden urn, its eyes blindfolded. The giant fish floating in the air with large, crazy eyes darting all around.

"The Zodiac welcomes Oughtred of Atlantea, the new ruler of the fabled kingdom," said the Aries ram beast.

It was as it was at the Feast. Stars above intensified in brightness then beautiful dancing waves of light, first orange, then yellow, green, and blue washed over the night sky. Hundreds of the Gwragedd Annwyn ancient fairies fell from the sky to the ground. Their glowing porcelain skin, their long blond hair flowing down to their bare feet, their long, sheer dresses covered in flowers— their large transparent wings, and their crowns made of roses. They bowed their heads to King Oughtred.

Oughtred saw the old banner of the kingdom of Xenhelm—the colors of orange and white, its symbol of a majestic griffin in the center.

"Will the flag of the Four Kings of Xenhelm be Atlantea's, our ruler?" an ancient fairy queen asked.

King Oughtred raised his arms in such joy. "Yes, it shall be so."

"Then that is what will be forevermore," the Atlantean said.

Oughtred found himself back on the shores of Atlantea with his armies. He looked at the Atlantean and the armies of Titan's alliance under the human, Traveler.

"I no longer even wish to look upon any of you. Go cower within the walls of the city while you can."

A whirlpool of magic engulfed them, and they were all standing miles away within the ante-city.

REVENGE

THE GIANTS OF ANTAEUS

Caravans of true giants in Atlantea to the treasured lands always took longer than all other fae and much longer than human ones. The ten-foot-tall Atlantean giants who became part of Titan's Caravan planned to spend a year gathering their treasures for their kingdom. Theirs would have more wealth than any other giant kingdom. As they marched with their original Antaean war hammers slung on their backs, they raised the massive, dwarven-forged mauls by the human weaponsmaster high in the air in song. Grakdar led his comrades Barg, Arteus, Aronir, Alceir, and Alebar. Barg sang the loudest and held his maul, with its painted dragon symbol, higher than the others.

The realm had a gray sky with not a single cloud in sight. The path they walked had a sole megalith in the distance towering over the harsh, barren mountainous lands. According to legend, the large stone was a monument to a fallen giant. But the megalith was of no interest to them.

Ahead were the great caverns rumored to contain the treasure troves they sought. In Atlantea, they spoke to many guides: lamias, blue caps, troglodytes, and dwarves. But they chose to stumble around the lands and find the treasure themselves.

"What is that?" Barg said, looking into the dark gray sky as the other giants turned.

"Oh, no," Grakdar said. "Tell me my eyes are seeing an illusion."

The other giants grunted and made other sounds of disapproval. A familiar man, hooded cloak, sword on his back, on a dog-headed griffin flying to them.

"Maybe if we hide, he won't see us," Barg said.

The other giants looked at him.

"Giants are fae too. Don't any of you have a spare concealment spell in your pocket somewhere?"

"Master Traveler," Grakdar said to the little smiling human in front of them. His giant dog griffin was at least back to its normal size. "Don't take offense, but we were hoping not to see you again."

"No offense taken. I almost didn't think I'd find you. Guides told me that once you got to the underground caverns, no one could find you, even a dwarf or kobold," Traveler said.

"Lucky you that you found us before we got there," Barg said sarcastically.

"No guides?" Traveler asked.

"No. We didn't find any we wanted."

"We wanted to be left alone in peace," Grakdar added.

"Typical for a giant. You must be more like your cyclops brothers. Plan ahead," Traveler said.

"Brothers? All my brothers have two eyes." The giants laughed again. "Plan? What's that?" Barg asked.

"Where did you come from?" Grakdar asked, sniffing the air.

"Spices is what you're smelling. I was in a merchant shop. I did a bit of shopping, but I was there to use a looking glass to talk to an old master, a cyclops in the city of Cyclopes."

"Very uninteresting story. Please do not tell us any more, so we can get back to treasure hunting. We have treasure to get, lots of it."

"I came for your help."

"Help? Master Traveler, we are not leaving this realm until we get our treasure. We'll be here six months to a year, and then we will return to our lands. You'll have to find others to accompany you on your journey."

"What of the circle of darkness that surrounds the water outside Atlantea's waters?"

"The kraken wall?"

"No, Oughtred's fleet of fiends. No concern at all?"

"Why should we be? We had already forgotten about them. Master Traveler, no one sails from Atlantea to traverse back through Titan's Trail again to return home. When you sail to depart, you are sailing to be transported by Atlantea's great magic back home in mere blinks of an eye. You know this."

"I do, of course."

"What does it matter what creatures sit outside the fabled kingdom? It's not the first time."

"I still need your help but not any journey. I need to know about giants."

"Giants? We may know a little something about them," Grakdar said.

"I thought so."

"Funny you ask," Barg said.

"Why?"

"We encountered these evil giants since entering the Oceans of Faë-Land and Atlantea rarer than a purple unicorn," Barg said. "Fomorians."

"The goat-headed sea giants are not part of decent giant-kind," Grakdar said. "Fomorians are evil. More of demons than giants or any fae."

"I never encountered them directly but I once met gnome travelers who did. They said the sea giant brought droughts and blight to their lands. Have your people ever encountered them?"

"Our power is only on land. Upon water, we are as helpless as pups. Formorians are the opposite. Our kingdom met them once. Centuries ago, in battle. The result was what every giant warrior loathes. Stalemate."

"Master Traveler, the smallest of Fomorians are twice our size and where they go darkness and death follow. They can summon much more than blights and droughts. Your big-nosed sprites sighted them in their giant ship with an argus giant headed here."

"Sailing towards Atlantea but have they entered the kingdom? Surely, we would know."

"Would we?" Grakdar asked.

"And we cannot forget the Athos giants," Barg said.

"The mountain throwers responsible for the death waves that caused the kraken wall beyond the City of Kraken's Falls. The krakens will be there for decades, maybe much longer. What other giants do you want to talk about?"

"Tell me about demi-titans."

"They are dead as the dragons."

"Where did they come from?"

"The Titans. They were their offspring."

"But the Titans are dead."

"Yes, they are the descendants of the Titans, and don't try to figure it out. It is like asking where the fae came from or the heavens or the stars. They did not exist, then we did. That's all there is to know."

"What happened to the demi-titans?"

"They had to be exiled to the realms where the Titans were buried. Brobdignagian."

"The land of giants. But that is the name of your lands."

"There's is the first and ancient Brobdignagian, which

no longer exists on the magical lands of Pan-Earth. Only ancient giants know where. But it is a realm forever cut off to Pan-Earth. But they're all dead too like the Titans. Our Brobdignagian you have visited."

"Why were they exiled from Pan-Earth?"

"They swore they'd destroy the world that killed their progenitors."

"You mean Atlantea, the Atlanteans."

"Yes, but what does it matter. They are all long dead," Grakdar said.

"Why are you asking about them?" Barg said. "They do not exist."

"A merman told my cyclops former teacher that one was walking along the bottom of the Oceanus Omnis to Atlantea. That its foot was so large that it crushed an entire kraken as it passed through the kraken wall."

"We told you they don't exist," Grakdar said. "If it were a real demi-titan, it's one foot would reach from there to here. They would be no walking. One step. Here."

"What giant is that large then?" Traveler asked.

"We can think of a few. They're supposed to be extinct too," Grakdar said.

"Why did you come here to upset us?" Barg asked.

"You once told me that giants don't run, except for the Gegenees. Perhaps, you should run to the treasure caverns ahead."

"Those six-armed freaks are not giants either. We told you we don't run, and we don't walk fast either."

"Or hop like rabbits," Barg added.

"That's why we need a year to go and come back," Grakdar said. "We take our time and rest and relax often. Master Traveler, nothing is going to keep us from our treasure. Fly away on your dog-not-a-dog and leave us be. If we see any Fomorians, Athosians, Argans, Gegenees, or demi-titans, we promise to send them to you for a long chat and play."

ELVES FROM THE OCEAN DEPTHS

Traveler felt sadness as he secured the red cloth pouch within the magic pocket within his cloak. He hated to think that the magic bag of tricks, as fae called them, would be all that he had to remember his former trio of fae teachers. Mistress Wu and Masters Gorb, and Nigelle were fleeing Atlantea in fear. Their facial expressions would never reveal their true emotions, but their actions and the quickness of their departure spoke volumes.

But they would not be fearful of Oughtred or any draugr or dark fae fleet he could assemble. Even if the forces were greater in magic than their own, they would not be afraid.

The dragon horses (kirins) that he secured for the royals and Gwyness were from the magical lands of Mistress Wu. All three of the great majestic beasts—the one with golden fur and scales for King Aereth, Lady Aylen's lucent-blue fur and scaled one, and black kirin with antlers for Gwyness—had galloped off into the sky without any acknowledgment. The beasts were said to possess the gift of future sight better than most human and fae oracles. Did the beasts leave to return or flee and never come back? He did not know what to think.

He had spent some time with the man called Frog-Dor and would have him settle into the section of the city where he resided. Traveler returned to the crowded streets with his dog to seek out others who were part of his great caravan along Titan's Trail.

Elves lived in their section of Atlantea which they called New Elfheim. Land elves lived above, and water elves lived in the underwater section in the sub-city's center. Sky elves had their own section of Atlantea, high above in the sky. But not all elfin races lived in New Elfheim or Sky Elfheim.

Little was known of abyssal elves who lived in kingdoms so far below in the pitch-black depths of the Oceans of Faë-Land that they were strangers even to all other water elfin races. Traveler had seen them only a few times in life, the last rather recently. He enlisted the aid of water fairies to find them.

Their underwater vessel often was mistaken for a giant manta. He hired a triton crew to ferry him and his dog to these rarely seen elves. One of the strange-looking elves in black waited for them at the door as soon as they docked together. He had visible gills on the sides of his neck, and their bodies had a flatness to them.

"Greetings, human," the deep-water elf said.

"Greetings, may I speak with you?"

"We do not get many visitors. What do you require of us?"

"I need to know about giants of the seas and oceans of the magical lands."

"We know little of giants. Races said to be of the waters actually live on land. If they have two legs, they are land walkers, whether they can swim or breathe underwater."

"You have two legs."

"We walk on the ocean's floor, and after so many centuries, our legs are more like fish-tails. We are more like tritons than elves, which is why they are our good allies."

"Then what of a giant whose foot could crush a giant kraken against the ocean floor?"

"Yes, we felt its approach, but it could never pass beyond the magical barriers of Atlantea. No giant or giant beast, no matter how massive in size, no matter how great its magic or dark its core, could ever pass into Atlantea. The magic of Atlantea would shatter like common glass if such an impossibility were to happen."

THE FAIRY SISTERS OF CHRYSA

Traveler knew why the sky elves had joined Oughtred in his relentless quest to conquer Atlantea at all costs. They had been scheming to do the same for centuries. Oughtred's goblin allies joined simply because elves had and would not allow any elf to gain sole ownership of any region or plot.

Everyone had told Traveler that the air and water elementals joined Oughtred's dark alliance because they were allies to the sky elves, especially the celestial and star elves. But he never believed that to be the whole story. Why would beings so beautiful, indistinguishable from nymphs and fairies, ally with one so dark and so far removed from their Mother Pan–Earth, a world of life and green, blue skies and clear waters?

Oughtred marched into the Feast Gwragedd Annwyn with his sky elves, goblins, and gargoyles. However, the sylphs and undines that followed in a procession after him, some sitting on beautiful winged black horses, were so mismatched with the human lich king. Earth and fire elementals were patriarchal empires. But air and water were ruled by queens alone, like fairies, mermaids, and nymphs. But these matriarchal sylphs and undines fought for a fiend, a human—a man.

The cities of fairies in Atlantea rarely were visited by non-fairies for good reason. The moment one set foot within their section, one was bombarded by a visual frenzy of fairies, insects, especially butterflies and fireflies, birds, and flying things, such as fish, flowers, and vines of all sizes and colors. In fairy cities, often lots of pollen, petals, and leaves floated through the air. So much movement and chaos, even most fae would have difficulty knowing which way they were going in a virtual fairy-storm about them.

Traveler was immune to the chaos, and so was his dog. He understood fairies, their natures, their mischievousness. He didn't mind them, so they didn't pester him, though humans were their favorite targets.

After hours of inquiry, he stopped in a garden eatery of eight-foot tulips. Pretending not to notice them or know their true identity, he casually walked right up to them, looking around them until he stopped.

He smiled at the two young humanoid females of average human female height, one short blond, the other with short brownish hair.

"You look proper as human females, Wildglow and Sunpetal."

The two fairy sisters burst out giggling.

"How did you know?" Wildglow asked in a high-pitched voice.

In their caravan, Wildglow was two feet in height, and her sister, Sunpetal, half that. Both had two antennae poking out from their heads and large translucent insect wings from their back. Before, Wildglow wore a muted ivory frock and Sunpetal, a brown half-jacket that had the texture of a woolly caterpillar. Before him, they both wore matching yellow and white frocks.

"How did you know?" Wildglow asked again.

"Magic," he replied. They giggled.

"Where can we talk privately?" he asked, and should have known better.

Both human and dog were grabbed by the fairy sisters' swarm of multicolored insects, picked off the ground, and flown through the air. The fairy sisters couldn't contain their laughter.

When they landed on a cloud high above on the city's towers, he and the dog steadied themselves on the cloud, which had the texture of a super thick rug.

"You two are getting older, so you have to practice

acting adult more and more.”

“That's not fun!” Wildglow said.

“Which of you can pretend for the longest?” Traveler asked.

“Sunpetal is good at boring things,” the older fairy said.

“No, I'm not,” Sunpetal puffed.

Tree people had the attention span of centuries. Fairies, fairy children and pre-adults being the worst, could only hold their focus for mere moments.

“That evil Oughtred!” Traveler said.

“Yes! He's evil,” Wildglow said.

“He's a bad, evil human,” Sunpetal said.

“Let's send our swarms after him!” Wildglow said.

Traveler felt good. He had their attention on what he wanted.

“Why would the beautiful air elementals and water elementals be his friends? Why would they join his evil alliance?” Traveler asked.

“Yes, tell them,” Wildglow said to her sister.

“Revenge,” the little fairy said.

"What do you mean?" Traveler asked seriously.

"Yes. Our mother told us. The sylphs and undines wanted the Atlanteans to give them control of the great sky realms with worlds of plants and clouds and rain, but the Atlanteans refused. The sylphs and undines were mad."

"They became Oughtred's friend because they were mad at the Atlanteans."

"Yes."

"That is foolish," Traveler said.

"It may be foolish, but it is true," said an adult fairy floating above them with giant hummingbird-like wings.

"That simple?"

The adult fairy's eye narrowed as she watched him. "Yes, human, that simple. For all their great power, my air and water elementals sisters are as simple as a common nymph and as easily manipulated by their own emotions. You humans have much experience with that."

"We do. Humans and fae are alike there. Hopefully, humans and fae do not suffer for this foolishness, or worse, get killed."

"We can agree there, human. Next time have such conversations of import with adult fae rather than children."

"We are not children!" Wildglow and Sunpetal yelled.

"We know Traveler," Wildglow said.

"We were part of Titan's Caravan!" Sunpetal said.

"Traveler's Caravan!" Wildglow said.

"I know, little ones."

"We are not little!" the fairy sisters said.

"Well, you're not old," the adult fairy said.

"They are far older than me, even as children," Traveler said.

"Everything is older than humans. Come with me to my courtyard and pose your questions to adults. Or is there some other reason you want to speak to two little female fairies?"

Traveler instinctively knew the fairy wanted a rise out of him.

"What do you mean?" Wildglow asked.

"I'll ignore you," Traveler said to the adult fairy, "because you also know we marched under the banner of the Fairies of Chrysa, among others. I was their guardian who delivered on my promise to lead them safely to Atlantea."

"A promise you wisely kept."

"If we go to this courtyard, I'd like to get there on my own, though. My dog can fly, and I can ride his back."

It was too late.

"No, Traveler. It's our turn again," the fairy sisters said in unison, already giggling as their insect swarm picked human and dog off the cloud to follow the fairy, already in flight for another structure nearby. "We will get you and your dog there. You got us to Atlantea. We'll get you to the building over there."

FAE-BLOODS

From living in Atlantea, he had heard of its Lady of the Lake in the water world of Atlantea. He also learned the Lady was not as pure good as had been in the fables of the Lands of Man and that there existed other magical beings of water in other far away realms. Some were oracles, others were keepers, and others were guardians. Never did he know that the Lady of the Lake of the water realms in Atlantea was a dark decaelia.

The battle with the creature left Lady Aylen severely wounded. Without the intervention of the white elfess and The Old One, she or maybe all of them could have been killed as the decaelia, corrupted with dark magic, had become a gorgonic hybrid.

He was determined to enlist the help needed to protect the princess, Gwyness, and all of the new city of Faylen. However, the city streets of Atlantea were strangely almost empty. As he searched with his dog, he felt that all the residents of Atlantea knew something he did not. The oracles had fled the day Atlantea closed its gateway to all others beyond. As night fell, he felt that most of those living in Atlantea were secretly and quietly doing the same. What happened to the fabled kingdom of legend and as he had known it? So many caravans he had traveled with to the kingdom. So many caravans had he led to the kingdom. Atlantea was unique among all the kingdoms of Pan-Earth and beyond. There was nothing unique about the current Atlantea. A vast kingdom of realms that had lost its joy, wonder, and magical enchantment.

There was much for him to do as he wanted to be at the princess's side when she awoke. He and the dog turned down a quiet street with only a few fae passers-by.

"How long did you plan to wander the streets?" the fae-blood asked from behind him.

Traveler and the dog turned. "I was told all fae-bloods left Atlantea days ago."

"Not all of us."

The humanoid, Ursi, appeared as she always did clad in black clothing, including a cloak, and necklaces of brown stones. Upon her head, she wore a small golden crown.

"What do I owe the visit, Queen Ursi?"

"Please, Ursi is all. My people don't care for titles as you humans and fae do. We only adopted your customs for our stay here. I had ignored your inquiries, but much has changed, and we have changed our decision. The fae-bloods have been absent for long enough from the magical lands. We can flee like others, but with Atlantea closing for a thousand years, we must change too. We cannot allow ourselves to disappear into obscurity like so many other fae races."

"I do not know why your race has hidden itself for so long, even from other fae, but I would not want you to do so again."

"I ask to join you again. This new city of Faylen."

"Ursi, you wish to join a city that was destroyed once before, and already new forces plan its destruction again. A city that will specialize and dedicate itself to fighting practitioners and creatures of dark magic. The nature of fae-bloods seems to be more reserved, though when you do decide to fight, you are quite formidable."

"Thank you. You do not know our history, but we have more experience in fighting darkness than you know. We have decided. Will you speak to Lady Aylen on our behalf?"

"I will, of course. Who is we?"

"My bear clan and the others. We have formed our own alliance to this end. Atlantea is far from what we expected. Treasure is not the true value of this place."

"Far from it."

"You knew this."

"It is not for me to say, as a caravan master. Atlantea is not called the realm of realms as merely another name. Atlantea is not one place. It is many places all converging here."

"It is why the ancient fae remain here. Why the human Oughtred covets it. Why they all do. Why the darkness does."

"Not only the darkness."

"Then this new city of Faylen does need others on its side. We volunteer—all the fae-blood clans of our alliance."

"I will speak to Lady Aylen and Maiden Gwyness. They would welcome the addition to their ranks of warrior mages."

"Do you know there are many necromancers within Atlantea?"

"Yes, I do."

"Much darkness comes to Atlantea, Master Traveler.

Atlantea doesn't close its gateways because of Oughtred or his dark armies. We do not need any oracles to tell us. We can feel it, and I believe you know it too. Oughtred is taking the advantage, but he is not the cause."

A RAGE ALMOST AS ANCIENT

"The magic is gone!" had yelled Nagisa.

The ancient fae had waited so long for their chance. Oughtred had his armies, and so did they. They would kill Oughtred, and Atlantea would be theirs!

Their pocket-realm was an orange desert and had a yellow sky with many moons.

Nagisa was their eyes on the outside and would sound their clarion call to attack. Many lamia royals in silver iron-like armor gathered to the rear of columns and columns of their humanoid desert fae warriors with swords, scimitars, javelins, and archers. Before them all was a sea of poisonous snakes. The men were immune to their death poison, but not enemies.

Armies of spider centaurs with swarms of spiders and tarantulas. Armies of scorpion centaurs with swarms of scorpions. The sky above was thick with marrashi—the hybrid humanoid beasts had heads of jackals, eagle bodies the size of men, black wings that moved without noise, and razor-sharp talons—with their leather quivers and long golden bows at the ready with poison arrows.

Nearby the sky was thick with wild hieracosphinxes (heads of hawks and bodies of a lion) and ram-headed sphinx creatures (criosphinxes). Below on the desert soil were armies of sphinx and andro-sphinx, attended by serpopards (heads of falcons on snake-like necks and bodies of winged leopards).

Behind them all were giant snake creatures, giant spiders larger than tarasques, and in the air came swarms of giant flying mantises. The lamia-sphinx alliance wanted to make any human, elf, goblin, or fae lose all courage and resolve at the sight of their army and flee in terror.

But rumbling forward were the greatest weapons of the ancient fae—taking centuries to be constructed from bronze and magic. Not one of the Talos giants but several fifty-foot giant humanoid automatons marched forward. All were identical—a humanoid male in battle armor and high-ridged helmet with one hand ending in a sword and the other a mace. Made of magic and impervious to it. Even Oughtred's draugr army would be unable to stop their attacks.

"The time is soon!" the sphinx queen said. "Oughtred approaches with his armies. We will destroy them, seize

Atlantea, and kill all others not of our alliance! Kill those ancient fae too weak to join us! Kill all the lesser fae! Kill the human who drove us from the Lands of Man ages ago! But not before we kill Oughtred and end the Four Kings forever!"

A cloud appeared and looked like the smiling face of...Oughtred. Then the cloud dissipated. A portal opened before their armies—a large perfect circle cut in mid-air. Burning bright and flames. The flying demons, some humanoid, some monstrous and gross, spilled out into the desert realms in endless numbers. Flames of such intense heat shot out from their realm at the Talosian giants, already melting their magical armor.

HALL OF ATLANTEANS

The Atlanteans' watchtower stood within its own realm of invisibility, built on a series of clouds and extending into the void of the heavens. Dozens of Atlanteans watched through the window. The celestial body that moved in front of the window could have been the moon, but it was the humanoid eye of a Titan, able to see through their magic into the Hall of Atlantea.

Hundreds of millennia ago, the war with the Titans raged. The being before the fae no longer wanted to share the realm of realms. They meant to conquer it.

The Titan's head moved closer until it blocked out all light, and the hall was thrown in darkness.

Tens of millennia ago, the war with the dragons raged.

Within the Hall of Atlantea, the Atlanteans watched as flames and fireballs engulfed the skies. The creatures flew higher than they ever did into the void of the heavens. The hordes of dragons meant to have all the realm of realms as their domain. They'd even burn all of Pan-Earth to conquer it.

The largest dragons dove for the Atlantean tower.

The Atlanteans' watch tower focused on the ground below. In the era of ancient fae, elves, drows, fairies, nymphs, mermaids, giants, dwarves, and goblins were all the same race with many, many clans. All the clans on land, sea, and air lay siege on the outermost walls of Atlantea. A century of war, dozens of millennia ago, and the fae's conquest of Atlantea would fail.

The war with the ancient fae would lead to the breaking up of their one race into many. Atlantea would be strengthened, fae would be forced to make retribution, and the foundling race known as humans would gain favor.

At the Hall of Atlantea, the Atlanteans greeted their guests. The translucent-skinned sylphs and their blue-skinned undine sister elementals entered through a magic doorway that appeared.

"Welcome to the Hall of Atlantea," one said.

"We may be an ancient race, but even we are younglings compared to the history of this place throughout the eons," the elementals said to the Atlanteans.

"Since the time of the Titans," an Atlantean said.

"We have done much to rebuild the trust between our peoples," the sylphs said, "yet you still deny our requests."

"Why not be content with all that you have?" the Atlantean asked.

"We are not the earth or fire elementals," the undine said. "We are greater than they and other fae. Only the sky elves understand among all fae."

"Yet you still give favor to the weak humans who possess no magic and have no power," the sylph said.

"May I speak?" another fae said who entered the hall.

"Welcome to the Hall of Atlantea," the Atlantean said. "We have not seen your kind in centuries."

"I would say longer," the fae said. An orange hooded robe walked on the roots of his feet, and his eyes glowed like stars. "We star leshies took to the heavens centuries ago with the celestial, star, sun, ice, and shadow elves."

"I dare say more fae than the elves you have named."

"Think of all that you Atlanteans have inspired. You have caused races to die, races to be born, and have inspired many more to explore the heavens beyond Pan-Earth."

"What do you wish of us?"

"All you care about is the humans," the sylphs said. "Never will you forgive us for a war that happened eons ago by ones who died and turned to dust eons ago."

"If all you care about is humans, then we will find the most evil of them to be our voice. We will do everything to help such a human," the undine said.

"In fact, we may have already found such a human to be our champion," the sylph said.

"We do not care what he does or how he does it. As long as the elementals of air and water have control over the many magical worlds through the gateways of Atlantea that favor us."

"We are so sorry to make you feel you must take this path. We did not defeat the Titans, dragon armies, or your fae armies because we were more powerful. We were simply more intelligent and more patient."

"We are not the young races we once were. So it is we who may be more intelligent, and we have been patient enough," the elementals said.

"Always remember whatever point you reach in time; we passed that same crossroad eons ago."

"Mages say that three is a lucky sign. No one says that of the number four," the sylph said.

"We should have our own champions too," the Atlantean said.

"When we triumph over Atlantea. We might ban you from its lands for a thousand years," the undine said.

"You can return to your original world," the sylph said.

"You don't understand," the Atlantean said, "but it does not matter. What matters is you learned nothing from the lessons that your ancestors bestowed upon you. That is why we have denied your requests."

Most fae knew of three entrances to the fabled kingdom: by land, across the Oceanus Omnis, past the stature of Titan's Point and through the final marker of Titan's Gate. For fae of the water, they had the underwater version of all above the surface with their own Titan's Gate. A third Titan's Gate rested on the clouds for those flying caravans that entered the realms of Atlantea from the sky and heavens.

The fourth Titan's Gate was unknown to all but a few fae. Ancient dwarves and fire elementals knew of this rare portal from the age when all fae were one race. Dark fae used the Gate now—and daemons. The Gate's entrance was in a gargantuan cavern hundreds of miles beneath the earth's surface.

The star leshy stepped from the portal.

"Welcome," an Atlantean said. "We knew we would see you again."

"You did recognize me the last time."

"We did."

"Do your allies know you actually work for others?" asked another Atlantean.

"No, they do not. They are as consumed with their revenge as you are with your arrogance," the star leshy. "You should have greeted me with an armada of your ships of light. You should not have allowed me to enter at all."

He reached out, his open hands filled with seeds.

"A gift from the heirs of the Titans."

He threw them at the ground. Most of the seeds vanished from the air, but one landed. The seed magically became alive as it burrowed downward.

"Then time will be frozen until we are ready to receive your vengeful gift," an Atlantean declared.

WAR OF GIANTS

PLANET FALL

Day became night as the object hurled towards them. The Atlantean and the alliances rose to their feet. King Oughtred yelled at his armies as the white moon fell to the earth.

Armies on both sides braced for the impact. If the planetoid hit the surface, likely many would die.

"What can we do?" Traveler asked the Atlantean.

"We need not do a thing."

Oughtred turned his head from upon his griffin steed, flashing rage at the Atlantean.

"King Oughtred, you rule Atlantea. You must defend it."

The human lich smiled and raised the Atlantean staff in the air. "Then I will," he said. "Destroy it!" his voice shook the air.

Celestial elves fired flames of celestial power; star elves

fired starfire, and lightning elementals shot their bolts of lightning. The planetoid slowed in its descent as black flames, yellow rays, and massive bolts of lightning bombarded it. The moon's surface crumbled away, and then it all exploded. The moon fragments showered the land, but some fragments were the size of cities. Sorcerers on both sides used shields of magic to protect their own on the battlefield.

King Oughtred laughed. "Was this your ploy, Atlantean? You have only seen a fraction of my armies. Your magic to pull the moons from the heavens has failed!"

"It was not us, King Oughtred. The moon did not fall. It was thrown," the Atlantean said.

For the first time, they saw concern on Oughtred's face.

Another larger moon became visible high above. The grayish planetoid arched to the center of the two armies. Oughtred's forces did not wait for the command. Waves of the white, pale, blue-haired lightning elementals flew into the sky and concentrated their collective lightning bolts at the falling planetoid. Another giant rock was blown apart by the wild, yellow and white charges of electricity from the beings. A shower of stone rained down, bouncing off magic shields and invisible barriers protecting those below.

Before Oughtred's forces could relax, three more moons appeared in the sky but not heading towards them—the cities of Atlantea were under siege. Beyond them in the heavens, more moons, followed by a flurry of giant comets, slowly headed towards them all.

HORDES OF EVIL

Oughtred's elementals were of far greater numbers than Traveler, or the alliance realized. The lightning elementals flew higher into the sky to fire their massive bolts of lightning at the now storm of moons raining down on Atlantea. Air elementals created a whirlpool of clouds to create a shield over the entire kingdom. However, every single sylph had to take on the effort straining with all their inner magic to repel the falling moons.

A sickening feeling came over Traveler as he saw the first one. For any of what was taking place to occur meant that the magic of the fabled kingdom was gone. Atlantea was completely defenseless. He and the alliance were so focused on Oughtred. Columns of giant draugr warriors appeared in the distance, walking through the sea, enshrouded in a mist, not of water but the evil magic of death their bodies emitted like fumes. But for the Atlanteans, it never was about the human lich and his dark allies. It was always about the other invaders.

The first Fomorian crawled out of the sea onto the shore ahead of the coming draugr. Its monstrous sea giant's goat head had a damp and dank pelt, a short twisted horn on each temple, and black eyes. Quickly it stood in its pot-bellied, shaggy fur and kelp-covered body. It yelled to reveal its crooked, fanged mouth, and it struck at those of Oughtred's army closest to them on the shore. One fist of black, twisted, claw-like nails slammed down, killing goblins, dire wolves, and Redcaps.

Draugr giants attacked the Fomorian. Three ten-foot undead giants against one fifteen-foot sea giant. The Fomorian swiped at the three of them and ripped them in half. But even dismembered, the draugr's upper torso was able to swing their axes and sword, cutting down the sea giant. But more of the sea giants rose from depths below.

Armies of the draugr shrunk their size to swarm over the head and torso of another Formian, inflicting damage with weapons and their claws. The sea giant ran onto the shore and allowed itself to fall as it was killed. The giant fell on dozens more goblins who were not quick enough to run.

Other Fomorians rose from the sea, but Oughtred's draugr armies kept growing and their frenzy of violence increased. An ax slipped from a draugr's skeleton hand and struck the barrier protecting the Seven Empires of humans and elfin armies with such force that all were knocked off their feet.

King Oughtred yelled triumphantly, "No one will take Atlantea from me!"

A Fomorian coughed a black cloud of pestilence at Oughtred. His griffin shrieked as its body decayed to bone and collapsed. Some of his elves, goblins, and beast men around him also fell dead. But Oughtred was untouched. The attacking Fomorian was hit in the head and back by multiple draugr blades and decapitated.

The Fomorians responded in kind by grabbing whole draugrs and ripping them to pieces.

Traveler remained at the front with the sole Atlantean. He glanced back at them to see the fear in the faces of Lady Aylen, Maiden Gwyness, Frog-Dor, and Dr'amal.

"What are we to do?" Lady Aylen asked. "This is not a war. It is a slaughter. And ours if we cannot retreat."

Gwyness called out. The skeletal body of a draugr warrior crashed against their magical barrier and once again knocked them on their feet.

"This is so far beyond us," Dr'amal said.

"Master Traveler!" Frog-Dor yelled.

The disembodied arm of the giant draugr reached out at Traveler. The barrier blocked it, but its skeletal hand pushed through slowly. Traveler swung his magic sword to sever the hand at the wrist that breached their magic barrier.

Gwyness stepped up to the decaying skeletal fingers and shot a white ray of light from her amulet. The fingers burst into dust. Traveler pushed his sword through the barrier to touch the rest of the draugr's arm, which burst into flames.

"Can you strengthen the circle?" Traveler asked Frog-Dor and Dr'amal.

"We will need the aid of the elfin and drow sorcerers to do so," Frog-Dor said. "But Lady Aylen is correct. We must escape here, or we will all die."

The earthquake exploded around them, and every member of Titan's Alliance fought to stay on their feet.

The giant walking from the region outside Kraken's Wake that was seen by a merman oracle stepped into Oughtred's Atlantea. The foot came down on dozens of draugr warriors. Giant krakens—mad krakens—still clung to the mega-giant's limb. Above, the giant's three heads peered down through the clouds at them all. The mega-giant may have lumbered across the Pan-Earth's ocean floor but it was a winged giant, and bat wings extended to take up the horizon.

"What monstrosity of evil is that?" Gwyness asked.

The Geryon, a three-headed demon of a giant, was besieged by Oughtred's armies. Its skin was leathery, lean, and muscular; the face of each head was humanoid and deformed.

"The allies of the Titans have returned to conquer Atlantea," Traveler said, more to himself.

"Atlantea has already been conquered," Lady Aylen said.

"Allies of the Titans?" Dr'amal asked. "But the Titans are long dead. What allies?"

"Demi-titans."

"Their children were far from our heavens and purported dead as well," Frog-Dor said.

"Who are these demi-titans?" Gwyness asked.

"Brace yourself!" Traveler yelled.

The Geryon flapped its black bat wings. The tsunami reached out from the sea, crashing along the entire shore to wash human, fae, and the cities away.

The human wizard king of the Seven Empires of humans held the Bident of Faylen in his arms as he marched to the head of their allied armies. He stabbed the earth with the staff's end to allow it to stand on its own.

"Tell everyone to remain within the circle of the bident's magic," he said. "Anyone who steps outside of it will have the choice to die by Oughtred's army or the coming new Titans."

The king wrapped his hands around the handle of the Faylen's Bident. The staff weapon grew as tall as the Fomorians and widened larger than four battle columns.

"Wizard, do you need us to strengthen the circle's magic?" an elfin wizard said as he approached with five others.

Dr'amal's father and other drows reached them. "Why remain cowering under a magic dome when we should collectively cast our magic to escape?" Dr'as asked. "The lands are completely submerged underwater."

The water covered the shore and flowed back into the sea. The land armies could be seen again. Oughtred and his forces were untouched by the waters. Draugr giants greatly outnumbered the advancing Fomorian giants, but the darkness of their magic was equally matched. Both races had to do much to kill the other, and both could increase their size.

The Geryon had stopped the flapping of its wings because it, too, was under greater attack. A mountain peak sailed through the sky and shattered on the creature's body. The giant turned to face the other oncoming mountains. A single giant kraken remained on its body, and it finally ended the annoyance by crushing it and throwing the lifeless body at Oughtred just as another mountain hit the Geryon squarely in the upper torso.

"Mountain throwers," an elf said. "They must be far, far away but still can hurl their mountain-size boulders across the face of Pan-Earth with the accuracy of the best of an elfin archer."

Oughtred's air elementals grabbed the kraken corpse and flung it back at the Geryon.

"Then the Athos giants belonged to Oughtred's dark alliance," said the high-elf wizard Lyre. "He caused the death waves and the kraken wall."

"Oughtred has giants," Pangolin the berserker said.

Traveler's eyes remained ahead as more of the alliance leaders joined the front, including King Aereth. Another giant crashed into the sea from the heavens.

"How strong is the magic of this circle?" Traveler asked the human wizard king.

"As long as we remain within the circle, we will survive," he replied.

"What of that?" Traveler pointed to the new humanoid giant approaching the warring draugr and Fomorians.

The magic barrier of the Bident was engulfed in flames hotter than what some of them experienced in the attack of the sun elves.

"Can we fire our arrows through the barrier?" an elf asked the human wizard king.

"Yes. The magic is to prevent attacks from outside; nothing prevents anything passing through from within," he answered.

"Even all our archers combined could not harm that beast," the moon elf Shadu-mun said.

The fire-breathing Cacus giant hadn't aimed his attack at them, but Oughtred and his forces deflected its hellish flames with their magic. But the giant did manage to set on fire scores of draugr giants on the ground and air elementals in the sky. If not for their own inherent magic, both draugr and sylph would have been totally consumed by flames.

At first, they thought the Cacus was silhouetted by the shadow of the Geryon or something else. However, from the flickering of fire in its eyes and from its mouth, they realized the giant's skin was coated in black soot. Whether naked or clothed was hard to tell as it let loose another blast of fire at attacking elementals, elves, and gargoyles in the air around it. Oughtred's forces fired arrows and magic at it.

One of Oughtred's high-goblin generals sat on the back of a winged dire wolf that came at the Cacus giant. A cloud of giant bats descended from the sky at the giant commanded by the goblin beast lord—goblins with the greatest magical power to summon and control malevolent beasts, but not only one—many all at one time.

The giant bats landed or circled its head and body and clawed at it with their feet or bit into its flesh. The Cacus giant responded by breathing fire. Many bats were burnt alive, but many more dodged its attack, as did the high goblin.

Gargoyle swarms increased their own attacks so the flying sylphs could remain back.

The lightning elementals continued to destroy the endless barrage of falling moons. In the sea, Oughtred thought his giant draugr army would overwhelm the Fomorian invaders, but then a virtual army of the sea giants began rising from the sea. The Geryon had its attention focused on the volley of mountain thrown at it from far away, but the mega-giant either destroyed the mountain or grabbed it to throw at Oughtred's forces on the ground or air. The last mountain he threw at the lightning elementals hit and killed dozens of them before they knew it.

Not all the falling moons were destroyed. Some got through and obliterated the remaining parts of the Atlantea kingdom or hit the ground with such force to create massive craters or chasms. The very continent the fabled kingdom stood upon was being destroyed.

Oughtred watched the battle, waiting, thinking. He turned his attention to the Atlantean and Titan's alliance within their protective magic circle. All of Atlantea would be destroyed.

"Kill them!" he yelled. "There will be no mercy after all, for any enemies of my Atlantea!"

Red goblins and shadow goblins raced or rode their dire wolves to them.

Goblin archers had already begun firing at the Oughtred's goblins. The abilities of the red goblins were not known, but magic arrows bounced off their armor and passed completely through the shadow elves.

"Elves, kill their death archers!" Traveler yelled at the elves. "Drows, help our goblins stop the red and shadow goblins!"

"Our goblins," Dr'as said but moved quickly to defend the circle.

Traveler raised his sword and moved in front of the Atlantean.

"I do not need your protection," the Atlantean said.

"Yet we will do so anyway," Traveler said.

The death archers were Oughtred's celestial elfin archers who fired arrows of pure celestial magic. The magic could pass through most other magic and pierce even the strongest of elfin steel.

"Music to a berserker's ears," Pangolin said as he joined Traveler and the others. "A battle to be had."

The first red goblin breached their circle, and then they learned what made their sub-race so deadly. Red goblins were shape-shifters. One transformed into a hideous red dire wolf with bony spikes when Pangolin's axe-mace crashed onto its chest. Pangolin's magic weapon was known as the Mountain Breaker, and he had used it to send flying away, and kill, creatures and giants many times his size. The red goblin was obliterated and showered his attacking fellow red and shadow goblins in blood.

Sickening, maddening screams of the draugr warriors shook the air the moment a shadow goblin leaped over Traveler to dodge his blow. Lady Aylen's war trident passed right through the dark fae but not so with Gwyness's war hammer. The maiden struck the dark goblin again and, with a look of astonishment, he fell dead.

Red goblins attacked in the form of red manticores, pouncing on humans, elves, drows, and allied goblins. An illusion of Dr'amal. The red goblins hadn't pounced on anything but empty ground. Arrows ripped them apart from elfin and a flurry of double-blades from the drows.

Their magic circle was hit with a flurry of celestial elfin arrows as their own elves fired an endless volley at the floating celestial elves in the sky, soon joined by star elves.

Then the magic of the Atlantean realm shattered again. King Oughtred looked up. For the first time, with fear. He yelled in rage.

"Atlantea is mine!"

He flew into the dark sky. "Rise from the sea! Rise from the Nether-Lands! Descend from the hell of the heavens!"

DEMON CENTAURS, WAR WIZARDS, AND NECROMANCERS

With the over-magic gone, Atlantea was being overrun by hordes of sea giants. Draugr were the favorite warriors of lich lords, unrelenting undead fighters capable of much dark magic. However, Fomorian were indeed more demon than giants and capable of far greater dark magic.

A giant helmeted face appeared in the sky like a sun.

I'll arrive soon, Atlantea! Vengeance of the Titans will be ours.

"I am King Oughtred and I alone rule Atlantea! You will cease your attack upon my kingdom, or it will be you who will be destroyed."
Who are you?

"I am the new ruler of Atlantea!"

You are nothing, little animal.

"I am a lich lord, and my armies even now will destroy your forces."

You throw mountains at us. We throw worlds. You are creatures of decaying death. We are beings made of the power of the cosmos. You crawl upon the earth like insects. We walk among the earth crushing cities beneath our feet. When the bridge connects our worlds, I will slide down and remove you from existence. No magic of light or darkness can defeat the magic of the universe's creation.

"No bridge will ever connect our realms."

The bridge was created before you were born. The Atlantean spell to stop time is cracking, thanks to you. You are the birth of your own death.

The demi-Titan's image vanished from the sky.

"Now! Now!" Oughtred yelled madly.

The human lich king unleashed all his forces at once.

The Bident of Faylen towered above the one part of the

Atlantean ante-city still standing. The human wizard king stood with the object to his back, watching the battle between Oughtred's forces and the giants. Traveler, Lady Aylen, Pangolin, Gwyness, Frog-Dor, and Dr'amal waited at the main entrance. The bodies of red and shadow goblins littered the path.

The Atlantean joined the caravan master at his post.

"If not for the giants, we would have fought Oughtred's forces and died," Traveler said.

"If King Oughtred hadn't conquered Atlantea, the giants would have destroyed Atlantea," the Atlantean said.

"The Fates laughing at us both?" Traveler asked.

"Or protecting us in spite of ourselves," the Atlantean said.

"But you defeated the Titans," Dr'amal said.

The Atlantean smiled. "We did."

"Those giants were more powerful than these, were they not?" the drowess asked.

"The Titans were not giants. Humans and fae wrongly believed they lived on Pan-Earth. They were beings who walked the heavens. They only visited our world. They did not try to conquer Atlantea. They tried to conquer Pan-Earth and all its races, including those not born."

"Forgive me, Atlantean, but you are not saddened or fearful as their war destroys your kingdom?" Traveler asked.

"This is not the war. The war only begins."

"This is not the war?" Pangolin asked, looking at all the destruction around the city.

Traveler looked at them. "He means the demi-Titan hasn't arrived yet."

Titan's Caravan had seen the quasi-demons before. Their blackened ships rose from the sea depths, a hill of earthen soil in the center of each ship's deck. The spider centaurs swarmed out from a hole at the top of the hill. Upper torso of drow-like males with purplish skin, unkempt hair hanging in front of their faces, long, protruding elfin ears, and the lower torso of a giant black spider.

They immediately fired arrows in rapid fashion at the Fomorians as they crawled out. With so many spider centaurs and so many arrows, Fomorians had both the draugr giants and demonic centaurs to battle.

Other spider centaurs leaped onto the bodies of the sea

giants. But they were not alone. From below the sea, the spider centaurs' evil allies swarmed over the Fomorians too. Crab centaurs, with thick shell armor over their humanoid upper torsos and giant crab lower torsos, stabbed the sea giant's skin with their giant pincer claws of tremendous power. Both spider and crab centaurs covered the entire body of the first Fomorian. The sea giant frantically tried to wipe them off his body as he dove back into the sea depths.

A whirlpool opened above in the sky, appearing like a black lake of choppy water. Oughtred's new army of war wizards descended through the portal. Many different human and fae races, every one with sickly yellowish eyes, comprised the wizard army. They joined the battle against the fire-breathing Cacus giant with the gargoyles, giant bat swarms, and goblin beast lord. The Cacus giant threw a raging fireball at the war wizards killing dozens of them. He could create a deadly fire within his own hands, too, besides breathing it. But hundreds of the wizards descended from the sky lake portal.

A whirlpool of clouds appeared above the ground. The wizards that rose through its portal were also of many different fae races. The necromancers chanted in unison as they animated the Geryon's wide shadow on the sea. The shadow became alive as it took form and rose to be of equal height and breadth. Its shadow wings extended out. The Geryon's shadow grabbed the real Geryon giant, and both wrestled each other just as another mountain struck them and shattered to pieces.

Oughtred smiled with his striga, in her elfess form, at his side. He would destroy the invading giants before their master arrived. "The demi-Titan spoke of a bridge between worlds. Anything that appears that could be it, attack with all the magic and warriors that you can, even sacrificing your own lives."

THE ACCORD

The Fomorian giants dove into the sea, sending a tidal wave smashing to the ground, but Oughtred's floating war wizard protected their armies with magic. The giant draugr army screamed wildly in victory. The Cacus rose into the sky, followed by the larger Geryon taking flight just as another mountain fell and barely missed him. Falling to the sea were spider and crab centaurs like dust from the Geryon's body. Giant bats pursued the Cacus but were called back by their beast lord. Gargoyle warriors circled the skies in a circling flock. All that remained was the shower of planetoids continuing to fall from the heavens.

Oughtred felt triumphant.

"I can do anything," he said to himself.

He could feel the power of the staff. The land of Atlantea magically began to heal itself. The ground reconstructed itself—craters filled in, chasms closed. The destroyed Atlantean cities in the distance began rebuilding themselves. Green returned to the land. The blueness returned to the sky.

"I can do anything!"

He looked at the giant draugr army standing on the seashore.

"Go to the threshold of the kingdom. Guard it as you would guard a great treasure for your king. Kill anyone or anything who seeks entrance without permission. Block the gateways with dark clouds of pestilence and madness. Destroy even the gateways to Atlantea if any force threatens to overwhelm you.

"Here it begins. All of Atlantea, all its realms, then all of Pan-Earth. Each of you, every member of our alliance, will have your own kingdoms to rule...forever."

The draugr turned and marched out to the borders of the fabled kingdom.

From the sole remaining city of Atlantea, surrounded by rubble, their alliance watched Oughtred and his armies. The armies beyond their walls formed up before the human lich king—common, high, red, and shadow goblins, including beast lords; Redcaps; sky elves, nymphs, elementals, and gargoyles; drows, night drows, and shadow drows.

Humans peered through telescopes. The fae used magic mirrors. Mages used seeing eyes.

Traveler had not left his place at the city's walled entrance.

"Where is your dog?" Lady Aylen said.

"I gave him a mission, princess. Could not risk losing him."

"Is this not the time when a powerful shape-shifting animal would be of most benefit to us?" Lyre the elfin wizard asked.

"Lyre, not all the Seven Empires of humans, Thirteen Houses of elves, Three Kingdoms of drows, and the Towers of Ten goblin clans here in Atlantea could have defeated Oughtred's forces. We are only their representatives."

"Then your great spell to remove fear and aggression from our hearts was for naught?" Lyre asked.

"Lyre, it saved our lives."

"The human speaks correctly," Nagisa said. "If the reality is clear to us ancient fae, it should be clear to you child-race fae."

"Child-race?" elves and drow said.

"We arrived in the fabled kingdom to see its end," Traveler said.

"Do not give up so easily, Master Traveler," the Atlantean said to him.

"Atlantea no longer exists. Without the existence of an Atlantea on Pan-Earth, its races will return to their strife against each other," Traveler said.

"Possibly," the Atlantean said.

"Also, the magic is gone from the kingdom," Traveler said. "The magic of Atlantea enchanted all who resided within its realms."

"Kept us drunk with a magical reverie of indifference, you mean, human," Nagisa the lamia said.

"Mr. Traveler, should we not focus our attention on Oughtred?" Pangolin said. "He pushed back the attack of those giants. He will then re-focus his attention upon us. There is a pile of dead goblins outside the circle. Goblins he sent to kill us. No offense to the goblin here."

"He sent them to kill us too. No need to apologize, human," goblins said. "Land and water elves hate sky elves. Those goblins are outcasts to us for allowing a human to lead them. No offense to the humans here."

"Mr. Traveler?" Pangolin repeated.

"We must stay here within the circle of the city under the protection of the Bident of Faylen. It is the only protection we have in Atlantea now."

"The berserker is right," the wild elfin king said. "We will be in battle soon again, and whether Oughtred has superior forces doesn't change the fact that we will have to fight to the death. For a knight, that is not a bad way to die."

"No one is supposed to die in Atlantea," Traveler said.

"Yet here we are," the wild elf said.

"We must ready ourselves," King Aereth said. "Mr. Traveler, you did create this alliance."

"Not for this, sire. The alliance is not for here. It was for our caravan to get here. It is for when we all return to our lands to last for as long as we nurture it. Oughtred did make the giants retreat, but giants such as they only retreat for one reason. They are like gnolls in the magical lands."

"Reinforcements," Pangolin said.

"Yes, Mr. Pangolin, and the only reinforcements that giants have are more giants. Oughtred will have his attention re-focused again. I did say the demi-Titan hasn't arrived yet."

"But we saw it," Lady Aylen said. "The giant with the

three heads and bat wings the size of a roc."

The humans and fae agreed, but the lamia laughed.

"That was a Geryon," Traveler said. "The fire-breather, a Cacus giant. The demi-Titan still comes."

The Atlantean remained emotionless, but every human and fae saw the horror flying through the air at Oughtred's ground armies.

DEMI-TITANS

Traveler thought of Atlantean's history and the meteor storm of giant rocks that destroyed much of the continent that the Colossus of Titan's Point stood upon. Was it actually an attack eons ago? They watched as Titan's Gate, the circular structure, a thick ring of metal-like stone, fifty or so feet in width, sail through the sky like it was all a dream. But the final marker of Titan's Trail had shrieking bodies of several draugr giants clinging to it.

When the circular Gate crashed, even the magical barrier created by Oughtred's war wizards shattered. War wizards fell to the ground or into the sea. Oughtred and other fae in the air dodged the monument by flying through its center. Then the draugr bodies landed—on the ground, in the sea, and another crashed just before their city.

"Send the creature to whom it belongs," the Atlantean said to Traveler and the others.

Frog-Dor raised his arms just as the other elfin wizards were about to act.

"May I?" he asked them.

The draugr giant rose to its feet, saw them, and moved to them. Frog-Dor conjured an arrow in his hand. It flew from his palm. As it passed through their magic barrier, the arrow became a hand and shoved the draugr into the sky. The creature flew towards Oughtred. Bolts of celestial fire from his elves reduced it to ashes.

"Look," Gwyness said.

The pile of dead red and shadow goblins began to shake on the ground.

"He's changing them," Dr'amal yelled.

"Traveler, I'd set them ablaze with your sword," Dr'as said.

"Do not leave the circle," the Atlantean said.

"I can accommodate from here," the human wizard king said. The dark fae corpses erupted in intense red flames.

Then the flames were blown out.

They thought it was Oughtred. But quickly saw it wasn't the human lich king.

The giants had returned—with more.

The blue of the sea was gone. The green of the lands was gone. The blueness and clouds of the sky were gone as the hurricane winds rushed through the realm. As the new Wind Giants marched through the sea, the Fomorians rose from the depths for the shore. The hurricane winds bellowed from the open mouths of the Wind Giants.

"Armies—"

Suddenly, King Oughtred found himself pinned to the ground on his back under the giant hand of another new giant. More human than the others, fair-skinned, golden hair, and smiling. But his red eyes glared at him. His body had no clothes, no features, no skin or flesh. None in the alliance could readily describe it, other than he was made of solidified air. The Antaean giants that traveled with Titan's Caravan told them that there was only one race of giants that ran, but there was only one race of giants known as the fastest of them all, giants that moved at the speed of the wind—the Damysos.

Oughtred engulfed the giant's hand crushing him in dark, dead magic. But Oughtred's attempt to necrotize the giant's hand was futile. The giant laughed, grabbed Oughtred up, held him in his hand, then threw the human lich king to the heavens. The war wizards fired magic bolts at him, but the giant moved faster than they thought possible.

A portal door opened, and Oughtred stepped through it to step back onto the ground.

The spider and crab centaurs resumed their attack on the returning Fomorians. Spider centaur arrows fired in a rapid frenzy. Crab centaurs swarmed over the Fomorian from below. In the distance, the draugr giant army marched back to them. More and more of them entered the realm; their giant weapons held high.

The Cacus giant flew back down to the center of the first wave and incinerated all of them. Oughtred's army of war wizards floated to it to resume their attack, joined by the swarms of gargoyles and giant bat of the goblin beast lord. The Cacus giant blew fire at them, but the war wizards reflected it and shot rays of ice at its open mouth.

The Geryon returned, flapping its wings as it dropped into the sea. Oughtred's necromancers chanted in unison to once again animate the Geryon's shadow to help in their attack. The Geryon, this time did allow its shadow doppelgänger to attempt to strangle him.

The lightning elementals continued to fire their massive bolts of lightning at the still raining planetoids down on Atlantea. The air elementals that had created a whirlpool of clouds to shield the entire kingdom had to battle the hurricanes of the Wind Giants. No longer could they focus on the falling moons. But Oughtred's unseen Athos giants returned to their own, raining down whole mountains at their targets of the Geryon, Fomorians, Wind Giants, and Cacus. The second and third waves of his draugr giants advanced on the invaders. Some seized up a Fomorian and threw the sea giant into an oncoming planetoid. The Fomorian was crushed as it shattered the falling moon to pieces. Another whirlpool of clouds appeared on the ground, and out crawled an endless advance of humanoid ghouls. Whether they had been humans or fae could not be determined. All they desired was to kill anyone or thing that their lich lord commanded.

"Watch for the bridge of the demi–Titan," Oughtred said to the striga witch.

The Atlantean watched war once again engulf Atlantea.

"Our war with the Fae lasted a century. The war against the dragons was five hundred years. Our first war with the Titans lasted ten centuries. Oughtred is beginning to realize that if he wishes to keep Atlantea to rule its lands and realms, a war cannot be waged and won in a day. The time needed will be much, much longer."

"But he is not mortal anymore," Lady Aylen said.

"He is impatient. Because one is immortal doesn't mean one wishes to use every moment of all that time in the furtherance of only one thing," the Atlantean said to her.

However, the gemstone being's eyes were sad.

"Do Atlanteans cry?" Traveler asked.

"Yes, we can and have."

FURY AT TITAN'S END

Hundreds of miles beneath the earth's surface at the entrance of Atlantea's rarely used fourth Titan's Gate, within its gargantuan cavern, the star leshy reached out his open hands filled with seeds.

"A gift from the heirs of the Titans."

He threw them at the ground. Most of the seeds vanished from the air, but one landed. The seed magically became alive as it burrowed downward.

"Then time will be frozen until we are ready to receive your vengeful gift," an Atlantean declared.

"For how long do you believe your magic can sustain such a spell?" the star leshy asked.

"We can receive your gift now," the Atlantean said.

The first of the seed's vines pushed through the ground.

A giant vine burst through the ground changing from white to light green to a darker green as it grew into the heavens. The vine expanded in size as the top of it disappeared from view. The ancient star leshy crawled up the vine, riding it upward. First the size of a tall human, the star leshy grew to ten feet and more, becoming less humanoid and more tree-like. Its feet of roots shot down into the earth, and its roots expanded through the land to attack Oughtred's army too.

The star leshy realized the change by the stars in the heavens. "How long have we been frozen in time?"

The Atlantean city was also under the attack of the giant leshy's roots as the main vine grew wider than even the Geryon. What little light shone was being blotted out.

The demi-Titan fell to Atlantea from the giant vine in slow motion. The fattest giant they had ever seen, barrel-chested, twice the size of the Geryon. Argan giants had one-hundred eyes. The part-giant, part-creature had one-hundred arms. They saw the gold of its skin or armor, but the true size of its full body was not yet perceptible.

Fae especially had always heard of the legends of the

demi-Titans, the descendants of the ancient and long-gone Titans. However, none had ever thought how massive a true demi-Titan was. The second demi-Titan did not need to climb down the vine. The being was so large its full body was never seen. A foot alone came down on all of Atlantea's region and day became night. When it landed, all of Pan-Earth must have shaken in a quake never before experienced during or before any of the races were born. The continent of Atlantea no longer existed, only a myriad of islands.

Oughtred screamed in defiance, and all his war wizards collectively cast their spells. Sprites and other beings, including the draugr, could increase their size. The magic of the war wizard army began to shrink the demi-Titan. The humanoid became perceptible—clad in liquid gold armor, a golden helmet, and golden sandals. The monstrous giant was greater than one hundred feet, even with the dark magic trying to shrink it. His body was humanoid and upon his shoulder was the helmeted head that they saw in the projected image upon the sky. But his neck and shoulders were a mass of snake-like heads and tentacles. In the center of its chest was a great eye.

Oughtred yelled with a rage that shattered the realm again. The demi-Titan caught one of the falling planetoids and threw it at the human lich king. The giant rock vanished and then came out of a portal behind the demi-Titan to crash futilely into the mega-giant's body.

More whirlpools of black waters appeared in the sky as more of Oughtred's dark armies came—lampads, goblins, shadow elves, shadow goblins, shadow drows, more sun elves, more ice elves, more war wizards.

A portal opened in the sea—a large perfect circle emitting burning bright light. Flying demons, some humanoid, some monstrous and gross, spilled out into the dark sky. The Cacus giant spat a giant ball of fire and incinerated so many of the demons as they had just taken flight.

Within the sole Atlantean city floating in the sea, Titan's alliance watched in horror as all of Atlantea had been utterly destroyed, but Oughtred's armies and the demi-Titans continued their war.

As a true warrior all his life, Pangolin had seen it in battle many times. He knew it shone in his face too. Every human, elf, drow, fae, goblin was in the deepest of shock. Many of them were on the verge of tears or outright crying. The reality was too painful, too overwhelming. Nothing could be done. Die, live; it was all far beyond their control. They were in a world of two titanic forces, and no one and nothing else mattered or could touch them. All was lost. The magical, wondrous, exquisite, mesmerizing, mysterious, eons-old fabled kingdom to all humans and fae on Pan-Earth was lost. Atlantea was gone.

"They will fight forever," the Atlantean said.

"Then that is all the time I need for my revenge," Nagisa said.

The lamia flew through the circle followed by all the ancient winged goblins, seemingly hundreds of them. None knew there were so many of them hiding in invisibility. In mere moments, she killed the striga witch-elfess at Oughtred's side with two magic javelins that appeared in her hands. Whatever mask spell she covered herself with was gone. Her form was an even more serpentine form with a gaunt green humanoid face, long fangs, and slits for eyes. She was not the neutral race of lamias she pretended to be but the more sinister malevolent kind fond of devouring human children and small animals.

So much subterfuge, Traveler thought. Oughtred and the younger fae races. Nagisa and the ancient fae races. The battle for Atlantea would have been between their evil forces, not any battle between Titan's Caravan and Oughtred. But none knew of the coming demi-Titans whose obsession with destroying the fabled kingdom began before all of them were even born. None knew except the Atlanteans.

Her winged goblins were met by attacking animals of darkness conjured by necromancers standing on the air. A giant draugr arm rose from the sea and blocked as the lamia threw a volley of more javelins at Oughtred. She landed on the draugr's arm and still lunged at the human lich king as her size grew and her arms, fingers, and claws elongated. She managed to claw the crown from his head, but nothing more.

"And you will have all the time that you desire," the Atlantean said to the lamia.

Then the demi-Titan's hand smashed the sea over all of them.

"They will fight forever," the Atlantean said again as the tidal wave rose higher and higher, about to crash down on the one city and all that remained of the fabled kingdom of Atlantea.

For a brief moment they saw Oughtred fly out of the sea into the air.

The Atlantean reached out with his hand into the sky. Suddenly everything that was around them was within a clear globe in the Atlantean's hand. "Two forces. One of ultimate destruction. One of ultimate evil. Both immortally obsessed with the fabled kingdom of Atlantea. We will let them fight forever."

All around them was the empty void of the heavens as the city floated in an empty sea. Everyone and everything was gone save them.

"Atlantea is gone," Traveler said sadly. "Was I the cause?"

"Why would you think so, Master Traveler? This all began before humans were born. Atlantea is not gone. Atlantea is wherever we wish it to be, and as long as we sustain it with magic, it will be."

"But what happened?" Traveler asked.

"Our wars are over. Atlantea can live into the future without fear of the return of any of its enemies from time's past."

"The fabled kingdom is not dead?" Traveler asked.

"The fabled kingdom is not dead. It is a realm of realms, so all we had to do is move our realm to another." The Atlantean held up the globe. "They have their Atlantea. We have ours."

The Atlantean threw the crystal globe into space. It became a comet and flew away in a streak of light.

THE REALM OF
REALMS

THE RETURN

Traveler caught himself staring at his own reflection in the blade of his magic sword in his hand. For him, a tiny shard of a far greater Titan's sword, or so wizards told him. Its translucent flame rippled with renewed power. He looked up.

They were in the same city, but everything was different, or it had returned to the reality before, but better. Every human and fae saw everything, including him, with the same eyes of wonder and excitement as if they had beheld the fabled kingdom for the first time.

Their city floated on the back of some submerged beast. An aspidochelone. It could be no other giant aquatic creature. Its back unmistakable for the rocky shore of an island thick with trees, other plant life, and wildlife. Whether the species of titanic sea turtles or shell-covered whales, it moved through the sea with no ill intent.

They were definitely in the waters of Atlantea's Sea with a hallucinatory haze of cloudy mist behind them and…the fabled kingdom ahead of them—again?

"Steep drop!" Mr. Elman's voice rang from the top of a tower rising from the small city's wall.

Their floating city crossed the invisible barrier. The sky and everything around them winked out. Their lead ship sailed on black waters with the darkness of the heavens around them. Stars in the distance seemed only several hundred feet above and around them. The sun was behind them. Ahead of them, the ocean dropped off. But no one was afraid.

A controlled descent down a waterfall rivaling that of even Titan's Fall. At the bottom were distant stars, and the water raged as it plummeted. They crashed into the black waters. The splash drenched the city but evaporated instantly. Like before, they moved forward in near darkness then the massive oval portal appeared in the distance. Within its realm, the normal sky resumed and the real castle peaks at Titan's End—Atlantea.

Traveler turned to the Atlantean standing with them at the city entrance. "I don't understand. Was it real?"

"Yes, very much so," he said.

The glowing city was made of solid white gold and rose from the horizon into the heavens, with both the sun and the moon at opposite ends in the sky.

Everyone smiled at the sight of the Atlantean light

ships in the sky as they drifted by. Seemingly the same tall Atlantean on the deck of the light ship with his skin of blue gemstone. He bowed to them.

"It was never about me or us," Traveler said to the Atlantean. "But I was truly concerned for Atlantea."

"We know, Master Traveler. You were focused on evil. Significant to you, but unimportant to us."

"I thought Atlantea did not see good and evil."

"Of course, we do. We always have. But judging the concepts is difficult. Judging the actions is simple. That is what we watch for. Actions, not words."

"Nothing that we did mattered."

"We did tell you not to trouble yourselves about him and to enter the fabled kingdom for your riches."

"But Oughtred and his dark forces weakened the magic of Atlantea," Lady Aylen said.

The Atlantean smiled. "They weakened nothing. We transferred our magic elsewhere."

"It's more than just Atlantea; it is the Realm of Realms," Traveler said.

"You are beginning to understand. Atlantea is not one place. It is many places. It is wherever we say it exists. Wherever you say, it exists."

"Where Oughtred and demi-Titans fight...is that not Atlantea?" Traveler asked.

"It is. It is one true Atlantea out of many, many more. That is the best I can explain for you to understand."

"Atlantean oracles predicted the arrival of Oughtred, didn't they?" Traveler asked.

"I am surprised. I thought you rejected most of the myth of oracles, and rightly so," the Atlantean said. "We did not need to predict his arrival, nor even be an oracle or any being of magic to know what we would do. We saw his actions. He didn't need you to be given entry to Atlantea. We simply wanted him to believe it. The formation of his dark alliance began before his birth. He simply seized control of it at the end. We knew of him and his dark alliance as we knew of the demi-Titan and his."

"You needed him to destroy the demi-Titans for you?"

"No, not so. Of all the possibilities, they would never have triumphed in the end. We fought the Titans, the dragons, the ancient fae, and others."

"More than three wars?"

"Yes. You only know of the three because those are the three of Pan-Earth. Atlantea is beyond Pan-Earth. The price of this war, had we fought as we did in the past, would have been too great for us to bear. You and others would have attempted to defend us from Oughtred and been destroyed. You would have attempted to defend us against the demi-Titans and would have been destroyed. All humans and fae would have come to our aid and been destroyed. We had to end it before they ever started. Atlantea lives, and so do you all."

The enormous circular structure of Titan's Gate stood tall before them, coming out of invisibility.

"There isn't simply one Titan's Gate."

"There are many of them, but this one, for Pan-Earth, is yours and it never was destroyed by demi-Titans or quadri-Titans."

Once again, the shadow of the one-hundred-foot-tall Colossus of Titan's Point towered behind them on a single flat island. The statue honoring the Titan, or myth thereof, was the penultimate marker to Atlantea. Known as the Maker of All Mountains, the statue depicted the helmet over his saddened face, clad in chest armor, and dragging his fabled weapon, the Star Slayer, upon the earth.

The final marker of the ancient Titan's Trail to Atlantea, Titan's Gate, was the circular structure, a thick ring of stone, fifty or so feet in width. Three-fourths of the Gate was above the waterline, and over a mile high. The material of the gate appeared to be carved out of a single piece of solid stone but really was an ancient metal of some kind. Atlantea's shore was clearly visible under the mirror-like blue sky but was at least a hundred miles away.

The moment their moving city crossed the threshold like they had experienced in so many other magic cities before, they passed into another realm. The sky was thick with billowy white clouds and flocks of perytons, far more than when they first sailed into Atlantea.

"They're here!" Quilllen yelled.

To their left, were mountains with steep cliffs. Their outward appearance seemed hazy as if an illusion. They were many miles away, but how far was not clear. The side of the cliffs reached beyond the height of the Colossus outside the gateway, possibly higher, but where they ended on either side was not certain.

With both Titan's Point and Titan's Gate behind them, all that was left between them and the shores of Atlantea was a bright blue sea. An evenly-spaced network of large white stone piers jutted out from the land. As they got closer, the shore looked to be crystalline and sparkled under the sun, with the land sloping up to a field of lime green grass swaying in the breeze. Beyond that was a smaller version of Titan's Bridge, which was the first official marker of Titan's Trail. At the other end of the bridge was the open entrance of a castle wall of towering keeps into the sky.

"Mr. Hobbs," Traveler called out.

Their steward ran to him. "Yes, sir."

The two men looked at each other.

"You know what I'm going to say, don't you?"

"Same as before?"

"Yes."

"Say it anyway, sir."

"Mr. Hobbs, we will march into Atlantea as we did on the land Trail. Have the flag bearers fly our banners high, our Brothers Brimm playing loud, and Mr. Pangolin and his Cut-Throats can lead us in."

"I think you said something like allowing me and my vanguard to do the honors?" Pangolin said.

"And you said something smart like it took me long enough to get us here."

Only moments before Titan's alliance held their heads low under a cloud of horror and depression at the sight of a decimated kingdom, and the very continent it rested upon turned to pebbles in the vast sea. Most still didn't understand what had happened. All they knew was that the kingdom stood tall, just as they had seen it before, and they returned as if for the first time. Both human and fae erupted in cheer, laughter, and giddiness.

There was no Oughtred fleet, no draugr-filled ships, no killer giants, or falling mountains or moons. The city sailed on Atlantea's bright blue sea under a mirror-like sky. The land ahead mesmerized all with many brilliant colors. Besides the perytons, birds, normal-sized and giant-sized, giant insects, tiny sprites, and flying beasts filled the skies. Bright green, yellow, and blue trees towered on the land ahead, filled with fruit. As they neared, they saw the fairies, sprites, and birds sitting on their branches or on their leaves. Swarms of butterflies flew all around.

All the sights were new for most because they had been under the slumberous, trance-like reverie of the land's magic as first-time visitors. But they were not first-time visitors to Atlantea anymore. Nearing the shore, fish hopped in and out of the water with its myriad of floating water lilies.

Every human and fae could feel the magic of Atlantea coursing through them again. The over-magic that permeated every grain of soil, every droplet of water, every particle of air, and all its realms lived. They could see the crowds of fae and beasts moving about within the ante-cities. Half-lings, brownies, greenies, imps, pucks, hippopodes (humanoid fae with horses' hooves), panotti (humanoid fae with large elephant-like ears), fish men, sylvans (part-fae, part plant), fairies of different forms, "normal" giants of ten-feet and under and many fae never before seen by any human or fae of their Titan's caravan. Even within its special sheath on his back, he could even feel the slight heat of magical flames from his sword as the power of inanimate objects of magic was also magnified.

"Will Atlantean still be closing its kingdom?" Traveler asked.

"Yes," the Atlantean said, surprising them. "The moment Titan's Caravan and all your allies depart. You have been in Atlantea for a year."

"A year? We haven't been here in Atlantea for a year," Lady Aylen said. She realized. "Yes, Mr. Traveler, you do not need to tell me. Time moves differently in lands of magic."

"Yes."

I-wulf raised a hand. "May I ask a question?" he said to the Atlantean.

"I-wulf, do not embarrass us," Pangolin said.

"It is an important question," I-wulf said.

"Of course," the Atlantean said.

"If Atlantea hasn't been destroyed. Does that mean all

our treasure sits in their storehouses for us to retrieve? I mean, it is why we came to Atlantea, risking our lives. Not that Atlantea isn't a beautiful and enchanting and magnificent place. And you Atlanteans are such great people. Magical and powerful and wise. Uh, that treasure, our treasure, still here?"

Every human and fae waited for the response.

The Atlantean said, "Of course."

ATLANTEA'S FEAR

"They're here too!" Quillen yelled.

Scores of the dobhar-chú, the adorable half dog, half fish animals, floated on their backs in the water or waddled onto the shores.

Traveler cast his eye to the goblins. "Why didn't you join the lamia and her winged goblins?" he asked the goblin king.

"We knew she was using them and us. Ancient fae of their kind view us as beneath them, like elves, including those ancient, winged goblins. With you at least, we are equals, even though you don't care for us."

"Though no great alliances in our future."

"I think we all have had our fill of supposed alliances. I don't want to ever hear the word again."

"Can't blame you there. But did you join her alliance then?"

"She joined ours. We let her act as if it were the reverse. Do you know that the Feast of Gwragedd Annwyn or the Feast of the Ancient Fae did not allow goblins, but we did not care since they didn't allow elves?"

"Hopefully, that is one tradition that will be changed."

"I would hope so with so many of their numbers being killed by Ough—"

Traveler put his finger to his lips.

The goblin smiled. "So many of their numbers being killed."

"Always the same with goblins."

"Yes, our motivations are that simple. Wherever exists the elves, will exist goblinkind. If the forces of darkness have their goblins, with their elves, then we goblins will not cede the forces of light to elves."

"Strangely, goblin, that makes sense to me," Traveler said.

"That is why you were allowed to live among goblins unmolested," the goblin said. "You understand us."

"I was allowed to live among goblinkind because they were amused by the prospect of training a human to kill elves by the sword."

"That too," the goblin said with a smile.

The island city floated up to the continental land and came to a stop, flush. The path of their city seamlessly connected to a path on land. The Atlanteans led the humans and fae from the small city towards the giant castle of this new Atlantea.

"Are they waiting for us?" humans and fae asked, seeing the crowds at the giant castle's open entrance.

"Of course."

The fae they thought escaped the devastation of the old Atlantea actually traveled through portals to the new Atlantea. Queen Geneva of the Mermaids, Queen Oluania of the Oceanids, King Centauro of the Sea Centaurs, King Traerio of the Tritons, and then the water elfin royals Kings Finlor, Elfred, Agis, Queens Amphitrite, Leena, and Eriana. Queen Atopia of the Cecaelia, "standing" on her tentacles. All of the fae royals having formations of warriors, nobles, and attendants behind them.

Lady Aylen smiled as she approached with Gwyness. The two selkie leaders, Queen Nori and King Otari were at their side greeting the water fae.

Also waiting, were the four Tree Shepherds of their former caravan and many more of the old leshy clans, with many crawling trees resting behind them, branches extended wide and high. Gnomes, brownies, and gnomoids stood among the trees waving and cheering. Then there was Ammon, the faun chief, with his daughter,

Zafea, and many fauns moving as a group.

The elfin questing knights were glad to see their animals again—their giant falcons, leopard axes, flying horses and unicorns, flying wolves, large birds, giant weasel-like beasts (ichneumon), and even more gigantic beasts larger than elephants—lionlike creatures with bodies covered in rock-like turtle shells with spikes (tarasques). But then the elfin questing knights saw the woodland leaders Chief Ethor. As on the Trail, without their kings of the Woodland Elf Kingdom of Bravehowl, Desert Elf Kingdom of Falconbright, Moon Elf Kingdom of Nightshade, he was their designated leader.

The caravan's humanoid animal men—frogmen, lizard men, squirrel-like men, fae that looked like raccoons, possums, foxes, rabbits, birds and mice—who left them so quickly when the caravan first arrived, marched to them. With them the frogmen with their giant crabs, the possum men with their giant turtles, the raccoon men with their giant porcupines, the bird men with their large jackalopes (rabbits with antlers as hounds) or enfields (animals with the head of a fox, forelegs like an eagle, and the hindquarters and tail of a wolf). Others guided the group's giant ducks and cranes. Finally, to great cheer was the animal men's own sorcerer, the surly mole-looking fae with his giant carnivorous moose companion. The return of so many familiar animals made Mr. Nirgund's thirteen alphyn hounds and the Cut-Throats flying chamroshes run and fly around in circles in playful joy.

The animal men began singing, and they greeted all the humans, elves, and drows of the alliance.

The dwelf Bragg and his elfin comrades riding their carnivorous Diomerian Mares galloped to them. Pangolin and the Cut-Throats cheered and ran to them. Bragg's eight-foot-tall metal golem, Mr. Glog, lumbered to them as best he could. The fae berserkers had joined Bragg's men, so they were there too.

Sprites flew down from the castle's towers. Brownies, pech, gnomes, and horned gnomoids—all from their former caravan.

Someone pointed, and there everyone saw in the fields adjacent to the castle the large noble Strag with his great antlers, elaphine archers, rusines, and cervids around him. Also, their races traveled and lived as a herd.

The sky filled with laughter and giggling. First, the two fairies, Wildglow and Sunpetal, appeared, then clouds of armored fairies, one by one.

"Traveler!"

The giant Grakdar was the only giant the alliance ever cared to see in their lives. He and all of the great Antaean armored ten-foot giants—Barg, Arteus, Aronir, Alceir, and Alebar—marched forward in song with their even longer warhammers triumphantly in the air.

Traveler, Hobbs, Pangolin, and berserkers hugged the

man who traveled with the caravan, training to be a healer as good as their caravan master, who came out of the crowd.

"Good to see you, Mr. Gresham," Traveler said.

"Can't say I know what has happened," he said.

"You are not alone," Pangolin said.

Above them all, cackling black birds flew over them—birds with the smiling heads of bats. Mr. Traveler's pookas had also returned.

"Spiders and snakes! Snakes and spiders!" they sang.

Lady Aylen shot a disapproving look at Traveler. Gwyness laughed.

The same Atlantean watchtower stood on its secluded solid clouds and extended into the void of the heavens. Dozens of Atlanteans watched through its window, but they weren't alone.

"You should know all the truths regarding the human king, Oughtred," an Atlantean said.

"The human lich," Lady Aylen said.

The Atlanteans gave King Aereth, Lady Aylen, and Gwyness a tour of the hall. Traveler peered out of the window.

"Again, we are honored to be invited to this sacred place of yours," King Aereth said. "Why are we so honored?"

"A balance. The last visitors were of what you call evil. Goodness should also grace the Hall."

"We aided in Oughtred's plot to conquer Atlantea," the Atlantea over-seer said.

"In what way?" Traveler asked.

"The Great Alliance of Faë-Man."

"Oughtred's sun and snow elfin allies."

"The idea did not come from Oughtred but originated with us. He did what we knew he would. Plot to use it to destroy your allies. But it served our purposes in that it would expose his allies to you and force you to re-form your own alliance. We needed to keep you occupied, keep you in Atlantea so he, Oughtred, and his alliances, would keep occupied in trying to destroy you. If not, he might have sensed the coming demi-Titans and their allies."

"You said we didn't understand," Traveler said. "That Oughtred didn't weaken the magic of Atlantea to conquer it. That you transferred its magic to Atlantea here."

"We were more concerned with Oughtred than you were," King Aereth said. "In fact, I don't believe you cared about him at all."

"It was always about the coming demi-Titans," Traveler said.

"How could those giants live on Pan-Earth?" Gwyness asked.

"They never lived here," the Atlantean said. "They visited. Their world is of a size beyond your imagination. That was their land and is their tomb. We did more than transfer the magic of Atlantea. We removed the magic of Atlantea because if that protection was in place when the demi-Titan attacked, stepped from its realm into ours, it would have crushed Pan-Earth and killed all life on this world."

All of them stood silent at the shocking revelation. The gravity of the Atlantean's words stunned them to the core. As they looked towards the window overlooking their wonderful world of Pan-Earth, the true life and death stakes of things were made clear.

"Oughtred, then, was definitely not your primary concern," King Aereth said.

"No. Oughtred was a means to an end for the sake of Pan-Earth."

"You used him as he used his own allies," King Aereth

said. "Your noble end. His fitting end."

"Ordinarily, we would not have intervened, but we had to this time."

"Pan-Earth thanks you," King Aereth said, "though few will ever know this truth."

"Nor should they ever know," the Atlantean said.

"Mr. Traveler, where is your dog?" Lady Aylen asked.

"I sent him on an errand which now is no longer needed," Traveler said.

"Atlantea thanks you, Master Traveler. We knew what he would do, but we also knew your heart."

"We could have upset your plans," Traveler said.

"Never a chance. We only hoped, more than hoped, that you would not get killed, that none of you would die in your efforts."

"Were you ever afraid?" King Aereth asked.

"Atlanteans are a reserved race, but we have emotions too. We can know fear, and have. Not for ourselves, but for all life on Pan-Earth. That was only the stakes for us. That had to come before even the fabled kingdom, as you call it."

FAYLEN'S LEGACY

None of Titan's Alliance left immediately. For them, they were in the New Atlantea, and they meant to explore as much of it as they could, having already secured all their treasure. All was exactly as before, but the ominous signs and the presence of Oughtred or his forces were gone—forever.

Lady Aylen awoke again, staring up at the high vaulted white ceiling from her bed. Her eyes were pools of swirling water. She looked at her bluish-tinted skin and then across the room. Gwyness was already gone to prepare. The day had come.

Their room was the same with the spacious balcony with the view overlooking a lake and beyond it at the bottom of a row of giant statue heads dozens of feet in the air with a thunderous waterfall flowing from their open mouths. Above the waterfalls was a circular archway whose edges were almost beyond their periphery. On the other side of the archway was another realm with floating white cities resting on the air, and above them were three moons.

Atlantea. The realms within realms within realms.

She had always liked the fae-blood, Ursi. The fae was of the bear clan, and on the Trail, they found out exactly what that meant. From Traveler, she learned that Ursi was a royal of her clan, possibly a princess or even queen.

Ursi, all in black with a necklace of brown stones stepped from her boat to the newly formed island city of Faylen. Every detail, through magic, was reconstructed as if it hadn't been ripped apart by the collapse of its realm and falling miles down to crash on the land of another. Its magic Bident, back on the top of the tallest tower, enveloped the island in its own protective barrier.

Ursi was not alone. Lady Aylen waited at the gatehouse entrance with Gwyness, the selkie royals, Nori and Otari, and the three "lost warrior" leaders.

"Welcome, Ursi. Mr. Traveler told me of your proposal, and the city of Faylen graciously accepts."

"Thank you, Lady Aylen. You remember the fae-blood wolf clan."

The group of fifteen men, also all in black attire and

cloaks. Human in every way except for a tint of yellow in their brown wolf-like eyes. The fae had been a part of Titan's Caravan too.

"This will be interesting," Lady Aylen said. "Fae-blood wolf clan and faoladhs. Do you know of each other?"

"No," Ossarian said.

"We know of his kind," one of the fae-blood men said.

"Is that good?" Lady Aylen said.

"We are here," the fae-blood said.

"The other fae-bloods are the clans of fish, bird, and cat," Ursi said.

All the fae-bloods wore black; some had cloaks, others not. The piscines had eyes very much like a fish with a necklace of blue stones, and the felis had cat-like eyes with yellow stone necklaces. The avians had bird feathers in their hair and clear bird-like eyes.

"There are many other fae-blood clans who may wish to join in the future. Our race is very cautious," Ursi said.

"I know. I am honored that you wish to help restore Faylen to protect both human and fae alike."

"We have seen with our own eyes horrific sights few will ever see, even in nightmares. We know what happens when evil is allowed to gather."

"Yes, we have, and we do."

"We are interested in the codes of this new Faylen. A city of warrior mages."

"Slayers and seers," Lady Aylen said. "But why not more?"

"Mages are more than the magic," Ursi said. "They have a higher purpose than beyond themselves. That is what we seek. Without that code, we are no different than what other fae or human can do, their sorcerers."

"I agree," Lady Aylen said. "We will be the same as our predecessor city, but more."

"Which is which with you," one of the fae-blood men asked of Lady Aylen and Gwyness.

"I am the seer and Lady Aylen, a slayer, but it would seem we could both be the opposite too, based on our abilities," Gwyness replied.

"We should get the fae-bloods settled in, Lady Aylen," Nori said.

"Yes, immediately."

"Once settled, I can give you a full tour," Otari said.

"Will Mr. Traveler be joining us?" Ursi asked.

"He may assist us at the start," Lady Aylen said. "With Atlantea closing for ten centuries, he does need a new vocation."

"Good," Ursi said.

"The sorcerer on our caravan, the one called Frog-Dor, will join us too, though I will insist he get a better name, and the drow sorceress, Dr'amal, I hope will join us."

"They are very knowledgeable in fighting darkness, and especially well-suited since their embrace of it almost destroyed their race. They are well-motivated," Ursi said.

"And to follow our former caravan master's lead would be our little alliance here within our walls. Elves and drows."

"Yes."

"We will need weapons," said one of the other fae-blood clans. "Weapons against the living, the dead, the solid, and the ghostly."

"But only the malevolent," Lady Aylen added suspiciously.

"And self-defense," he said.

"We will also need animal companions but not from the lands of humans but of fae," Ursi said.

"As long as no wolves," the fae-blood male said.

"Hear! Hear!" Ossarian said.

AS ATLANTEA SLEEPS

Before the sun had risen, human and fae parties had gathered in front of their hired castle-pyramids floating in the air, guarded by the giant griffins. Men carried their treasures down lowered drawbridges to the ground.

Hobbs directed their three-thousand man party down the drawbridge, carrying the large packs. King Aereth looked on with Pangolin and the chief Cut-Throat leaders.

Mr. Elman, of course, saw the beasts first and called out. From the Faylen party at their castle-pyramid, both Lady Aylen and Gwyness ran out.

"Sire, you have an honored visitor," Pangolin said.

The kirins appeared, galloping on the air and down to them. The dragon-horses had returned.

Lady Aylen hugged her dragon-horse with its lucent-blue fur and scales, single unicorn horn sprouting from its head, and catfish whiskers around its nose and mouth.

Gwyness did the same with her own kirin, bigger than the others, with black fur and scales, its head adorned with full antlers, and unlike the others, her kirin had a tail not unlike a lion.

King Aereth joined them and rubbed his beast's strong neck. His kirin, with its golden fur and scales, horse-like, powerful muscles, cloven hooves, a thick mane of hair, and dragon-like head, closed its eyes in contentment.

An Atlantean herald appeared on the path to the docks.

Traveler also joined them. The kirins looked at him with twinkles in their eyes. "I'd say that Traveler's Caravan is ready to depart the fabled kingdom," he said.

"Yes, we are, Mr. Traveler," King Aereth said.

"What is that?" Pangolin asked looking up.

Commotion grew in the Atlantean ante-city among humans, elves, drows, giants, and other fae at the city of the castle-pyramids. A dark giant whale flying with large black feathered wings prancing along the air with four large lion-like limbs; the hybrid creature flew as point to a massive armada following behind it.

"My dog has returned," Traveler announced.

The air was filled with sky ships, and the sea was thick with city-ships. All the vessels flew giant banners of their kingdoms. From the city, human and fae royals stood aghast.

Ships of the Seven Empires, including the Kings on Helm-Earldom and allied kingdoms of Strongbridge and Eastmoor. Flying ships of the Thirteen Great Houses of Elves. City-ships of the Three Kingdoms of Drows. City-ships of the Towers of Ten of Goblins. Flying ships of fairies and nymphs. Sea ships of centaurs and sky ships of cat centaurs. Flying ships of the Cyclops City of Mímir-Spring. Sea city-ships of the mermaids, cecealia, sea centaurs, and tritons. Sea ships of giants.

Pangolin looked at Traveler first. "This is your doing," the berserker leader said.

They'd learn when they returned home that Traveler sent his dog to all the major empires of the magical lands with hand-written letters to their rulers. The caravan master made a very unique plea on behalf of Atlantea. For the fae of Pan-Earth to make the ultimate retribution and come to the aid to save the very kingdom they made war against so many eons ago when all fae were one. None of the kingdoms refused, and many thought it was the caravan master himself delivering the letters when, in fact, it was his shape-shifter.

"Oughtred knew that the magic of the old Atlantea was gone, and he could allow his forces in. I knew the same."

"Titan's caravan. Titan's crew. Titan's army," Pangolin said with a grin.

Berserkers did not fear dying on the battlefield; most thought it was the most noble way for a man to die. Pangolin and the Cut-Throats did not like the notion that had it not been for the demi-Titans, their battle against Oughtred would have ended in crushing, horrible defeat. Now they knew that a war against such evil would not have been hopeless—far from it. Pangolin looked at his sub-leaders, I-Wulf and Nirgund, and the men smiled.

"We would have defeated Oughtred and his armies of darkness!" I-wulf said triumphantly.

"We did not know of the demi-Titans," Traveler said. "It was supposed to have been him versus us. Oughtred thought he would be unstoppable in seizing Atlantea and then Pan-Earth. He was gravely mistaken."

Pangolin couldn't help smiling and hugged the caravan master. "We would have beaten him."

"Yes, in a century or two," Traveler said.

Titan's Caravan and all their allies, their ships heavy with treasure, departed.

King Aereth had spent his previous night meal with a few of the Atlantean heralds, eating under the stars in what would be the last camp of Titan's Caravan. Like all, he was saddened that they would never see Atlantea again in their lifetime.

"Whether Atlantea was closed to us or not, my kingdom would not have made this journey ever again. We acquired what we set out to in the name of our kingdoms and build our empires and better our peoples. However, it is a bittersweet end nonetheless."

"You should see it as an honor, King Aereth. Few humans have ever set foot in the fabled kingdom. This respite will be of great benefit to you. Your people can focus their attention inwardly rather than on lands of magic far away and across great distances filled with danger and often death."

"All so true. But many of my people would gladly risk it and have. To be here in this kingdom and realize the fraction of its realms and even other worlds exist," King Aereth said.

"Why worry of other realms and other worlds when you a have a good one of your own to take care of and nurture," said the Atlantean. "Be like Atlantea, not by joining our kingdom. Be like Atlantea by transforming your own world so that if one were to stand in either kingdom, one could not tell the difference which is which from its splendor, contentment, and magic."

King Aereth nodded. "Wise words from a wise race."

Traveler also spent time with Atlanteans as he glanced back at the cities for a final time.

"Do not be sad, young human," an Atlantean said to him. "You have traveled here and beyond many times. Think of the quest beginning anew. Cultivate your new allies and the new alliances you forged."

"Yes, I will. But it's hard not to be sad that when I leave Atlantea this time, it will be for good. Never to even see the many realms of Atlantea ever again."

"Atlantea will be closed for a thousand years. No one said anything about any of the many realms that exist beyond it."

Traveler looked at the being with the skin of gemstone.

Through magic, Lady Aylen and her party watched their magic island city rise into the sky. A floating Atlantean stood at her side.

"You have decided then?" he asked.

"Yes," Lady Aylen said. "The city of Faylen will rest between Faë-Land Major, the lands of fairies, sprites, and giants, and Faë-Land Minor, the lands of elves, hoofed fae, and goblins."

"Atlantea is pleased that the city of warrior mages will live again," the Atlantea said.

"We are pleased to be able to fulfill our legacy," the princess said, looking at Gwyness.

"All will be ready when you return from wrapping up your affairs at your human city of Sirnegate," Nori said to them.

"Will this hurt?" Lady Aylen asked.

The Atlantean smiled. "One moment you will be floating in the sky. The next, your city will be in its new home descending to the ocean in your lands of home."

The men waved as the floating city of Faylen vanished. All that remained was their Atlantean attendant, who floated back to the sea.

Traveler saw them! Tunik and his crew of sea kobolds, toad men, and fish men in a new boat. Tunik cackled as he waved goodbye to them all from the bow of the ship. Nifle, standing at Tunik's side, touched his forehead in a final salute. They had told the truth. They would all be remaining in the fabled kingdom.

Their own ship sailed out. They would pass Titan's Gate, the Colossus of Titan's Point, and across the threshold between Atlantea and Oceanus Omnis of Pan-Earth for the last time. A floating fleet of Imperium vessels of light hung in the air, as a final farewell. Their ship would lead all their allies' ships in the sea and air followed by the entire armada of the fae of Pan-Earth. Once beyond the threshold, they would all be teleported by the Atlantean over-magic home.

"We did it, Mr. Traveler," King Aereth said.

"We did, sire," Traveler said, looking down at his dog, especially affectionate. The caravan master briskly rubbed his neck and back.

"We survived, Mr. Traveler," the berserker leader in his earthen armor said.

"We did, indeed, Mr. Pangolin."

"Gentlemen, not to be indelicate," Mr. Hobbs began, "but who will I be working for when we return home?"

The men laughed.

"Won't you be in the City of Faylen, Mr. Traveler?" the king said.

"Very likely, sire."

"Yes, very," Pangolin said with a grin.

"Bird man!" one of the men on the deck called out.

The same icarian, part human, part bird with large, eagle-like wings, large bird eyes, and feathers for hair, that Traveler had done business with for their journey to Atlantea landed on the deck. Dressed as royalty in a golden-brown tunic, coat, trousers, and sash as before.

Quillen walked right up to the fae. The icarian looked at the boy with large eyes quickly scanning him, with his upper and lower lips pointed like a bird's beak. He saw their caravan master.

The icarian let out a deafening bird-like shriek.

"Good morning to you, too, Icarian."

The men had forgotten that the shriek was how the bird-like fae greeted and said goodbye.

"So glad I reached you in time, Master Traveler. Though Atlantea will be closed for some great time, it does not mean a human of your skill and experience will not remain in high demand. The caravan master of the great Titan's Caravan, the last to enter and depart the fabled kingdom. Already the stories are being told far and beyond. I already have a party who wishes to hire you, and I may tag along this time too."

"No!" Traveler yelled, and before the icarian could ask the question. "To both!"

The End of the Fabled Quest Chronicles...Volume One!

CONTINUE THE ADVENTURE

<u>Get Your Next *Fabled Quest Chronicles* Books!</u>

<u>Through Titan's Trail</u> (Book 1)
<u>In the Shadow of the Kings</u> (Book 2)
<u>Comes the War Wizards' Wrath</u> (Book 3)
<u>The Forest of Ancients</u> (Book 4)
<u>Siren Storms of Madness</u> (Book 5)
<u>Kingdom at Titan's End</u> (Book 6)

<u>Fabled Quest Chronicles Box Set</u> (Books 1-3)
<u>Fabled Quest Chronicles Box Set 2</u> (Books 4-6)

<u>Prequels</u>

<u>Quest Master</u> (Prequel to the Fabled Quest Chronicles)

<u>Also by Austin Dragon</u>

See all my books in fantasy, science fiction, and horror:
<u>http://www.austindragon.com/books</u>

643.

GLOSSARY / BOOK SIX

Quillen's List of Races, Beasts, and Monsters of Myth and Magic

A.

Alkonost - a woman-headed bird creature, often confused with their sister race of harpies.

Alphyn - a fae wolf-hound with black fur and a knotted tail, a ridge of knotted fur along its back, lizard-like underbellies, and eagle-like forelimbs. Alphyns are rumored to be able to spit fire.

Anemoi - a face of ancient male fae, winged humanoids related to sylphs (air elementals) capable of blowing strong winds of hurricanes, rainstorms, or snowstorms from their lungs.

Animal Men (Animaloids) - human-like fae that have the features of a specific animal. In Titan's Caravan, one animal man has the features of a lion, others are cat-like, another reptile, and another is boar-like.

Aspidochelone - colossal aquatic creatures often mistaken for rocky islands thick with trees, other plant life, and wildlife such as birds. Actually, they are giant sea turtles or shell-covered whales, and the visible "island" is their back. They spend most of their life sleeping, and feed on fish and water life passing underwater beneath them. Malevolent ones have been known to lure sailors to land on their backs to drown or destroy their ships, but likely the rare behavior is to play, rather than any ill intent.

Axex (pronounced A-Z-E-X) - they were popular in the Lands of Man before the griffins. They had the head of a hawk and a body of a very slim, sleek lion and were swift runners. Smaller ones are used as hunters and watch dogs; larger ones are used as steeds. There are also different feline species such as leopard axex.

B.

Beast Man - a race of violent hybrid humanoids that are part simian, part reptile. Often, their heads resemble baboons, as do their upper torso and arms. Their eyes, clawed hands, and feet are reptilian, along with a lizard tail.

Bluecap - a race of fairies that live in mines and underground. If treated well, they can lead treasure hunters to precious minerals and gems in those mines. They can change to blue flames to light a path to guide miners. Also, they can forewarn miners of impending cave-ins.

Brownies - halfling sprites who look like old men with short curly dark hair and wear brown clothes with pointed brown conical caps. These fae are nocturnal, coming out at night to do their daily chores. They make their homes in enclosed dwellings or traveling wagons.

<u>Bukavac</u>—a six-legged monstrous lizard with gnarled horns on its head that lives in dark lakes, rivers, and bodies of waters.

C.

<u>Cecaelia</u> (also known as a Mermaid Octopus) - a sister race of the mermaids who also live in matriarchal civilizations deep underwater in cities governed by queens. They are beautiful female humanoids with large octopus tentacles instead of bipedal legs, with their upper torsos clothed in material tunics or battle dress. Their skin is luminescent light blue but chameleon-like, able to change color due to mood or to blend into their surroundings. Their hands are webbed, and their fangs may barely be noticeable but can elongate when angry or in battle. Their hands can also become claws in battle. They have long, flowing hair down their backs or kept in a beehive style on top of their heads.

Cecaelia are said to have bodies free of bones (though not true) because of their seemingly impossibly fast movements, flexibility, reflexes, and speed. Their tentacles can act independently, as if each possesses its own free will, or as a single unit. Since they live deeper in the waters, their night vision is superior to mermaids, and their skin can also glow in the dark at will. Their regenerative abilities are superior to not only mermaids but most water fae.

Like mermaids, cecaelia can summon and direct aquatic life, but a far more diverse range of species and those that dwell in the ocean, unlike mermaids.

Centaur - one of the major races of fae who live in patriarchal societies. They are half-man, half-horse; having the torso of a man extending where the neck of a horse should be.

[Crab centaurs and spider centaurs are actually more related to demons. Sea centaurs (ichthyocentaurs) and scorpion centaurs are unrelated fae races.]

Sub-Races of Centaurs:

Cat centaur - instead of a horse body, they have the giant body of a cat. There are lion centaurs (liontaur), tiger centaurs, and panther centaurs.

Cyprean centaur - centaurs with large bull horns sprouting from their heads.

Flying or winged centaur - centaurs with massive eagle or angel wings capable of flying at great heights and great speed.

Hippogriff centaur - centaurs that are part hippogriff—forelegs of a giant eagle and hind half of a horse.

Stag centaur - centaurs with massive antlers.

Unicorn centaur - has a dark complexion with a single ivory-like horn pointing upwards from its forehead.

Cerberus - a three-headed demon dogs with snake-like tails.

Cervid - one of the race of deer-folk, a hoofed fae of normal human height with small horns, one above each brow. As archers, they carry short dark wooden bows.

Chamrosh - a fae hound with an eagle head and bird wings sprouting from its back. They particularly hate hippogriffs.

Crab Centaur - a dark fae race more related to demons than fae. They have thick shell armor over their humanoid upper torsos and giant crab lower torsos with giant pincer claws of tremendous power.

Criosphinx - a ram-headed beast with the body of a lion and wings of a falcon.

Cù-sìth - the name means "fairy dog" and it is as large as a small horse with a shaggy, green coat. It has pointy green ears and a long-curled tail. Some have a long tail rolled up in a coil on its back. Often, it has other animals such as birds and squirrels resting on its back. Forest fae, especially leshies, have them as watch dogs or guardians.

Cyclops - a sub-race of giants with a single eye in the center of their forehead. There are different clans, both civilized and savage. Some are gifted builders, craftsmen, and merchants. Others are scholars and artisans. Rare ones are seers and oracles, able to see what cannot be seen with the normal eye or the future. There are also savage clans known for their ferocity and cannibalism.

D.

Dark Fairy - a sub-race of evil fairies who look like other fairies but wear dark colors and prefer shadowy regions. They are practitioners of dark magic and are mortal enemies of fairies of light.

Darkling - the name given to the phooka by Traveler when he first encountered them in Faë-Land as a lad.

Deer-folk or Deer People - one of the races of fae who live in patriarchal or matriarchal rustic, nomadic societies. They are a pack society who live and travel as a group at all times. They are part of the hoofed-fae races, which includes fauns, satyrs, and centaurs.

Sub-Races of Deer-folk:

Cervid - a hoofed fae of normal human height with small horns, one above each brow. As archers, cervid carry short dark wooden bows.

Elaphine - the largest species of deer-like fae with deer noses, ears, eyes, and huge antlers sprouting from their heads. As warriors, they wear armor and chainmail. They carry long bows as tall as they stand—over six feet and made of smooth, immaculately polished white wood. They are fae archers as gifted as elves and centaurs.

Rusine - are deer-like in appearance—large eyes, a black deer nose, and cloven feet. These humanoid fae are short compared to most humans, no taller than five feet in height. Most prominent is their large deer-like ears that are in constant motion.

Darkling - the name given to the phooka by Traveler when he first encountered them in Faë-Land as a lad.

Decaelia (or Squid Mermaid) - a sub-race of the Cecaelia who are squid-like rather than octopus-like, meaning they have ten tentacles, two of which are longer and larger, rather than only eight equi-length tentacles.

They possess all the abilities of their mermaid octopus sisters and possibly more.

Diomedian Mare – a carnivorous horse-beast with wolf feet rather than hooves. Elves have been domesticating them for ages for benevolent purposes.

Dire wolf – a large black wolf-beast used as steeds and attack animals by goblins.

Dobhar-chú (or "water hound") – resembles a dog-like otter with a large fish-like tail. A very curious, benevolent animal that lives in lakes and streams. Its fur has magical traits which protect the animal from most physical attacks.

Domovoi (or Domovoy) – a sub-race of brownies. Halfling sprites who look like old men with thick gray mustaches and beards touching the ground, wearing dark caps and clothes. There are both day and nocturnal clans, who spend their time keeping the home dwelling they share with humans or fae tidy and clean and see to other housework. They are also protective of the children or animals of the household. Female domovoi are called domania.

Some are said to be able to foresee and warn of coming calamities that threaten the household. However, despite their unwavering loyalty and protection of a household, they can get angry or even leave if the family engages in behavior or language they view as unacceptable or corrupt.

Draugr – are the species of undead warriors more formidable than ghouls. Animated corpses through dark magic, they are foul-smelling skeletons covered with the remnants of their perpetually decaying flesh, tinged in a shade of blue, green or gray, and clad in rusting battle armor. With the empty eye sockets in their skull, they can see clearly, day or night or in the deepest of fog. Known for their superhuman strength and murderous fury in battle. They slay their victims not with weapons but by crushing them with their arms or bodies, eating them in part or whole, or drinking their blood. The very presence of the undead creatures in battle can drive people and animals mad. Stories exist of even birds dropping dead from the sky at their appearance.

Some say they can increase their size like sprites. Others say they can pass through rock or walls; however, their bodies are always extremely heavy in weight. Their intelligence is more than a zombie, their cunning is less than a ghoul, but they often attack in groups. Many physical or magical weapons have no effect on draugr. The undead creatures are said to live in or near their graves, but they can carry the dirt of that grave with them and make a "home" anywhere. They exist to guard treasure and wreak havoc on all living beings. Often, they are in the service of a more powerful dark magic being such as a lich, the most powerful of the undead, or a wizard. Rarer fae stories say that draugr are shape-shifters able to transform into vicious animals.

Drow - or dark elf (not to be confused with a night elf) is a member of an elfin sub-race characterized by dark bluish skin, most often white hair—though some have black hair, and their eyes often have irises of a bright color, such as blue or purple. Drows wear only dark colors like black, dark blues, and dark purples. The original Drow sub-race had separated from high elves due to embracing dark magic. Drows abandoned the practice long ago but remain enemies to all elves, and most fae.

Night drow - sub-race of drows, and historic enemies of the common drows, characterized by their dark purplish skin. They are mostly a nocturnal race and their magic is strongest during the night. They still believe that magic is neither light nor dark, but both can be used for any purposes.

Shadow drow - a rare sub-race of drows characterized by their pure black skin. They are mostly a nocturnal race and their magic is strongest during the night. They left Pan-Earth for kingdoms in the void of the heavens a long time ago. Shadow drows are accomplished warlocks.

Dwarf - a race of thick, brawny halfling fae who live in villages and kingdoms deep underground or within great mountains only accessible from below ground. They are known among all fae as the best precious metal prospectors, miners, blacksmiths, and metal craftsmen. Though slow moving on land, they are also some the strongest of fae for their size and are fierce in battle.

Dwelf - a fae who looks like an elf but has a large, brawny, wide frame and is very tall. Elves have tall sleek bodies; dwelves are bulky like that of a dwarf, but aren't halflings.

E.

Elementals - powerful beings able to manipulate one of "original" elements of Pan-Earth: air, earth, fire, and water.

Air Elemental (Sylphs) - the beautiful nymph-like elementals of the air. In appearance, women with pale, almost-transparent skin, clear eyes, and long, flowing blue-white hair. With their immense power, they can manipulate air and weather at will, making them the most powerful of all elementals.

Earth Elemental - a race of male humanoid living rock, stone, and earth. They are large, bulky, and slow moving. However, they can manipulate the earth in any form in any way they wish. Also, they create earthquakes and avalanches.

Fire Elemental - also known as Vulcans, a race of beings of humanoid, animated fire. They can summon and manipulate fire.

Water Elemental (Undines) - the race of powerful elemental beings of water. Beautiful tall, thin women, who wear sheer, flowing dresses of nature. They live in the oceans or in giant sacred waterfalls. They possess the ability to summon and control water in any way. As their power comes from the oceans of Pan-Earth itself, only the sylphs of the air are ultimately more powerful than they among all elementals.

Elf - one of the major races of fae and the one most resembling humans in appearance. They are humanoids characterized by pointed ears, taller than the average human, and slim in build. They have fair to porcelain-like skin—though there are sub-races with darker skin. Their eyes can be one of many different colors, depending on their sub-race and clan. Their senses, strength, and stamina are far superior to humans. As with many fae, they can make themselves invisible through magic in their natural environment, can move at extreme speed whether running or fighting—almost seeming to jump from one point to another in the eyes of humans, and are very long lived. Along with centaurs, they are known as the top archers in Faë-Land. They fight with blade weapons never bludgeoning weapons, and bows, never crossbows.

Different sub-races of elves have additional physical and magical abilities.

<u>Sub-Races of Elves</u>:

<u>Celestial Elf</u> - one of the elfin sub-races and the most powerful race of elves as they are celestial elementals, said to be able to summon, manipulate, and create solid objects or fire of black celestial magic. In appearance, they look like high elves but have black eyes. Unlike other sky elves, they live, and have lived, on other worlds from Pan-Earth for some time. As such, view those of Pan-Earth, including other sky elves, as beneath them, and all other elves, humans, and other fae as inferior.

<u>Cloud Elf</u> - an elfin sub-race very similar in appearance to high-elves but are also powerful air elementals able to create, summon, and control clouds.

<u>Desert Elf</u> - one of the elfin sub-races of the outer desert lands of Faë-Land.

<u>Drow</u> - or dark elf (not to be confused with a night elf) is a member of an elfin sub-race characterized by dark bluish skin, most often white hair—though some have black hair, and their eyes often have irises of a bright color, such as blue or purple. Drows wear only dark colors like black, dark blues, and dark purples. The original Drow sub-race had separated from high elves due to embracing dark magic. Drows abandoned the practice long ago but remain enemies to all elves, and most fae.

<u>Fairy Elf</u> - one of the flying elfin sub-races with greenish or bluish skin, the tips of their pointed ears are at least six inches tall, their foreheads have long antennae above each eye, and they have large insect wings, invisible to humans.

<u>Forest Elf</u> - one of the elfin sub-races of the large forest lands of Faë-Land.

<u>High Elf</u> - one of the elfin sub-races of tall, regal elves, exceptionally beautiful/handsome in appearance. High elves consider themselves the most royal and highest of all elves. They dwell exclusively in highly advanced and magical cities.

<u>Moon Elf</u> - an elfin sub-race very similar in appearance to high-elves with snow-white hair. They are powerful elementals able to summon, manipulate, and create magical objects of moonlight. They were once part of the sky elves but forsake this status to ally with land elves.

<u>Mountain Elf</u> - one of the elfin sub-races who live in the mountain lands of Faë-Land.

<u>Sky Elf</u> - the collective term for any race of elves that live in the sky or heavens. They include wind elves, cloud elves, star elves, and celestial elves. Among elfin-kind, there is great animosity between land and water elves with sky elves. Moon elves forsake their status as sky elves to ally with land elves.

<u>Shadow Elf</u> - ancient high-elves who left Pan-Earth for other worlds before even the celestial elves. They have used cosmic magic for dark purposes for so long that their skin and body have become more of magic than physical flesh. They appear almost as living shadows.

<u>Snow Elf</u> - ancient wind elves whose powerful air elemental magic is able to summon and control snow and ice. They have total resistance to all cold temperatures. It is unclear whether Ice Elves are the same or a separate elfin race.

<u>Star Elf</u> - an elfin sub-race taller than most other elfin races, typically with silver white hair and gray eyes. They are power elementals able to summon, manipulate, and create objects of magical starfire. Historically, they were known for their benevolence but after their alliance with celestial elves, are now regarded as ruthless and malevolent, especially by land and water elves.

<u>Subterranean Elf</u> - a seclusive elfin sub-race, also known as nether-elves, who live in underground kingdom and are said to also have earth elemental powers.

<u>Sun Elf</u> - ancient high elves whose magic allows them to conjure and manipulate sunfire magic in any manner they wish.

<u>Water Elf</u> - elfin sub-races who live in seas, oceans, rivers, and lakes.

<u>Wild or Savage Elf</u> - they have light brown hair, bigger pointed ears sprouting from the sides of their heads, fanged teeth and clawed nails on their hands. They are tall, muscular, and their eyes had the look of a wild animal.

<u>Wind Elf</u> - an elfin sub-race very similar in appearance to high-elves but are also powerful air elementals able to summon and control the wind.

<u>Winged Elf</u>- an elfin sub-race thought extinct, and often called "angels" for the large, beautiful, white feathered wings on their backs. They are said to be able to fly into the heavens without the need of air and fly at incredible speeds.

<u>Woodland Elf</u> - an elfin sub-race known as the best trackers in the forests with strong societies built around hunting. They have eyesight more powerful than eagles and magically can see the "after-presence" of prey they are tracking. There are two main divisions: Rustic—who live in wooded lands of modest hamlets, and Hunter—who fashion themselves after high elves and live in large tree cities.

Enfield - a fae animal with the head of a fox, foreleg like an eagle, and the hindquarters and tail of a wolf. Domesticated ones are primarily used for hunting.

F.

<u>Fae</u> - the sentient and dominant humanoid species of the realm of magic known as Fäe-Land.

<u>Fae-Blood</u> - a member of a fae race rarely seen by humans who appear to be visibly indistinguishable from an average human. They wear black attire and colored stone necklaces. There are many clans named after a specific animal, such as bear, wolf, cat, chameleon, hawk, etc., and each clan has its own unique magical powers. As their name suggests, they are fae whose very blood is pure magic.

<u>Fairy</u> - one of the major races of fae who live in matriarchal societies governed by queens. Fairies are often insect-like, but there are also bird-like, reptile-like, amphibian-like, mollusk-like, snail-like, and plant-like races. They are shape-shifters able to take the form of other animals, such as smaller mammals, birds, or insects. Like sprites, their different sub-races and tribes have differing magical powers. Like many fae, they possess the ability of "sizing" wherein they can magically increase or shrink their size to defend themselves. Fairies live and work with animal companions, most often birds and insects.

<u>Faoladh</u> - human shape-shifters with the ability to transform into giant wolves and fight evil. They are also immune to the dark magic bite or scratch of any lycanthrope, including the frightening werewolf.

Faun - one of the major sub-races of hoofed-fae who live in patriarchal, rural societies governed by kings and chiefs. Fauns and satyrs are very similar, but they are not the same race. Fauns are shorter than the average human, often with a goatee, and both male and female fauns wear tops. They are peaceful, reasoned, and congenial. They often act as guides.

Sub-Races of Fauns:

Common - have pointed ears, goat horns sprouting just above their eyes, legs of a goat, and cloven hooves.

Grand - have large curving ram's horns sprouting from their head and are above average human height.

Flying Horse - a horse with the wings of a giant bird and capable of flying. They can be of any color and different kinds have differing magical properties. They are also (incorrectly) called a pegasus by humans, but Pegasus was the name of a specific legendary flying horse.

G.

Gargoyle - a humanoid reptilian race with a tall and elongated body, gray, earth-like skin, and large bat wings they fold behind their back when not flying. They live and nest in the highest mountain domains in the region with or near flowing water.

Ghoul - an undead creature but, unlike a zombie, are intelligent and calculating. They are extremely strong and only special magic or physical force that can destroy their entire physical form at once can kill them. They can also turn another into a ghoul with physical contact, such as with a scratch or bite. Ghouls serve dark masters and "live" to commit acts of evil.

Giant - one of the major races of fae who live in patriarchal societies governed by kings and chiefs. The majority of the giant races are warriors, all possessing great strength, but others have kingdoms of diverse occupations. Giants can range in height from ten to one hundred feet.

Sub-Races of Giants:

Antaeans - members of the sub-race of giants regarded as great warriors, ranging in height from eight to twelve feet. Antaeans wear shining armor and helmets. Their greatest magical power is that when they directly touch the earth in a deliberate stance, no force in the world can move or harm them.

Argus - a sub-race of seer giants whose bald heads are covered in a hundred eyes. They are greater oracles than even the cyclops seers.

Athos - a sub-race of brutish giants who possess the magical strength to rip whole mountains from the earth and hurl them great distances. Hence, their common name: "mountain thrower."

Cacus - an ancient fire-breathing mega-giant over fifty-feet tall. Besides breathing their hellish flames from their mouth, they can throw their fireballs from their hands.

Cyclops - a sub-race of giants with a single eye in the center of their forehead. There are many different clans, both civilized and savage. Some are gifted builders, craftsmen, and merchants. Others are scholars and artisans. Rare ones are seers and oracles, able to see what cannot be seen with the normal eye, or the future. There are also savage clans known for their ferocity and cannibalism.

<u>Damysos</u> (or Damysus) - an ancient giant of more than one-hundred feet tall and said to be the fastest of all giants.

<u>Fomorian</u> - an evil race of sea giants. Humanoids with the head of goats more related to demons than actual fae. They are giants of chaos and death whose dark magic emits disease, blight, and drought to any lands they visit.

<u>Gegenees</u> - a sub-race of six-armed, twelve-foot-tall giants who wear blackish war-paint over their entire body. Their favorite weapon of choice is the double battle axe. They are mortal enemies of the Antaeans.

<u>Geryon</u> - an ancient monstrous giant well-over one hundred feet with three humanoid heads and has giant bat wings.

<u>Talos</u> - an ancient giant of bronze, silver, or gold. Humanoid in form, the automaton either act with its own evil will or the will of its creator or master.

<u>Typhon</u> - the most frightening, monstrous, and largest of the ancient demi-Titans. Part-giant, part-creature it has one-hundred arms; its humanoid head sits in the center of a fleshy stalk, and a multitude of arm-long snakes and tentacles grow from its neck and shoulders.

<u>Zodiac</u> - a group of twelve ancient giants said to have established the codes of justice and law among all ancient fae.

<u>Giant Animals</u> - domesticated ones are used as steeds, guard animals, or beasts of burden. Titan's Caravan includes giant crabs, giant turtles, giant porcupines, giant ducks, giant cranes, and a giant moose.

<u>Gnome</u> - fae halfling sprites known for their perpetual happy-go-lucky personality, amiability, and love of dancing, singing and music. They often have beards but not always. They often look older, but there are baby-faced clans. They always wear hats, though gnomes exclusively wear pointy, often red, conical hats.

<u>Gnomoid</u> - there are many races of sprites similar to gnomes, though not as good-natured. They also wear hats but not the pointy conical ones of gnomes.

<u>Goblin</u> - one of the major races of dark fae that resemble a kind of elves in appearance. They are the mortal enemies of elves.

<u>Common</u> - their skin is green, their frame stout and muscular, their noses flat, and their pointy ears are larger.

<u>High</u> - more refined facial features, and body types more elfin than what humans would call goblin.

<u>Shadow</u> - a sub-race of goblin whose use of dark and celestial magic has turned their skin so black that they appear as humanoid shadows.

<u>Winged</u> - an ancient race of goblins with whose green skin has turned tan as desert sand can fly with their bat-like or owl-like wings.

Golem - a humanoid automaton made of metal, wood, or clay animated by magic. Their intelligence and abilities are based on that animating magic.

Griffin - a fantastic beast with the body, tail, and hind legs of a lion and golden yellow fur. Its head and foreleg talons are that of a giant eagle. The animal is known for its echoing roar. Griffins are often used by fae as royal steeds or guardians of treasure. Like hippogriffs, they have a fondness for eating horses of the Lands of Man.

Sub-Races of Griffins:

Equine-like griffins:

Zebragriff - griffins with zebra stripes.

Unigriff - part unicorn, part griffin.

Bird-hybrid griffins:

Aloniegriff - hybrids of griffins and peacocks, with colorful feathers on the front half, and peacock-like tails.

Kolimbregriff - hybrids of griffins and hummingbirds, with front halves of hummingbirds and leonine hindquarters and tails with feathers on the ends.

Owl griffins - are griffins with the head of an owl.

Feline griffins:

Tigregriff - have distinctive stripes of a tiger.

Leopardalogriff - have leopard-like spots.

Sabergriff - part griffin, part smilodon, larger and more muscular than any other feline griffin hybrid, with saber-tooth tusks.

Mammaloid griffins:

Elefantagriff - are hybrid beasts, part griffin and elephant. They have tough grayish skin covered with feathers—mostly around their joints, back, and rear, tusks growing from either side of their beaks, elephantine ears, elephant feet-like talons on thick legs.

Kamilopardalogriff - hybrids of griffins and giraffes with long necks, long legs, giraffe horns, hoof-like talons, and the distinctive spots of a giraffe.

Lupagriff - hybrids of griffins and wolves.

Taurogriff - hybrids of griffins and bulls with bovine hindquarters, with feathers at the tips of their tails, taloned front legs, and horns on their heads.

Ursagriff - hybrids of griffins and bears with large, stocky builds, bear-like back paws, short tails, and a slightly bear-like face, but still being avian in appearance.

Griffinoids - griffin-like beasts.

Axex (pronounced A-Z-E-X) - they were popular in the Lands of Man before the griffins. They had the head of a hawk and a body of a very slim, sleek lion and were swift runners. Smaller ones are used as hunters and watch dogs; larger ones are used as steeds. There are also different feline species such as leopard axex.

Hippogriff - a fantastic beast that has the hind half of a horse and the front half, including head and forelegs, of a giant eagle. It is known for its loud eagle shrieks. Like griffins, they have a fondness for eating horses of the Lands of Man.

Keythong - forehalf of a giant eagle, hind-half of a lion and spiky protrusions on its back and head

Opinicus - griffin-like beast with a full lion's body with an eagle's head and wings.

Gwragedd Annwyn - an ancient race of powerful fairies who reside in lakes and rivers of land and the heavens.

H.

Half-Elf - humanoid with one elfin parent and one human parent. They have pointed ears but often not as pronounced as a full elf. They are far stronger than an average human and possess superior senses. Many often have the same magical abilities as their elfin lineage or to a lesser degree. They have a much longer life span than humans, and some have the ability to communicate telepathically with other half-elves, suggesting that elves, secretly, have the same ability.

Half-Goblin - one parent is goblin and the other human. They have pointed ears, green skin, and its goblin features vary: one or more horns, a large pointed nose, and a larger chin.

Haltija - a sub-race of sprites that guard, help, or protect something or somebody. Haltijas appear as frowning full-bearded halfling men with pointy hats. They are nocturnal sprites like brownies, coming out at night for their daily tasks. They are ill-tempered, rude, surly, and hate being talked to directly. They are also shape-shifters. A clan of haltijas is called a väki and there are many different clans in Faë-Land. See Väki.

Harpy - an evil female creature much larger than the average human. They are humanoid females from the waist up—matted hair, gaunt facial features, black eyes, and jagged teeth—and the legs of a bird below, with fearsome talons. Their arms are the wings of a large bird, and their human halves are covered in hair and feathers. They are fiercely territorial of specific structures or places where they live and protect together as a flock.

<u>Highborn</u> - a sub-race of harpies who are more humanoid. The hair on their heads are feathers but styled to appear as human hair running down their backs. Their human arms are also wings with feathers reaching the ground. Their entire body below the neck is covered in thick dark feathers. Their eagle feet end in menacing, retractable claws.

Hieracophinx - a hawk-headed beast with the body of a lion and wings of a falcon.

Hippocampus - aquatic beasts with the upper body of a blue horse and the lower body of a fish. They are the chosen transport by many royal water fae races.

Hippogriff - a fantastic beast that has the hind half of a horse and the front half, including head and forelegs, of a giant eagle. It is known for its loud eagle shrieks. Like griffins, they have a fondness for eating horses of the Lands of Man.

Hippopodes - a race of humanoid fae with horses' hooves for feet.

Hobgoblin - the creature is about three feet in height. Their pointy ears are longer and thinner, sprouting from the sides of their heads. Their noses are hooked. Their teeth are long and sharp like piranha, and have beady little eyes. They wear dark clothes—tunics and trousers—and curled pointed shoes.

Humanoid Animals

Sub-Races of Humanoid Animals:

Frog men, lizard men, squirrel men, raccoon men, possums, fox men, rabbit men, bird men, and mice men.

Hydra - a snakish creature with a lizard-like body and several, long snakes as heads. It is said that if one snake head is cut off, two will grow in its place.

I.

Ichneumon - a giant weasel-like beast able to wrestle and kill beasts ten times their size. They despise any snake creature and can kill a wurm many times their size. They are impervious to fire attacks.

Ichthyocentaur (or Sea Centaur) - cousins to merfolk and tritons, they are a race of fae with a bluish-skinned humanoid upper torso and lower torso of a horse's forelegs and the tail of a giant fish. Despite their strange form, they can swim faster than mermaids and longer than most water fae.

Imp - this dark fae is a small, gray, ugly humanoid creature, with bat-like wings, big ears, and tiny horns poking out above its eyebrows. Its skin is either stone-like or scaly. Imps are known for their destructive mischief against unsuspecting fae or humans. Their wild pranks are often a result of boredom rather than evil. When discovered or caught they are given to wild outbursts as they run or fly away. Imps can also be very territorial—bound to a specific region or love to hide in specific objects, especially magical objects. Though most of their pranks are harmless, they have been known to engage in more serious acts such as taking babies or small animals, leading people astray to their death, and starting fires. They are also shape-shifters, which they often take full advantage of in their pranks, and can turn invisible as they escape. Imps have been used as spies or agents for evil wizards.

Ipotane - a fae race of half-horse, half-humanoids. They have a man's body, hoofed feet, and the head of a horse, and they wear trousers alone. They are a semi-intelligent race similar to minotaurs and are not regarded as part of the hoofed fae races of fauns, satyrs, or centaurs.

J.

Jackalope - a fae animal that is a rabbit with antlers. Domesticated, they are used as watch dogs and for hunting.

Jörmungandr - the largest sea serpents of the great oceans of the magical realms, said to have even existed in the age of the Titans. They are so large and long they can shoot up to touch the void of the heavens above. Since very few living creatures are large enough to even get their attention, any destruction they inflict is purely accidental.

K.

Kilmoulis - a race of shy but good-natured sprites with huge noses that cover most of their faces. They always stay together in their group and do not mingle with others, human or fae. They are regarded as lazy creatures by most fae, others view them as disgusting, eating by stuffing food up their noses. Magically, they can smell and distinguish animals or beings leagues away; an ability not possessed by any other fae.

Kirin (also Ki-rin or Quilin) - a fantastic beast from the magical lands beyond Faë-Land, and is often called a dragon-horse (though there is another magical beast by that name). These intelligent animals serve as companions, guardians, and protectors. They have varying characteristics of other animals to match their environments and varying magical abilities. They can fly, whether they have wings or not, and can swim or gallop under water.

They never harm benevolent life or pure souls, but they are swift and fierce to attack if threatened or to protect a defenseless or pure person threatened by a malicious thing. They are thought to be a symbol of luck, good omens, protection, prosperity, success, and longevity. They are also rumored to see future events before they happen.

Klabautermann - a race of water kobolds (sprites) that are larger than the average human, hunched over, thick bodies, ugly faces, and usually missing teeth. In the Lands of Man, they are known to assist sailors and fishermen, even rescuing them from sea wrecks or those who are washed overboard. In the magical lands, they command their own vessels, as they are exceptional sailors. Like all sprites, they are given to merriment and music, but are hard workers. Like their land cousins, they can sense treasure of any kind near them and eagerly seek it out.

Kobold – a race of shape-shifting sprites who can take the form of an animal, fire, a human being, and a candle, or become invisible. In their humanoid form, they appear as figures the size of small children, little, wrinkled old men wearing caps. There are three major types of kobolds.

Though harmless to the benevolent, when angered kobolds have been recorded as cutting victims to pieces and eating them.

House – most commonly, the fae are house sprites of ambivalent nature. They sometimes perform domestic chores, but can play malicious tricks if insulted or neglected.

Underground – another type of kobold haunts underground places, such as mines. Mine kobolds are expert miners and metalworkers, often drilling, hammering, and shoveling dirt to claim metals or precious stones. Evil ones are blamed for accidents, cave-ins, and rock slides that harm or kill human or fae miners. A favorite kobold prank was to fool miners into taking worthless metal ore or gems, or, sometimes even, when smelted, could be deadly poisonous. Benevolent ones warned miners not go in a dangerous direction, led miners to veins of metal or richer ones.

Seafaring - a third kind of kobold, the Klabautermann, lives aboard ships and helps sailors. Those that live in human homes wear the clothing of peasants; those who live in mines are hunched and ugly, and sometimes are said to have black skin. Kobolds who live on ships smoke pipes and wear sailor clothing.

Koerakoonlased—half-human, half-dog cyclops creature.

Korrick - a race of small dwarf-like spites, said to love dancing around water.

Korrigan - a race of fairy-like fae known for their long, red silky hair and glowing red eyes. Like nymphs, human men are helpless to their powerful, magical attraction; fae men can also be susceptible to this enchantment Like mermaids and sirens, they can lure and attract humans and other humanoids with their enchanted singing. Like fairies, they are fond of dancing, especially by moonlight and around bodies of water.

L.

Lamia - one of the major races of ancient fae with the upper torso of a beautiful female humanoid and the lower torso of a large snake tail instead of bipedal legs. Often, they have long, flowing hair, and their eyes can be similar to a snake or human.

Evil ones stalk and eat children or small animals. Others are said to be like vampires who feed on the blood of humans. Benevolent ones are said to be oracles or sorceresses.

Lampads - are a sub-race of nymphs of the Nether-Lands, land of demons. They are fond of enchanting and haunting travelers in their path. Their glowing skin is also a reflection of the power of their inner light; magic they use to create torches to drive men to madness.

Land Kraken - a giant squid-like creature than moves through the earth and attacks with multiple giant tentacles pushing through the ground, ripping apart or crushing victims.

Landvættir - another race of ancient beasts of tremendous size often described as "walking land masses." The smaller ones are as large as a mountain or even an entire mountain range. The largest ones, existing before the birth of fae or humans, can be as large as a continent in perception. Regardless, their size is so vast that a precise description of their form is difficult. They are beings that protect the lands they inhabit, or they feed off the flora and fauna of that land.

Leokampoi (also known as a Sea Lion) - a large lion beast with the lower half of a fish. The aquatic beasts are found in the wild or are often domesticated to serve in water fae kingdoms as guards and companions. They are fierce fighters, and their claws are especially deadly to skin or metal, leaving wounds extremely resistant to magical healing, though not impossible.

Leshy - known as guardians of the forest, they are male fae with white skin and hair and full beards of living grass and vines. They have bright green eyes and hoofed feet, and some have horns and tails. They are shape-shifters known for the ability to take the form of any animal or plant. They can shrink to the size of an insect or grow to the size of the tallest tree. They can imitate the voice of any human or humanoid, make the sound of any animal, and can scream horribly to frighten enemies. They often keep animals as companions, the favorite being a cù-sìth.

There are also dark leshies given to leading travelers astray, kidnapping, or making people sick.

Tree Shepherds - are leshies who control any number of magical, sentient trees—walking, crawling, or flying.

Lich - the most powerful and intelligent of all undead beings, either created by a master necromancer or the result of a such transforming himself into the fiend in a quest for immortality. Most look like decaying or skeletal humans, but more powerful ones can appear as normal at first look.

They are able to summon and command hordes of undead creatures, such as zombies, ghouls, and draugr, to use as servants or fighters. Those that transformed themselves to liches retain and increase their powers of dark magic.

Lunatishee - a sub-race of dark fairies. They are wingless fairies covered in sharp thorns over their entire bodies, no taller than gnomes, and look more like devilish males than fairies.

M.

Marrashi - are a race of hybrid beasts with heads of jackals, eagle bodies the size of men, razor sharp talons, and fly with their wings. They are great archers.

Melusina - a nymph-like fae with the upper torso of a humanoid female and the lower torso were tails of fish below the waist with fish-scales instead of legs. Their backs have bat-like wings which they can fly through the air or water.

Merfolk or Merpeople - one of the major races of fae in Oceanus Omnis who live in matriarchal underwater cities governed by queens.

Mermaid - are beautiful female humanoids with a large fish tail instead of bipedal legs. Their skin is an almost luminescent light blue. They have long, flowing hair, and their eyes can be similar to fish or human. The only clothing they wear are a type of brassiere—like cloth wrapped around their breast area several times.

Malevolent mermaids love storms and floods, and are present at shipwrecks and drownings. Also, like sirens, they can lure and attract humans and other humanoids with their enchanted singing, often to crash sea-going vessels onto rocks. Benevolent ones can help victims of natural disasters at sea and have been known to fall in love with humans, giving up their fae lives to live as humans.

<u>Merman</u> - there are two main species: Ugly male sea humanoids that look like a brown fish but with the head of a man—blue-green hair, unsightly teeth, and slits for eyes. They enjoy storms and being present at sinking ships. Despite their appearance, they can magically cure sickness and lift curses. Others are sages and oracles.

The other species look like attractive blue-skinned male humanoids. Like mermaids, they can appear in their true form, with their lower torso that of a giant fish, or transform them to be human legs to walk upon land. They have the speed, strength, and agility of mermaids but not the same level of enchantment as mermaids.

<u>Minotaur</u> - a race of semi-intelligent fae that are humanoid bulls. Minotaurs have sharp, pointed or jagged, dual horns protruding from their heads, large bull ears, and extremely muscular necks. They wear loincloths and sometimes use weapons such as axes, maces, and clubs.

N.

<u>Nemean Lion</u> - a vicious gigantic lion beast with claws sharper than most human or fae swords and able to cut through most armor. Their golden fur is impervious to the attack of human or fae metals.

<u>Nisse</u> - a sub-race of sprites who are very friendly and gregarious little people, knee-high, wearing bright green pointy hats as long as their bodies. They are never without a smile on their face. There are both men and women. The bearded men dress in standard dark tunics and trousers;

the women dress in lighter colored dresses with their blond or brunette hair braided behind them. Other nisse wear red or orange hats, too. They are believed to have shape-shifting abilities too.

Despite their size, they have tremendous strength, like all sprites. Often they are protectors of farmlands, livestock, and animals. They are easily offended by rudeness, laziness, and the mistreatment of animals.

<u>Nymph</u> - one of the major races of fae who live in matriarchal societies. They are enchanting, beautiful women with long hair. They look human, but have an angelic glow. Human men are helpless to their powerful, magical attraction; fae men can also be susceptible to their enchantment.

Sub-Races of Nymphs:

<u>Aurae</u> - nymphs of breezes.

<u>Crinaeae</u> - water nymphs of fountains.

<u>Dryads</u> - nymphs of the trees.

<u>Hamadryads</u> - nymphs that live in the trees themselves.

<u>Hesperides</u> - celestial nymphs of the heavens.

<u>Hydriades</u> - water nymphs.

<u>Limnades or Limnatides</u> - water nymphs of lakes.

<u>Naiads</u> - water nymphs of fresh water.

<u>Napaeae</u> - nymphs of wooded valleys and glens.

<u>Nephele</u> - a cloud nymph.

<u>Nereids</u> - powerful water nymphs of the seas and oceans.

<u>Oceanids</u> - water nymphs of oceans.

<u>Oread</u> - a mountain nymph.

<u>Pegaeae</u> - water nymphs of springs.

<u>Pegasides</u> - nymphs associated with water holes.

<u>Potameides</u> - water nymphs of rivers.

O.

Ophiotaurus - fantastic fish-scaled beasts with the upper torso of a bull and the lower half of a fish with a long tail. They swim and live together in packs (or schools), and sightings of the peaceful animals are seen as good omens by fae.

Opinicus - griffin-like beast with a full lion's body with an eagle's head and wings.

Orthurus - a giant two-headed wolf.

P.

Panotti - a race of benevolent fae with giant ears that resemble those of an elephant.

Pech - halfling sprites with wild, bushy eyebrows, big noses, and even bigger forearms bulging from their tunics. They wear off-white tunics, dark trousers and boots, and dark caps. They are some of the strongest sprites in Faë-Land.

Pegasus - a horse with the wings of a giant bird and capable of flying. They can be of any color and different kinds have differing magical properties. They are also (incorrectly) called a pegasus by humans, but Pegasus was the name of a specific legendary flying horse.

Peryton - often called a "deer bird," the large flying beast has the antlered head and legs of a deer and wings and body of bird.

Phoenix - a bright orange-feathered bird glowing and flickering in flames, with wings twelve feet wide or more. It makes its habitat in volcanos, the Nether-Lands, and lands of earth and fire elementals.

Phooka (also known as Pooka, Púca, Phouka, Phooka, Phooca, Puca, or Púka) - they are fae shape-shifters that always take the form of some humanoid animal or animal but always black in color. The malicious ones are violent and dangerous, taking the form of frightening black animals. The benevolent ones are given to mischief and harmless pranks, not unlike fairies, but they can be quite helpful and are only dangerous to evil beasts and beings. All phookas can take the form of dogs, foxes, wolves, cats, horses, goats, rabbits, birds, and much more to frighten and shock their enemies. They are especially fond of changing into distorted versions of those animals or a combination of more than one or changing into humanoid forms with animal features.

Pixy - a tiny sprite that appears as an insect-winged man with a child-like face and pointy ears, who wear a green pointed hat and a green outfit. They are prone to mischievous but harmless pranks. They like to play with animals, especially horses, often to torment them; enjoy music, gathering in groups for dancing or horseplay, and their favorite pastime is pestering humans, which includes leading them astray and stealing children.

R.

<u>Rat-bats</u> - the swarming flying rat creatures used in battles by goblins and other dark fae.

<u>Redcap</u> - are a sub-race of evil, murderous goblins. They appear as short, old-looking humanoid males with coarse, graying hair down to their shoulders, long prominent teeth, skinny fingers ending in talons like eagles, large fiery red eyes, and grisly hair streaming down their shoulders. They wear iron boots, carry pikestaff weapons, and, more prominently, wear red caps on their heads, said to be red from soaking it in the blood of their victims.

<u>Rusine</u> - are deer-like in appearance—large eyes, a black deer nose, and cloven feet. These humanoid fae are short compared to most humans, no taller than five feet in height. Most prominent is their large deer-like ears that are in constant motion.

S.

<u>Salamander</u> - an orange elemental amphibian of fire continuously ablaze in flames. Like the phoenix, the creatures that thrived in fire. They are companions to fire elementals.

<u>Scorpion Men</u> (or Scorpion Centaurs) - evil creatures with the head, torso, and arms of a man and the body of a giant scorpion. The giants are larger than elephants and their deadly poisonous scorpion tails are longer than their body.

<u>Sea Centaur</u> (or Ichthyocentaur) - cousins to merfolk and tritons, they are a race of fae with a bluish-skinned humanoid upper torso and lower torso of a horse's forelegs and the tail of a giant fish. Despite their strange form, they can swim faster than mermaids and longer than most water fae.

<u>Sea Goblin</u> - the seafaring cousins of land goblins. Stout and muscular, in frame, their green skin is similar to that of an eel, both ridged and scaled. Their noses are flat, and their pointy ears and clawed hands are larger than their land cousins'. They are the mortal enemies of water elves.

They are called sea goblins exclusively, but exist in the oceans, seas, and deep underwater in different sub-species.

<u>Sea Lion</u> (also known as Leokampoi) - a large lion beast with the lower half of a fish. The aquatic beasts are found in the wild or are often domesticated to serve in water fae kingdoms as guards and companions. They are fierce fighters, and their claws are especially deadly to skin or metal, leaving wounds extremely resistant to magical healing, though not impossible.

<u>Selkie</u> - a race of humans, also known as sealfolk, who can transform into seals or sea lions. Little is known of their people outside of fae-kind, but they are a benevolent race respected by all five main empires of the Oceanus Omnis—merfolk, water nymphs, water elves, sea centaurs, and tritons—as advisors and seers.

Serpopard - a beast of the desert lands with the head of a falcon, a snake-like neck, and the body of a leopard with falcon wings. Some have the head of a lion.

Shape-shifter - any fae or creature capable of changing its appearance or form at will. Human shape-shifters are rare and possess this ability through dark or light magic.

Spell-Talker - a rare demon that looks like a pale human male with pure black eyes. On either side of its mouth are holes—used to magically lock its mouth closed by its master. It can kill any living thing by simply speaking words of dark magic over a steady but short period of time unless stopped.

Sphinx - a giant creature with the head of a women and body of a lion with the wings of a giant eagle. Malevolent ones are carnivorous. Male sphinxes are called androsphinxes.

Spider Centaur - are related to demons before with the upper torso of drow-like males with purplish skin, unkempt hair hanging in front of their faces, long, protruding elfin ears, and the lower torso of a giant black spider.

Sprite - one of the major races of fae who live in patriarchal rural societies governed by kings, chiefs, or clan chiefs. Sprites are human-like halflings or smaller but like all sprites and fairies, they possess the ability of "sizing" wherein they can magically increase or shrink their size to defend themselves.

Striga - an evil cursed, carnivorous powerful witch filled with a hate for all living things from its practice of dark magic. Some are often confused with vampires.

Stymphalian Bird - a race of carnivorous birds, twice the size of storks, with beaks of metal and metallic feathers. They can be unrelenting predators of any who trespass into their territory, and are feared by fae and human alike.

Sylph - the beautiful nymph-like elementals of the air. In appearance, women with pale, almost-transparent skin, clear eyes, and long, flowing blue-white hair. With their immense power, they can manipulate air and weather at will, making them the most powerful of all elementals.

They live high above in the clouds and work closely with their sister elemental race, the undines, or water elementals.

Sylphid - tiny nymph-like fairy air elementals.

T.

Tarasque - the lionlike beasts are larger than elephants with bodies covered in rock-like turtle shells with spikes, they have six clawed legs and long ridged snakelike tails ending in spiked ball. Some have scorpion tails, others forked tails.

Taurus - the winged, flying bulls of the magical lands.

Tree People – a race of fae tree humanoids with bark for skin, wide eyes, and loosely foliated branches for hair. Known for their ancient wisdom and ability to speak with all fae flora and fauna.

Tree Shepherd – a special clan of leshies who control any number of magical, sentient trees—walking, crawling, or flying.

Triton – a noble race of water fae with an upper humanoid half and a lower half of two green-scaled fish tails for legs. They are one of the five main races of the Oceanus Omnis along with merfolk, water nymphs, water elves, and sea centaurs. They have a main fin on their heads and fins along their spines, arms, and sometimes legs. Their skin is blue or green in color, and they have pointed ears like elves.

Their weapon of choice is the magic trident. They are also able to communicate long distances to one another with large shells, often conch, or use them to magically summon various water animals or beasts. Wizards use the same method to calm or create storms.

Tritons' main allies are the sea centaurs, the other patriarchal race of the five main races.

Troglodyte – a race of fae known as "cave dwellers" or "trogs." Descriptions vary, but most often resemble bulky lizard-like humanoids. They are larger than the average human but walk hunched over, or slither on the ground. They also can see in the dark.

U.

Undine - the race of powerful elemental beings of water. Beautiful tall, thin women, who wear sheer, flowing dresses of nature. They live in the oceans or in giant sacred waterfalls. They possess the ability to summon and control water in any way. As their power comes from the oceans of Pan-Earth itself, only the sylphs of the air are ultimately more powerful than they among all elementals.

Unicorn - a magical horse with a large single horn one to two feet long protruding from his forehead. They can be of any color and different kinds have differing magical properties; some are also winged and can fly. Unicorns are a favorite steed of elves and an animal companion to fairies.

V.

Väki - a clan of haltijas. Besides the tulen väki or väki of fire there are also väki of specific trees, forests, mountains, water, precious metals or gems, underground lands, etc.

Väki of forest (metsän väki) - possess the magical powers of the forest.

Väki of water (veden väki) - can use their magical power of water to make people sick or heal them.

Väki of woman (naisen väki) - clan of female vaki known for their nurturing and restorative magical powers.

<u>Väki of death</u> (kalman väki) – rarely seen clan whose power comes from ghosts and spirits.

<u>Väki of fire</u> (tulen väki) – the clan of haltijas who wear charred brown and orange fabric clothing. They are a race of guardians with the elemental magically ability to conjure and control fire and use warm air to heal or burn.

<u>Väki of mountain</u> (vuoren väki) – possess the earth elemental powers of mountains.

<u>Väki of wood</u> (puun väki) – the haltijas of trees.

<u>Väki of iron</u> (raudan väki) – possess the magical powers to summon, shape, and control iron.

Z.

<u>Zodiac, The</u> – a group of twelve ancient giants said to have established the codes of justice and law among all ancient fae. There are Aquarius, Aries, Cancer, Capricorn, Gemini, Leo, Pisces, Libra, Sagittarius, Scorpio, Taurus, and Virgo.

ABOUT THE AUTHOR

Austin Dragon is the author of over 20 books in science fiction, fantasy, and classic horror. His works include the cyberpunk detective *LIQUID COOL* series, the epic fantasy *FABLED QUEST CHRONICLES*, the international epic *AFTER EDEN* Series, and the classic *SLEEPY HOLLOW HORRORS*. He is a native New Yorker but has called Los Angeles, California home for more than twenty years. Words to describe him, in no particular order: U.S. Army, English teacher, one-time resident of Paris, ex-political junkie, movie buff, Fortune 500 corporate recruiter, renaissance man, futurist, and dreamer.

He is currently working on new books and series in science fiction, fantasy, and classic horror!

http://www.austindragon.com/books